Cmr

Always the
BACHELOR

Wedding Party Collection

Michelle
CELMER

Amanda
BERRY

Barbara
HANNAY

D0727107

Always the
BACHELOR

Wedding Party Collection

Michelle
CELMER

Amanda
BERRY

Barbara
HANNAY

MILLS &
BOON

Published in Great Britain 2017
By Mills & Boon, an imprint of HarperCollins*Publishers*
1 London Bridge Street, London, SE1 9GF

WEDDING PARTY COLLECTION: ALWAYS THE BACHELOR
© 2017 Harlequin Books S.A.

Best Man's Conquest © 2007 Michelle Celmer
One Night with the Best Man © 2014 Amanda Berry
The Bridesmaid's Best Man © 2007 Barbara Hannay

ISBN: 9780263931068

09-0617

BEST MAN'S CONQUEST

MICHELLE CELMER

*I dedicate this work to my future
Great Niece or Nephew,
who will make his or her appearance
at roughly the same time as this book.
You have five brothers, so naturally
your mommy is hoping for a girl.
Try to work on that okay?*

USA TODAY bestselling author **Michelle Celmer** has written more than twenty-five books for Mills & Boon. You can usually find her in her office with her laptop, loving the fact that she gets to work in her pyjamas. Write her at P.O. BOX 300, Clawson, MI 48017, USA visit her website at www.michellecelmer.com or find her on Facebook at Michelle Celmer Author.

One

Is your ex hanging around and making noise like he wants to reconcile? Does he think he can sweet-talk his way back into your life? Don't fall for it! Repeat after me: men don't change.
—excerpt from *The Modern Woman's Guide to Divorce (And the Joy of Staying Single)*

Ivy Madison was not a violent person, but as the "surprise" man she'd been hearing about for the past three months—the one who looked disturbingly similar to her gazillionaire ex-husband—unfolded his long, lean body from the backseat of the limo, she quietly began plotting her cousin Deidre's murder.

No, it couldn't possibly be him.

Blake, Deidre's fiancé, was supposed to be off

picking up the best man from the airport. There was no way that the surprise Deidre had repeatedly enticed her with, the mystery best man Ivy was just going to *love,* was Dillon Marshal! Never in a million years would Deidre expect Ivy to stand up in a wedding, much less spend the week before the ceremony in the Mexican villa, with the biggest mistake who had ever walked in, then walked back out of, her life.

Would she?

Maybe the surprise was that the best man only looked like Dillon. Yeah, that was probably it. They would have a good laugh, then Ivy could relax and enjoy the first real vacation since the release of her book.

It was just one of those weird, quirky coincidences.

The man who couldn't possibly be her ex slipped off his Ray-Bans, revealing a familiar pair of heavy-lidded, come-hither, steel-blue bedroom eyes. Eyes that had been known to melt her with a mere glance, reduce her knees to mashed potatoes and her head to scrambled eggs.

Oh shi—

A blast of emotions tore through her insides with the velocity of a tropical storm, misfiring the synapses in her brain and tangling her intestines into knots.

She turned from the front window and looked to her cousin for an explanation. For an assurance that there was no way the man standing in the driveway was who he looked like.

Deidre flashed her a look seeped in guilt and offered a weak, "Surprise."

Oh, no.

Ivy's heart slid down from her chest, weaved around her internal organs and settled just north of her ovaries.

Her knees felt as if they might give out, and the bagel she'd had for breakfast was in danger of making a repeat performance all over the southwestern-theme rug. This could not be happening. There was a damned good reason she'd spent the last decade avoiding Dillon.

Feeling woozy, she lowered herself onto the couch. She glanced out the window and saw that men were at the back of the limo now, collecting Dillon's luggage. Soon they would be coming inside.

Her stomach launched into an Olympic-caliber backflip with a triple twist.

Deidre sat down on the opposite end of the couch, far enough away to hopefully avoid any flying fists. "I know you probably want to kill me right now, but I can explain."

Oh, yeah, she definitely had to die. And it would be slow and painful. Stung to death by African bees, or drained by a million leeches. "Deidre, what did you do?"

"I have a very good explanation."

There was no good explanation. And there was only one thing Ivy could do. She needed to grab her things, slip out the back, and catch the next flight back to Texas.

She made a mental list of her belongings and tried to estimate how long it would take to shove them back into her bag.

Oh, to hell with her clothes. She had plenty more back home. All she really needed was her laptop and purse. She could grab them both and be out the back door in two minutes. Dillon would never be the wiser. Unless...

Oh, no, she wouldn't have. "This was a surprise for him, too, right?"

Deidre clamped her bottom lip between her teeth, eyes pinned in her lap, and Ivy felt the bagel creeping farther up her throat.

"Deidre, *honey,* tell me he doesn't know I'm here."

The color leached from her cheeks.

"Deidre?"

"He knows."

Wonderful. Just *freaking* fantastic.

That meant running was not an option. No way she could let Dillon know he'd scared her off. Even worse, he'd had time to prepare for this. He would do and say all the right things.

Oh, who was she kidding? Dillon was not the type of guy who needed to prepare.

Oh boy, she was in big trouble.

The front door opened, and Ivy's heart sped up triple time. With an excited squeal Deidre dashed from the room to greet them, leaving Ivy alone.

Traitor.

She wasn't ready for this. Had she not been forced, she didn't know if she would have *ever* been ready to face Dillon again. Too much bad blood. Too many regrets.

She heard voices from the other room, enthusiastic greetings and the unmistakable hum of Dillon's deep, easy voice. Her heart started going berserk in her chest.

No matter what, she could not let that man see her this rattled.

She rose from the couch on rubbery legs and turned to look out the window at the taillights of the limo as it pulled down the driveway. Something was said about taking the luggage to the bedroom, then she heard the sound of footsteps on the stairs—more than one set. She closed her eyes and clung to the breath in her lungs until her head began to swim from lack of oxygen, praying Deidre was showing Dillon up to his room and she could put off a little longer the inevitable confrontation.

She needed time to prepare. Ten or fifteen minutes. Or a week.

For several long seconds the house was still and silent. She exhaled slowly, felt her heart rate returning to a somewhat normal pace, and sucked in a fresh breath.

Then a familiar feeling—something warm and complicated and unpredictable—poured over her. It soaked through her clothes and drenched her skin and she knew without turning that Dillon was in the room. She could feel his presence, the pressure of his gaze on her back, like some creepy sixth sense.

Goose bumps broke out across her arms, and the fine hairs on her neck started to shiver.

Oh, boy, here we go.

Gathering every scrap of courage she could dredge up, she fixed what she hoped was a disinterested look on her face and turned to confront a past that up until today she thought she'd seen the last of. The man recently dubbed one of the country's most eligible bachelors.

He leaned in the arched doorway, arms folded over his chest. Arms that somehow managed to appear muscular and lean at the same time, a chest wide enough to impress but not overpower. Memories of those arms around her, her cheek pressed to that warm, solid chest breathing in the clean, subtle scent of his aftershave, rushed up to choke the air from her lungs.

In faded blue jeans, a white T-shirt and cowboy boots, the billionaire oil king looked just as he had in college. Yet there was an air of authority and importance that emanated from inside him, from every pore. An arrogance that said he knew exactly what he wanted and he wasn't afraid to go after it, and pity the person who dared get in his way.

Beginning with her pink-tipped toes, his eyes embarked on a leisurely journey, working their way up her body. Slowly they climbed, no shame, no apology, as if he had every right to be mentally undressing her.

Over her hips, across her mostly flat stomach…

She clasped her hands behind her back, so he wouldn't see them tremble. What was wrong with her? She was no longer the naive, sheltered girl who had been swept away by a trust-fund rebel. She was a strong, self-confident professional. She had co-written the definitive guide on divorce for the modern woman. She was a *New York Times* bestselling author, for cripes' sake. She could handle Dillon Marshall.

She hoped.

He finally reached her breasts and took his sweet ole time, caressing them with his eyes. She felt the tips tingle and tighten against her will. The urge to cross her arms over her chest was almost unbearable, but she wouldn't give him the satisfaction.

This inspection, this violation, was all a part of the game he played.

She narrowed her eyes and raised her chin to a don't-even-mess-with-me angle. When he finally reached her face, his eyes locked on hers and held, and one corner of his mouth tipped up in a familiar, cocky smile.

He shook his head, eyes simmering with male appreciation. "Damn, darlin', you look good enough to eat."

If looks could kill, Dillon would be knocking at the pearly gates. His ex-wife's whiskey-colored eyes impaled him like razor-sharp daggers.

Talk about a blast from the past. It was the same look she'd given him ten years ago, the day she walked out on him.

Though the particulars of that morning were still fuzzy, he remembered stumbling in stinking drunk at 7:00 a.m. after an all-nighter with his buddies. His third all-nighter that week...and it had been only Wednesday. He'd tried to coax her into bed, to show her how sorry he was—hell, it had worked before—and she'd lobbed an empty beer bottle at his head.

Lucky for him that her aim had been as bad as her temper.

But damn, did she look good now—tall and willowy and soft around the edges. The kind of pretty that crept up on a man slowly, then dug its claws in deep and held on.

Too bad she was a major pain in the behind.

He turned up the charm on his smile, knowing it would irritate the hell out of her, since that in large part was the motivation for this trip. He intended to make her suffer. "What, no kiss?"

Sure enough, that telltale little crease formed between her eyebrows. She always had taken life too seriously. He used to admire her confidence, her determination. The woman knew exactly what she wanted, and she hadn't been afraid to go after it. Too bad she'd never learned how to have fun. He'd tried his best to teach her, to loosen her up, and what had it gotten him?

A lot of grief.

It would be that much more satisfying when he finally broke her spirit.

"You don't look happy to see me," he said.

Her eyes narrowed, like maybe she thought that if she concentrated hard enough she could wish him out of existence.

"Oh, right, you still think I'm a…now, how did you word it in that little book of yours?" He scratched his chin thoughtfully. "Something to the effect of me being a self-centered, pigheaded horse's ass?"

Her chin rose in that familiar, stubborn tilt. "Not once did I use your name in that *little* book, so you can't say one way or the other who I was referring to."

She might not have used his name, but the implication had been more than clear.

Clear to him.

Clear to his family and friends.

And clear to the millions of women who had flocked to the bookstore to get their hands on the new must-read self-help guide.

Nearly every negative little story and anecdote she'd included in the text had been plucked right out of their marriage. Talk about social devastation. The class of woman he normally dated wouldn't give him the time of day, and the women who would, the morbidly curious and monetarily motivated, he wouldn't wish on his worst enemy.

"Besides, it was self-*absorbed* and *bull*headed," Ivy added. "And I never used the term horse's ass. Even though you were one."

He flattened a hand across the left side of his chest. "Darlin', you're breakin' my heart."

"Look, you can cut the *good ole boy* crap. I don't imagine you're any happier than I am about being stuck together for a whole week."

It was just like her to cut through the bull and get right to the point. And as usual, she was wrong. He couldn't be happier.

"For Deidre and Blake's sake, I'm going to try to make the best of it," she continued in that master-of-the-universe tone. "I expect you to do the same."

He just bet she did. Was she under the impression they were going to pick up where they left off? With her issuing orders?

Had she forgotten that he didn't take orders from anyone?

"How do you s'pose we go about doing that?" he asked in the same *good ole boy* twang, since it clearly annoyed her.

"I think we should agree to avoid each other whenever humanly possible. I'll stay out of your way and you stay out of mine. After this week, we never have to see each other again."

The *never seeing each other again* part sounded just fine to him. But that was only a fraction of the good news. He'd been looking for a way to irritate her, to make her as miserable as humanly possible, and she'd just served it up on a silver platter.

The worst thing he could do to a control freak like Ivy was take away her control.

A corner of his mouth twitched, but he held the smile inside. He pretended to give her demand some thought, then gave her a solemn nod. "Sounds like a good idea."

She narrowed her eyes at him. "So that's it?"

"Sure." It did sound like a good idea. For *her*. That didn't mean *he* had any intention of doing it.

She had no idea the flack his family had taken after her book was released. Call it childish and immature— hell, he'd been called worse—but the way he saw it, he was long overdue for a little payback. Some good old-fashioned revenge.

If keeping his distance was what she really wanted, for the next week he would be stuck to that woman like glue.

TWO

Feeling helpless, hopeless? Stand up and take control! Show that man who's boss.
—excerpt from *The Modern Woman's Guide to Divorce (And the Joy of Staying Single)*

Ivy sat outside on the private balcony of her bedroom, at the cute little wrought-iron patio set, reading the novel she'd started on the plane. The sun felt warm on her skin, and a damp, salty ocean breeze flipped the ends of her ponytail.

What better place to relax? To kick back and put her feet up? Yet she was so tense she'd read the same paragraph half a dozen times and still had no idea what it said.

She marked her page and set the book down, rubbing

at the beginnings of a headache in her temples. This was supposed to be a vacation. It was supposed to be fun.

She heard her bedroom door open, and her cousin called to her. "Are you in here?"

Ivy looked at her watch. It had taken Deidre a full hour to work up the courage to face her again.

"I'm out here," she said.

Several seconds passed, then she heard Deidre behind her. "Are you mad at me?"

Mad?

Mad didn't scratch the surface of what she was feeling. She felt hurt and betrayed and *humiliated*. They were supposed to be best friends. The sister neither had ever had.

A *team*.

How could Deidre pull a stunt like this? How could she lie by omission?

She turned to her cousin. Deidre stood in the bedroom doorway wringing the color from her hands, looking like the poster girl for guilt and remorse.

She'd been a nervous wreck for weeks, sure that at any moment Blake would come to his senses and finally accept the truth. Deidre, with a family history of obesity and bad skin, would never be a supermodel. Then he would undoubtedly start listening when his parents and brothers assured him that, for all his money and family connections, he could do much better.

Deidre also had what looked like a smear of chocolate in the corner of her mouth. Just that morning Ivy had confiscated a six-pack of chocolate bars and a half-empty box of Ding Dongs from Deidre's bedroom. She didn't want to venture a guess as to how much weight

Deidre had gained back in the last month or so, but a few more pounds and she would look like an overstuffed sausage in her ten-thousand-dollar designer wedding gown. Even worse was the random acne that had begun to spring up on her chin. Which of course only made her more upset, and more likely to stuff her face with junk.

She'd been a neurotic mess for weeks. Still, that didn't excuse what she had done.

Ivy concentrated on keeping her voice calm and rational. "How could you do this to me?"

"I'm so sorry. But I knew if I told you, you wouldn't have come. Without you as my maid of honor, it would ruin *everything*."

Deidre was one of those women who had begun planning her wedding the instant she left the womb. She'd accumulated a ceiling-high stockpile of bridal magazines and catalogs by the fifth grade.

After a few miserably failed false starts, she had finally snagged Mr. Right. Ivy got the feeling Deidre saw this as her last chance and that, if everything didn't go exactly as planned, she was destined to spend the rest of her life alone and childless and die a bitter spinster.

"I told you the best man was a buddy from college, and you knew he and Blake went to school together."

Ivy knew they had shared an apartment at Harvard, until Dillon had been expelled, that is, but she hadn't known they were that close. Her and Dillon's quickie Vegas wedding had been too last-minute for a best man or maid of honor.

Or a cake.

Or even a wedding dress.

It had been more of a *we'll show them* when their parents had tried to interfere in their relationship. Proving that not only is love blind, it's downright idiotic.

The sad truth is, she and Dillon had barely known each other when they'd gotten married. Out of bed, anyway. Only after their vows had she realized her mistake.

The day after.

"I know you probably won't believe this," Deidre said, "but Dillon has changed."

"You're right. I don't believe it." Men like Dillon never changed. Not deep down, where it counted.

"Maybe it's time you…" Deidre paused, her lip clamped between her teeth again.

"It's time I what?"

She shrugged. "Maybe…get past it."

"Get past what?"

"What I mean is, maybe it's time you…forgive him."

Forgive him?

Was Deidre joking? Had the wedding jitters short-circuited her brain? Had she forgotten what Dillon had put her through?

Did a woman ever get past having her heart stomped on and filleted into a million pieces? Did she forget losing an academic grant, being tossed out of college and having her reputation decimated?

And how did you forgive someone who showed no remorse? Someone who sat back and watched with a smile on his face while her world fell apart? A man who had promised to love and honor her until death? "What Dillon did to me was unforgivable and you know it."

Deidre lowered herself into the chair beside Ivy's, a look of genuine concern on her face. "I just hate to see you so unhappy."

Her words nearly knocked Ivy out of her chair. "What are you talking about? My book is selling millions, my private practice is flourishing. Why in the world would I be unhappy?"

"You're the psychologist. You tell me."

Ivy had everything she'd ever dreamed of. A good career and an impressive stock portfolio. Personal and financial independence.

She was not unhappy. In fact, she was freaking ecstatic. "For your information, I am very happy with my life."

"When was the last time you were in a committed relationship? When was the last time you had sex? Hell, when was the last time you were on a date?"

"I don't need a man to complete me." The words spilled from her mouth automatically. It was her mantra, the basis for her book. The only constant in her life.

"Maybe not, but they sure can be fun to have around."

And so not worth the hassle. She had her career and her friends. That was enough. For now. "Setting me up like this has put me in a terrible position. Considering all the people who will be at the wedding Saturday, it's bound to get out that I spent a week in Mexico with my ex. You know how brutal the media can be. What if they start spreading rumors that we're getting back together? What do you think that will do to my reputation?"

"I guess I never thought about it like that." Deidre's lower lip began to quiver and tears hovered just inside her eyelids. "I was only trying to help. If you want to leave, I understand."

Ivy sighed. As mad as she was at her cousin, deep down she knew her intentions were pure. Deidre didn't have a vindictive bone in her body. If she said she was trying to help, it was the truth, and it was executed out of love and concern.

Oh, hell.

She reached over and squeezed Deidre's fisted hands. "I'm not going anywhere. This is the most important week of your life, and I wouldn't miss it for anything."

The tears spilled over onto Deidre's cheeks and rolled down, leaving wet dots on the front of her shirt. "Thank you."

"Besides, Dillon and I talked, and we've reached somewhat of an agreement. I'll avoid him and he'll avoid me." She gave Deidre's hands a reassuring squeeze and forced a smile. "Really, how bad could it be?"

It could be bad, Ivy realized fifteen minutes later after Deidre left to see about dinner. Really bad.

She experienced the same eerie, familiar feeling as she had downstairs when Dillon had entered the room, and she looked up to find him a stone's throw away, leaning on the edge of his own balcony on the opposite end of the house. His eyes were on her, steady and intense, as if he was biding his time, just waiting for her to notice him there.

"Howdy!" he called, wiggling his fingers in a casual, friendly, good-ole-boy wave. He looked out across the ocean, his chest expanding beneath his T-shirt as he drew in a long, deep breath. "Hell of a view, isn't it?"

Oh, yes it is, she agreed silently, her eyes wandering over his solid frame. And she could feel it coming on, that little shimmy thing her heart did whenever he was near.

Here it comes…

No, no, no!

She lowered her eyes back to her book. Don't look at him. Don't encourage him in any way. Maybe he would take the hint and leave her alone.

He didn't.

"Whatcha' doin'?"

"Reading," she answered, not looking up from the page. Maybe if she kept her answers short and succinct he would get a clue. He would realize she wanted him to leave her alone. Like he promised he would.

He didn't.

She could still feel his eyes on her, feel him watching. Goose bumps shivered across her skin, and she felt fidgety and uncomfortable.

Ignore him and he'll lose interest, she assured herself. Keep reading and he'll get bored and go away. But she could feel her anxiety level climbing again. Her foot had begun to tap, the way it always did when she was nervous, and she was grinding her teeth.

She forced herself to relax.

"Good book?" He used a tone that suggested he was making friendly conversation. Maybe to break the ice, so the situation would be a bit less awkward.

He was wasting his time. The only conversation she was interested in having with him was the nonexistent kind. She didn't want to break the ice, and she had no desire to make things less awkward.

She just wanted him to go away.

There was also the distinct possibility that, despite his promise to leave her alone, he was doing this to annoy her.

Either way, she was beginning to feel like a specimen under a microscope.

She took several deep, cleansing breaths, tried to concentrate on her book and not on the man staring at her.

After a few very long, tense moments he said, "Must be a good book."

"It is." Up until a few minutes ago, anyway. Now, as she tried to focus on the small print, the words ran together in a nonsensical jumble. Was a few minutes of peace really too much to ask for?

Several more minutes passed quietly by, but she knew without looking up that he was still watching her. The question was, why?

When she couldn't stand it any longer she looked up and met his gaze. "Was there something you wanted?"

"No, ma'am," he said, his eyes never straying from her face. "Just enjoying the scenery."

Something in his eyes, in the intense way he stared, suggested that the scenery he was referring to was her. He was beginning to annoy the hell out of her, and she had the sinking feeling that was exactly his intention.

"Do you think you could possibly enjoy it from somewhere else?" she asked as politely as possible, despite her rapidly mounting irritation.

"What's wrong, Ivy?" He leaned forward on his elbows, deeper into her personal space. "Do I make you uncomfortable?"

That was the last thing she wanted him to think. He

no longer had *any* power over her. She was strong and independent. She answered to no one but herself. "No, but I would like to read a few more chapters before dinner. If you don't mind."

"Not at all. You go on ahead and read."

"Thank you." She turned her attention back to her book. He was quiet for several minutes, but in her peripheral vision she could see that he hadn't moved from his spot. He was still watching her.

He was definitely doing it to annoy her. There was no other logical explanation.

"I saw your mom a few weeks ago," he finally said.

She sighed and gathered her patience. So much for sitting outside, reading and enjoying the view.

She very calmly marked her page, shut the book and looked up at him. Ten years ago she would have thought he looked damned good standing there, the sun reflecting bluish-black off his dark hair, eyes slightly squinted against the glare and crinkled in the corners. The distinguished kind of crinkles that men got. The same things that on a woman were just plain old ugly wrinkles.

Dillon had that special something, a physical appeal that was impossible to ignore. Or resist. In the short term, anyway.

As she'd quickly discovered, looks aren't everything. What he needed was the personality to go along with it. One that wasn't quite so...*annoying*.

"You still fold your page over to mark your spot," he said. "No matter how many bookmarks you bought, you always misplaced them."

For a minute she was speechless. How had he re-membered such a mundane, trivial detail about her? She honestly didn't think he'd been paying attention.

"Anyway," he continued, "I was in downtown Dallas for a meeting, and I saw your mom through the window of her shop. She looks as though she's doing well."

"She is." It had taken a while, but her mom had finally gotten her life together.

"I would have stopped in for a trim, but I was running late."

Only a complete fool would go to his former mother-in-law for a haircut. And while Dillon may have been a big pain in the behind, he was not a fool. Complete or otherwise.

"I figured I would stop in after my meeting instead. But then I got to thinkin', she may not have the highest opinion of me."

"Gosh, you think?" Her mom had *never* liked Dillon. Not even when they'd been dating. She'd always said he was too much like Ivy's real dad. Arrogant and unreliable.

After Ivy's dad took off, she and her mom had been forced to stay with Deidre and her parents until they got back on their feet.

He hadn't bothered to stick around, and her mom had been sure Dillon wouldn't, either. She'd warned Ivy re-peatedly that she was asking for trouble, just begging to get her heart broken.

Ivy had wanted so badly to prove her wrong. But her mom had been right, of course, and to this day she'd never let Ivy live it down.

What would her mother think if she could see her

now, stuck in the same house with Dillon for a week? She would probably be worried that Ivy would be foolish enough to fall for him again. The way she had repeatedly fallen for Ivy's dad, trapped in what she liked to call an on-again, off-again trip through the house of horrors that had spanned nearly a decade.

Ivy was smarter than that. If there was one thing she'd learned from her mother, it was how not to repeat her mistakes.

She would worry about her mom Saturday when she flew in for the wedding. Right now she had other, more pressing problems, like the man still staring at her.

It was clear Dillon didn't intend to leave her alone. Rather than spend an hour or so before dinner enjoying the sun, she would instead have to remain indoors, where he couldn't bug her.

Ivy rose to her feet and grabbed her book. "I guess I'll see you at dinner."

"I thought you wanted to read."

"It's been a long day. I think I'll take a quick nap." It was a lie, but there was no way she would admit that he'd irritated her to the point of driving her away.

She hoped this was just his misguided way of trying to make amends. She hoped she was wrong and he wasn't actually doing this to annoy her.

"See ya'll later," he called, and as she was shutting the door, she could swear she heard laughter.

Three

Bitterness can be handled in many ways. The worst is to pretend it isn't there. Recognize it, identify it, embrace it. Then get over it.
—excerpt from *The Modern Woman's Guide to Divorce (And the Joy of Staying Single)*

Dillon was a big, fat liar.

Ivy sipped her champagne and glanced up at him through the pale pink, lingering light of sunset across the patio table. Eyes as blue and crisp as the ocean stared back, tangling her up in their gaze like a fish in a net.

A shivery zing of awareness started in her scalp and rippled with lightning speed down to her toes. And though she mentally squirmed and flopped, she couldn't seem to break loose.

Instead, she stared him down with a cool, disinterested look. Hoping he couldn't see the frantic flutter of her heartbeat at the base of her throat. The goose bumps dotting every conceivable inch of her flesh.

He was *supposed* to be avoiding her. He had *agreed* to leave her alone, hadn't he? Yet, as she feared earlier on the balcony, it was crystal clear that he had no intention of keeping his promise. In fact, he was doing everything he could to make her as uncomfortable as humanly possible.

And he did it damned well.

Throughout dinner, every time she looked up from her plate of mostly untouched food, his eyes were on her. He wasn't even attempting to be subtle, the big jerk.

At this rate she would be leaving the country a total basket case.

Blake kept shooting Ivy apologetic smiles, and Deidre had started stress eating. She had finished her own meal and was stealing bites from Blake's plate when she thought no one was watching. Blake's brothers, Calvin and Dale, observed with blatant curiosity.

Deidre's bridesmaids were another story. The motor-mouth twins—or as Deidre liked to call them, Tweedle Dee and Tweedle Dum—were too busy flapping their jaws to notice Ivy. Or anyone else for that matter.

They weren't actually twins, although they may as well have been. They had the same burnt-out blond hair and surgically enhanced, anorexic, size-one bodies. They even shared an identical flair for mindless, irrelevant conversation. Ivy was guessing that their collective IQ's ranked somewhere in the low double-digits.

"A toast to Deidre and Blake," Dillon said, raising his

glass, his eyes still locked on Ivy. She couldn't help but notice that he'd dropped the good ole boy twang. Tonight he sounded decidedly more upper-crust Dallas. "May you have a long, happy life together."

Like we didn't, his eyes seemed to say. Was he suggesting that was her fault?

Yeah, right.

Around the table crystal stemware clinked and everyone sipped. Ivy downed the contents of her glass in one long swallow. She'd never been much of a drinker, but the champagne felt good going down. It tickled her nose and warmed her nervous stomach.

One corner of Dillon's mouth tipped up and his eyes sparked with mischief. He was mocking her.

She sat a little straighter, pulled her shoulders back, all the more determined to see this through. She refused to let him win.

Maybe the trick to making it through this week was to drink alcohol. Lots and lots of alcohol. Hadn't that been Dillon's method of coping with stress? Hadn't he spent the better part of his time in college intoxicated?

Although she did notice that he drank only mineral water with dinner and had barely touched his champagne. Was it possible he'd given up drinking?

As if reading her thoughts, Dillon reached for the bottle of champagne the housekeeper had left chilling beside the table. He rose from his chair and circled to her side, moving with a subtle, yet undeniable male grace that was hypnotizing. Even the Tweedles, deep in some inane conversation about the difference between clothes sizes in the U.S. as opposed to Europe—in

Europe Dee had to buy a size three, *gasp!*—stopped to watch him with unguarded interest.

Ivy sat stock still, resisting the urge to turn in her chair as he stepped behind her. His aura seemed to suck the oxygen from the air around her, making her feel light-headed and woozy.

He leaned forward, resting a hand on the back of her chair—his fingers this close to her skin but not quite touching her—and filled her empty glass. As he poured, his arm brushed her shoulder.

His *bare* arm. Against her *bare* shoulder.

Time ground to a screeching halt, and the entire scene passed before her eyes in slow motion. A twisted, messy knot of emotions she couldn't even begin to untangle settled in her gut, and a weird, this-can't-possibly-be-happening feeling crept over her.

Why didn't she do something to stop him? Bat his hand away or jab an elbow into his gut? Why was she just sitting there frozen? It was not as if she was enjoying this.

Yet she couldn't deny that there was something about him, about the feel of his skin that was eerily familiar.

Not just familiar, but almost…natural. Which was just plain freaky, because there was nothing *natural* about her and Dillon being anywhere near each other.

Silence had fallen over the table and everyone stopped what they were doing to stare at her and Dillon.

Which Ivy realized was exactly what he wanted.

Under the table, her foot was tapping like mad. If she didn't calm down, she was going to wear away the sole of her sandal.

She forced herself to relax, to pretend she didn't care when in reality she was wound so tight she could crack walnuts on her rear end.

What felt like an eternity later he *finally* backed away, making it a point to run the length of his arm across her shoulder while the hand that rested behind her chair brushed ever so softly against the back of her neck. If this was what she had to look forward to every time she emptied her glass, maybe the heavy drinking wasn't such a hot idea after all. She was much better off keeping him at the opposite end of the table, where he could only touch her with his eyes.

"Anyone else?" he asked, offering a refill to the rest of the table.

Dee raised her glass. "I'd love some."

As he poured, Ivy couldn't help noticing that he didn't rest his hand on her chair, nor did he brush against her with his arm. Everyone else seemed to notice, too.

It confirmed that he had only been trying to antagonize her. Hadn't he caused her enough grief? Couldn't he act like an adult and leave her alone?

Just as she'd suspected. He hadn't changed a bit.

"Dale told us you guys used to be married," Dee said as Dillon returned to his side of the table and slid easily into his seat.

The way he could look so relaxed and casual, yet emanate an aura of authority, boggled the mind.

He retrieved his napkin from the table and draped it in his lap. "That's right."

Dee's eyes widened a fraction and she looked to Ivy for affirmation. "Really?"

"We were," Ivy confirmed. "For about a year. A long, *long* time ago."

"*He* married *you?*" Dum asked, looking first at Ivy, then to Dillon, shaking her head as if she couldn't believe what she was hearing. "Wow. I really thought Dale was kidding."

Gee, thanks, Ivy wanted to tell Miss Tactless. Just go ahead and say what's on your mind. Don't worry about my feelings.

"She left me and broke my heart," Dillon said, flashing Ivy a wry grin.

A look passed between the twins, like sharks who had just smelled blood in the water and were gearing up for a feast.

"*She* left *you?*" Dee, who obviously missed the sarcasm oozing from his words, clucked sympathetically, shooting Ivy a look of disdain. She reached across the table to pat Dillon's hand and assured him, "You deserve better."

Oh, please. Ivy experienced a severe mental eye roll. Even if she had wronged him somehow, which she absolutely hadn't, it had been ten years ago.

"It's no wonder," Dum said. "Blake, didn't you say she hates men?"

Deidre's jaw fell and she shot Blake a look.

"That's not what I said," Blake told her, shifting uncomfortably in his seat. He turned to Ivy, looking as though he wanted to disappear. "I swear, that's not what I said. I was just telling them about your book. Man-hating never entered the conversation."

Ivy believed him. In all the time she'd known Blake,

she'd never heard him say a disparaging word about anyone. But she could see the needle on Deidre's stress meter creeping into the red zone. Deidre eyed the Tweedles' untouched chocolate mousse with ravenous eyes and asked, "Would anyone like seconds on dessert?"

"Not me," Dillon said, rubbing a hand across what Ivy was sure was still a washboard stomach. "I'm stuffed."

"Like *she* needs seconds," Dee mumbled under her breath, but conveniently loud enough for the entire table to hear. Dum snickered and Blake's brothers exchanged a look, one that said Deidre's fluctuating weight had been a topic of conversation in the past.

That didn't surprise Ivy. The Tweedles hadn't exactly been Deidre's first choice for bridesmaids. In fact, they weren't her last choice, either. They ranked somewhere just below the never-in-a-million-years category. But Blake's brothers were the groomsmen, per their gazillionaire father's demands, and they had refused to stand up in the wedding without their girlfriends.

Since Deidre would be stuck as a part of the family for the next fifty years or so, and Daddy was footing the bill for the wedding—and the house they were moving into after the honeymoon, *and* the cars they would be driving—Deidre felt it best to acquiesce.

The whole arrangement set off warning bells for Ivy, but she was keeping her mouth shut. Deidre seemed happy, and Ivy didn't want to burst her bubble. There was a very slim chance it would all work out, and Ivy was clinging to that hope.

An uncomfortable silence fell over the table, and Deidre lowered her eyes to her lap, shame flaring in red-hot splotches across her cheeks. Blake looked awkwardly around, everywhere but at the woman he should have been speaking up to defend. Ivy felt torn between defending her cousin and not wanting to make things worse.

Blake was a genuinely nice guy, and he loved Deidre. Unfortunately, he didn't have much in the way of a backbone.

Of the three brothers he was the youngest, and while he hadn't taken a beating with the ugly stick, he wasn't what you would call a looker, either. He was sort of…nondescript, and he let everyone, including his family—*especially his family*—walk all over him.

Which is why Ivy feared Deidre would be bowing to her in-laws' wishes for the rest of her natural life.

"So, Ivy, I hear you're a practicing psychologist now," Dillon said.

Uh-oh. She distinctly felt an attack coming on.

Wonderful.

At the very least, taking potshots at her would deflect the attention from Deidre. It would be worth a little humiliation.

"Yes, I am," Ivy said, unable to keep the defensive lilt from her voice. One corner of Dillon's mouth quirked up in a very subtle grin, and Ivy raised her chin, bracing for the onslaught of insults. The "shrink" jokes she'd already heard a million times. The "little book" jabs.

She fisted her hands in her lap, digging her nails in the heels of her palms, her foot tapping like mad under the table, steeling herself for the worst.

Bring it on, pal.

"I find it truly fascinating," Dillon said, and Ivy thought, *sure you do.*

Dee covered a yawn with fingers tipped in bright pink, clawlike nails, and Dum made a production of looking at her watch. Did they think they were the queens of stimulating conversation?

Dale and Calvin, on the other hand, looked thoroughly amused by the entire situation. Those two were even worse than Dillon. They needed to grow up and get a life.

"Her book has been on the *New York Times* bestseller list for months," Deidre said, a note of pride in her voice. "She's famous."

Unimpressed, the Tweedles rolled their eyes.

"I'm particularly interested in the study of self-esteem," Dillon said.

Self-esteem?

Was that some sort of veiled insult? Was he honestly suggesting that Ivy had low self-esteem?

She felt her blood pressure shoot up to a danger-ously high level, and her foot was cramping up from the workout it was getting.

She was incredibly comfortable with herself, *thank you very much.*

"I once read that people with a negative or low self-esteem will insult and belittle other people to boost their own egos." His expression was serious, but there was a spark of pure mischief in Dillon's eyes. His gaze strayed briefly to the Tweedles, then back to Ivy. "Is that true?"

It took a full ten seconds for the impact of his words to settle in, and when it did, Ivy was so surprised she nearly laughed out loud.

He *wasn't* attacking her. His observations were aimed directly at the twins.

"That is true," she told him, in her therapist's, I'm-not-speaking-of-anyone-in-particular-just-stating-the-scientific-evidence tone.

Dale and Calvin weren't looking so cocky now, and a grateful smile had begun to creep over Deidre's face. The Tweedles were a bit slower to catch on.

Ivy watched with guilty pleasure as the two of them digested his words with brains no doubt impaired by bleach overexposure. She relished the look of stunned indignation on their faces when the meaning hit home.

She had never been an advocate of "an eye for an eye" and preferred not to lower herself to the Tweedles' level, but it felt damned good to knock those two down a peg.

"In fact," she continued, "self-esteem is one of the most widely studied areas of psychology."

"Why is that?" Dillon asked, feeding the flames, while the Tweedles grew increasingly uncomfortable.

Her conscience told her that what she was about to do was childish and just plain mean, but she couldn't deny the satisfaction she felt watching the Tweedles squirm. And who knows, maybe her words would strike some sort of chord, and they would think of other people's feelings for a change.

Should she or shouldn't she?

Oh, what the hell.

"Because self-esteem plays a role in virtually everything we do," she explained. "A lack of it can have dire effects. People who are unsure of themselves sometimes have trouble sustaining healthy relationships.

Since they often feel embarrassed and ashamed without due cause, their irrational reactions tend to baffle and alienate others."

"That *is* fascinating," Deidre agreed, casting a grin Ivy's way.

On a roll now, Ivy added, "Even worse, low self-esteem can cause or contribute to neurosis, anxiety, defensiveness, eating disorders and even alcohol and drug abuse."

"How tragic," Dillon said, looking pointedly to Blake's brothers. "Don't you think?"

Dale and Calvin exchanged an uneasy look, but neither uttered a sound. It was clear they were of the collective opinion that they shouldn't mess with the billionaire oil man.

The balance of power had just been established. At least for once Dillon had used that clout and influence for someone's benefit other than his own.

She would have to thank him later.

"Well, I think I'll take a walk on the beach before it gets dark," Dillon said, rising to his feet, and with his eyes on Ivy asked, "Anyone care to join me?"

As if. She wasn't *that* grateful.

"I will!" Deidre said, popping up from her chair with such enthusiasm that she bumped the table and sent her champagne glass teetering precariously. Blake grabbed it before it could topple over and shatter against the glass-top table. It was a nice save and, if Deidre's doe-eyed smile was any indication, might just compensate for his letting her down earlier.

Blake stood, brushing remnants of his dinner from the front of his clothes. Clothes that hung on his narrow, gangly frame. No matter how well he dressed, he always looked a tad…untidy. "I'll come, too."

"We're going into town to hit the bars," Dale said, answering for that side of the table. All four of them looked as though they could use a stiff drink. Or maybe five. Hopefully, in the future they would take the time to think about what they were saying before they opened their mouths, and realize there were certain people you just didn't mess with. Not without getting burned.

Ivy rose from her chair. "I'm going to head up to my room. I have to check my e-mail."

"But you promised no work this week," Deidre said with a pout.

"I know, but I'm expecting a message from my editor," she lied. The truth was, she'd told her editor, agent and writing partner that this week had been reserved strictly for relaxation.

What a joke. There would be nothing relaxing about this week. She would be lucky if she didn't return to Texas a certified Froot Loop in need of intensive psychotherapy.

Deidre clutched Ivy's hand in a death grip. "Come with us. *Please*."

Ivy knew what she was trying to do, and it wasn't going to work. She wanted Ivy to forgive Dillon. To "get past it," whatever "it" was.

Yes, Dillon had done something nice, shown that he had an unselfish side, but it didn't excuse the way he'd taunted her all evening. It also didn't change the fact that he would most likely continue to taunt and harass her until she boarded the plane Sunday morning.

She pried her hand free. "Next time. I promise."

Deidre looked as if she wanted to press the issue but let it drop.

Everyone went their separate ways, and Ivy headed upstairs, feeling uneasy and not quite sure why. Something weird had just happened down there. Something disturbing that she couldn't quite put her finger on.

She stepped into her room, closed the door and leaned against it.

A disaster had been diverted, thanks to Dillon. She would go so far as to say the entire situation, while childish and petty, had actually been fun—

Wait a minute. *Fun?* With *Dillon?*

The truth grabbed hold and shook her silly for a second.

That's what was so weird. Tonight had reminded her, if only for a few seconds, that at one time she and Dillon had made a good team. They used to have fun.

Even worse, she was pretty sure she actually disliked him a little less than she had this morning.

Oh, this was bad.

Hating Dillon was her only defense, her only ammunition. She depended on it.

Without that hate, she could no longer ignore the fact that he'd irreparably broken her heart.

Four

Do you suspect your man is lying to you? Trust your intuition. Odds are, he probably is.
—excerpt from *The Modern Woman's Guide to Divorce (And the Joy of Staying Single)*

Ivy learned two important lessons that night.

The first was that the only thing worse than having to face her ex again was having to face him in her ratty old nightshirt with the sleeves torn off, wet, tangled hair and no makeup.

The second, more valuable, lesson was always lock your bedroom door.

"Whoops," Dillon said from the open doorway when he saw her lying in bed on her stomach, on top of the covers, her laptop open in front of her.

She scrambled onto her knees, tugging the shirt down over her pale, sun-deprived legs, kicking herself for not visiting the tanning bed a few times before she left. Then kicking herself a second time for caring what he thought. "What are you doing in here?"

He looked genuinely baffled. "Guess I got the wrong room."

She couldn't help wondering how he'd managed that, since Deidre had had the decency not to put them in adjacent rooms and his was located at the opposite end of the house.

"Huh." Dillon glanced down the hall in the direction he'd come from. "I must'a made a wrong turn at the stairs."

She dragged her fingers through her knotted hair, cursing herself for not running a brush through it. Her mother, the cosmetologist, had spent years hammering into her head that to avoid damage to the ends and give her thin hair more body, it should be brushed *after* it dried. Which shouldn't have been a problem since she hadn't been anticipating company.

Or in Dillon's case, an intruder.

You don't care, she reminded herself.

"Well, as you can see, this isn't your room, so…good night."

He looked casually around, as if he had every right to be there. "Hey, this is nice."

"Yeah, it's great." And she knew for a fact it was not much different than his room.

Rather than leave, Dillon stepped farther inside, wedging his hands in the front pockets of his jeans. A move completely nonthreatening, but she felt herself tense. "I think your room is bigger than mine. And damn, look at that view."

Without invitation, and in a move arrogantly typical of him, he crossed the room to the open French doors and stepped outside onto the balcony.

Ugh! The man was insufferable!

Forgetting about her unsightly white skin, she jumped up out of bed and followed him. Staring at her from a balcony a dozen yards away was one thing. She could even live with the teasing, but this was her room, her only refuge this week, and he had no right to just barge in uninvited. "What do you think you're doing?"

The sun had dipped below the horizon, leaving only a hazy magenta ghost in its wake, and specks of glittering light dotted the heavens. And in the not so far distance she could hear the waves crashing against the bluff. Add to that the cool breeze blowing off the water and it was a perfect night. If not for the man standing there.

He whistled low and shook his head. "Yes, ma'am, quite a view."

"Your room faces the same ocean, so I doubt the view is all that different at the opposite end of the house. Hey, I have an idea. Why don't you go check."

Ignoring the razor-sharp edge of irritation in her voice, he propped both hands on the railing and made himself comfortable. "No, sir, you don't see stars like this in Dallas." He sucked in a long, deep breath and blew it out. "No smog, either."

She wasn't quite sure of the point of the "aw, shucks"

routine, but it was getting really annoying. "Dillon, I want you to leave."

He turned to her, his face partially doused in shadow, wearing that crooked grin. "No, you don't."

Damn him. He still knew exactly which buttons to push. But she wasn't going to take the bait. She wasn't the young, emotionally adolescent girl he remembered. She was going to stay calm. "Yes, *I do.*"

"It's been ten years. We have a lot of catching up to do." His eyes strayed to the front of the threadbare, oversize shirt and the grin went from amused to carnal.

Exactly what kind of catching up did he think they would be doing? And was he familiar with the phrase, *when hell freezes over?*

"You always did wear T-shirts to bed. Usually mine." He hooked his thumbs in the front pockets of his jeans and something dangerously hot flickered in his eyes. "You said you liked 'em 'cause they smelled like me."

She crossed her arms and shot him a chilling look.

Undaunted, his eyes wandered over her. "And I see that you still wait until your hair is dry to brush it."

She hated that he still knew her so well. That he'd bothered to remember anything about her at all. And the only reason he had was to use it against her. To make her uncomfortable. To knock her off balance and lower her defenses so he could go in for the kill.

She wouldn't give him the satisfaction.

"I'll bet you do all those things subconsciously," he mused. "Because deep down you still love me and you want me back."

The mercury on her temper began a steady climb, and

she clamped her teeth over the sarcastic reply that was trying like hell to jump out of her mouth.

You will not show this man how angry he's making you, she chanted to herself. *You will not let him get the best of you.*

"Isn't there a technical term for that?" he asked.

Yeah, there was a term for it.

Nuts.

Which he was if he honestly believed she had any feelings left for him. Favorable ones, that is.

"Don't we have a high opinion of ourselves," she said.

He grinned. "Maybe, but you can't say that I'm not consistent."

No, she definitely couldn't say that. He'd never once failed to let her down.

And this conversation was going nowhere.

"Look, I appreciate the way you defended Deidre against the Tweedles at dinner, but let's not pretend that I don't know exactly what you're doing and why you're doing it."

Amusement quirked up the corner of his mouth. "Tweedles?"

Ivy slapped a hand over her mouth. Oh, jeez. Had she really said that out loud?

"Like Tweedle Dee and Tweedle Dum?" A deep rumble of infectious laughter rolled from his chest and had a grin tugging at the corners of her own mouth.

And just as quickly it fizzled away.

Ugh!

He was doing it again. Softening her up. Lowering the ick factor of just being near him.

"You need to leave," she said. "I have work to finish."

He didn't move. "I guess you got that e-mail from your editor, huh?"

"That's right," she fibbed. "I'm incredibly busy right now."

"Why don't I believe you?" He eased away from the ledge, and she resisted the urge to step back. "You know, I could always tell when you were lying."

"I guess it takes one to know one," she snapped.

The humor slipped from his face, and she could see that she'd hit a nerve. Well, good. He had it coming.

Then why did she feel like such a louse?

He took another step closer. "Did I ever lie to you, Ivy?"

"I am not doing this." She turned and walked to the closet. She flung the door open and snatched her robe from the hanger. "I refuse to get sucked into a conversation about a relationship that has been over for ten years."

She thrust her arms through the sleeves and bound the belt securely at her waist. She swung around and nearly plowed into him. He was right behind her.

"The truth, Ivy." Every trace of playful cockiness had disappeared from his voice. "Did I ever once lie to you?"

Her heart rattled around in her chest. She remembered this man. The quiet, serious, alter ego. His appearances had been rare, but they had always intimidated the hell out of her. And Dillon knew it.

Had he been hiding in the background all this time, waiting for just the right moment to pounce?

"I don't owe you a thing."

He stepped closer, his eyes locked on her face, and

every cell in her body went on full alert, every neuron in her brain lit off like fireworks on the Fourth of July.

"Did I *ever* lie to you?"

Don't do it, she warned her traitorous subconscious. Don't you dare say what you're thinking. It doesn't matter anymore. It will only make things worse.

Don't say a word.

He stepped closer, until he was only inches away. His hair was a little windblown from his walk along the beach, and she could smell the scent of the ocean on his skin and clothes. Steel-blue eyes bore through her, stripping her bare, and her feet felt cemented to the floor.

She couldn't move.

"Ivy?"

"No!" she shrieked, no longer able to contain the anger and frustration and hurt that had been festering for far too long. "You never lied to me, Dillon. In fact, you made it distinctly clear just how little our marriage meant to you."

She regretted the words the instant they left her mouth, but it was too late to take them back. She was still bitter and hurt by the divorce and now he knew it. And she didn't doubt he would use it against her.

For several long seconds he just stared at her, his expression impossible to decipher. Finally, his voice neither warm nor cold, he said, "I wasn't the one who walked out the door."

His words felt like a slap across the face and literally knocked her back a step. He wasn't suggesting the demise of their marriage was *her* fault, was he? There was only one person to blame, and he was standing right in front of her.

Who had repeatedly stayed out every night and come home drunk while she had done her best to get an education? Who had blown his money gambling week after week?

And who had sicced his father on the grant committee and had her scholarship revoked?

Maybe he hadn't lied, but what he'd done was worse. He'd let her down.

For a second they just stood there looking at each other, then he shook his head, so subtly she had to wonder if she'd really seen it or if it had been a trick of the light.

"Good night, Ivy." He turned and left, closing the door quietly behind him.

And for some stupid reason she felt like crying.

She didn't care what he believed. What had happened to their marriage was not her fault. She may have been the one to physically walk out the door, but emotionally, Dillon had already been long gone.

Ivy dove into the pool, limbs slicing across the still water like a hot knife through cool butter. Thanks to Mr. I-never-lied-to-you, she'd slept like hell and woke at dawn. But with each stroke she could feel the stress from the previous night begin to evaporate, burned away by the adrenaline and endorphins coursing through her bloodstream.

She'd always had something of a love/hate relationship with exercise. She'd been blessed with a naturally slim figure, so her sporadic visits to the gym never caused her concern. In the last few years, however, she'd noticed things gradually beginning to expand and spread.

Hence her daily morning swim. It was the one thing that felt the least like real exercise. And while it wouldn't bring back the figure of her youth, she was able to comfortably maintain her present weight.

She only wished some of that extra weight had been redistributed to her less than impressive bustline.

She completed her laps and surfaced, and there, not three feet away, lay Dillon in a lounge chair beside the pool, a mug of coffee in one hand. Watching her, of course.

Here we go again.

She couldn't see what he had on from the waist down, other than the fact that his feet and calves were bare, but from the waist up he wore a deep tan and a sleepy smile. One that said, *hmm, how can I mess with Ivy today?*

She ignored the sudden lightness in her chest, the jittery, nervous feeling in her stomach. She repressed the *why me* groan working its way up her chest.

"Morning," he said. Dark stubble shadowed his jaw and his hair had that mussed, just-rolled-out-of-the-sack look.

She wondered how long he'd been sitting there watching her. She'd never seen him crawl out of bed before ten in the morning. Usually it was closer to noon.

She swam to the ladder and climbed out, facing away from him, feeling uncomfortable despite her modest one-piece suit. It was still too revealing. Too likely to show off the changes in her body, when his own physique appeared to have only improved with age.

And really, why did she care?

She wrapped herself in a towel, squeezing the excess water from her hair. "You're awake early."

"I'm an early riser these days."

Just her luck. More time he could spend harassing her.

Yet nothing good would come of letting him see that he was irritating her. Last night was an unfortunate setback. It was imperative that today she play it cool. She had to be patient.

She grabbed her iced coffee from the table where she'd left it and turned to her ex. When she realized how he was dressed, the cup nearly slipped from her grasp.

Deep down in the rational part of her brain, she knew he was going for shock value. She knew the appropriate reaction was no reaction at all.

Unfortunately, at the moment, her rational brain was not calling the shots. *"What are you wearing?"*

He looked down to his lap, at what appeared to be a pair of very expensive black silk boxers. "Skivvies," he said casually, as though there was nothing at all inappropriate about walking around a strange house in his underwear. "I would have put on pajamas, but as I'm sure you recall, I don't wear any. Besides," he said, with a slight wiggle of his eyebrows, "it's nothing you haven't seen before."

"There are six other people in this house, you know."

"And they're all sound asleep."

"Not to mention the housekeep—" She stopped abruptly and spun away from him. "For pity's sake, at least have the decency to button your fly."

"Whoops," she heard him say, although he didn't sound all that concerned with his faux pas. The man would go to any lengths to make her uncomfortable. "No wonder the housekeeper looked at me funny when I was pouring my coffee." There was a short pause, then he said, "The stallion is locked back in the stable. You can turn around now."

Facing him meant he would possibly see the red patches of embarrassment blooming across her cheeks. But not facing him would be even worse.

She turned, keeping her eyes above neck level. Looking at his bare chest reminded her of touching his bare chest, which reminded her of other things they used to do. Which would only make the blush burn brighter.

"When did you start swimming?" he asked. "I seemed to recall you hating exercise."

"I still do, but some of us have to work at it."

"And you're assumin' I don't? Would it surprise you to learn that I go to the gym every morning before work?"

Being surprised wasn't the issue. She didn't want to know about his life. It humanized him, made him seem like a regular guy. She preferred to keep him in the niche she'd carved out for him. That place in her mind where he would always be arrogant and cocky and totally unappealing.

"Although I never did learn how to swim," he said, which she found incredibly hard to swallow. True, she'd never actually seen him swim, but his home had been highlighted on some decorating show on cable television—or so someone had told her. From what she heard he owned a big, fancy mansion—she might have even driven past it one time, accidentally, of course—where he'd installed an Olympic-size indoor pool. He wasn't married, didn't have children. Why install a pool if he didn't plan to use it?

"You should try it sometime," she said.

"Are you going golfing today?" he asked, referring to the golf outing Blake and Deidre had scheduled.

Apparently, he didn't remember everything about her. She did not golf.

She was about to tell him no, she didn't plan to go, but caught herself. There was only one thing Dillon had loved more than drinking and gambling. That was golfing. But if he knew she wasn't going, he might very well skip it and spend the entire day harassing her.

"I'm going," she lied.

"Blake said we're meeting in the foyer at ten-fifteen."

That could be a problem. If she didn't show, he would know she wasn't going. Of course, if she was already gone by ten-fifteen, he would have no idea where to look for her. It shouldn't be all that tough to slip away. "Well then, I should hurry back to my room and get ready."

"Wear something cool," he called after her as she rushed inside. "It's going to be a scorcher."

"Will do!" she shot back. She could sneak out of the house by ten, and Dillon would never be the wiser. And she would have the entire day all to herself.

Five

*Is your ex harassing you? Trying to intimidate
you? Take action and beat him at his own game!
It's easier than you may think.*
—excerpt from *The Modern Woman's Guide to
Divorce (And the Joy of Staying Single)*

He'd reduced himself to stalking.

Dillon followed several yards behind Ivy as she
browsed the merchandise lining the streets of the
shopping district. He'd been following her since she
snuck out of the house this morning.

He couldn't help thinking that he'd sunk pitifully
low, but he had to keep his eye on the prize. Seeing Ivy
broken and begging for forgiveness.

The sun brought out the reddish-gold highlights in

her hair, and a cool breeze blowing off the ocean ruffled the full, filmy-looking skirt she wore, playing a tantalizing game of peek-a-boo with those long, toned, milky-white legs.

She wore a simple, pale blue tank top that settled nicely on shoulders that, on someone else, would have been too narrow and angular. But everything about her body fit just right. He wasn't the only one who noticed, either. As she wandered down the cobblestone street, dignified and maybe a touch aloof, heads turned and eyes looked on with interest.

But he knew something they didn't. He knew the feisty, passionate girl she hid behind that curtain of quiet grace. There were times when he missed that woman. But she had disappeared the moment they'd said *I do*.

He wondered what it would take to draw her out. If she even existed any longer. Somehow he doubted it.

It might be fun finding out though.

Ivy picked up a bottle of something from a table, perfume maybe, and lifted it to her nose. She closed her eyes and inhaled deeply, a dreamy look on her face.

The vendor behind the table said something, and she smiled and shook her head. A genuine, easy smile. One he hadn't seen in a very long time. Even on the inside jacket of her book, which he had grudgingly skimmed at Barnes & Noble, she'd been all business. And near the end of their marriage neither had done much in the way of smiling. Not at each other, anyway.

That had always been Ivy's problem. She was too repressed and too driven. She'd never learned how to have fun. At least, not out of the bedroom. And it wasn't as if he hadn't tried to teach her. They had been making good progress, then they got married and she did a one-eighty on him.

After a bit of haggling, she reached into the pack she wore around her waist, pulled out several bills and handed them to the vendor. She slipped her purchase inside her pack and moved on to the next canopy.

She looked so relaxed and serene. At peace with herself and the world.

A grin curled his mouth. What better time to mosey up and say hello?

"Well, well, what a coincidence," he drawled from behind her in that counterfeit twang he knew grated on her nerves.

Her hand stilled midair, just short of the colorful silk shawl she'd been about to look at, and every inch of her went rigid.

This was too easy. Better than greeting her this morning in his underwear, although that had been pretty damned funny. She obviously hadn't noticed the robe draped over the chair beside him.

Still only seeing what she wanted to see, believing what she wanted to believe.

Ivy paused and took a deep breath, as if gathering her strength—or maybe her patience—then turned to face him. She'd sufficiently wiped any trace of emotion from her face, but she forgot who she was dealing with. He picked up on the subtle signs no one else noticed. The crinkle in her brow and the slight tightening of her jaw. The way she ground her teeth and narrowed her eyes the tiniest bit.

Things she probably wasn't even aware she was doing.

She could pretend she wasn't annoyed, but he knew better.

"Why do I sincerely doubt this is a coincidence?" she asked.

He shrugged. "It wouldn't have anything to do with you bein' somethin' of a pessimist, now would it?"

"What are you doing here?"

He flashed her a grin and held up the bag he was carrying. "Souvenirs. For my secretary."

"Lingerie?" she guessed.

"Nah. My preferences in sleepwear lean toward the casual. Oversize T-shirts…" He leaned closer, lowering his voice. "Or nothing at all."

She rolled her eyes.

"Not to mention the fact that my secretary is sixty-eight."

"Aren't you supposed to be playing golf?"

"Shopping sounded like more fun."

She let an undignified snort slip out. "Now I *know* you're lying. You love playing golf, and you always hated shopping."

"That is true. It's the company I wasn't all that thrilled about. What was it you called them? The Tweedles?"

It wasn't a lie. He'd had more of those two than he could stomach at dinner last night. And torturing Ivy won out over golf any day of the week. He just had to accidentally bump into her, the way he'd "accidentally" walked into her room. What he hadn't counted on last night was getting himself sucked into a touchy-feely debate about their failed marriage.

She was still trying to pin the blame on him. No big surprise there.

Miss Perfect. Miss Nothing-is-ever-good-enough-for-me. Maybe he'd made a mistake or two, *minor ones,* but if anyone was ultimately responsible for the divorce, it was her.

And why had she assumed that what he'd done at dinner last night had anything to do with her? He was merely helping a friend. Blake was a good guy, the kind who would give a stranger the shirt off his back in the middle of a blizzard. But as long as Dillon had known him, Blake let his family walk all over him. With golf cleats on.

Deidre was the perfect match for him. Soft-spoken and demure, and maybe a little awkward. Although Dillon sensed there was more to her than met the eye, the spark of something more complex. A confidence that she hadn't let herself explore. If that was the case, Dillon suspected that she would only take so much more from his family before she blew a gasket.

He hoped so. Otherwise, they would eat her for breakfast.

"Well," Ivy said with a forced smile. "It was…nice seeing you again."

He chuckled. "Now, that's a lie if I ever heard one."

"You're right, it is a lie. Goodbye." She turned and marched off, weaving her way through the crowd of people clogging the streets. Did she really think he was going to let her off that easy?

This was a vacation, and he intended to have fun.

* * *

Ivy zigzagged her way through the crowd, resisting the urge to break into a run and let Dillon see her desperation.

The market was hot and noisy, the air filled with the spicy scent of unfamiliar and delectable foods she had been hoping to sample. There were a million different things to see and do, places to explore.

And she'd planned to do it alone.

Barely thirty seconds passed before she heard Dillon say, "Where's the fire?"

She groaned to herself. He wasn't going to leave her alone. He was going to dog her all afternoon, like a joy-sucking leech. And how had he managed to find her? She'd waited until no one was around to sneak out of the house, and she hadn't told anyone, not even Deidre, where she was going.

Had he lied about golf? Had he hidden somewhere and waited for her to leave, then followed her? Would he be that devious?

Dumb question. Of course he would.

What had she done to deserve this?

She could play this two ways. She could act as though she didn't care, or she could bluntly tell him to leave her the hell alone. But she knew Dillon. Admitting he was annoying her would only fuel his determination. The best way to possibly get rid of him, the *only* way, was to pretend she didn't care either way. Eventually he would get bored and find someone else to torture. She hoped.

Either way she would be stuck with him for the rest of the afternoon. Maybe longer.

Yahoo. She could hardly wait.

She cast him a sideways glance. He walked beside her, thumbs hooked loosely in the front pockets of his jeans, casual as you please, and for an instant she felt a tiny bit breathless. He wore a pair of faded Levi's, polished cowboy boots and a white tank top that accentuated the golden tan of his shoulders, the lean definition in his biceps. His hair had that casual, slightly mussed look, as if he'd just rolled out of bed and run his fingers through it. Which is what he used to do ten years ago.

But when a person looked at him, really looked, it was clear there was more to him than just a pretty face. You could see the breeding, the auspicious roots.

He wore his status well. It complemented, but didn't define him.

"So, you're a hotshot author now," he said.

"If you say so." She tried to keep it light and brief. She didn't want to say the wrong thing and give him a new round of ammunition to fire her way.

"I heard you're writing a followup to that little book of yours."

"Did you?" He could condescend all he liked, but that "little" book had made more money than she and the coauthor, Miranda Reed, had ever imagined possible.

Having both endured grueling, nasty divorces, the project had been more therapeutic than financially motivated. They hadn't even been sure anyone would want to publish it. In fact, they had been fairly certain the manuscript would sit untouched on some apathetic editor's desk, yellowing at the edges and gathering dust.

Not only did it sell, it became ensnared in a bidding

war between several publishing houses. Since its release it had been topping the bestseller lists. It was a pure fluke that it had struck a chord with so many readers. And disturbing to discover the staggering number of women who had endured, or were presently experiencing, painful divorces.

It had solidified Ivy's belief that happy, successful marriages were a rare anomaly not experienced by the majority of the population. And with very few exceptions, women were better off staying single.

"I would think you'd have run out of material by now," Dillon said.

Was the hotshot billionaire afraid he would be seeing his checkered past in print again?

Well, well. This was interesting.

"Do I detect a note of concern?" she asked.

"The truth is, I was thinkin' maybe I'll write a book, too."

If he was trying to scare her, he would have to do better. "Good luck with that."

"A tell-all with every intimate detail of our marriage." He grinned and nodded his head, as if he was really warming to the idea. "Yeah. Or better yet, maybe I should send a letter or two to *Penthouse Forum*."

"Sex with you was not that exciting," she said, knowing as well as he did that it was a big fat lie. Near the end, their sex life had been as volatile as their tempers, as if they had been taking out all their frustrations in bed.

"Are you forgetting the time we got creative with that bottle of hot fudge and you let me lick it off your—"

"I remember," she interjected, fighting the blush that

had begun to creep up from her collar. Hot fudge hadn't been the only food they'd experimented with. She had fond memories of a can of whipped cream and a bottle of maraschino cherries.

"And if memory serves, you had a particularly sensitive spot, right here…" He reached up and brushed the tip of his index finger against the spot just below her ear.

She instinctively batted his hand away, but not before a ripple of erotic sensation whispered across her skin, making her feel warm and shivery at the same time. She shot him a warning look.

His victory triggered a triumphant, smug grin. "Yes, ma'am, it's still there."

"Try it again and you'll lose that finger." Verbal torment was one thing. Touching was off limits.

"I think I just figured out your problem."

So had she. He was walking right beside her.

But she had to ask, "Which problem would that be?"

"Sex."

Sex? Oh, she couldn't wait to see where he was going with this. "My problem is sex?"

"I'll bet you haven't had it in a long time."

She thought back to Deidre's comment about Ivy's less than active sex life. The truth was, she hadn't been with a man, hadn't had time for a relationship, much less a one-night stand, in so long she wasn't sure she remembered how. But as she told Deidre, she didn't need a man to complete her. And if she was looking for sexual release, she didn't need a man for that, either.

"And you're basing this assumption on what exactly?" she asked Dillon.

"Though you try to repress it, you're a very passionate person. Passionate people need sex regularly or they get cranky. And darlin', you are about as cranky as they come."

Did it ever occur to him that *he* was the one making her cranky?

"It can't be just any sex, either," he went on. "It has to be damned good, preferably with someone who knows exactly what it takes to light their fire."

And she was pretty sure he was offering to do the job. Did he honestly think he could charm his way back into her bed? Could he possibly be that arrogant?

Of course he could.

The real question was, what did she plan to do about it? How would she put him in his place and teach him a lesson he should have learned a long time ago?

She would do the one thing he would never expect. The only thing that would knock *him* completely off balance.

She stopped abruptly, right in the middle of the street, in front of God and everyone, and turned to face him. Before he could get his bearings, or she had a second of clarity to talk herself out of it, she reached up and curled her fingers into the front of his shirt. She wrapped her other hand around the back of his neck and tugged him down to her level.

He smelled of soap and shampoo and his hair was soft around her fingers. His wide-eyed surprise was the last thing she saw as she planted a kiss right on his damp and slightly parted lips.

* * *

Just when Dillon thought he had Ivy pegged, she did something completely off the wall and totally out of character. He'd expected some sort of reaction from her. One of those cool, deadly stares or a snippy remark. The last thing he'd expected was a kiss.

And he sure as hell hadn't expected to enjoy it.

One brush of her full, soft lips, one taste of her sweet mouth, and the memory of the fighting, the bitter, angry words they had flung at each other like daggers, misted like the ocean spray, then evaporated in the hot, dry Mexican air.

It came on swift and sudden, like a sniper attack, and before his brain had a chance to catch up with his body to process the acute physical response, it was over.

In a flash he was back on the noisy, crowded street. Ivy stood with her hands propped on her hips, looking up at him. Her eyes cold. In that instant he understood exactly what she was doing and what she meant to accomplish. And for reasons he didn't understand—or didn't want to admit—he felt cheated.

No one had looked at him with the same genuine and honest admiration as Ivy had. As long as he could remember, his family name had afforded him certain privileges. With little more than a snap of his fingers he could have had any woman he desired.

Ivy had been the only one he'd ever *needed*.

She saw through him, to the real man inside. She understood him in a way no one else had. Or maybe she had been the only one who bothered to try.

She studied him for a good thirty seconds, looking almost bored, then shrugged. "Nothing."

Ouch. She'd scored one on him, no doubt, and it had been a direct hit.

"I guess you just don't do it for me anymore," she said apologetically. "But I appreciate the offer."

She spun away, skirt swishing around her legs. Only then did it register; the slight tremble in her voice, her pulse throbbing at the base of her throat and the smudge of color riding the arch of her cheeks.

A man didn't spend a year of marriage without learning a woman's signals. And he could read hers loud and clear. He wasn't the only one turned on by that kiss. She wanted him, too.

This called for a slight change of plans. There was only one thing that could possibly be more fun than annoying Ivy, and that would be getting back into her panties. That would be the ultimate payback.

He was smiling as he set off after her. It looked as if they would be taking this competition to an all new level.

Six

*Divorce recovery typically takes two full years.
Take it day by day. Trust me, the time will soon
come when you'll look back and wonder what you
ever saw in him.*
—excerpt from *The Modern Woman's Guide to
Divorce (And the Joy of Staying Single)*

Kiss your ex-husband. Brilliant idea.

As fast as her wobbly legs would carry her, Ivy
headed blindly in what she hoped was the general direction of the villa, praying that Dillon didn't follow her.

Weathered stucco buildings, brightly colored can-
opies and an ocean of moving bodies blurred together
like smudged oil paint on a three-dimensional canvas.
Voices and sounds echoed through her ears and jumbled

around inside her head, disorienting her. Her hands were trembling and her heart beat hard and fast in her chest.

One stupid kiss and she was a walking disaster area. *What had she been thinking?*

It wasn't supposed to happen this way. She was supposed to be proving how over him she was. She wasn't supposed to *enjoy* kissing him.

She wasn't supposed to *feel* anything.

And if she had to feel something, why couldn't it have been hate? Disgust would have been a good one, too. Or good old-fashioned anger.

And what if by some remote chance someone recognized them? Someone who had read her book? What if word got out that she was messing around with her ex? What would people think of her? How could her readers, not to mention her patients, trust her if she couldn't even follow her own edict?

This was bad.

Really, *really* bad.

Although she had to admit that seeing the stunned look on his face, knowing that for once *she* had flustered *him,* had almost been worth it. In a sadistic sort of way. Like cutting off her nose to spite her face.

"You sure move fast when you have something to run from," Dillon said from behind her, and Ivy cursed under her breath.

Oh, crud.

She needed a minute to pull herself together. She couldn't let him see her thrown so far off-kilter.

This was just a fluke. She'd been too immersed in her

career, too swamped promoting her first book and writing the second to even think about sex, so, yeah, she'd overreacted a little.

Okay, she'd overreacted *a lot*. But she would have gotten the same result from kissing any number of men.

She tried to conjure up a name, an appealing, eligible man in her life. Maybe one in the office building where she worked, or at the club where she used the pool. Or even at the grocery store. There had to be *someone*.

Yet not a single one came to mind.

Oh, hell, who was she kidding? She could continue to blame her busy schedule, but deep down she knew that was bunk. The reason she hadn't slept with anyone in…well, longer than she wanted to admit, was because she hadn't met anyone she wanted to sleep with. Up until today.

Oh, no. She did *not* just think that. She didn't want to sleep with Dillon. Not now, not ever.

"And what is it exactly that I'm running from?" she asked. She even managed to keep her voice steady and vaguely disinterested.

The deep baritone of laughter that followed rubbed across every one of her nerve endings until they felt raw and exposed.

He knew. He knew exactly what that kiss had done to her, and he would spend the rest of the week rubbing it in her face.

Would this nightmare never end?

She was about to turn, to face Dillon, still unsure of exactly what she wanted to do or say—and resigned to the fact that whatever it was it would probably only make things worse—when she spotted Deidre and Blake walking down the opposite side of the street like two angels of mercy.

"Deidre!" she called, waving frantically to get her attention. The instant Deidre looked her way Ivy knew something was wrong. Her skin looked pale, and the way she leaned into Blake gave the distinct impression he was holding her steady.

Forgetting Dillon and every other horrible thing that transpired that morning, she rushed across the street to her cousin. As she drew closer she noticed the bandage on Deidre's forehead.

Her grotesquely *swelled* forehead.

Ivy's horror and surprise must have shown, because the first thing out of Deidre's mouth was, "It's not as bad as it looks."

"Let me see." Without waiting for permission, she lifted Deidre's bangs to get a better look. The area over her left eye looked swollen and tender, and hints of purple peeked out from under the edge of the bandage. "Oh, my God, what happened to you?"

"An alleged golfing mishap," Blake said bitterly.

Deidre ducked away from Ivy and shot him a look. "It was an accident. And the doctor at the clinic said the swelling should be down in time for the wedding."

"You had to see a doctor?"

Deidre nodded. "I needed three stitches."

Why did it have to happen this week? It was just one more thing to put a damper on the most important day of Deidre's life.

"Who did this to you?" Dillon asked, and Ivy jolted

at the sound of his voice. She hadn't even realized he'd followed her.

"Dale's girlfriend," Blake all but spat out. "She swung her club and lost her grip. It went flying and pegged Deidre in the head."

"But it was an accident," Deidre said with a forced cheeriness that wasn't fooling anyone. "Believe me, her aim is not that good. She can barely hit a ball much less a person standing fifteen feet behind her."

Dillon looked from Deidre to Blake. "Which one is Dale's girlfriend? Tweedle Dum or Tweedle Dee?"

Blake shrugged. "Who knows. I can't tell them apart. When it happened, I was more concerned with stopping the bleeding than figuring out who was at fault."

The only thing concerning Ivy was Deidre's pasty-white pallor and the dark circles under her eyes. The way she clung to Blake's arm, as though without him there she might topple over.

Dillon's eyes mirrored Ivy's concern. "Maybe you should go back to the villa and lay down for a while."

"No! I refuse to spend the week of my wedding in bed feeling sorry for myself." Deidre sounded awfully close to tears, and Ivy had the distinct feeling there was more to this than she was admitting. "I don't want to talk about my head anymore."

Blake looked curiously between Ivy and Dillon. "So, what are you guys up to?"

What he really meant was, what were they doing together.

"We were shopping and we bumped into each other," Ivy said, shooting Dillon a look that said she knew damn well their meeting had been no accident. And if he said one word about what had happened, he would die a very slow, agonizing death.

He just smiled. "That's right, and I was just about to invite Ivy to lunch."

"Perfect!" Deidre gushed, perking up instantly. "We were looking for somewhere to eat." She wove an arm through Ivy's and clamped down. Hard. "We can all eat together."

The death grip on Ivy's arm said very clearly that this was not a matter of choice. Ivy was going, even if Deidre had to drag her there.

Seeing there was no way to get out of this without making a scene, and making matters worse in the process, Ivy plastered a smile on her face and said, "Great. Let's eat."

The second they were shown to a table inside the bustling, noisy café, Deidre said something about needing to freshen up, then dragged Ivy with her to the ladies' room. Her grip on Ivy's arm was so tight she was cutting off the circulation. When they were safely inside with the door shut Deidre finally let go.

Ivy shook the blood back into her tingling fingers. "All right, what's going on?"

"I hate them," Deidre spat with a ferocity that was completely unlike her. Angry tears pooled in her eyes. "I hate the Tweedles and I hate Blake's brothers."

Deidre didn't *hate* anybody. She was too sweet. But apparently even she had limits.

"What happened?"

"After I got hit, Blake went to go get the rental car. While he was gone, the four of them were—" Her voice broke and tears dribbled down her cheeks.

Ivy rubbed her shoulder. "They were what? What did they do?"

Deidre sniffled loudly and wiped the tears away with the heels of her palms. "They were…making fun of me. They were whispering and laughing."

Was it possible that they could be that rude? That cruel? "Could you hear what they were saying? I mean, maybe you misunderstood. Maybe they weren't talking about you." As she said the words she suspected they weren't true.

"They were looking right at me, and I heard Dale say it was my own fault for standing too close while she putted."

No, this was *Ivy's* fault. She had been afraid that antagonizing the Tweedles at dinner last night would only make things worse. That they might retaliate. She never should have lowered herself to their level.

And who had encouraged her to do that?

Dillon.

It didn't excuse her behavior. Or make her any less accountable, but in a roundabout way this was as much his fault as hers.

The thought made her feel a little bit better.

"Does Blake know about what they said?"

She sniffled and shook her head. "He already feels so bad. This would only make things worse."

Ivy didn't know if things could get much worse. That would take a tropical storm or a tsunami.

"She didn't even say she was sorry." Deidre wiped her eyes. "What did I ever do to them? Why are they so mean to me?"

"It's not you, Deidre. It's like I said at dinner last night. They're insecure. Cutting you down makes them feel better about themselves." She stepped into one of the empty stalls, pulled a length of toilet paper off the roll and handed it to Deidre. "It's also very possible that they're jealous."

"Yeah right," Deidre said with an indignant snort. She dabbed at her eyes and wiped her nose. "I'm sure they're both dying to be overweight and have my lousy skin. I'm like an ugly duckling next to them."

"It has nothing to do with looks or weight. They're jealous because no matter how skinny they are, or pretty they are, or how blond they dye their hair, they'll never be as happy as you and Blake. Hell, *I'm* jealous and I don't even want to get married."

Deidre shrugged.

"I'm serious. Blake is crazy about you. Anyone can see how happy you two are, how much you love each other. And no matter how mean and nasty the Tweedles are, they can't take that from you."

A grin teased the corners of Deidre's mouth. "You really think they're jealous?"

"I honestly do. Those two may be aesthetically attractive. Maybe even beautiful. But on the inside they're the worst kind of ugly."

"Blake's brothers don't think so."

"They're no better than the Tweedles. I sometimes

wonder how Blake turned out so normal when the rest of his family is completely wacky."

The smile spread to her cheeks. "Wacky? Is that an official diagnosis?"

Ivy laughed. "Absolutely."

Deidre may not have been conventionally beautiful, but she had a warm, genuine smile and a good heart. Ivy hoped Blake realized just how lucky he was.

And maybe somewhere deep down, she *was* a little jealous. But not everyone was lucky enough to find what Deidre and Blake had.

Some people weren't capable.

Deidre wiped her eyes one last time and tossed the tissue in the trash. "You know, no matter how lousy things seem, you always manage to make me feel better."

"It's what I'm trained to do."

"No, it's always been that way, even when we were really little. It's a gift."

If that were true, Ivy wished she could bestow that gift on herself.

"That's the reason I got you and Dillon together," Deidre admitted. "I wanted to help you the way you always help me. I wanted you to be happy."

"I am happy." The words spilled out automatically, but they sounded dry and hollow. Like maybe she wasn't so convinced anymore.

"Speaking of Dillon," Deidre said, "what's *really* going on with you two?"

Ivy shrugged. "Just like I said, we bumped into each other."

"You're sure about that."

Something in Deidre's expression said she knew something Ivy didn't. "Of course I'm sure."

"So what you're telling me is, you were just walking along and accidentally ran into him with your lips?"

Ivy winced.

Oh, crud. Didn't it just figure that not only had her plan backfired, but of the thousands of people roaming the city, Deidre had to be there to witness her mistake.

"Did Blake see?"

"Lucky for you he was looking the other way. And before you ask, no, I didn't say anything to him. And if you ask me not to, I won't. But do not think for a second that I'm going to let you off the hook. I expect an explanation."

Ivy opened her mouth to speak, but no sound came out. She didn't have a clue what to say.

"Well?" Deidre asked, all but tapping her foot, waiting impatiently. "What's the deal?"

"You know, if we don't get to the table soon, the men are going to send in a search party." She made a move toward the door, but Deidre blocked her way.

"I'm not letting you leave until you tell me the truth."

Ivy sighed. She may as well come clean. The worst Deidre could say is I told you so. "Okay, so I kissed him. But I did it to prove I was completely over him. That I'm not attracted to him anymore."

Deidre nodded. "I see. And did it work?"

"Umm…" She bit her lip.

"The truth, Ivy."

"I may have been a little…*flustered.*"

"I saw your face, honey. You were more than a little

flustered. You looked as if you'd gone ten rounds with the ghost of Christmas past."

Okay, so maybe I told you so *wasn't* the worst she could say.

If her feelings had been so clear to Deidre, Dillon must have known exactly what she was feeling. The man always did have an uncanny way of reading her thoughts, her body language.

"Proving that what you said was right," she told Deidre. "I haven't had sex in a long time. Too long, obviously. And it had nothing at all to do with Dillon."

"That's good, Ivy." Deidre reached for the knob and pulled the door open. "If you keep telling yourself that you might start believing it."

Seven

*Want to discover the secret (and dirty!) tactics
men use to make our lives hell?
(Shh...don't tell them we know!)*
—excerpt from *The Modern Woman's Guide to
Divorce (And the Joy of Staying Single)*

The man clung to her like lint on a black wool blazer.

After lunch, which she grudgingly admitted was not as bad as she'd anticipated, Deidre, Blake and Dillon took off to sightsee. Ivy headed back to the house and found it blissfully empty. No Tweedles, no ex-husbands or neurotic battered brides. Only tranquil silence.

Thirty seconds later Dillon strolled through the door.

She felt like throwing up her hands in surrender, breaking down and crying, and shoving Dillon over the balcony, down the rocky bluff and into the ocean below. All at the same time.

Just remember, he's doing this on purpose, she reminded herself. He's doing it to annoy you. Do not let him know it's working.

"I thought you were going sightseeing," she said in a flat, I'm-only-asking-to-be-polite voice.

He just shrugged—a slight hunch of his shoulders and an almost imperceptible tilt of his head. "Changed my mind."

No, he hadn't. This had been the plan all along.

Tease her with a hint of freedom, a few precious moments of peace, before he was back annoying her again.

Despite how many times she brushed him off, cosmic static cling kept drawing him back.

Just like lint.

Only, in this case, a dryer sheet wouldn't be much help. They didn't make one big enough or powerful enough to get rid of someone like him. The way to avoid Dillon, Ivy realized, would be to shut herself away in her room for the remainder of the week.

It couldn't be any worse than spending a week with him.

"I'm going up to my room to rest. I'll see you later." Much, *much* later.

"I understand why you might need some time alone," he said, a devilish glint in his eyes. "That kiss did get you pretty hot and bothered. You go ahead and take care of business."

"Business?" For a second she was confused, then it

hit her. She realized exactly what he meant by *business*. Did he really think she was going upstairs to—

"I have nothing against going solo." He stepped closer, eyes sparking with desire. His voice dropped a few decibels, even though they were the only ones there. "In fact, you might not remember, but I love to watch."

Oh, she remembered.

The things he'd talked her into doing back then still made her blush. Unlike past boyfriends, he'd never played the if-you-loved-me-you-would card. He'd been patient. A tender, generous lover. The kind of man who never failed to put her needs before his own.

The memory poured over Ivy like melted milk chocolate. Rich and sweet and warm. And her head had begun to get that light, fuzzy feeling…

Damn, damn, damn.

He was pulling that sexy, simmering thing he did so well. And like an idiot she was falling for it. *Again!* How could someone she disliked as much as Dillon be so darned appealing? Could it be that she didn't dislike him as much as she thought?

Or was she just losing her mind?

The worst part was he knew it. He knew exactly what he was doing to her, and he was loving every second of it.

Someone needed to cool that man's engines.

Since tossing him over the balcony into the ocean wasn't an option, she would have to settle for the next best thing.

"On second thought, maybe I'll dip my feet in the pool for a second and cool off." She switched direction, heading instead for the French doors that would take her to the pool deck. She knew he would follow, and he didn't disappoint her.

The man's libido had been bound to get him into trouble one of these days. She was just glad she would be around to see him get a dose of his own medicine. And even better, she would be the one to dispense the bitter pill.

He reached past her, like the gentleman he'd always been, and opened the door.

She stepped outside, a wall of dry, sweltering heat drawing her into its grip.

"Damn!" Dillon said. "Sure is hot out here."

Not to worry, he would be cooled off soon enough.

"I could use a cold drink," he said. "Can I get you something?"

"Whatever you're having."

"Two mineral waters comin' right up."

His arrogance, his unshakable self-confidence, would be his undoing.

She walked to the deep end of the pool, hiked her skirt up to the midthigh region so it wouldn't get wet— and hell, why not give him a decent view before he went down—and sat on the edge, the hot tile scorching the backs of her legs. She dipped her feet in and cool water lapped around her ankles. The midday sun reflecting off the surface strobed in her eyes and made her squint.

She watched as Dillon stepped around the bar and fished two bottles of water from the refrigerator. With the exception of a sip of champagne, she still hadn't seen him drink a single alcoholic beverage.

"You don't drink anymore?" she asked.

He opened both waters and added a wedge of lime to each one. "Occasionally."

Keep a casual conversation going so he doesn't suspect, she told herself. Act as if everything is normal. "What made you quit?"

"You ever try to run a billion-dollar corporation with a raging hangover?" He carried them both over to where she sat, and the anticipation was killing her.

"So it was interfering with your work?"

He shrugged. "The truth is, I didn't make a conscious effort to stop. I guess I just outgrew it." He leaned slightly forward to hand her a bottle. "Here you go."

"Thank you." She cast him a bright smile. This was going to feel *so* good.

She reached up to grab it, but instead she wrapped her hand around his wrist and yanked as hard as she could. He teetered for a second, trying to catch his balance, then he laughed and cursed and let himself fall.

He landed with a noisy, messy *kersploosh,* bottles and all, splashing her from head to toe with pool water.

"Yes!" She jumped to her feet, cherishing her victory. Maybe now he would stop messing with her; he would see she meant business. And even if he didn't, it had been a lot of fun.

She gazed down into the water. Any second now, he would rise to the top and see her smug smile, the satis-faction in her eyes. Maybe the kiss idea had been a disaster, but this would be her moment of triumph.

Yep, any second now.

She squinted to make out his shadowy form against the

dark tile lining the bottom of the pool. He was still *way* down there. Maybe he was looking for the water bottles. So someone didn't accidentally step on one and cut their foot. Only thing was, he didn't appear to be moving.

A pocket of air rose and bubbled to the surface but still no Dillon.

What if he'd hurt himself?

No, that was silly. She had seen him go in. He hadn't hit his head or twisted anything. At least, she didn't think so. He was fine. He was just trying to get her to jump in after him.

Well, she wasn't falling for it.

But how long could someone hold their breath? It had already been a while, hadn't it? Close to a minute even. At least it seemed that way.

As every second ticked past, her confidence began to fizzle.

What if there was something really wrong? What if he wasn't breathing? What if he'd been telling the truth and he really didn't know how to swim?

He'd told her he never learned how and she'd pushed him in regardless, meaning she would be responsible if he was hurt.

If he *died*.

Her heart dropped hard and fast, leaving a sick, empty hole in her chest as a dozen gruesome images flashed through her brain at the speed of light. Dillon being dragged from the pool, his tanned skin gray and waxy, his lips a deathly shade of blue.

Dillon's funeral. Having to face his family and admit it had been her fault.

She thought of all the things she could have said to him, *should have said,* and had never gotten the chance.

Her stomach churned with the possibilities, and her head swam with disbelief. She didn't like Dillon, but she didn't want him dead, either.

And what if no one believed it was an accident? She could see the headlines now. *Bestselling author murders ex-husband after publicly berating him in her tell-all book.*

Dillon had floated closer to the surface, but he still wasn't moving, and she was running out of time. There was no way he could hold his breath for that long.

Oh, hell.

She kicked off her sandals and dove in, the cool water swallowing her up like a hungry beast, numbing her senses. All she could feel was the dull throb of panic squeezing her chest, hear the beat of her own pulse in her ears, louder and louder as she descended. She opened her eyes, blinking against the burn of chlorine. Her gaze darted back and forth as she searched, desperate to spot his floating form. She would have to hoist him from the pool and do mouth-to-mouth, get his airway cleared. She'd been certified in first aid and CPR for years, but she'd never actually had to use it. She only hoped she remembered how.

But she would have to find him first. He was gone, as if he had vanished into thin air, or been sucked into an alternate universe.

She hit the bottom at the ten-foot mark and flipped over, her long skirt tangling around her legs. She looked up and saw a pair of booted feet and blue jeans and the lower half of a male torso. The rest of him was out of the water.

And he was very much alive.

She heard a muffled noise above her and realized it was laughter. He was laughing.

He was okay. All this time he'd been okay, and now he was *laughing* at her.

She pushed off the bottom of the pool and sailed to the surface, her lungs screaming for air.

A minute ago all she could think about was saving his sorry behind. Now she wanted to kill him.

Dillon hoisted himself up onto the pool edge beside the ladder, wiping water from his eyes and sweeping his dripping hair back from his forehead. His wet jeans clung to him like a cloying second skin, his boots were toast and his lungs burned like the devil from holding his breath for too long. But it would be worth it. Worth the look on Ivy's face when she re-surfaced.

Would she never learn? No matter how dirty she played, he always sank an inch lower. He always won.

Ivy popped up out of the water, blinking rapidly to clear her eyes. Her auburn ponytail hung lopsided and limp and one side of her tank top drooped down her arm.

She looked like a drowned rat.

He smiled and said, "Gottcha."

She didn't yell, didn't call him a jerk. She didn't even look at him. She just swam to the ladder in a few long, easy strokes and grabbed the rail. For a second he thought she might try to dunk him, but she only pulled herself up from the water. Her wet skirt stuck to her legs and was considerably more transparent than it had been before.

Was that a pink thong she was wearing?

Her eyes were rimmed with red, her mouth pulled into a rigid line.

"Hey." He reached out and grabbed her arm but she jerked it away. Without a word she walked across the patio to the house, wet feet slapping, clothes dripping.

He knew every one of Ivy's expressions and he could swear he'd just seen her on-the-verge-of-tears face.

Of all the reactions she could have possibly had, why would she cry? Anger he could understand. He'd expected her to be furious. But tears?

Or maybe she was crying because he *hadn't* drowned.

No. If she'd wanted him dead, she wouldn't have jumped in to rescue him. Maybe she was just embarrassed that once again he had bested her. The gentlemanly thing to do would be to apologize, even though she'd started it, then maybe rub it in her a face one more time for good measure.

He jumped up and went after her, his feet squishing in his sodden boots. "Ivy, hold up."

But she didn't stop moving. If anything, she walked faster. She flung open the door, but, thanks to a much longer stride, he caught her just inside the threshold.

"Come on, Ivy, stop." He reached for her, wrapping his hand around her wrist. Once again she jerked free and marched through the living room. She wasn't just a little angry that he'd gotten the best of her. She was seriously peeved.

"Come on, Ivy, it was a joke. Lighten up."

She stopped abruptly and swung around to face him. Her eyes were bloodshot, her face pale, and tears hovered just inside her eyelids.

"A joke?" she asked incredulously. Her lower lip quivered and her hands were trembling. "You call *that* a joke?"

He shrugged. "I was just fooling around."

"Fooling around?" She took a step toward him, raising both her arms. For a second he thought she was going to deck him, or wrap her hands around his throat and squeeze. Instead she planted both hands on his chest and gave him a good, hard shove. Because he was prepared and outweighed her by almost half, he didn't go very far.

"Fooling around?" she repeated. Then she gave him another shove, harder this time, knocking him back a couple of inches and darn near forcing the air from his lungs. "You scared me to death, you idiot! I thought you drowned! I thought you were *dead.*"

The tears flowed over and rolled down her cheeks, and whatever pride remained of his victory fizzled away. "I didn't mean to scare you."

An explosive combination of fear and fury burned hot and lethal in her eyes. She wound up again, but before she could shove him he grabbed her wrists. She tried to jerk away, but this time he held on.

"Let go of me!" She twisted and yanked, struggling to break free, and he began to worry that she was so hysterical, she would hurt not only him, but herself.

"Ivy, calm down! I didn't mean to scare you." He

pulled her against him, managed to get his arms around
her, pinning her close to his body to protect them both.
She was cold, wet and trembling all over. *"I'm sorry."*

Eight

Has your ex frustrated you to the breaking point? Physical violence, though tempting, is not the answer. Try a punching bag or a voodoo doll instead.
—excerpt from *The Modern Woman's Guide to Divorce (And the Joy of Staying Single)*

Ivy wrestled with him another second or two, then went still in his arms.

"I'm sorry," he said again, since that seemed to do the trick. He pressed his cheek to the top of her soggy head.

Her body went lax, as if she'd burned up every last bit of energy, and she all but collapsed against him. Her arms circled his waist and she clung to him, a dripping, trembling, emotional catastrophe.

It wasn't supposed to happen this way. The game had gotten way out of hand this time. Hadn't they hurt each other enough?

"I'm sorry," he whispered, and her arms squeezed him tighter. He would say it a million times if it would take back what he'd done.

"I th-thought you were dead," she hiccupped, her cheek pressed against his wet shirt. His throat felt tight with emotion.

Jesus, what was wrong with him?

Maybe it was a little crazy—or a lot crazy—but he liked her this way. Soft and sweet and vulnerable. She was usually so independent, so driven, he'd rarely had the opportunity to play the role of the hero. The protector.

He stroked her soggy, tangled hair, and for one of those brief, fleeting moments remembered all the reasons he'd fallen in love with her. And wondered why in the hell he'd let her get away.

But it was tough to keep someone around who didn't want to be there.

"You're going to wish you had drowned, because when I stop shaking, I'm going to kill you," she warned him, but she didn't let go. Didn't even loosen her grip.

Why would she get so upset if she didn't still care about him, didn't still love him somewhere deep down?

And what difference would it make if she did? They'd had their go-around, and it had been a disaster. They may have loved each other, but that didn't mean they could get along.

That didn't mean there hadn't been good times, too.

He cupped a hand under her chin and lifted her face to his. She gazed up at him with watery, bloodshot eyes, mascara running down her face, and he couldn't stop himself from smiling.

"I must look awful," she said with a sniffle.

He rubbed his thumbs across her cheeks, wiping away the last of her tears. "Not at all."

In fact, he couldn't remember her ever looking more beautiful, more appealing than she did at that very second.

He brushed his thumbs over her full lips. Her mouth looked soft and inviting. He tried to recall what it felt like to kiss her, and not that taunting little peck she'd laid on him earlier. A real, honest to goodness, I'll-go-nuts-if-I-can't-have-you-this-second kiss.

When he looked in her eyes he could swear she was thinking the exact same thing.

In that instant he knew he needed to kiss her. Not wanted. He *needed* to.

It wasn't about revenge or breaking her spirit. It wasn't even about sex. It was just something he *had* to do.

He lowered his head and she rose up to meet him halfway. They came together swift and firm. With purpose. As though they both knew what they wanted and they weren't afraid to take it, the consequences be damned.

She took him into her mouth, against her tongue. She tasted warm and familiar and exciting.

He didn't know what he was expecting, but it wasn't for Ivy to grab his ass and drive herself hard against him. He was so surprised and so turned on, he just about embarrassed himself. He didn't even know it was possible to get a boner wearing ice-cold wet denim.

He bit down on her lip, the way he used to, and she moaned her appreciation. The sound slipped over him like exquisite Italian silk, cranking his level of arousal up yet another notch. Then she slipped her hand between their tightly fused bodies and rubbed it over his crotch, and he was the one moaning.

He knew without a doubt that kissing her was not going to cut it. He needed to get her naked. He wouldn't be satisfied until he was driving himself deep inside her. Watching her shatter in his arms.

He tugged at her soggy shirt, trying to push it up and out of the way, so he could get his hands on some skin. She must have had the same idea, because he could feel her wrestling with the hem of his shirt. At least they were on the same page.

But these wet clothes had to go.

He nipped her lip again, and Ivy moaned. She fisted her hands in his shirt, her nails scraping his skin. Everything in her body language begged, *take me now,* and he couldn't come up with a single reason why he shouldn't. Not that he was trying all that hard to come up with one.

Then he heard a door open and voices in the foyer. An obnoxious, earsplitting cackle of laughter rang through his ears. That was the laugh of a Tweedle. He could feel his hard-on instantly begin to deflate.

Looked as if they were about to have company.

Why the hell hadn't he swept her up and carried her to his room? Or her room. Or the bathroom? *Anywhere* that they would have a little privacy.

As abruptly as they had come together, they broke apart. Both dazed and breathless. And still soaking wet.

Ivy blinked a few times, gazing around as if she'd completely forgotten where she was.

The Tweedles and Blake's brothers appeared in the hallway a second later, like crashers at a private party. *His* party. They were still dressed in their golf gear, and Dee, or was it Dum—he still couldn't tell them apart— was laughing. Awfully jovial, weren't they, considering what had happened to Deidre?

He absently wondered which one had pegged her, and if she felt even a modicum of regret. If she cared about anyone but herself.

All four stopped abruptly when they noticed Ivy and Dillon standing there. The one he was pretty sure was Dum inspected them from head toe, a look of revulsion on her face. "Oh, my God. What happened to you?"

Ivy looked from Dillon, to herself, then back to their captivated audience. He couldn't wait to see how she explained this one.

She shrugged, the picture of innocence, and said, "We went swimming." As if that was obvious, and not at all unusual despite the fact that they were both fully dressed.

She always did have a way of making the ridiculous or unlikely seem completely rational.

Not that he gave a damn what the four Musketeers did or didn't know.

Of course, at some point the news would have gotten back to his mother. He didn't really give a damn what she thought, either. But the business of trying to explain and assuring her that there was no way in hell he and

Ivy would ever try to reconcile would be a big pain in the behind. A hassle he didn't need. Or want.

If they were going to do this, it would be best to keep it to themselves.

And they were. Even if Ivy didn't realize it yet.

"You're dripping everywhere," the other Tweedle said, mirroring her counterpart's distaste.

Those two really needed to lighten up.

Ivy looked down at the growing puddle of water around her feet. "Oops. Guess I should go change into some dry clothes."

Gathering her wet skirt, she bolted for the stairs, but not before he saw the mildly shocked, what-the-hell-have-I-done look on her face.

"Guess I should change, too," Dillon said, heading after her, leaving the others looking thoroughly confused.

"Who's going to clean up this mess?" one of the Tweedles called after him, but he was more concerned with the pound of Ivy's footsteps up the stairs. She was moving awfully fast.

By the time he reached the foot of the stairs she was already at the top.

"Ivy, wait," he called to her, but either she didn't hear him or she was ignoring him.

He was guessing the latter.

She disappeared down the hall and a second later he heard her bedroom door slam. From where he stood he couldn't actually hear her turn the lock but knew that she had.

It didn't take a genius to realize she was running away again.

* * *

Dillon was worse than lint, Ivy decided as she stepped out of the shower into the steamy bathroom and dried off with a soft, fluffy orange towel. She'd scrubbed and scrubbed, run the water as hot as she could stand, and she could still feel the ghost of his touch. She could still smell his scent on her skin.

She'd brushed her teeth twice and rinsed with mouthwash, but she could still taste him.

He wasn't just clinging to her sleeve or the leg of her slacks. He was under her skin, coursing through her bloodstream. She could feel him inside her head, making things she used to believe, things she counted on, hazy and unclear.

She rubbed the steam from a section of the mirror and looked at herself. Really looked. Same hair, same eyes, same nothing special body.

Then why did she feel so...*different?*

Confused and frustrated and scared...and more *alive* than she had in years.

She slipped her robe on and opened the bathroom door, letting out a startled squeak when she realized she wasn't alone.

No, Dillon wasn't lint.

He was a virus. A full-blown flu that made her feel weak and feverish and blew her judgment all to hell. A highly contagious bug who had broken into her room while she showered and made himself comfortable on her bed.

"Howdy." He lay on his back, propped up on both elbows, one leg crossed over the other. Like he had every right to be there. He'd showered and changed into casual slacks and a slightly transparent, white linen pullover that all but screamed, look at my tan! The scent of freshly scrubbed man reached across the room and wrapped itself around her like a tentacle, tempting her closer.

Did viruses have tentacles?

She tugged the belt on her robe a little tighter. Just in case.

She didn't trust Dillon, and even worse, she didn't trust herself. That kiss downstairs would have knocked her out of her shoes had she been wearing any. She never thought the day would come when she would say she was happy to see the Tweedles, but thank goodness they had walked in, jaws flapping. They were the only thing that had stopped her from making another huge mistake.

"Good shower?" Dillon asked, looking her up and down with warm, blue bedroom eyes.

Every one of her billion or so nerve endings went on full alert. Her brain kicked into overdrive to compensate and threatened a complete shutdown.

Why in the hell had she kissed him again? Hadn't she learned her lesson the first time? Hadn't she learned it *ten* stinking years ago?

The lack of oxygen from staying under the water so long had clearly damaged her brain.

Or maybe he really was a virus, and she just didn't have the antibodies to fight him off.

"I know I locked the door before I got in the shower," she said, doing her best to sound stern. So he wouldn't know that she was thinking of how much better he would look out of his clothes than in them.

He looked at the door, then back to her. "What's your point?"

Could he be more arrogant? Any cooler or more composed? More of a pain in the behind?

"A closed, locked door generally means the person on the other side doesn't want to be disturbed."

He just grinned. The frustratingly charming grin she both loved and hated. She would order him to leave if she thought he would actually listen. Hell, she'd even try hosing him down with Lysol. But she knew it was a futile battle. All the disinfectant and antibiotics in the world wouldn't fend him off. Like every other virus she'd had, he would simply have to run his course.

This time she wouldn't give in and let him become a full-blown epidemic.

She shoved her wet, tangled hair back from her eyes. "Do I even want to know how you got the door unlocked?"

He reached into the pocket of his slacks and pulled out a credit card. "I used my Visa."

So much for her plan of staying barricaded in her room for the rest of a trip. Not even a locked door could keep him out. Besides, wouldn't that be like letting him win?

This game he was playing was getting more complicated by the hour. It would be so much easier if she knew the rules, but she had the uneasy suspicion that there weren't any.

She tried to work up the enthusiasm to be annoyed but didn't see the point. Her anger was wasted on him. If anything, he seemed to enjoy getting her riled up. "Was there something you wanted?"

He flashed her that sexy, simmering grin and wiggled his eyebrows. "You know what I want, darlin'."

Oh, *that*. And here she had been hoping he wanted to play checkers.

Then he—*Oh, my God*—pulled his shirt over his head and dropped it on the bed beside him.

Hunk alert.

All that bronzed skin and lean muscle was making her eyes cross.

He patted the mattress. "Why don't you slip out of that robe and squeeze in here beside me."

If only he knew how tempting that was.

The bedroom was the one place he had never disappointed her. And it wasn't just the sex, although, Lord knew that had been out-of-this-world marvelous. But, being something of a nerd, one of her favorite things had been to just talk. Back then, few people had had the privilege of meeting the intellectually intriguing man lost behind the rebellious, party-boy facade. Some nights they had made love for hours, then had lain awake until dawn discussing social issues and politics and world events.

She wondered when that had stopped. When going out to the bar with his buddies had become more appealing than spending time with her. When the discussions had turned into arguments, the arguments to angry sex. Until even that had no longer been able to connect them. Until they had been just plain angry.

When she didn't move, he sighed and let his head fall back. His neck was lean and tanned, and she could see a tiny mark under his chin where he'd nicked himself shaving. "Is it safe to assume that we're not going to pick up where we left off downstairs?"

"What happened downstairs was a mistake." A huge, monster-size, "ginormous" mistake.

"Wouldn't be my first, and I doubt it'll be my last."

"That doesn't justify what we did. It's pretty obvious we have some unresolved issues, but I don't think hopping into bed is the way to fix them."

Not that it wouldn't be fun.

He flashed her that hungry, devilish grin. "The only thing unresolved between us is that we still make each other hot. And hopping into bed together, right here, right now, is the perfect way to fix that."

"Maybe that was the problem with our marriage. Maybe it was only about the sex."

"Who could blame us, since we did it so well."

She shot him a look. One he would no doubt recognize as exasperation. "I'm serious, Dillon."

"So am I." He reached over and pulled back the covers. "Come here, I'll remind you."

She just stood there, arms folded over her chest. He blew out an exasperated breath and fell back against the pillow. It was so typically Dillon, so familiar, her heart ached the tiniest bit.

"Darlin', you're sending so many mixed signals I'm getting whiplash. Did you or did you not kiss me? Twice in fact."

"Call it temporary insanity. Let me say this loud and clear so there's no confusion. We are not having sex. Not today, not tomorrow, not ten years from now."

"How about Saturday? Could we do it then?"

"Never."

He considered that for a second, then asked, "When you say sex, do you mean intercourse only, or are you lumping foreplay in there, too?"

She wasn't going to justify that with a response. "No wonder our marriage went to hell. You can't be serious for two seconds."

A muscle in his jaw twitched, and she knew she'd hit a sore spot. She seemed to have a knack for doing that. "How's this for serious? I can tell you *exactly* why our marriage went to hell. You didn't trust me."

So, they were back to blaming her. How typical. And to think that only a few minutes ago she had seriously been considering sleeping with him. "If I didn't trust you, Dillon, I had a damn good reason. You weren't exactly reliable."

"Reliable?" Now he looked downright resentful. "Did I ever make you a promise I didn't keep?"

She wanted to be able to say yes. But the honest truth was, he'd never broken a promise. When he gave his word, he'd never failed to follow through. The tricky part was getting him to make the promise in the first place.

Did that make him unreliable or self-centered? Or simply smart enough to know his own limitations?

And what difference did it make now?

"No," she admitted. "You never made a promise you didn't keep, but like always, you're grossly oversimplifying. It wasn't about lies or broken promises. In all the time we were together you never once showed an ounce of incentive. A drive to succeed."

"How do you figure?"

Was he kidding? "Dillon, you were flunking out of school! All you did was drink and gamble."

He shrugged. "So?"

So? Was that all he had to say? Just *so?* "You had so much potential. You could have gone so far."

"*Could have?* I run a billion-dollar corporation, Ivy. How much further did you expect me to go?"

"You know what I mean," she said, although he did have a point. But turning out okay despite his behavior didn't make it right. It just meant he was lucky.

"What I know, Ivy, is that my future was set. My parents had been priming me since the day I was born. I knew that when my dad retired I would take his place. You may find this hard to swallow, but I considered it an honor. One I took *very* seriously."

He sat up, closer now. Too close. His eyes serious. It was unsettling because Dillon didn't do serious very often. "But, damn it, if I was going to be chained to that company for most of my adult life, I was *not* going to spend my youth with my nose buried in a textbook. I was going to have fun."

"How was I supposed to know that?"

"You *did* know that. You knew it because I told you a thousand times. Every time you rode me because I skipped class, or blew off studying to hit a party. I never lied to you, I never made a promise I didn't keep. I never gave you a reason to not believe what I said was true, but that wasn't good enough for you. Which brings us right back to where we started. You. Didn't. Trust. Me."

He was turning everything around, making it look like it was her fault.

Maybe he was right. Maybe she hadn't trusted him completely. But it was more complicated than that. "You may not have given me a reason to mistrust you," she told him, "but trust has to be earned. You have to *make* promises to keep them."

"If you didn't trust me, Ivy, why the hell did you marry me?"

"I wish I hadn't!" she shot back, regretting the words instantly. It was one thing to be angry, but that comment had been downright mean. A vicious low blow.

Dillon gave her this look. Not cold or warm, annoyed or insulted. His face was a blank page. A blank page in a book whose language she had never been able to translate. "I'm real sorry to hear that our life together was such a disappointment for you."

Awkward silence echoed through the room like thunder.

It had happened again. No matter how hard they tried, they just couldn't seem to get along. As usual, nothing had been resolved.

Their relationship was like a long string of Christmas lights rolled up in one big, knotted ball. There was a very short beginning and a sharp, stubby end, but the middle part was so densely tangled and riddled with missing bulbs, she wasn't sure if they could ever make sense of it.

Maybe they weren't meant to resolve anything. Maybe the trick was to throw the old set out and shop for a new one. Or stop hanging the lights altogether, even if it did make life drab and colorless at times. Boring even.

Boring, but safe.

The air was thick and sticky with tension, and she had no idea what to say to him. Thankfully, Deidre chose that second to knock on the door.

Nine

Move forward and don't look back. The best part of your life lies ahead. Life's not about the destination, it's about the journey.
—excerpt from *The Modern Woman's Guide to Divorce (And the Joy of Staying Single)*

"Hey, Ivy, you in there?"

"Come in," Ivy called. Deidre's timing couldn't have been more perfect.

The doorknob jiggled and she said, "It's locked."

She shot Dillon a look. He had broken in, then relocked the door? The man gave himself far too much credit.

She crossed the room and let her cousin in. Deidre looked considerably better than she had earlier. The color had returned to her cheeks, and she'd lost that muddled, slightly dazed expression. She always had been quick to bounce back.

"I can't find Dillon and I was wondering—" She spotted Dillon lounging on the bed. "Oh! There you are."

Curiosity leaped like wild flames in her eyes, but she played it cool. Ivy could just imagine what she must be thinking. Dillon half-naked on her bed, Ivy in her robe.

It looked pretty bad.

He didn't even have the decency to look guilty or uncomfortable. Or maybe that was a good thing, since they had no reason to feel either. As useless as this conversation had turned out to be, it hadn't been in any way inappropriate. "Yes, ma'am."

"The tailor is here to do the final fitting on the tuxedos. They're waiting for you in the master suite downstairs."

He pulled himself to his feet. "Guess I should get down there."

Taking his time, he grabbed his shirt, turned it right side in, then pulled it over his head. There was something hypnotizing about a man getting dressed, the easy flex and pull of muscle. Yards of smooth skin.

Too bad it wasn't anyone but him.

He crossed the room to the door, but instead of leaving, he stopped. Right by Ivy. He stood there, closer than she was comfortable with. Close enough to look suggestive and raise even more questions.

Which was probably what he wanted. It was probably his way of getting back at her for hitting so far below the belt. She would apologize, but really, hadn't he brought it on himself? Wasn't he the one following her around, breaking into her room, harassing her?

And if that was true, why did she feel so guilty?

Their eyes locked, and his gaze was so intense she could swear he was seeing straight through her skin to her insides. And for some stupid reason she couldn't look away.

Could he really see inside her? And if so, could he see how bad she felt? Did he know that she wanted to apologize?

He leaned toward her the tiniest bit, tilted his head a fraction, and for one brief, horrifying, *exhilarating* second she thought he was going to kiss her. Right in front of her cousin. Her pulse began to race and her mouth went dry.

Explaining to Deidre why they were in her room together, and getting her to believe it, would be difficult enough.

She stood there frozen, holding her breath, waiting to see what he would do. If he would make matters worse.

"It's been...*enlightening,*" he finally said, then turned and walked out.

She didn't really see how he considered this interlude enlightening. Nothing had been resolved. Nothing was *going* to be resolved. Not until he took responsibility for his actions and stopped blaming everything on her. And she knew that would never happen.

Deidre waited several seconds, until they could hear the sound of his footsteps on the stairs, then she shut the door and turned to Ivy. "Enlightening?"

"It's not what you think," Ivy said.

"I'm not sure what I should think."

"Nothing was going on. We were just talking."

"*Talking?* Oh, my gosh!" Deidre squealed. "That's so awesome!"

No. Not really. "I was trying to take your advice. I wanted to resolve whatever it is we're still hanging on to."

"And?" she pressed, her eyes bright and enthusiastic. And so full of hope it nearly broke Ivy's heart.

Deidre was so excited, Ivy hated to disappoint her. But as her mother used to say, part of growing up is accepting disappointment and realizing that there are some things you just can't change.

When it came to Ivy and Dillon's relationship, Deidre would have to learn to live with defeat.

Ivy had.

"We don't seem to be making much progress." Maybe they weren't meant to resolve anything. Maybe what they needed was to simply forget the past and go their separate ways.

Tough to do when the guy followed her everywhere.

"But you're trying," she gushed, undeterred. She took both of Ivy's hands and squeezed them. "That's what's important. I know that you guys will work things out!"

Ivy wished she could share Deidre's optimism, but it was tough to resolve anything with a man who refused to admit he may have made a mistake.

Dillon didn't say two words to her at dinner.

That had been what she'd wanted all along. For him to leave her alone. So why did she feel so lousy?

Clearly it was the I-wish-I'd-never-married-you statement coming back to bite her in the behind. Not only had it been mean and uncalled for, it wasn't the least bit true.

For every good day, they may have had two lousy ones. And if she had a dime for every night she'd cried herself to sleep she could buy herself a Mercedes.

But if not for Dillon, for their marriage—the good and the bad—she wouldn't be the person she was today. She was stronger because of him. She may have learned the hard way, but she knew how to take care of herself. To beat any odds.

And for some stupid reason she couldn't bring herself to tell him so.

The men went for a guys' night out that evening while the women had the final fittings for their dresses. Six months ago Deidre had gone through fifty different styles of bridesmaid dresses before the Tweedles would agree on one they'd be willing to be seen in. And as Ivy spun in front of the mirror she had to admit the color and design were flattering. Not just flattering, but sexy.

She wondered what Dillon would think. If he would like the way she looked.

Not that she cared, of course.

"Gorgeous!" the seamstress gushed after making a slight adjustment to the spaghetti strap. Of course the Tweedles' size ones were a perfect fit. They were like Stepford bridesmaids. Only scarier.

"We need our bride!" the seamstress called impatiently in the direction of the master bath, where Deidre had disappeared to put on her dress. She had been in there an awfully long time.

The bathroom door opened a crack and Deidre called back, "Ivy, I need you for a minute." Then it slammed shut again.

The seamstress sighed loudly while Dee and Dum exchanged an exasperated look.

"At this rate we're going to be here all night!" Dum groaned.

"I'll see what the problem is," Ivy told them. She lifted the skirt of her dress, so it wouldn't drag on the floor as she crossed the room. She knocked lightly on the door. "Deidre? You okay?"

The door opened and a disembodied hand shot out. It latched on to Ivy's arm and yanked her inside. She barely had time to pull her skirt in before Deidre shut and locked the door.

With her free hand Deidre was holding her partially fastened dress up, clutching the bodice to her breasts. Her face and chest were flushed and beads of sweat dribbled down the sides of her face and into her cleavage. She looked as though she'd just run a marathon.

"What's wrong?" Ivy asked. "The natives are getting restless out there."

Tears hovered just inside her eyelids. "I'm too fat."

Ivy sighed. Not this again. "You are not too fat. You're going to look beautiful."

"No," she insisted. "I mean I'm really too fat." She turned, showing Ivy her back, and the gap between the two sides of the dress between the zipper. "I can't get the dress zipped up."

Oh, crap.

"I pulled and pulled until I heard the fabric start to rip."

Yep. Ivy could see a small tear where the lace had begun to pull away from the silk.

Double crap.

"What am I going to do?" she half whispered, half shrieked. "I can't go out there like this. If Blake's mom finds out it doesn't fit she will *kill* me! This thing cost a fortune!"

In Deidre's defense, Blake's mom was the one who had insisted Deidre order a size smaller, assuring her that it would be a perfect fit after she lost a few pounds. At least at the last fitting she'd been able to zip it up all the way. She'd have been fine if she didn't eat, or move. Or *breathe*.

As far as Ivy was concerned Blake's mother was getting exactly what she deserved for being such a demanding, controlling twit. But Ivy *did not* want to see Deidre unhappy.

"Turn around," she ordered and her cousin complied, her lip clamped so hard between her teeth Ivy worried she might bite clear through. "Don't worry. We'll make it fit."

She grasped the zipper tag. It was slightly disfigured from the workout Deidre had given it. "I want you to inhale and suck it in as far as you can. You ready?"

She nodded.

"On the count of three. One…two…three!"

Deidre sucked, and Ivy pulled for all she was worth. Deidre grunted as Ivy managed to get her zipped about halfway. Then there was an earsplitting rip, and the zipper tag popped loose and flew across the bathroom.

The little tear was now a gaping hole.

Oh, shit.

"That sounded bad," Deidre said, her voice small and frightened.

"It was bad." Ivy was no expert, but she was pretty sure it would take at least an inch of fabric to fix it.

At *least*.

There was no way this dress was going to fit Deidre by Saturday. It wouldn't fit by next week, either. She would have to starve herself and work out nonstop for a month just to get it zipped up.

Ivy had to wonder if all this was worth it. All this frustration and compromise, just to be married.

Not for her. She liked being single and intended to keep it that way.

There was a loud bang on the door. "Are you planning on staying in there until the wedding?" Dee snapped.

All the color had drained from Deidre's face and her eyes were wide with terror. "What am I going to do?" she whispered.

Ivy didn't know, but they had to do *something*. Deidre started to hyperventilate and her face was ashen.

"Give us a few minutes!" Ivy shouted back, and told her cousin, "Relax. We'll figure out something."

Deidre started to cry. Big, fat tears ran down her cheeks. "This is an omen."

"Everything will work out," she assured her, but Deidre wasn't listening.

"This whole stupid week, my whole *life* has been one big, bad omen!"

"Deidre, shh—"

"And I hate this stupid dress!" she shrieked. She tugged it down and shoved it to the floor then proceeded to stomp it flat with her bare feet. "I've hated it from the second that witch forced me into picking it."

Oh, jeez. The stress was too much. It had finally happened. She had come completely unglued.

There was another loud bang on the door. "We're waiting!"

Deidre snatched the dress from the bathroom floor and, wearing only panties and a strapless push-up bra, ripped open the door.

"Here I am! Are you happy?"

Ivy cringed and followed her out. There wasn't much she could do at this point. Other than hold Deidre back if she tried to strangle one of the twins.

The Tweedles stood there in their identical size one dresses with identical stunned looks on their faces.

"Yes, I'm fat!" Deidre all but screamed at them, wild-eyed and sweaty, spinning in a circle so they got the full view. "Does that make you feel better?"

The seamstress looked downright frightened. Apparently she'd never seen a bride-to-be have a total nervous breakdown. She flinched and cowered when Deidre thrust the tattered, wrinkled dress at her.

"This dress does not fit me. I wear a size sixteen. Not a fourteen, not a twelve. A *sixteen*. Find me a size sixteen or I will hurt you. Understand?"

The seamstress nodded, her head wobbling on her neck like one of those bobble-head dogs in a car window. She grabbed the dress and scurried out of the room. The Tweedles, their pea-size brains apparently sensing danger, weren't far behind her.

Then it was just Ivy and Deidre.

Deidre sat on the edge of the bed looking shell-shocked. "I can't do this. I thought I could, but I can't."

Ivy wasn't sure what *this* was. If she meant she couldn't go through with this particular wedding, or if she couldn't marry Blake at all. And honestly, she was afraid to ask.

"Do you know what I need?" she asked.

Wow. The list was so long Ivy wasn't sure where to begin. But if she had to pick one thing, she would start with Valium. "What do you need?"

"I need chocolate. Lots and lots of chocolate."

It took two hours and an entire box of Ho Hos to calm Deidre down. By the time the men returned, Ivy had managed to get her into her pajamas and tucked into bed. And thanks to one of the emergency sleeping pills Ivy kept on hand, she was resting peacefully.

She explained to Blake what had happened.

"What should I do?" he asked, looking so hopelessly baffled she wanted to hug him. She had several suggestions, but it would be better if Blake figured this one out on his own. He'd gone too long letting people run his life for him.

He needed to grow up.

Or Deidre needed to find herself a new future husband.

"Deidre isn't feeling well," Blake announced the next morning at breakfast, when he came to the table alone. His brothers and the Tweedles looked from him, then to each other, and snickered. Didn't they feel the least bit guilty for what had happened? Didn't they realize they had pushed Deidre just a little too far this time?

She'd been balancing precariously on the edge of a cliff, and they had poked and prodded until she'd finally lost her balance and gone over it.

Dillon stood in the kitchen, coffee mug in hand, quietly observing. He still hadn't said a word to Ivy, but she could feel him there, watching her. Yet every time she glanced up, he was looking the other way. Either he was trying to make her feel uncomfortable, or it was her own guilty conscience gnawing at her.

"Is there anything I can do?" Ivy asked Blake.

"I don't think so. The week has been pretty…stressful. I think she just needs some time to rest."

Blake was living in the land of Deep Denial if he thought Deidre could *rest* this one away. He was going to have to face the fact that he needed to make some changes.

If he didn't, he was going to lose Deidre.

"She said you guys should take the boat tour without us. It starts at eleven."

Six hours trapped on a boat sailing up and down the coast with Blake's brothers, the Tweedles and Dillon. *Don't think so.*

"I wouldn't feel right going without her," Ivy said.

Blake shrugged. "The charter is already paid for and it's too late to get a refund. It would be a waste not to use it."

"We made other plans," Dale said, but he wouldn't look his brother in the eye. Blake just shook his head. How many more ways could they let him down this week?

"Ivy and I will go," Dillon said.

She was about to say, *I will?* But she had to wonder if this was his way of saying no hard feelings. And if she said no, what message would that send to him?

Besides, if the charter was nonrefundable, it was a shame to see all that money go to waste. And Deidre might feel better knowing that Ivy and Dillon were taking some time alone together and could potentially work things out.

Not that Ivy thought there was a chance in hell they ever would.

Blake shot her a questioning look. Normally she wouldn't tolerate anyone telling her what to do, but in this case she would make an exception.

"Sure," she told Blake. "We'll go."

Ten

Most women are brought up to believe that their husband will take care of them for the rest of their lives. But that's only true 50% of the time. The other 50% end in divorce.
—excerpt from *The Modern Woman's Guide to Divorce (And the Joy of Staying Single)*

Ivy was flirting.

Shamelessly flirting with a member of the crew. A kid who looked as though he was barely out of high school. Or maybe still in high school for all Dillon knew. Since they'd left the marina she had been cozying up to him, and the kid was practically drooling over her form-fitting tank top and short-shorts.

Okay, maybe the shorts weren't *that* short, but they seemed to show an awful lot of leg.

She'd worn her hair down, and it rested in soft chestnut waves on her shoulders and tumbled down her back to just above her bra strap. Everything about her screamed *pick me up*.

Since Ivy was not, and never had been, the type to flirt—she was way too uptight—Dillon guessed this little show was entirely for his benefit. To make him jealous. Though he had no idea why she thought he would be. Because he wasn't.

At all.

She'd made her feelings pretty damn clear yesterday. She regretted ever marrying him. Wasn't that just great.

Well, it hadn't been all roses and sunshine for him, either. Did she think she'd been easy to live with? Always complaining, her panties always in a twist over something. If she thought he gave a damn what she felt about their marriage, she was mistaken.

And people wondered why he stayed single. Sheesh!

It had been her idea to "talk." Her telling him they needed to resolve things. Far as he could figure, she was pretty gung ho about *resolving* things, until she heard something she didn't like.

He was all for working things out, but how could they if she refused to admit she was wrong?

He had the feeling they were just going to have to agree to disagree and leave it at that. He would go his way and she would go hers and they could forget they ever knew each other.

Although he had to admit, it would have been really nice getting her under the covers one last time.

When they reached the dock later that afternoon, he saw Ivy slip her new boyfriend what appeared to be a business card. It looked as though the lovebirds planned to hook up later. Did she have the slightest clue how ridiculous a woman her age would look dating an adolescent? Did she have no dignity?

He had dated a lot of women in the past couple of years, but never one young enough to be his daughter. Or at the very least, a young niece.

A car waited to take them back to the villa. As they were rolling out of the parking lot he said, "Looks like you made a new friend today."

Ivy cast him a sideways glance, a grin on her face. "You could say that."

Didn't she see how foolish she looked? Pining over some kid. And obviously the kid in question was only in it to get some tail. And what a fine tail it was, he couldn't help noticing.

But that was beside the point.

In college, Ivy had always had been on the naive side. She probably had no clue this kid was using her. She was not the type to settle for a one-night stand. She'd made Dillon wait three excruciating months before she would sleep with him.

Maybe he should point out the obvious and save her a bit of humiliation.

"You don't think he's a little young for you?" he asked.

She was looking out the car window, but he could see her smile widen a fraction. "Just the way I like 'em."

"I hate to break it to you, but he's only after one thing. When you leave Mexico, you'll never hear from him again."

She turned to him, her expression blank. "What's your point?"

She wasn't fooling him with her casual attitude. "I know you, Ivy. You don't do casual. You're a commitment kinda' girl."

She shrugged. "Go ahead and tell yourself that if it makes you feel better."

"This has nothing to do with me. I don't care what you do. I just don't want to see you get your pretty little heart broken."

"I think men should be like tissues," she said. "Soft, strong and disposable. The jealousy is flattering, though."

He snorted. "Jealous of what? You're a complete pain in the ass."

"Maybe, but you still want to sleep with me." She looked over at him. "Admit it."

Great, now she was stealing his material. "Why would I want to sleep with a woman who regrets marrying me?"

Only after the words were out did he realize how pathetic that sounded. Like she'd hurt his feelings or something.

Which she hadn't. He didn't give a damn what she thought about their marriage.

She looked out the window and said in a soft voice, "I didn't mean it."

Was that some sort of veiled apology from Miss Perfection? Miss I'm-Never-Wrong. "You didn't mean what?"

She fiddled with the strap of her purse, eyes downward. "As bad as things got between us, there were good times, too."

"What are you trying to say, Ivy?"

She took a deep breath, looked up and met his eyes. "I'm trying to say that I'm sorry. I'm sorry if I hurt your feelings."

He waited for a sarcastic remark, a caustic dig to pop into his head. Instead he was drawing a blank.

What the hell was wrong with him?

Ivy was proud, so he knew that hadn't been easy for her. He settled for, "You didn't, but apology accepted."

"He's a twenty-two-year-old psychology major," she said, and it took him a second to realize she was talking about the cupcake on the tour. "Really smart kid. He's engaged to a lovely girl that he is absolutely crazy about and plans to marry after they both graduate. They're considering moving to Texas. I told him to give me a call when and if he's ever looking for an internship."

"A bit of advice. Next time you might want to tone down the flirting."

"I was not flirting."

"I saw you, darlin'. You were most definitely flirting, and laying it on thick."

"Okay, maybe a little. But you were jealous. Admit it."

"If I say yes, will you sleep with me?"

She just grinned and turned back to the window. "I knew you were jealous."

He didn't see any point in arguing. Once she set her mind to something she rarely backed down. And what the hell, maybe he had been a *little* jealous.

If anyone was going to sleep with Ivy on this trip, damn it, it was going to be him.

When they got back to the villa everyone else was gone. Since dinner had already been prepared, they figured it would only be polite to sit down and eat. And it wasn't so bad.

Ivy would go so far as to say it was darn near pleasant. Something strange had happened on the ride back from the marina. The tension that had been dogging them since their fight yesterday afternoon seemed to wither away. They seemed to have come to some sort of understanding.

And she began to think that when he followed her around, incessantly bugging her tonight, it might not be such a bad thing. Since there wasn't much else to do.

After dinner he pushed back his chair and stood. "I'm going to call it a night and head up to my room."

Sure he was. "It's barely eight o'clock."

"I'm a little tired, and I have some work I wanted to catch up on."

Did he really think she was that gullible? That she didn't know exactly what he was up to? He was pulling the same routine he always did. He would pretend he was going to leave her alone, then dog her relentlessly all night.

But just to make him happy, she played along. "I guess I'll see you tomorrow, then. Sweet dreams."

Dillon walked around the table, stopped beside her chair and held out his hand. She looked at it suspiciously. He stood there patiently waiting, and finally she slipped her hand in his. She assumed he meant to escort her from the table. Instead he turned her hand over, exposing her wrist, and he leaned forward.

Unsure of what he was doing, but curious to find out, she sat motionless. Even though her heart had begun pounding out a faster and slightly erratic rhythm.

His eyes closed and he inhaled the scent of the perfume she'd dabbed there. The bottle she'd bought in town yesterday.

He looked up at her, his eyes like a hot spring ready to bubble over. "I like it."

Her hand felt small and warm wrapped in his and his breath was hot on her skin. Then his lips brushed just below her palm and tiny jolts of awareness, like little static shocks, rippled up her arm.

Oh, my God.

She found herself looking forward to the time he would spend nagging her, and figured, if today was like every other day this week, she wouldn't have to wait long.

He let go of her hand, then walked inside. She didn't doubt that he'd be back in a minute or two. He would find some ridiculous reason he should keep himself glued to her side.

Yep, *any* minute now.

She sat at the table several minutes, then got up and walked to the balcony railing and looked out over the ocean, at the sun sinking slowly below the horizon. Several minutes passed before she heard a noise behind her.

She couldn't help grinning. The man was *so* predictable.

She wiped the smile from her face and turned to him. "I thought you were going to—" The words trailed off when she realized it wasn't Dillon, but the housekeeper, preparing to clear the table.

"Ma'am?" she asked in a thick Mexican accent.

Ivy's cheeks blushed with embarrassment. "Sorry. I thought you were…someone else."

She scurried past her into the house. The poor woman must have thought she was a loon. Although, compared to Deidre, who scarfed chocolate and had nervous breakdowns, and Dillon, who walked around in his underwear with his winkie hanging out, and the Tweedles—she wouldn't even go there—Ivy was definitely one of the most normal of the bunch.

Apparently Dillon was going to wait until Ivy went to her room, or maybe he was there already, lounging on her bed. The way he had been when she got out of the shower.

That was probably it. All this time she'd been waiting for him, he was probably waiting for her.

She headed up to her room, making sure her footsteps were just heavy enough, so he would know she was coming. The hallway was quiet and dim. Her bedroom door was open, just the way she'd left it, the room dark. No doubt he was going to try to startle her again.

She stepped in the room and switched on the light, eyes on the bed where she expected him to be.

It was empty.

Was he on the balcony? In the bathroom?

She checked everywhere. Even in the closet, but the room was as empty as she'd left it that morning. Besides the bed being made and the bathroom cleaned spotless, not a single thing appeared to be out of place.

Huh.

She was surprised, and even worse, disappointment tugged at her conscience. Why had he picked now to stop being a pest? When she was finally getting used to having him around? When the idea of spending a little time with him didn't repulse her?

Maybe she was just being impatient. Maybe he was going to give her time to settle in, then he would show up, all prepared to annoy her.

She could wait.

She kicked off her sandals and fluffed her hair with her fingers. Besides the times that it was wet and snarled, today was the first time Dillon had seen her hair down. Not that it looked all that different than it had ten years ago. It was a little longer, but still had a hint of unruly curl to it. Her mom used to nag her incessantly about it.

"Would you please do something with that mop," she would complain when Ivy would let her hair dry loose and wavy. Which she did ninety-nine percent of the time.

Looking back, she remembered her mom nagged her constantly. She still did. About her hair and her clothes and her makeup. Her *posture*. Areas in which she considered herself an authority.

"If you learned to use eyeliner correctly your eyes wouldn't look so small," she would say, or, "I saw you interviewed on CNN and as usual you were slouching. Would it kill you to sit up straight?"

Most people would be proud to have a daughter who even made it on CNN. But her mom didn't see it that way. Nothing was ever good enough for her.

Ivy wondered if her mom had nagged her dad like that. That might have been enough to drive him away. Or maybe he just hadn't been ready for the responsibility of a family. And still wasn't if the rare Christmas card and occasional birthday call were any indication. After years of trying to build some sort of relationship with him, Ivy had come to terms with the fact that it would probably never happen.

She wondered, if she had stayed with Dillon, would the same thing have happened to their children? Would he have been an absentee dad? He'd made it all too clear that he hadn't been ready for children then. Maybe he never would be.

It was one of those subjects that they'd never brought up. One of many.

She glanced over at the digital clock beside the bed. It was eight-fifteen and he still hadn't shown up. How much longer did he plan to make her wait?

Until she was tucked into bed and sleeping?

If that was how he wanted to play this, fine. If he could wait, so could she.

To pass the time she opened her laptop and launched her e-mail program. Might as well do something constructive while she waited.

There were the usual three hundred or so e-mails for male enhancement drugs guaranteeing her a larger penis in six months, erectile dysfunction drugs at a deep discount and replica watches for rock-bottom prices. There was also a message from her writing partner, Miranda Reed, marked Urgent. The body of the e-mail was a series of question marks and exclamation points.

There was a second message that simply said, *call me!* in fifty-point, hot-pink type.

Ivy had promised to call her the instant she learned the identity of the mystery best man. She'd been so far off-kilter, she'd completely forgotten.

She dug her cell phone from her purse, and, sure enough, there were a dozen missed calls and half as many voice messages.

She dialed the number and Miranda answered on the first ring. "Who is he?"

Ivy laughed. "Hello to you, too."

"Have pity. The suspense is killing me. Is he dark and sexy? Does he bear a striking resemblance to Johnny Depp or Antonio Banderas?"

In the weeks before the trip they had speculated who the mystery man might be, coming up with both the best-case scenario—he looked like Johnny or Antonio with a body to die for—or worst case—he would look more like Johnny Cash but older. And he would have a beer gut, thinning hair and ingrown toenails.

In some ways, what she'd ended up with was worse.

"Yes, yes, no, no."

"Okay, dark and sexy is good. Is he nice?"

Rather than play twenty questions, she decided it best to just blurt it out. "He's Dillon."

There was a pause, then, "Like, Matt Dillon?"

"Nope."

"Ugh, not *Bob* Dylan."

"Dillon Marshall."

Another pause while she digested that, then, "You mean, he *looks* like Dillon?"

Oh, didn't she wish. "I mean he *is* Dillon. In the flesh."

"Holy crap."

"Yeah. Surprise." She gave Miranda a blow-by-blow of the trip so far. The way he'd been following her and how they couldn't be together five minutes without arguing. She left out the kissing parts, since they were completely irrelevant, and the way she'd made him jealous today. Oh, and the fact that she actually wanted him to intrude on her. "Deidre thinks I need to let the past go and forgive him."

"Maybe that's good advice."

"Miranda, we can barely say two words to each other without an argument starting. How are we supposed to resolve anything if we can't talk to each other?"

"Maybe you're not trying hard enough."

For a moment she was too stunned to reply. Surely Miranda of all people would be on her side. She would understand what Ivy was going through. Finally she managed a baffled, "Excuse me?"

"Don't take this the wrong way. But you can be stubborn sometimes. Maybe you're just not listening to what he has to say."

"I listen to people for a living. I would not be where I am today if I didn't know how to listen. And you think *I'm* stubborn? You should try having a serious conversation with this man. He's *impossible!*"

Her tone softened. "I swear I'm not saying this to upset you. I'm just worried that the past is holding you back."

"Holding me back how? Is this about my sex life?"

"Well, no, not exactly, although you've got to admit, it *has* been a while."

"Next you're going to tell me that you think I'm unhappy." There was silence at the other end. "You do, don't you? Why is everyone so convinced I'm not happy? I'm a psychologist, for God's sake. Don't you think I would have noticed? If I was so miserable, don't you think I would have done something about it?"

"Maybe you're so used to feeling that way, you don't even realize it's happening. I think...oh, shoot! The other line is ringing." She paused, and Ivy knew she was checking the caller ID. "It's our publicist. We're supposed to make the final arrangements for my trip to New York, for that radio interview. I really should answer."

"That's fine," Ivy said. She'd heard enough, anyway.

"I'll call you right back. I promise."

"I'll talk to you later." Ivy disconnected and shut off her phone. She didn't want to talk to her again. Calling Miranda was supposed to make her feel better, not worse.

If everyone else was so convinced she was miserable, what about Dillon? What did he see when he looked at her? Did he think she was unhappy?

She looked at the clock. It was half-past eight, and she was tired of waiting. If everyone was so darned convinced her unresolved issues with Dillon were ruining her life, then damn it, she was going to resolve them. Once and for all.

Eleven

Self-esteem take a hit? Get past the hurt and move on.
Find a new activity or group to get involved in.
Exercise! Walk! Look in the mirror every day, and
say, "I like that person looking back at me."
—excerpt from *The Modern Woman's Guide to*
Divorce (And the Joy of Staying Single)

Ivy flung open the bedroom door and peered down the length of the hallway. No Dillon. But a narrow sliver of light shone through his partially open door like an written invitation. She marched down the hall, intent on barging in on him before he had the chance to do the same to her.

Rather than knock, since such gestures hadn't been high on his list of priorities, she shoved the door open and stepped right inside.

The first thing she noticed was the binders and loose papers strewn across the bed. The second was Dillon sitting in the middle of it all, back propped against the headboard, reading some official-looking document. He didn't look as though he was preparing to barge in on her anytime soon.

"Problem?" he asked, watching her expectantly.

She just stood there, mouth hanging open, probably looking like a trout stuck on a hook. He was wearing a pair of jogging pants, a Texas A&M T-shirt, and his feet were bare.

He really hadn't been going anywhere. When he said he was going to his room to stay, he'd been telling her the truth. He hadn't been planning to bug her after all.

He set down the papers he'd been reading. "What's wrong? Cat got your tongue?"

She said the first thing that popped into her head, and she said it with…*enthusiasm*. "I am very happy with my life."

He shrugged, looking more than a little confused by her outburst. "Okay."

Now what? Now that she'd just made a complete ass out of herself. "I just wanted you to know that. Because I'm finding out that some people don't think I am."

"Really. Do these people have names?"

"That's not important. The thing is, these people seem to think that my unresolved issues with you are holding me back somehow."

He folded his arms across his chest, looking intrigued now. "Oh, yeah?"

"In case you're wondering, they're not. But, to shut

them up, I'd like us to sit down and talk and figure out what it is that's unresolved, and resolve it. Without arguing or fighting," she added. "In other words, I want us to get along."

"There's only one problem with that," he said. "Your idea of getting along is when I shut my mouth and agree with everything you say."

The accusation stung, and she was about to snap right back at him when she realized that would only start a fight. If they were going to do this she had to be willing to listen to what he had to say, even if it was sarcastic and snotty. Maybe it was the only way he knew to communicate his feelings.

"So what you're saying to me is that you feel I don't listen to you."

He narrowed his eyes at her, as though he wasn't quite sure what to make of that. "Active listening, right?"

The man never ceased to surprise her. "How do you know that?"

"I did go to a few of my classes, you know. And I dated a psychiatrist a couple of years ago."

"Then think how easy this will be."

"For some reason I doubt that," he said. "You sure you want to do this? You want to dredge up the past and try to sort it out after all this time?"

She did and she didn't. All she knew was that Deidre's thinking she was unhappy was an annoyance, but hearing the same thing from Miranda had scared her a little. And though she'd denied it, deep down she couldn't help wondering if they were right. What if they were seeing something she wasn't? What if there was something better out there and she was missing it? What if all this time she'd just been slogging through life, not really living it?

"We at least should try," she said.

"You might not like what I have to say."

She was well aware of that. "I'll take my chances."

"Okay," he agreed. He gathered the papers and tucked them into the binder, then gestured for her to sit.

She perched on the edge at the foot of the bed. "So, where do we start?"

"Since we're new to this communicating thing, maybe we should practice first. Maybe we should try talking about something we never fought about."

That subject did not exist. "Dillon, we fought about *everything*."

"Not everything."

"See, we're fighting already!"

"This is not fighting. This is discussing."

"Name one thing in our entire relationship that we didn't fight about."

"Money," he said.

"Money?"

"Money was never an issue. You nagged me about school and rode me relentlessly about my drinking and my weekend excursions. But never money. Even during the divorce it never came up."

He was right. She may not have approved of the way he spent his money, particularly the trips to Vegas and Atlantic City that would put him back thousands of dollars. But she hadn't felt she had any right to dictate where and how he spent—or wasted—his fortune.

And when the divorce happened, she didn't ask for a penny. She just wanted it to be over fast. And it might have been if his father hadn't gotten involved. Apparently, he hadn't trusted her to fade away quietly. Either that or he was just pissed off that he'd been wrong about her, that she really hadn't been after Dillon's money.

"And sex," he said. "We never fought about sex."

Oh, but they had. One time. It had been *the* argument. The one that had hammered the final wedge between them.

"The day I told you I thought I might be pregnant, we argued. Sex...pregnant. Can't have one without the other."

"And I've been trying for the first one for days now, but you're not cooperating."

Clearly, he used humor as a defense mechanism when she came close to hitting a nerve, to making him face something he didn't want to deal with.

"Don't do that," she said. "Don't make a joke out of this or nothing will get resolved. Just talk to me. I know you're not used to talking about your feelings, but you're going to have to if we really want this to work."

He was quiet for a second and she could see the wheels spinning, see him working things through, trying to decide if this was worth the hassle.

What would it be?

"I had every reason to be upset," he finally said. "Neither of us was ready to start a family."

"You were more than upset." He had been furious.

How could she let that happen, he'd shouted? How could she be so careless? As if he'd had no part in it.

The pregnancy test she later took had been negative, but by then the damage had already been done.

After that it had been as if they were afraid to touch each other, afraid there might be an accident that would bind them together for life. And without the sex, there had been nothing left to hold them together. She knew that it was only a matter of time before everything fell apart. But admitting it was over was as good as admitting that her mom was right. So she had hung on until the bitter end.

"I overreacted," he admitted, then he really blew her away by adding, "I think that deep down I knew I was a lousy husband and thought I would be an even worse father."

It was the most honest thing she had ever heard him say. The first time he'd ever admitted he wasn't flawless, that he had doubts just like everyone else.

"You weren't a lousy husband."

He got that stubborn, sulky look. "You sure as hell made me feel like I was."

Her first instinct was to lash out and deny the accusation. But Dillon was not the kind of man to admit to having feelings he didn't really have. He was too damned proud.

"I didn't mean to," she said.

"It wasn't always that way. After we got married, you changed."

Another denial sat on the tip of her tongue. Why was this so hard? Why was her gut reaction to go on the defensive?

Instead, she asked, "How did I change?"

He shrugged. "You were just…different."

Well, that wasn't much help.

She tried another angle. "What was I like before we got married?"

He thought about it a second, and the hint of a smile pulled at the corners of his mouth. "Fun. You were a little repressed at first, but you were willing to try new things."

They did have fun. So much that she used to believe it was too good to be true. She wondered why a rich, handsome man was even remotely interested in someone as boring and plain as her. Dillon had brought her out of her shell. He'd made her feel good about herself. At least for a while.

The next question was harder to ask, since she was pretty sure she wouldn't like the answer. "And after? What was I like then?"

"You were so…*serious*. All you did was study."

That was entirely unfair. Not everyone had the luxury of screwing around. "I didn't have an eight-figure trust fund to fall back on and a ready-made job being handed to me. I needed to get my degree. And I had to maintain my GPA or I would lose my scholarship. Which, as you know, I eventually lost anyway."

"Because of my father," he said.

She nodded. He'd pulled a few strings and her full scholarship had mysteriously been revoked. She'd worked hard for that money. She'd busted her butt all through high school and graduated at the top of her class.

With the snap of his fingers, Dillon's father had snatched it away. To this day she wasn't exactly sure why.

Was it because she'd never been impressed by his money and power? Because she couldn't be bought? Not for any price.

Maybe he'd done it to put her in her place. To prove the power he held over her.

To add insult to injury, no one would give her a student loan, not when she was married to a billionaire. She'd had to go to work full-time to cover her tuition and living expenses until the divorce was final, and Dillon's father saw to it that it took a very *long* time. By then she was so far behind, she'd graduated two years later than she'd originally planned.

"I didn't find out what he'd done until it was too late," Dillon said. "If I had known at the time I would have stopped him. Or at least I would have tried."

She'd convinced herself that he'd known all along and had let it happen, and she'd hated him for it. But the truth was, he'd never been vindictive. Just arrogant and misguided.

And she believed him. If he could have stopped it, he would have.

"Working harder for it just made me appreciate it more," she told him, and it was the truth. It taught her to be independent and self-sufficient. She learned she was tough enough to handle just about anything.

"I would have paid your tuition if you had only asked."

She knew that, too, but she'd been too proud to go looking for a handout. Too embarrassed to admit how badly she had screwed up. She had to do it on her own. As Miranda had said earlier, Ivy had a stubborn streak.

"You didn't even have to go to school," he told her. "I would have taken care of you."

"I'm sure my dad said the same thing to my mom. Then he walked out the door. Besides, if I had quit school, we both would have been bored silly within a month."

"Probably," he agreed.

"So, I guess our marriage failed because I was a good student," she said, half joking. He didn't return her smile.

"It wasn't just that."

Oh, great, there was more? Was there anything she did right?

"You sure you want to hear this?"

She wasn't sure of anything anymore. "No, but tell me anyway."

"After we got married you nagged me constantly."

Oh, *ouch*. That one really stung.

Her mother's nagging had driven her nuts. Had she really done the same thing to Dillon? "I nagged you?"

"No matter what I did, it wasn't good enough."

That wasn't true. Although she did recall thinking that being married hadn't been what she'd expected. In fact, it hadn't been any different than when they'd been dating. Dillon hadn't changed at all.

Maybe *that* had been the problem. She'd been expecting him to change. To mature overnight.

"I think I had certain expectations about being married," she told him. "I thought we would settle down and get serious. Start acting like grown-ups. But things didn't happen the way I planned. You were so…irresponsible. I think maybe it scared me."

"I wasn't ready to grow up," he said. No apology, no excuses. Hadn't that always been his M.O.? This is the way things are and if you don't like it, tough cookies. But that wasn't the way it worked.

"Part of marriage is learning to compromise," she reminded him.

He opened his mouth to argue, she could see it in his

eyes. That stubborn, I'm-right-and-you're-wrong look. Then he caught himself.

Jeez, were they both that stubborn?

He sighed and rested his head back against the headboard. "You're right. It is. I guess maybe I felt as though you were asking me to be something I wasn't."

"And the harder I pushed you to change, the more you rebelled and acted the complete opposite."

He nodded. "Yeah, I guess so."

"And the more you rebelled, the harder I nagged and pushed, making things even worse."

"Until we self-destructed."

"Exactly."

And there it was. Their entire relationship in a nutshell. It was a genuine "lightbulb" moment.

Two stubborn people, neither willing to meet the other halfway. She had never considered the possibility that it wasn't entirely his fault. It had never even crossed her mind.

"All this time I've had myself convinced that it had to be either your fault or mine. But the truth is, we both screwed up. It's both our faults, isn't it?"

"I guess so."

"We were young and stupid and had no clue what we were getting ourselves into."

He shook his head. "Well, damn. I guess I'm not as perfect as I thought I was."

Neither of them were.

Knowing that, accepting it, seemed to lift the weight of the past ten years from her shoulders. She felt free.

Until the meaning of it, the repercussions, dropped

on her like a ten-ton block of solid steel. Then she just felt like she wanted to barf.

She'd been basing her life's work on her own experiences, her own failed marriage. All this time she held herself up on some sort of pedestal. She'd been wronged, she was the victim. The real truth was, she had been just as responsible.

She was a statistic. Just like everyone else.

Even worse, she was a fraud.

Half of what she'd written in her book had turned out to be untrue, and the other half was skewed so far out of proportion it was hardly credible.

How many times, as a form of therapy, had she suggested her patients write down their feelings in a personal journal, or in a letter that they would later shred? To accept and validate their emotions. Which is exactly what she'd done. Then she'd sent them off to a publisher and printed them for the whole world to see.

And the really frightening part was people had actually listened. They had taken the ranting of a hurt, embittered woman and made them sacred.

What had she done?

And how could she justify doing it again?

She had a contract. She'd taken an advance. It was too late to back out now. To say, oops, I was wrong. What I said before, just ignore that. *This* is what you should really do.

She didn't even know what *this* was. What if she never figured it out?

"You look disturbed," Dillon said, genuine concern in his eyes. "I thought you would be happy."

"I am," she lied, because to admit what she was really feeling was a humiliation she just couldn't bear. And she owed him a *huge* apology. "I'm sorry for all those things I wrote about you."

He shrugged. "Like you said, you didn't write a single thing that wasn't true."

"Maybe, but I had no right to publish it in a book. If I had issues about our marriage, the only person I should have talked to was you or my shrink."

"I guess we've both made our share of mistakes. What do you say we forget what happened in the past and start fresh. Right here, right now."

He had every right to hold what she'd done against her. Instead, he was willing to forgive and forget. And she would be wise to do the same. "I'd like that."

He looked at her for a second, just looked at her face, as if he were seeing it for the first time. She wondered what he saw. If he could tell how conflicted she felt.

"You want to get out of here?" he asked.

"And go where?"

He shrugged. "Does it matter?"

He was right, it didn't matter. As long as she was anywhere but here, torturing herself.

She couldn't run from the past any longer, and she couldn't change the fact that her life was in total chaos. But this was a vacation, darn it.

She would worry about fixing this mess after the wedding. Tonight, she just wanted to forget.

Twelve

It can be very tempting, particularly on lonely nights, to look up your ex. But the more you fall back on your old ways, the harder it will be to truly move on.
—excerpt from *The Modern Woman's Guide to Divorce (And the Joy of Staying Single)*

It began as a walk on the beach. The air was warm and a full moon hung low in the sky, lighting their way. They didn't say much. Just strolled quietly side by side. Then Dillon suggested they walk to the village for a drink, and alcohol in any form sounded pretty good to her.

When they got there they found themselves in the middle of a Mexican carnival. Colorful lanterns and twinkling lights lined the street, and the air was scented with a mouthwatering combination of sugar and spicy fried food.

They snacked on authentic Mexican treats, drank salty margaritas and danced to a live salsa band. The evening was a blur of bodies, bumping and grinding, laughter and fun. Ivy couldn't remember the last time she'd felt more relaxed and…*alive*. Hadn't it always been that way with Dillon? The man excelled at having a good time.

It was well after midnight when they headed back to the villa. They were halfway there before she realized Dillon was holding her hand. She'd obviously been impaired by the alcohol, because she liked the way it felt. She didn't pull away. Not even when they went inside. If someone saw them that way, they could get the wrong idea. Or maybe it was the right idea. Either way it could get very messy and complicated for both of them. But mostly for her.

It wasn't fair. It wasn't right that after everything they had been through, after all the pain he'd caused her, Ivy still wanted him this much. Of all the possible men in the world, why did it have to be him? Why did he have to be the one?

It was dark and still in the villa. Probably everyone else was already in bed. As he walked her up the stairs, disappointment began to tug at her insides.

She didn't want this night to end. She wanted to make this last, to feel happy just a little while longer. She didn't want to fall asleep and wake knowing that it wouldn't happen again.

She wanted to invite him into her room. She wanted

him naked in her bed. One last time before they said goodbye forever.

That was a terrible idea. She should be trying to figure things out, not make them worse. And being caught sleeping with her ex would definitely make things worse.

Ivy would never hear the end of it from her mother. There was nothing she loved more than reminding Ivy of the mistakes she'd made, and finding new ones to nag her about.

So the decision that suited her best interest was to say good-night and go to sleep.

When they reached her bedroom door, she turned to him. To tell him she'd had a good time, and she was glad they could part from this vacation on better terms. Heck, maybe they could even be friends. But before she knew what was happening, Dillon was kissing her. And even worse, she was kissing him back. Not just your run-of-the-mill making out, either. They were ravaging each other, as if they were battling over who wanted it more.

His mouth still on hers, he backed her into the room and shut the door. She couldn't comprehend much over the moans and breathless sounds she had begun making, but she was pretty sure she heard the lock turn. Then Dillon was walking her backward. She wasn't sure where until the backs of her thighs collided with the mattress.

She was vaguely aware that she was pulling at his clothes. She wanted skin. Didn't matter where. Just something to put her hands on. She *needed* to put her hands on him.

Before she could get his shirt pulled from the waist

of his slacks, she was on her back lying sideways across the bed, her calves dangling over the edge. And she couldn't touch Dillon because he had her wrists pinned over her head with one of his hands.

Then he was kissing her, pushing her clothes out of the way so he had more area to explore. More to touch. Her stomach, her rib cage, and…oh! Her breasts. First through her bra, then he pushed that out of the way, too. Somewhere in the back of her mind she was thinking how small she was there, how he must have had much better, much bigger. Then she felt his mouth, hot and wet, and as long as he kept touching her, just like that, she didn't care what size they were.

She felt his hand on her thigh and the sensation was so foreign to her, so exquisitely intense, she gasped and jerked with surprise.

Dillon stopped what he was doing and looked at her, his lids heavy. "Do you want me to stop?"

Oddly enough, his asking was even worse than if he were to ravage her without her permission. If she didn't take this opportunity to stop him, she would only have herself to blame. And at the same time, she couldn't stop herself from thinking it would be worth every bit of grief it caused her.

"Yes or no?" he asked, his eyes dark and intense. And she had no doubt that if she told him no, he would stop. No questions asked.

"Don't stop."

A hungry smile curled his mouth and the hand on her thigh began to slide upward.

At that point she knew there was no turning back. It was a done deal. She was going to sleep with Dillon. She was going to have sex with her ex-husband.

She really was crazy.

His breath was hot on her skin as he nibbled and kissed his way down her body. Touching, tasting. His fingers slipped inside the leg of her shorts, brushing against her panties...

At that point things began to get fuzzy. One minute her shorts were on, the next they had mysteriously disappeared. The same thing happened to her panties. Then Dillon was touching her. Slow, steady pressure. Warm and slippery.

She closed her eyes and gave herself permission to relax and enjoy. How could she have thought she didn't need this? How had she gone so long without a man's touch?

And no man knew her body the way Dillon did. No one made her feel as good. And what the hell was wrong with feeling good every now and then? Who better than a man who needed no road map to please her, who would never expect or want more than a very brief physical relationship? A fling.

Without warning Dillon pressed her thighs open, lowered his head and took her into his mouth. The sensation was so wickedly intense she cried out. Her hands fisted in his hair and she was making sounds, raspy and nonsensical. She didn't seem to have any control left. She was flying on autopilot, and about to crash and burn.

Her breath was coming hard and fast, and the room

slipped in and out of focus. Each individual sensation merged and tangled and fused together like the wick on a stick of dynamite, then it sparked and ignited.

The flame hissed and licked its way up, building and climbing. And when it reached her core, she blew apart, splintered into a million pieces.

She hovered there, somewhere between pain and pleasure, conscious and unconscious.

It seemed as though she melted back together, one little piece at a time, slowly, gradually, her pulse returning to normal. When she finally opened her eyes, Dillon was there, leaning over her. Watching. Waiting for her to return from the outer stratosphere. Then he leaned down and kissed her. So gently, *so* sweetly.

"I'll see you later, Ivy."

Wait. What?

Later?

She sat up, still dizzy and a little disoriented. "Where are you going?"

"My room."

"But…" They had just gotten started.

"I don't understand," she said. "Did I do something wrong?"

He looked almost…sad. Which made no sense at all. "No. You did everything right."

"Then why are you leaving?"

"You know where I'll be if you need me."

Then he left, closing the door quietly behind him. For several minutes she was too stunned to process what had just happened. To make sense of it.

Was this just another part of the game for him?

Wasn't it enough that she'd let him into her room? That she'd let him touch her?

Apparently not.

What did he want? For her to chase him? Would he settle for nothing less than total surrender?

And wasn't that just like him?

She didn't know if she should feel angry or hurt or disappointed, so she allowed herself all three. Was he honestly that arrogant? He had chased her relentlessly for days; now he was just going to turn his back on her?

Unless...

Maybe Dillon wasn't as sure of himself, as self-confident, as she'd assumed. Maybe he needed her to come to him. Maybe, like her, he'd spent so long pushing people away, he had no idea how to let someone back inside.

Was it possible that under that arrogant facade he was just as lost and confused as she was?

And lonely.

Very, very lonely.

The idea was as sad as it was empowering.

And she knew exactly what she needed to do.

Ivy stepped into Dillon's room. The light beside the bed was on, but he wasn't lying there.

Her eyes were drawn to the curtains blowing in the open French doors. Dillon stood on the balcony, his back to her, leaning on the edge. He wore nothing but a pair of loose silk pajama bottoms.

She walked up behind him, and though she didn't make a sound, he sensed her there.

"You lost?" he asked, not turning around.

Lost?

She'd been lost for the last ten years and was only now beginning to realize it.

"No," she told him, hearing a quiver in her voice. Everything about him, about being close to him, both frightened and excited her. "For the first time in a long time I know exactly where I am."

He just stood there, facing the ocean. She knew what he was waiting for. He wanted her to make the first move. He needed that validation.

The idea gave her an unfamiliar but exhilarating sense of power.

She stepped up behind him and lightly touched his bare back. He didn't tense, didn't flinch, as though he'd been expecting it. She flattened her hands, smoothed her palms across warm skin, feeling only lean muscle underneath. His back rose and fell steadily as he breathed, while her own breath seemed to be coming faster. She could feel the steady beat of his pulse while her own fluctuated wildly, knocking around inside of her chest like a Mexican jumping bean.

She slipped her hands around to rest over his solid abdomen just above his waistband, and felt the muscles contract. She pressed her cheek to his back, breathed in the scent of his skin, felt that rush of familiarity pour over her.

His hands didn't stray from their perch on the railing but he said, "You're trembling."

"I'm scared," she admitted and she let her hands wander higher, across his chest.

"No reason to be scared."

She had every reason to be scared, to be terrified, even.

She was falling for him again. She was falling for a man she knew she could never have. They were stuck in a hopeless situation. A vicious cycle of piss-poor timing.

But she'd come too far to stop now. She was going through with this. She'd never wanted anything more.

She undid the tie on her robe and let it fall to the balcony floor, then pressed the length of her naked body against him. He sucked in a breath and groaned somewhere deep inside. She could feel it rumble through him, through muscle and skin into her breasts and her fingers and the curve of her belly.

They stood that way for several minutes, neither moving or making a sound. It was…nice, but she wasn't looking for nice. She wanted fantastic. She wanted mind-blowing, rip-roaring ecstasy.

She dragged her nails lightly down his chest, from his shoulders all the way to his waistband, felt him tense. He was trying to be strong, trying to milk this for all he could but she could feel him losing it. And she liked it. She liked being the one in control.

She continued her exploration downward, just below his silky waistband, teased him there. "You told me you don't wear pajamas."

His reply came out breathy and uneven. "I lied."

"I know you want me. Are you going to make me beg?"

She could swear she felt him smile. "That's not a problem, is it?"

He turned abruptly, and before she knew it she was in his arms. Body to body, soul to soul. Then he was kissing her. And, oh, did he know how to kiss. He took control, possessed *her*. If he had wanted her to be the aggressor in this scenario, that moment had passed.

And what gave him the right? What if she wanted to be the one calling the shots for a change?

His hands wandered down her back, over her behind, his erection long and hard between them behind the slippery silk. He cupped her backside and squeezed so she bit his lip. Hard.

He gasped and jerked and for a second she thought she'd gone too far.

"Did I hurt you?"

His lids were heavy, eyes glassy and unfocused as he gazed down at her. "Yeah, but I liked it."

So she did it again. She wrapped her hands around his head, pulled him down for a kiss, and sank her teeth into his lower lip. Dillon groaned and tunneled his fingers through her hair, fisted his hands in it. He pulled her head back to look at her, hovering on the line between pain and pleasure. This time there was a smile on his face. "I'm not sure what happened to you in the past ten years, but I like it."

"It gets better." She reached into his pajama bottoms and circled a hand around his erection. He mumbled a curse and his eyes rolled up. But when she tried to pull the pajamas down she only got them halfway past his hips before he caught her hand.

"We're outside," he reminded her.

She knew that. And to top it all off the light from the bedroom was silhouetting their bodies quite clearly.

"Oh, yeah?" She shook off his hand and shoved his pajamas the rest of the way down. "What's your point?"

Then she was off her feet. She gasped as her back slammed hard against the villa wall beside the door. She was pinned between the door and the balcony railing, between rough stucco and Dillon's long, lean body. He hesitated for a second, went stone still, as though he was afraid *he* might have gone too far.

"Did I hurt you?" he asked.

She wrapped her legs around his hips and ground herself against him, so he could feel how wet she was. "Yeah, but I liked it."

He seemed to know exactly what she wanted, and he didn't hesitate. He drove himself inside her, hard and swift and so deep that she cried out. With pain and shock and pure ecstasy.

Dillon pulled out, hovered there for a second, torturing her. Then he plunged forward, and she gasped as the rough wall dug into her back. She'd spent such a long time dulling her feelings, pretending they didn't matter. Now all she wanted to do was feel. Pleasure and lust and pain. She wanted it all, right here, right now. There was no such thing as too much.

"Harder," she gasped and he drove hard against her, inside her. And when it wasn't hard enough, she dug her nails into his back, dragged them across his skin. *"Harder."*

He did as she asked. He may have been the one driving, but she had her foot on the accelerator. She was still in control.

She could feel him tensing, feel him losing it. Bit by bit.

She was doing that to him. *She* was making him lose control.

And when he took the plunge, when he shuddered and roared with release, she went over with him.

Thirteen

Nothing will change for you until you take control of your life and decide that you will be happy. You need movement in a positive forward direction.
—excerpt from The Modern Woman's Guide to Divorce (And the Joy of Staying Single)

There were orgasms, and then there were *orgasms*. The kind that grabbed hold and didn't let go until the absolute last bit of energy had been wrenched out. The kind that released so many endorphins and pheromones that it took several minutes for her body to realize it was twisted like a pretzel, to register that the tingling in her back was not from arousal, but the sharp stucco facade shredding her skin like cheddar on a cheese grater.

"Ow."

Dillon lifted his head from her shoulder, where he'd dropped it a few minutes ago while he caught his breath. He shifted and she winced. "Problem?"

"Wall...sharp."

Only then did she notice the grimace on his face. "Disengage your claws and I'll let you down."

Oh, jeez! She hadn't even realized she was still clinging to him. She loosened her grip and he eased her away from the wall and set her on her feet.

He pulled her into the bedroom, into the light. "Turn around. Let me see the damage."

He examined her back and she watched him over her shoulder, trying to gauge his expression. "How bad is it?"

"Is the dress you're wearing for the wedding backless by any chance?"

"Yeah, why?"

"Then it's bad."

"How bad?"

"It looks like someone ran a belt sander across your back. And you have pieces of the wall still stuck to your skin."

"That would explain the pain, I guess."

He touched her lightly between her shoulder blades and the sting made her wince. "We need to get this cleaned up."

He turned her again and nudged her in the direction of the bathroom. When they were inside he switched on the light. Just like her bathroom, it was really bright with lots of mirror space. Miles of it. The floor-to-ceiling kind that screamed out each and every detail, down to the tiniest imperfection. Ivy crossed her arms over her breasts and sucked in her tummy, wishing she could suck in her hips, too. And her butt.

Dillon had no imperfections, she noticed, as he rummaged through his shaving kit. Nope. He looked just fine. Nicely shaped butt, muscular thighs…

He turned and crouched down to check the cupboard under the sink. She had to slap a hand over her mouth to keep from gasping in horror.

He emerged with a first aid kit, and when he saw the look on her face asked, "What's wrong?"

"Your tuxedo isn't backless, is it?"

He turned to the mirror, inspecting the long red welts criss-crossing his back from his shoulders all the way down to his butt. "I never knew you had such a wild side."

She bit her lip. "Sorry."

He hooked a hand behind her neck, drew her to him and kissed her. Not quite passionate, but not a peck, either. "Darlin', that was not a complaint."

He let her go and set the first aid kit on the bathroom counter. He rummaged through it for cotton and antiseptic. How could he be so casual? Didn't he feel the least bit self-conscious standing there naked? She sure did.

"Turn around." He dabbed antiseptic on the cotton. "This might sting."

When the cool liquid touched her raw skin she tensed and sucked in a breath.

"Sorry." He dabbed slowly and gently, starting at the top and working his way down. She wondered what he was thinking. If he was looking at her and noticing the way her body had…*spread*.

"My body has changed," she said, in case he hadn't

noticed. So he wouldn't suddenly look at her and think *Ack, who is this cow I've been sleeping with?* "I don't look like I did in college."

"Good," he said, looking at her in the mirror. "I'm turned on by women, not girls."

Oh, well, lucky her.

He tossed the used cotton in the trash and fished out a fresh one. "Besides, you don't really look all that different."

"I think your memory is failing."

"My memory is crystal clear," he said, flashing a devious grin over her shoulder. "I have video."

Video? "What kind of video?"

"*The* video," he said.

Her jaw dropped and her heart bottomed out. She hadn't thought about *the* video for years. She had no reason to, considering he'd told her he erased it.

"Our *special* video?" she asked. "The one you absolutely *swore* you got rid of?"

"I lied."

There were things on that video that she'd done for him, done to herself, without him in the frame, that he could have at any time used against her. He could have ruined her career. Her *life!*

"All done." He tossed the used cotton in the trash and turned her toward him.

"Why did you keep it?"

"I wasn't planning on using it against you, if that's what you're thinking. We made that for us. No one else is going to see it. *Ever.*"

Well, that was good to know. And it made her feel

like even more of a slime for the things she'd written in her book. How could she have been so vindictive and immature? He'd had the ammunition to retaliate big-time, but he hadn't done it.

"I am such an ass," she said.

He sat on the edge of the counter and pulled her closer, between his slightly parted knees. God, he was beautiful. And she must be completely nuts, totally off her rocker to be standing here naked with him, casually chatting, as though they hadn't just had sex so wild and out of control that they'd required first aid afterward.

And it would be a lie if she said she didn't want to do it again.

"Are you angry?" he asked.

She wasn't sure what to feel.

He pried her arms from their position guarding her chest and took her hands in his, weaving his fingers through hers. "The truth is, I don't really know why I kept it. I didn't even remember I had it until about a week ago. It was stashed in the back of my safe."

A ripple of excitement, a shiver of anticipation, rippled across her skin. "Did you…watch it?"

He nodded.

Oh. My. God.

Just talking about it was getting him hard again. Not just getting. He was already there. And she was feeling that warm, fuzzy sensation. It started in her scalp and worked its way south toward her toes in a slow, easy rush.

She could hardly believe what she was going to ask next. Something was definitely wrong with her. "Then what did you do?"

A grin quirked up the corner of his mouth. "Are you sure you want to know?"

She did and she didn't. But mostly she did, despite the fact that it was a little depraved and incredibly kinky.

She nodded.

"I watched it…" He rounded his hands over her hips, pulled her a little closer. "Then I went up to my room…" He leaned forward and nibbled her neck, her shoulder. "I took off my clothes…" His breath was warm on her ear and Ivy felt hot and cold all over—

"Then I took a very long, cold shower."

Embarrassment burned her cheeks. She buried her face in the crook of his shoulder. "That was mean."

He laughed. "I had you going, though."

She took a moment to breathe in his scent, to enjoy the way their bodies fit together, every dip and curve. It felt exactly the same. It felt…*right.*

And *so* wrong.

"What are we doing, Dillon?" She looked up at him. "We're divorced."

"Last I heard there's no law against sleeping with your ex." He tucked her hair back behind her ears. It was such a simple, sweet gesture of affection. One you did after being with someone for a long time. And that was kind of what this felt like. As though they hadn't really been apart for ten long years. It was as if it had been a week or two and they were picking up exactly where they'd left off.

Only wiser.

"How's your back feel?"

Back? What back? With his arms wrapped around

her, his body warm and close, she hadn't even noticed. "It feels much better."

"I guess we got a little carried away."

"I guess we did."

"I pride myself on my stamina, but you took me down in seconds flat," he admitted. "Before tonight, no one has ever managed to do that."

"Is that a fact?" She took his hands and pulled him backward toward the door. "Well, then, maybe we oughtta' go into the bedroom and see if I can do that again."

It mystified Ivy how some things never changed. She and Dillon had fallen easily back into their old routine. They made love, talked for a while, then made love again. Repeating the cycle until the hazy light of dawn crept up on them.

It was as frightening as it was settling. To know someone so well, but not really know them at all. To realize that as good as it could be, they had nowhere to take this. No future.

They lay curled up in the dark under the covers facing each other, arms and legs entwined, as though they couldn't bear the idea of not touching each other. Not being close. Not looking each other in the eye.

Maybe because they both knew that after this week it might never happen again.

"Why didn't you ever remarry?" she asked him.

He shrugged. "I guess once was enough. How about you?"

"I guess I never met anyone I liked enough to make that kind of commitment."

"You always were a little commitment phobic," he said, but she could tell by his smile he was teasing. "How many times did I have to ask you out before you finally said yes?"

"Enough that I realized you weren't ever going to stop asking. I was so nervous on that first date. I was so afraid you were going to try to take advantage of me. But you were a perfect gentleman."

"And it nearly killed me. The way I wanted you." He smiled and shook his head. "That was the longest three months of my entire life."

"I never told you this, but you were my first."

"Yeah, I sorta figured."

"You never said anything."

"I thought that if you wanted me to know you would have said so."

"Right from the start we didn't talk to each other, did we? We couldn't be honest. Maybe we just didn't know how."

"I guess we finally figured it out," he said.

"Yeah, ten years too late."

"Is it?"

"Is it what?"

"Too late."

He couldn't be serious. She propped herself up on her elbow. "You know that after this week, this has to end. It can't go any further than this bedroom. If it were to get out, that would be the end of my career. My writing, my practice. I would lose everything."

He sighed and rolled onto his back. "I guess that is a lot to ask, isn't it?"

"Besides, my mom would disown me if you and I ever got back together."

He grinned. "She never did like me much."

"And how would your mother react if you brought me home for dinner?"

"I'm thinking…stroke, heart attack."

She scooted up close to him and rested her head on his chest, sighed as his arms went around her. She had gone far too long without this. When she got back to the States, she would have to start dating again. Start living her life instead of watching it roll past without her. "We have until Sunday. Three more days. Let's just enjoy them while we can."

"Sounds like a plan."

It was a *good* plan, so why couldn't she shake the feeling, the fear, that three days with Dillon wouldn't be nearly enough?

A loud, insistent pounding roused Ivy from a dead sleep. She tried to open her eyes but the room was too bright.

What time was it?

She squinted at the clock. They'd been sleeping for a whole three and a half hours.

The pounding stopped, then immediately started up again. Beside her, Dillon groaned and stuffed the pillow over his head.

She gave him a poke. "Someone is knocking on your door."

"No kidding," he said, his voice muffled and cranky. He never had been a morning person. Of course, they hadn't gone to sleep until after seven, so this was technically like the middle of the night. "They'll go away."

They didn't. Whoever it was pounded harder, then Dale called, "Dillon, wake up! It's important!"

Dillon mumbled and cursed. He flung the covers off and rolled out of bed, naked and beautiful. She couldn't have asked for a better view. A full moon in the morning.

She watched as he grabbed his robe and shoved his arms through the sleeves, then stomped to the door. He flung it open and in his cranky voice asked, *"What?"*

"Have you seen Blake and Deidre?"

"Of course not. I was sound asleep."

"Well, they're not here," Dale said. "No one knows where they are."

"And you think they're in here with me? You picked a hell of a time to pretend you give a shit about your brother. They probably went out to breakfast or something."

"I don't think so. They left yesterday afternoon, and they haven't been back."

Ivy sat up in bed, instantly awake.

"Are you sure they haven't been here?" Dillon asked. The crankiness was gone and concern had crept in to take its place.

"The rental car was gone all night and their bed wasn't slept in."

Fear lodged in Ivy's gut. Deidre had been in pretty bad shape the other night. Ivy should have checked on her yesterday. She should have made sure she was okay.

What if she'd had another meltdown? What if she was in a hospital somewhere?

"I thought Ivy might know where they are," Dale said, "but I can't find her, either."

"I haven't seen her," Dillon lied.

Something was definitely not right. Deidre wouldn't just take off. Not without telling someone.

Ivy wrapped herself in the sheet and joined Dillon at the door. "Did you try calling her cell?"

It was almost funny the way Dale's mouth fell open, how he looked from her, to Dillon, then back to her.

"Oh, there you are, Ivy," Dillon said, acting surprised to see her. "How did you get in here?"

She shot him a look, then turned to Dale. "Did you call their cell phones? Deidre always keeps hers on and charged. She's fanatical about it."

"I tried calling them both and the calls go straight to voice mail."

"Did you try calling your parents?" Dillon asked.

He shook his head. "I didn't want to worry them."

"Something isn't right," Ivy said.

"You know my brother. With our parents flying in tonight, there's no way Blake would just take off."

"Give us five minutes to get dressed," Dillon said. "Then we'll figure out what to do."

"The only thing left to do is call the police," Dillon told everyone an hour and a half later.

They had called everyone they could think of who might possibly know where Deidre and Blake went. Friends, family, coworkers. They called the local hospital to see if anyone matching their descriptions had been admitted, and checked CNN just in case any accidents or unidentified tourists had been found. They had covered all the bases, and they had come up with nothing.

Deidre and Blake were gone.

"We shouldn't be so quick to jump to conclusions," one of the Tweedles said. Dillon still couldn't tell them apart.

"Yeah," the other one added. "I'm sure they're fine."

Everyone else was worried, while those two had done nothing but sulk. Probably because the attention was no longer focused on them.

Ivy was handling it the worst. She couldn't sit still. Dillon would convince her to sit down and relax, and she would be back up again in a minute or two, peering out the window for a sign of their car. Checking her cell phone for a missed call, even though it hadn't once left her hand.

"We should make the call," Dale said, and Calvin nodded in agreement.

Dillon flipped open his phone and was getting ready to dial when they heard a car coming up the driveway.

Ivy dashed to the window. "They're back!"

Relief hit Dillon hard and swift, like a sucker punch in the gut. He snapped his phone shut and slipped it back into the holster. Blake had better have had a damned good excuse for scaring them all half to death.

Tweedle number one followed Ivy to the window and peered out. "See, I told you they were fine."

Ivy turned and shot her a look. One that would have scared Dillon had he been on the receiving end.

"She's got a lot of nerve just taking off," number two said indignantly. "Does she think *we* actually want to be here?"

No, Dillon thought, they had made it pretty clear they were there under duress.

Ivy didn't say a word, but he could see her temper rising. Her cheeks were getting red and blotchy and her fists were clenching and unclenching. And her foot was tapping. Bad sign. If those two knew what was good for them they would quit while they were ahead. Especially with Ivy standing within swinging distance. He knew from experience that you could only push her so far before she blew, and she looked as though she was more than halfway there already.

"Enough, Heather," Dale said.

They actually had names. Go figure. And he was getting kind of attached to Dum and Dee.

"Why are you getting mad at me?" Heather snapped back. "I'm not the one with the problem. You should have seen the way she flipped out the other night."

"Yeah," number one agreed. "It's not our fault that she's too fat to fit in her dress."

The last word had barely left her mouth and Ivy was already in midswing. Dillon scarcely had time to cringe before she connected. One quick, solid right jab, and Tweedle number one was on the ground, holding her jaw.

Everyone else stood in stunned silence. Even number two, aka Heather, didn't seem to know what to say. Or maybe she just didn't want to be the next one to go down.

Then the door flew open and Deidre burst through, Blake close behind. "Hi, everyone! We're back!"

Fourteen

Is the new man in your life pressing for a commitment? Consider wisely. When it comes to relationships, three out of four women make the same mistake twice.
—excerpt from *The Modern Woman's Guide to Divorce (And the Joy of Staying Single)*

They had *eloped*.

Apparently, the dress incident had been the last straw. When Deidre pulled herself together she'd told Blake that if they didn't get out of there, if he didn't make some serious changes, the wedding was off. And thank goodness Blake was smart enough to know what he would have been giving up if he'd let her go.

If Ivy didn't love Deidre so much, she would kill her

for scaring them. But put in the same position, she wouldn't have done things any differently. At least she knew everything was going to be okay. Deidre and Blake would make it. They would be happy.

Now, if only she could feel so confident about her own life.

"You couldn't wait until I got inside the house," Deidre said, handing Ivy a new bag of ice and taking the melted one. "You had to take her down right *before* I walked in."

Ivy set the ice over her swollen, purple knuckles. "It's not as though I planned to hit her. It just sort of happened."

She barely even remembered doing it. One minute she was just standing there, the next Dum was on the floor and Ivy's hand was throbbing. She'd never hit another person in her life. There had just been the beer bottle incident, and luckily for them both she had missed.

When Dee recovered from the shock, she'd begun to wail about calling her attorney and pressing charges, then the four of them had packed up and left. The villa had been blessedly peaceful ever since.

"How's the hand, Sugar Ray?" Dillon asked. He sat in a chair across from Ivy, a goofy grin plastered on his face. He was enjoying this far too much.

"I think I'm going to cut my boxing career short."

"It looks as though you two are getting along better," Deidre said, looking back and forth between them.

"I guess you could say we're working things out," Ivy told her.

"I'm glad. At least this trip wasn't a total waste."

"Have you told Blake's parents?"

"We called them from the road and caught them just as they were leaving for the airport."

"I'm a disgrace to my family," Blake said. "And I'm probably out of a job. And a house."

"And you guys are okay with that?" Ivy asked.

He shrugged and sat on the arm of the couch, beside his new wife. She smiled up at him. "They'll get over it."

"Do you have anything lined up?" Dillon asked him.

"Not yet," Blake said.

"I've said it before and I'll say it again. If you need a job, there's always a position open for you in my company."

"I'll definitely think about it." He looked down at Deidre and grinned. "Right now I just want to enjoy being a newlywed."

"We've decided to leave early for our honeymoon," Deidre told them. "We're going to drive up the coast, then be back in time for the cruise when it leaves Saturday night. Either of you is welcome to stay for the rest of the week." She shot Ivy a smile. "Or both of you."

Ivy struggled to suppress the depraved excitement clawing its way to the surface. She glanced over at Dillon and saw that he was trying really hard not to smile. She didn't doubt they were thinking the exact same thing.

Three days alone, with this big house all to themselves. Did it get any better than that?

Sunday came way too soon.

After spending every waking hour together for the past three days, the idea of being apart was almost impossible for Dillon to fathom.

As he helped her carry her bags out to the limo that would take her to the airport—his flight wasn't scheduled to leave for another few hours—it occurred to him that he had gone and done something really stupid.

He had fallen in love with Ivy all over again.

And Ivy had made her position very clear. Her career was the only thing important enough to fill the number one spot in her life right now. She'd worked too hard, for too long, to throw it all away on a man she wasn't sure she trusted.

Well, she hadn't actually said that, but he knew that was what she was thinking.

It was kind of ironic. Ten years ago she'd been ready to settle down and start a life with him, but all he'd wanted was to have fun. To goof off. Now that he was finally ready to slow down and be with her, she had already moved on to bigger and better things.

And if it were his career in jeopardy, he couldn't say for sure that he wouldn't make the same decision.

They had genuine feelings for each other. Their timing was just *way* off.

For some reason that didn't make him feel any better.

The driver put the bags in the trunk, and Dillon opened the door for Ivy. "I had a good time this week."

She set her purse on the seat and turned to him, the car door between them. "Me, too. Do you think Dale will tell anyone he saw us together?"

"I doubt it. And if he does say anything, I'll deny it. Your career is safe."

"Thank you," she said, but instead of sounding relieved, he could swear he heard disappointment in her voice.

The driver got in and started the engine.

"I guess this is it," she said.

Dillon nodded. "I guess it is."

He kept his hands clamped down tightly on the car window, so he wouldn't touch her. Because he knew if he got hold of her again, he might not be able to let go. And that would be a mistake.

It hadn't worked the first time, and they had no guarantees it be any better now. Odds were they would have ended up right where they'd been ten years ago. Divorced and bitter and hating each other. At least this time they were parting as friends.

She had a life, and he had a life, and they were both better off keeping it that way.

"Have a good trip."

"Goodbye." She rose up on her toes and pressed a kiss to his cheek, then she turned and climbed inside the limo. He stood and watched as the limo rolled down the driveway and disappeared around the corner.

It was the second damn time he'd watched that woman walk out of his life.

Ivy had two major problems.

Problem number one was that she was pretty sure her career was officially over.

For the seventh day straight she'd sat at her desk, staring at the computer screen, until her eyes burned with fatigue and strain. Instead of tapping across the keyboard the way they usually did, her hands lay limp and useless in her lap.

Seven days, and she hadn't written a darned word.

What was once so clear to her, so obvious and logical, no longer made sense. The magic was gone. And the explanation was simple. She was a fraud. A charlatan. She'd been giving millions of trusting, naive women lousy advice.

It was humbling and embarrassing to realize that everything she believed in, everything she knew about her life, was a lie. Or at the very least, grossly misconstrued. It was a wrong she needed to right or she feared it would gnaw away at her, little by little, until there was nothing left. Unfortunately, she didn't have the slightest clue how to fix it. What her next move should be.

Which brought her to problem number two. Dillon.

She missed him.

She missed him like she'd never missed anyone before in her life. The first time she'd walked away from him had hurt, but it had also been a relief. The fighting, the heartache—it had been over. All she felt this time was pain and loss. A deep, sharp ache in her chest, as though her heart had been ripped out, filleted, haphazardly sewn back together, then shoved back in the wrong way.

After she'd kissed Dillon goodbye and the limo had set off to the airport, it had taken her exactly three seconds to realize, to admit to herself, that she loved him. The same as the first time, but completely different somehow.

What they'd had back then was thrilling and complicated and volatile. It had burned hot and fast, but what she felt for him now was more mature and undemanding. Simple in its complexity. And deeper than she imagined possible.

They had come full circle, and by letting go the first time, they had somehow grown together. It was finally their time. She was sure, all the way down to her soul, that they could make it work and that they would both be happy.

At least a dozen times she'd opened her mouth to instruct the driver to turn around, to take her back. But she'd been too chicken to do it. How could she willingly destroy her own career? Admit to millions of readers that she was wrong? And how could she not?

But what scared her the most, was what if he rejected her? What if he didn't love her the way she loved him?

What a pathetic excuse for a strong, independent woman she turned out to be.

But damn it, she was sick of playing that role. And the honest truth was, that's all it had been. A role. An act. When she stripped herself down to the core, to the real her, she was still the same old Ivy. Only a little wiser, she hoped.

What it really boiled down to, the thing she had to decide once and for all, was would she rather be successful, or would she rather be happy?

The answer came to her instantly.

Definitely happy.

Well, that wasn't so hard.

And who knows, maybe someday she would be able to manage both. But one thing at a time. First she had to talk to Dillon.

It was a risk. It was possible that he wasn't willing to give her a second chance. He could have moved on by now. But she knew that was a chance she was willing to take. One she had to take.

Oh, my God, she was really going to do this.

She reached for the phone, hand trembling with anticipation. Nothing in her life had ever felt so scary. Or so right.

The instant her hand hit the receiver she realized that she didn't have his number. She could call directory assistance, but she seriously doubted he would be listed.

But she did know where he lived.

Besides, if she was going to grovel, she should at least give him the satisfaction of seeing her face.

She pushed away from her desk. She would go to his house and hope that she was able to get past the front gate. Even if that meant running into his horrible mother. Mrs. Marshall, as Ivy had been instructed to address her, would just have to adjust to having Ivy around again. The same with Ivy's mom. She would have to accept that Dillon had changed. And if she couldn't, if she still believed Ivy was making a mistake, Ivy would just have to learn to tune her out. In fact, she should have learned that a long time ago.

And who knows, maybe a couple of grandchildren to spoil would lighten them both up a little. Right now, she felt as though anything were possible.

She grabbed her keys off the table in the entryway and stuck her feet into one of the pairs of shoes she'd left by the front door. Her hands were shaking and her heart was about to burst from her chest it was beating so hard, but she was determined to see this through.

She turned the knob and swung the door open and— hello!—almost ran face-first into the wall of man standing there.

It took her brain a second or two to process who it was. "Dillon?"

He stood in the hallway outside her apartment, fist raised, as if he'd just been preparing to knock, and he looked just as surprised to see her as she was to see him. Several days' worth of dark, coarse stubble branded his face and his clothes were wrinkled. His hair was a mess and when he slipped off his sunglasses his eyes looked red-rimmed and tired.

Good Lord, he looked about as awful as she felt. For some reason that was a comfort.

He didn't say a word. He just gripped her by her upper arms and tugged her roughly to him. His lips came down hard on hers, rough and sexy and demanding. His beard chafed her chin, fingers dug into her flesh. He tasted like coffee and sex, smelled warm and familiar. Her body went limp and she heard her keys hit the floor.

The kiss was as hot as a flash fire and over just as fast. He set her loose and she stood there, dizzy and disoriented, clutching the door frame to keep from falling over.

Whoa.

If he was trying to knock her off base, he was doing one hell of a job.

He scooped her keys up from the floor. "Going somewhere?"

"Believe it or not, I was just on my way to see you," she said. "We must be on the same wavelength or something."

"No kidding. You were coming to see me?" He looked her up and down, and his brow crinkled. "Like *that?*"

Like what? She looked down at herself and snorted out a laugh. She was still in the baggy pajama bottoms and threadbare T-shirt she'd slept in last night. The sandals on her feet were each a different style and color. Come to think of it, she couldn't remember if she'd even brushed her hair. She hadn't grabbed her purse, either, meaning she didn't have her driver's license. Had she been pulled over, the police might have mistaken her for an escaped lunatic.

"I guess I forgot to get dressed."

"We have to talk," he grumbled. It wasn't a request. It was an order.

"Okay, let's talk."

"Can I come in? If I'm going to grovel, I'm sure as *hell* not going to do it in front of your neighbors."

Grovel?

Dillon laid down the law. He divided and conquered. But Dillon *did not* grovel.

Without waiting for an answer, and in typical Dillon form, he strong-armed his way inside and shut the door behind him.

"Make yourself at home," she mumbled, annoyed, but only a little.

"So here's the deal," he said in that Master of the Universe tone. "I'm not going to let you toss me away again."

So this was his idea of groveling? Ordering her around again?

She crossed her arms over her chest, stuck her chin up in the air. "You're not?"

He settled into an identical, defiant stance. "Nope."

"Do I have a say in this?"

"Nope. I love you, and you love me. Even though you're too damned stubborn to admit it."

Oh, she was, was she? Why in the heck did he think she was coming to see him? To tell him she *didn't* love him?

"For your information, I do love you. Although at times like this I have to wonder why."

"Great, so you won't object to the fact that you're marrying me."

A shiver of excitement scrambled up her spine. He wanted to marry her. "If that was a proposal, you really need to work on your delivery."

"You want me to get down on one knee? Fine." He dropped down in front of her. "How's that?"

"Better." A lot closer to the groveling he'd promised.

He looked her right in the eye and said, "Marry me."

Another demand. For Pete's sake, could he drop the macho act for two seconds?

"What about my work? My career? If we get married, professionally I could be ruined. You said yourself that it was too much to ask me to give up."

The cockiness never wavered. "Too bad. Because I'm asking."

No, he wasn't. He was telling. The way he always did. But knowing how hard it must have been for him to swallow his pride and come here in the first place, this time she didn't mind so much. He was just being Dillon, and she didn't expect him to change. She loved him, warts and all. This time she was going into the deal with her eyes wide open.

That didn't mean it wouldn't be entertaining to mess with him just a little. "And if I say no?"

"You won't."

"But what if I do?"

He blew out an exasperated breath. "I'll ask again. And again. And I'll keep asking until you say yes."

The odds of a normal, traditional proposal seemed to hover somewhere in the million-to-one range. "Well, then, I guess I don't have much of a choice. I guess I have to say yes."

He rose to his feet and pulled her to him, not so roughly this time, and kissed her again. This time it lasted longer, felt…sweeter. Tender, even. His hands cupped her face, lips brushing lazily back and forth across hers. She heard him sigh, felt him shudder with satisfaction.

The kiss trailed off slowly, his lips lingering above hers. And when she opened her eyes to look at him, he was smiling that lazy, happy smile.

"This could be complicated," she warned him.

He only shrugged. "We'll figure it out."

"Our mothers—"

"—will adjust," he finished for her. He glanced over her shoulder, down the hall. "Have you got a bedroom in this place?"

"I want kids," she warned him.

"Great." He lowered his head, nibbled the curve of her neck. A new round of shivers exploded across her skin.

"I'm serious, Dillon."

"Fine with me." He licked the shell of her ear, nipped at it with his teeth. Desire ignited in the pit of her belly and burned its way through her arms and legs and into her head.

"I want at least two," she told him, her voice coming

out breathy and soft. "And I want to do it soon, before I'm too old."

"Good idea." He walked her backward down the hall, his hands gentle yet determined as they circled her waist, easing her T-shirt up. "In fact, I think we should start trying right now."

Apparently she wasn't moving quickly enough, because he lifted her right off her feet and carried her the rest of the way.

He found the bedroom on the first try and shouldered his way through the door, then he all but tossed her on the bed and dropped down beside her. Instead of ravaging her, the way she expected, he just looked down at her and smiled.

"This is going to be good." He kissed her forehead, the tip of her nose. "This is going to be really good."

"Yes," she agreed, "it is." They really had come full circle, and wound up exactly where they were supposed to be. She wasn't going to try to fool herself into thinking it would be easy. They were still both stubborn as hell. But this time, at least, they had maturity on their side.

"You know we're going to have to work at this," she said, and he nodded solemnly.

"I know."

"We're going to have to keep the lines of communication open or we'll end up just like we were ten years ago."

"I understand that."

"You can't just—"

He silenced her with a kiss. A long, slow, mind-melting deep one.

When it was over, she felt hot and fuzzy-headed. "What was I saying?"

"Ivy, you don't have to worry. We'll do what we have to do. Whatever it takes." His eyes searched her face, filled with love and affection and respect. "I let you go twice, darlin'. That's a mistake I won't be making again."

Coming soon from Series Press—from half the author team who brought us the bestselling self-help book The Modern Woman's Guide to Divorce (And the Joy of Staying Single), Not All Men Are Pigs *or* What Was I Thinking?

ONE NIGHT WITH THE BEST MAN

AMANDA BERRY

To my husband and children,
Thank you for helping me follow my dream.

After an exciting life as an accountant, **Amanda Berry** returned to writing when her husband swept the family off to England to live for a year. Now she's hooked, and since returning to the States spends her days concocting spicy contemporary romances while her cats try in vain to pry her hands off the keyboard. Amanda moved from the Midwest to the Southeast coast with her husband, two children, two cats and a Beagle-Jack Russell mix. For more about Amanda and her books, please visit www.amanda-berry.com

Chapter One

"How's the bride?" Penny Montgomery stepped into the church dressing room, where her best friend since childhood, Maggie Brown, was getting ready to walk down the aisle. This church, one of five in the small town of Tawnee Valley, was the one Maggie's mother had dragged Maggie and Penny to when they were growing up.

"Nervous. Excited. Trying to remember to breathe." Maggie hadn't stopped smiling. Her gown was lovely and simple. Classically A-lined styled with no train. Her light hair was pulled up in a loose knot with tendrils left to play around her neck. She looked stunning and had the truest heart of anyone Penny had ever known.

"You look beautiful," Penny said. "Your mother would have loved to see you like this."

Maggie nodded. Tears sparkled in her eyes but they didn't fall. For years, Penny and Maggie had been each other's rock. Now Maggie had found her dream man and was forming a family. Penny had Maggie and that was enough family for her.

"Mom would be happy."

A lump formed in Penny's throat and she coughed to clear it. "Brady wanted me to give you this."

She held out the little gift-wrapped box.

"Thank you, Penny." Maggie held on to Penny's hand. "I mean it. For everything. For being with me when everything was so hard and for nudging me in the right direction when I needed a shove."

"What are best friends for?" Careful of her long slip dress, Penny stepped back and sat on the antique couch. The pale gold silk gown slid against her skin.

She ran a finger over the worn velvet of the couch. If it were refinished it might fetch a nice price in What Goes Around Comes Around, her antiques store, but it suited the old chapel the way it was. Years of wear from weddings to funerals to christenings had made this couch unique. The story behind antiques always made them more valuable in Penny's eyes.

"Well," Penny prompted, needing to lighten the mood. "Open the gift. I bet it's a ring. Probably the kind that vibrates. You know, the kind that goes on his—"

"Penny!" Maggie was too serious for her own good sometimes. Penny just smiled and shrugged. She hoped that she helped to corrupt her friend just a little.

"Just because that would be something *you'd* like for a gift…" Maggie took off the ribbon and opened the box. She drew out two diamond drop earrings. "Oh, my."

"Looks like someone is making up for lost time." Penny smiled, kicked off her heels and drew her already-aching feet under her. The devil himself had made those heels, but she wouldn't tell Maggie that.

"Brady being here now is all that matters." The light caught in the facets of the diamonds and burst into tiny dancing lights around the room. "They are so lovely."

"I'm so happy for you." And Penny meant it. If anyone deserved a happy ending, it was Maggie.

Penny wasn't made for marriage. Whenever she wanted a man, all she had to do was go out and find one. The clubs were only an hour away in Springfield. And if she just wanted to stay warm at night, Flicker, her new shaggy puppy, could help her out.

Maggie put the earrings on and turned to face Penny. "How do I look?"

"Like you are in love. Glowing. When Brady sees you, he's going to be the happiest man in the world." Maggie's bliss was contagious. It radiated from her like the brightest star. Maggie had made it through all the suffering and losing her mom.

After a moment, Maggie gave Penny a worried-momma look. "Luke made it in last night."

"Great." Penny gave Maggie a grin, even though her heart beat a little heavier. "It would look a little weird if I didn't have a best man to walk me down the aisle. Plus he's going to be part of your family soon."

"Are you sure you are okay with this?"

Penny took a deep breath and gave Maggie a reassuring look. "It was nine years ago, Maggie. Teenage puppy love. I'm sure he's over it by now. I am."

"So no drama?" Maggie raised her eyebrow.

"If there's drama, I won't be the cause of it." Penny uncurled from the couch and stood, shaking any wrinkles out of the floor-length gown. The energy levels in her body had suddenly surged and she couldn't sit anymore. Suppressing a whimper, she shoved her feet back in her shoes. She nervously checked the mirror. Her makeup hadn't smeared. Her red hair had been pulled into a tight bun, and at least one can of hair spray had plastered it into place. With the extra few inches the heels provided, she'd at least be able to look Luke Ward in the chin after all these years.

The noise level in the hallway picked up. Someone knocked on the door.

"Five minutes, ladies." The door muffled an older woman's voice beyond recognition.

"He's not seeing anyone," Maggie continued. She picked up her veil and worked the comb into her hair.

"Too bad for him, I guess." Penny held the end of the veil and straightened it to keep busy. "Seriously, Maggie, I'll be okay. Luke is here for one weekend. The worst thing that could happen is that I'll step on his foot during the bridal party dance with these fabulous heels and he'll have to bandage himself up."

"If you're sure…" Maggie didn't sound as if she believed Penny.

"I'm sure that if we don't get out there soon, the groom will think you ran away." Penny picked up the bridal bouquet and handed it to Maggie. "You worry about walking down that aisle and not about me."

Penny gave Maggie a once-over before picking up her own flowers. The last thing her friend should be worried about today was what would happen when Luke and Penny were in the same room for the first time since she had driven him away.

It was not as if they had the type of love that would last forever. Teenage love never did. First loves never did.

Luke had been heading off to college, and she'd barely earned the grades to graduate high school. If it weren't for What Goes Around Comes Around, the only work Penny would be qualified for was as either a gas station attendant or a fast-food worker. When she had inherited the quaint store along Main Street from her grandmother, it had been bleeding money, but the shop meant too much to Penny to let it fail. After her grandmother died, she had no family left to rely on. Her father had been a no-show since she was born, and her mother had ditched her years ago to continue boozing without a child in tow. But Penny was an adult now. She had managed to turn the shop around and make it a tourist attraction in their little one-stoplight town.

Through it all, she'd always had Maggie's support. Maggie and her daughter, Amber, were her family, and she wouldn't dream of making a fuss on one of the happiest days of Maggie's life. Even if that meant putting up with Brady Ward's younger brother.

The moment she stepped into the hallway, she saw him.

Luke stood about a dozen feet in front of her. The air around her crackled with energy. Dark hair, blue eyes, towering height, these were all features shared by the Ward brothers. Luke wasn't as tall as Sam, the oldest brother, but he still towered over her even in her three-inch heels. The lankiness of high school was gone, replaced by a filled-out but trim figure his tuxedo suited just fine. His dark hair curled slightly at the ends, where it touched his collar. If this were any other man, Penny would be placing bets that she would have him in her bed before the night was over.

But this was her Luke. At least he had been hers. Behind the bleachers, in the backseat of her car, in the field on a blanket looking up into a night sky that seemed to go on forever. They'd made promises neither of them were old enough to keep. Things had seemed so clear to her then. He loved her. He'd promised forever, but she knew forever was just a word. Love didn't matter. Back then it had been only a matter of time. And when—not if—he had left her, she would have been the one picking up the pieces. She straightened her shoulders and loosened the death grip on her flowers.

Plastering a smile on her face, she stepped forward.

"Penny!" Amber's voice burst out from behind Luke and the speeding golden bullet of eight-year-old energy raced toward her. "Penny! Penny! You have to meet my uncle Luke. I have two uncles now. And he's a doctor."

Penny was powerless as Amber grabbed her hand and dragged her toward Luke. Not exactly the image she'd wanted to project, but Amber didn't wait for graceful entrances.

"Amber, I've met your uncle Luke. We went to school together." Penny managed to not fall off her heels as Amber stopped in front of Luke.

"She's got quite the grip, doesn't she?" Luke smiled down at Amber as Penny tried to compose herself.

Amber spotted Maggie and took off in the direction of her mother.

"You should see her with my puppy, Flicker." Penny held her breath as Luke's gaze floated over her dress up to her face. She wasn't eighteen anymore. What if he didn't like what he saw?

Nonsense. She never let a man make her feel insecure.

Luke finally met her eyes. "I'm supposed to walk you down the aisle."

Her world was lost in a sea of blue, so rich and inviting that if she could, she would strip naked and dive into their warm depths. Warmth soaked through her body and her knees felt loose in their sockets.

She shook herself out of his spell and managed a smile that didn't feel entirely plastic. "Yes, you are."

"Or from the looks of those heels, keep you from falling on your ass?" That mischievous twinkle she'd always loved lit in his eyes.

"Oh, these little things?" Penny lifted her shoe to contemplate it.

Apparently the past was where it belonged: in the past. She smiled easier. Luke hadn't changed much since high school, but his shoulders seemed less tight. Maybe he'd finally learned to let things go. When she'd first noticed him as more than just another classmate, he'd been filled with anger and grief after the death of his parents. She knew what it was like to be left by the ones you loved. And even though his parents hadn't meant to leave, the pain he'd felt had seemed close to her own.

"Looks like we'll be spending most of the evening together," Luke said.

Penny blinked up at him as her stomach gave a little flip of joy at the remembrance of nights spent in his arms. Hot nights in the back of her beat-up Chevy. They'd laughed and forgotten about the rest of Tawnee Valley while they lost themselves in exploring each other. Fogged windows. Naked skin to naked skin. His hands and mouth had made her forget how to breathe.

"I'm the best man," he said, slowly. "And you're the maid of honor...."

"Of course." She tried to laugh it off, but it came out stilted as she tried to control the heat bubbling within her. "I'd hate to keep you from your date, though."

"I didn't bring one."

"She couldn't make it?" Penny fished just a little, knowing that if there was a *she,* Penny needed to shut down this attraction. She didn't mess with taken men.

"There isn't a she." He looked over her shoulder briefly before returning his gaze to her eyes. "What about your date? Won't it make him jealous that I'll have you in my arms most of the night?"

"If he existed, it probably would." The men she hooked up with were always free agents and never more than that. "I guess that means I'm yours tonight."

His dark eyebrow lifted as if his train of thought had just arrived at the same station. A spark of awareness raced down her spine.

"If everyone could line up," Beatrice Miller called out in her singsong voice. The kindergarten teacher helped out at the church for the wedding coordinator. She treated every wedding party like a group of five-year-olds who needed to get in line and wait patiently for their turn. Many of them had had her as a teacher, so it wasn't hard for her to rein them in.

Luke held out his elbow, and Penny hesitated for only a moment before slipping her hand over his jacketed arm. They were to be the first down the aisle.

"Mom and Dad should be here," Luke said so softly that she almost missed it.

Her fingers squeezed his arm and she leaned against him. "Yes."

As they stood by the door waiting for the procession music to begin, the crisp, clean scent of Luke wafted over her. He pulled her in tightly to his side. His warmth penetrated her silk dress. He was as solid next to her as he'd always been. Almost as much a safe haven to her as her grandmother's antiques store had been when she was young. Had he stayed in Tawnee Valley, would things have been different for them?

The doors to the chapel opened, and Penny straightened and put on her smile. This was Maggie's day. The past was gone. Only right now mattered. The entire town had turned out for the wedding. And they were all looking at her walking arm in arm with Luke Ward.

She could almost see the matchmaking gears in ole Bitsy Clemons's head turning on overload. Bitsy had brought every eligible man in Tawnee Valley to Penny's store. As if Penny would die if she didn't marry soon.

It was bad enough to be walking down the aisle with an ex, but to do so in front of everyone who had known how hot and heavy they had been…

They made it to the preacher and split ways. As Luke went to the other side of Brady, she turned and their eyes met. She saw a hint of humor and speculation in those eyes. She could definitely lose herself in him for a night or two. After all, he could only improve with age.

Amber started down the aisle and tossed wildflowers on the path before her. When she reached the front, she turned and sat in the pew next to Sam Ward.

The music changed and the doors reopened to reveal the bride. The congregation stood as she walked slowly down the aisle with a smile filled with such love that Penny couldn't stop the tears that sprang to her eyes.

As she reached the wedding party, Maggie passed her bouquet to Penny to hold and took Brady's hands.

Brady looked as if he'd just been handed the most precious gift in the world. It hit something inside of Penny, and she had to look away. Luke came into sharp focus.

Years ago, she'd thrown away what they had together, but she'd never forgotten. Every man she had been with, she compared to him, never truly letting him go. Once tomorrow came, she'd have to let him go again, but tonight was filled with potential.

Chapter Two

"Thought you were going to miss it," Sam said.

Luke raised an eyebrow but continued to stare out the truck window. "I was called to scrub in on a last-minute surgery."

Sam grunted. "Family's not that important."

If the reception had been any closer to the chapel, Luke would have walked rather than get in the truck with his oldest brother. Sam had helped raise him after their father died when Luke was fourteen. Two years later, their mother had succumbed to cancer and Brady had gone off to college, leaving only Luke and Sam.

"Of course family is important." Luke flicked a piece of lint from his tux sleeve. "Which is why I'm here today. When it matters."

Sam gave a noncommittal sound as he pulled into the parking lot of the Knights of Columbus. The hall was a standard block construction on the outside. It might not be big-city classy, but Tawnee Valley didn't offer much else in the way of reception halls.

The parking lot was already filled with trucks and cars. As soon as Luke stepped out of the truck, he could hear the music floating out of the double doors that were outlined with a pretty trellis of flowers.

"I don't know why Brady didn't just have the wedding in New York," Luke mumbled.

"Because the people in this town are as much his family as we are." Sam walked past and into the banquet room.

Luke followed him in and actually did a double take. If he hadn't just driven up to the concrete building, he would believe that he'd been dropped into a grand ballroom inside a five-star hotel. The stage had had a face-lift since the last time Luke had been here, which had to have been almost five years ago. One of his high school friends had his wedding reception here, but it had been a potluck with lots of balloons, not an elegant buffet with waiters bringing guests drinks and appetizers. The room was decorated to rival the most elegant of ballrooms, down to the artful arrangements of wildflowers on every table.

"Kind of blows your mind, doesn't it?" Penny appeared at his side.

"Definitely." Just as she did. His pulse quickened. Penny hadn't been at that wedding years ago, and they'd managed to avoid each other the few times he'd been back since their breakup. This was the first time they'd seen each other in nine years.

"Brady arranged most of it, but Maggie had the final say." Penny was every bit as attractive as he remembered, from her coppery-red hair to her brown eyes to a body with curves in all the right places to her full lips that begged for his kiss. "Come on. I'll show you the table and give you a quick walk-through of what you missed last night."

Her fingers threaded through his as she pulled him forward into the crowd. The heat of her worked its way from their entwined fingers to the center of him. Her gold dress seemed like more of a long negligee made of slightly thicker material. His fingers itched to run over her silk-covered flesh.

"The DJ is one of the best in the industry."

Luke followed her gaze to the DJ table. "Wyatt Graham?" Wyatt had graduated high school a few years after them.

Penny smiled and winked. "The local industry isn't that diverse. He'll be playing a mix of modern and oldies. We'll be required to dance together at the end of the bridal dance and for the next few dances after that."

As Luke glanced around, he noticed more familiar faces—from the waitstaff to the cooks in the opening to the kitchen. All local people, from either Tawnee Valley or the neighboring city of Owen.

"Brady could have flown the whole town to New York for what this cost."

"That wasn't the point." Penny pulled him behind a large curtain thing that gave the room its illusion of class, and leaned against the old paneled walls of the hall. The scent of musty wood overwhelmed the small space. The lighting barely filtered through the curtain. It even deadened the low roar of the crowd and the soft music playing in the background. Everyone disappeared. It was just the two of them. His imagination went wild with possibilities, but he reined them all in.

He opened his mouth.

Penny put her fingers over his lips. "Just because

you are a hotshot doc from the city doesn't mean that everything should happen in the city. Brady wanted to give the people around here a chance to be part of the wedding. It was important to both of them, so not another word about anywhere else but here."

The dim light caught and danced devilishly in her brown eyes. Her fingers were warm against his lips. They stood close together. It would take only a second to pull her into his arms and claim a kiss. He let out a breath across her fingers. Her breathing hitched, but she didn't pull away.

"Now." She sounded breathless, and his body reacted. "Do I have your promise to behave?"

The wicked glint in her eyes made her request comical.

"Do you want me to behave?" His words caressed her fingers.

He felt the tremor ripple through her. Her lips curled up in an invitation.

The music in the room suddenly changed and Penny's eyes widened. "Oh, crap, it's the entrance music."

She grabbed his hand once again and pulled him out into the open. It had been so easy to forget about the whole wedding reception happening beyond the curtain. He was half tempted to pull her back and forget about the party altogether.

Maggie and Brady walked into the hall and the crowd burst into applause.

"Brady looks happy." Luke couldn't contain that little bit of skepticism from his voice. Luke's memories of Brady were tainted with the death of his parents and the iron rule of his brother. Brady had been one of the reasons he'd finally calmed down enough to graduate high school. Penny had been the other reason.

"He should be." She leaned against his arm. "She's happy."

A wistfulness he could have imagined had entered her voice.

Luke became aware that Penny was still holding his hand while they stood watching the couple work their way through the crowd. "Are you happy?"

She gave him a mischievous smile and squeezed his hand. "I could be happier."

The suggestion was far from discreet. If it were any other time and any other woman, he might have walked away from her right then. He didn't play games. His career was his primary focus and it didn't leave time for anything else.

But tonight was his brother's wedding in his hometown, and he was standing next to the girl who had rocked his world as a teenager before she ripped his heart out and threw it back in his face. Tomorrow he'd be on a flight to St. Louis to continue his residency and Penny would return to his past, where she belonged.

"I could always tell when you were overthinking something." Penny's finger reached up and traced a line between his eyebrows. "You know that's going to form a wrinkle if you keep doing it, right?"

"So you're saying I shouldn't think?" Luke tried to read her facial expressions, but Penny had always been careful to mask what she was really feeling. He'd thought he had been behind her wall once, but he knew better now.

"Thinking is highly overrated." Penny winked at him. "We need to go to the table now. Do you think you can turn off that mega-powered brain of yours for the evening and just enjoy?"

Did she mean that he should enjoy her again? Or

was it just wishful thinking on his part? One thing was certain—he wouldn't make himself a fool for Penny this time. "I'll try."

Penny sat between Maggie and Amber, and Luke sat on the other side of Brady next to Sam at the hour-long gourmet dinner. Penny wanted to continue flirting with Luke during the meal, but it was fun talking with Amber and teasing Maggie. Her wineglass never seemed to empty and she lost track of how much she'd actually had. She felt a bit tipsy but not drunk. With her family history, she tried to be careful with alcohol.

When Maggie, Amber and Brady got up to go visit guests at their tables, Penny scooted over into Maggie's chair and leaned across Brady's.

"Having fun yet?" She batted her eyelashes at Luke in mock flirtation.

"I can say the view definitely just got better." Luke's gaze rested on her cleavage and her gaping neckline.

She didn't make any move to cover herself or even to sit up straight. "Do you have your toast ready?"

He patted his jacket. "Color-coded index cards and all."

"You really know how to get a girl's motor going." She purred and moved back to her seat. She straightened the top of her dress and winked at the elderly man sitting at the table in front of the head table. He blushed and turned away.

Penny and the town of Tawnee Valley hadn't always been on the best terms. As one of the juvenile delinquents most likely to be pregnant at sixteen and most likely to have an arrest record by the age of twenty, she'd surprised them all with the success of her store.

But that didn't mean she didn't enjoy poking at the town's notions of propriety now and then.

The wedding coordinator, Rebecca, directed Maggie and Brady over to the cake. Rebecca had performed miracles to turn this old men's club into a ballroom worthy of Maggie. Given it was the woman's first time coordinating an effort this big, she had done an amazing job. Penny was impressed with the transformation of the hall, and even the chapel had been given an overhaul.

Everyone watched Brady and Maggie cut the cake while the photographer took at least a dozen photos. When they gave each other bites, they were respectful of each other and didn't goof around as Penny would have.

The couple returned to their seats as the waitstaff brought everyone a piece of cake and poured champagne into their flutes. Down the table, Luke picked up his spoon and clinked it against his glass as he rose to standing.

"I'd like to say a few words." Luke reached into his pocket and pulled out a stack of index cards. He glanced her way slyly as he fanned through the colored cards.

Penny stifled a laugh. She'd thought he'd been joking.

"I could tell you lewd jokes or make fun of my brother for the way he used to run around the farm in his underwear and a cape when he was seven, but I won't. I could talk about the fights we three used to get into and the trouble we helped each other out of, but I won't. I could tell you about Brady's adventures overseas or his high life in New York City, but I won't." Luke set the cards on the table and his gaze went over the crowded room.

Penny found herself leaning forward to listen to

whatever he was going to say next. When Luke spoke, even back in grade school, he commanded his audience's attention. He made sure to meet everyone's eyes in the audience to make them feel included. His even tone and that deep voice kept her mesmerized. His raw emotion and honesty bonded him with the audience.

His gaze briefly met hers before settling on Brady and Maggie.

"Everyone in this room is aware of the struggles our family has had to endure. We didn't always make the right decisions, but in the end, it looks like Brady found the one thing that matters most. Someone who loves him and wants to share a life with him. A hidden treasure waiting for him to come home."

Penny could feel a thickening in her throat and blinked to hold the tears back.

"We brothers have lost so much, but Brady has finally found his family. Here's to many years of shared joy and love. To Maggie and Brady."

The crowd repeated, "To Maggie and Brady."

A pause lingered while everyone took a drink. Penny met Luke's eyes over the rim of her glass. As the crowd applauded the speech, Penny smiled at Luke before standing.

She waited for the noise to die down and then cleared her throat. "I may not be as eloquent as our doctor, but I'll give it my best shot."

She turned to Maggie. "When I was a little girl, there was one place I always knew I'd be welcome. Maggie has been my best friend, my confidante, my family for as long as I can remember. She's always been there for me and I've always tried to be there for her."

Maggie reached out, took Penny's hand and gave it a

gentle squeeze. They both had the battle scars on their hearts to prove their long-standing friendship.

"If anyone is capable of loving forever, it's Maggie, and I know I'm not the only one in the room thinking that Brady is the luckiest man alive." Still holding Maggie's hand, Penny looked at Brady. "There aren't many people I would trust with my best friend's heart, but I trust you to keep it safe and to love her until you are old and gray and need to yell at each other to be heard. I love you both and wish you happiness."

Clearing her throat, Penny blinked back the tears that had snuck up on her again. She turned to Amber. "Amber made me promise to wish you one more thing." She held up her glass and gave a grin to the rest of the hall. "To a wonderful family, and may they be blessed with a little brother or sister for Amber."

The crowd chuckled as they clinked glasses once more. Penny sank into her seat and took a drink. The DJ put on some background music and the low din of conversations grew again. Maggie and Brady were lost in their own little world. Amber had wandered off to the kids' table to be with her friends.

Suddenly Penny felt isolated. Maggie had always been the person she talked to at these types of things. Not that she needed constant attention. Lord knew she spent more than her fair share of evenings at home with no one to talk to but the dog.

She used to see Maggie everyday. But now... Brady, Maggie and Amber would be leaving to go on their two-week vacation slash honeymoon at Disney World in a few days. It would be only a few weeks, but Maggie had been preoccupied with the wedding and Brady for months now, giving Penny a lot more alone time than usual. Penny was happy for her friend, but it didn't make her miss Maggie any less.

"I think this empty chair is a better conversationalist than Sam." Luke sat in Amber's seat. His smile warmed her down to her toes.

Her heart pounded a little harder. The champagne must be going to her head because all she could do was smile at him.

"The chair has definitely improved since you arrived," she said. She could spend hours just listening to the sound of his voice. Her whole body flushed with heat and tingled in anticipation of just the slightest touch.

It was crazy. For years, she'd avoided the emotional and clung to the physical. But with Luke, it had been different. Still, that was a long time ago. They were adults now. She was more than happy to bask in the warmth of his smile for the hours they had together.

Chapter Three

"Presenting Mr. and Mrs. Ward for their first dance," the DJ announced.

Luke stood next to the dance floor with his hands in his pockets as the strains of some slow song pounded out of the speaker behind him. This was how Penny and he had started. A school dance. It had been the social hour after a football game. The student DJ was set up in the cafeteria. No fancy lights had lit the floor then. In fact, most of the lights had been turned off, making the small space feel even tighter. He'd been standing on the side with the other football players, and Penny had appeared out of nowhere in a pair of cutoffs that would have gotten her sent home from school and a T-shirt that hugged her young body.

He knew Penny Montgomery. They'd shared classes since fifth grade. In high school, she'd transformed into the kind of girl who was hard for a teenage boy to ignore. From her red hair to her smoking body to her devil-may-care attitude, she was a high school boy's fantasy.

"Dance with me." She'd smiled with her red lips and pulled him onto the dance floor before he could say anything. The music had heavy bass and a bump-and-grind rhythm.

"I don't dance," he'd managed to protest once they were in the middle of the floor.

She gave him a pout and the wicked glint in her eyes had made his pants tighten. "Don't worry. I'll show you what to do."

A touch on his shoulder brought him back to the present. Penny stood there with a smile on her lips. Her makeup was softer now, but she was just as beautiful. The slow song was about halfway through.

"Would the rest of the wedding party join in?" the DJ said over the speaker.

Luke shook off the past and held out his hand to Penny. She slipped her hand in his and followed his lead out to the dance floor. She moved into his arms like a missing puzzle piece.

Sam and Amber followed them onto the dance floor, drawing everyone's attention. Amber put her feet on top of Sam's and he held her hands. It was strange watching Sam with a child. As Luke's pseudo-parent, Sam had been distant but controlling. Now he seemed perfectly at ease talking with his niece, even if he didn't smile.

Luke's attention returned to the woman he held in his arms for the first time in almost a decade.

"Looks like someone's been practicing," she said. That flirtatious tilt was back in Penny's smile.

"I try to maintain appearances."

"I'm sure you have your admirers." A teasing glint

in her eyes and a soft smile on her lips betrayed nothing of what she really felt, but that was Penny.

"I do love compliments." He led them toward a darker area of the dance floor as other couples joined in.

"I bet you do."

Years ago, that first night, when the music had slowed down she'd moved into his arms and her breasts had pressed against his chest, her body close to his. Hormones had flooded him, making it hard to think… Why was he getting wrapped up in the past?

His fingers tightened into the softness of Penny's waist.

She closed the slight gap between them and whispered, "Stop thinking, Luke."

"Why aren't you with someone, Penny?"

"I'm with you right now." Her eyes may never reveal her inner thoughts, but he noticed a slight hesitance in her words. Her body pressed slightly closer until there was no more than a whisper between them.

"You know what I mean." Luke tried to hold on to the thoughts in his head as his body tried to make them all vanish. Her light perfume smelled like spring flowers, the scent's innocence at odds with the seductive woman. It surrounded him, begging him to bend down and breathe in. To touch the warmth of her neck with his lips.

"Who should I be with? The town drunk, the divorcé with the ex from hell—"

"Sam."

She stopped dancing and her lips drew tight. "Sam?"

Penny was in his arms and he wasn't about to back off. Not when her soft curves filled in his rough patches. This was important. He didn't want to step in between his brother and anyone, even if that anyone had been the only girl Luke had ever given his heart to.

"You two were pretty tight last time I saw you." The last time he'd seen Penny, at his graduation party, she'd been kissing Sam.

She pushed against his chest, but he didn't budge. Her eyes flashed up at him. Was that hurt? It had been there for a moment, but it was gone so fast he must have imagined it. It felt as if she was going to push again, but instead she softened. The walls closed in her eyes.

"Sam never meant anything to me." She placed her hands back on his shoulders. "We never had more than a kiss. I'm surprised he didn't tell you."

"Why would he?" Some of the tension released from his grip. Luke's brain was quickly losing the battle with his body's needs. It shouldn't matter why she kissed Sam or even that she did. It had been years ago. It had stopped him from making a major mistake.

Sure it had hurt then, but he'd brought it up now to draw out the woman he'd known from this seductress before him.

She shrugged. "You don't really want to talk about Sam, do you, Luke?"

He didn't know what he was trying to prove. He looked around the dance floor. Now wasn't the time to rehash the past. No time would be the right time. "No."

"How about a drink?" she said. Her gaze flicked over his face.

"A couple of glasses of wine between old friends? Why not. Wait here."

Penny's heart pounded as she sank into a chair and watched Luke walk away. Her knees had barely held her up. Without Luke's arms around her, she would have been down on the ground. She watched him move through the crowd.

Sam had been a means to an end. She'd hated herself for using him, but it had done exactly what she needed it to. Luke had to leave for college without her.

As the DJ cued up some fast dance music, Penny took a deep breath. Tonight had turned out perfectly for Brady and Maggie. They were dancing with Amber in the circle of people on the dance floor.

If her knees recovered, she might go join them. A glass of wine appeared over her shoulder and Luke's breath teased the hairs on the back of her neck. "I had to turn down a lot of eligible ladies to get back here."

Glancing over at the bar, she took the wineglass and felt him sit in the chair behind hers. All of her cells were attuned to whatever frequency Luke gave off. At the bar stood a gathering of white-haired women all giving Luke come-hither looks and finger waves.

Penny choked back a laugh. She tried her hardest to look serious when she turned to Luke. "I hope you let them down easy. It's just as hard to find a man at their age as mine."

Leaning in so he could speak in her ear and be heard over the music, Luke's cheek rubbed against hers, sending a wave of heat through her. "I always try to be gentle."

"I'm sure you do." She could feel his cheek lift in a grin. A shiver rippled down her back.

He moved back until they were eye to eye. "They were actually encouraging me to hit on the wedding coordinator."

Penny glanced over at Rebecca in her peach suit. She was a few years younger than Penny and looked as if the pressure of this wedding was about to make her explode.

"I suppose you could go for Rebecca...." Penny put on a pretend thoughtful look.

The music changed to a slow song again. "Come on. You can tell me all about what that look means on the dance floor."

Luke pulled her out of the chair and guided her into his arms. She'd given up on love songs when Luke left, preferring the rawness of modern rock. Slow songs messed with her brain and made her think about things she couldn't have.

"So are we for or against chatting up the wedding coordinator?" Luke raised his eyebrow as he looked down at Penny.

"I think she'd have an aneurysm if 'we' approached her." Penny mocked Luke's look.

Luke laughed. "Fair enough. Besides, I'm only here until tomorrow. Wouldn't be fair to get anyone's hopes up."

"No, you wouldn't want to do that."

He pressed his hand into the small of her back and she allowed herself to move closer to him. To breathe in his scent. To feel the heat of his body against hers. The song didn't matter as long as it didn't stop.

"Besides—" he leaned down as if he had a secret to whisper in her ear "—I always heard that the best man was supposed to hook up with the maid of honor."

Penny's breathing hitched as she met his eyes. "I think it's actually a written law somewhere that if both parties are single, it's required."

"So we'd be in a lot of trouble if we didn't at least attempt to..." He wiggled his eyebrows.

"Heaps of trouble." Her heart beat hard against her chest as she tried to keep a teasing tone.

"We wouldn't want that." Luke gave her a cocky

smile. "But then you were never the type to follow rules."

"I'll have you know I'm one of the upstanding citizens in Tawnee Valley now."

"Really?" His sarcastic tone made her laugh.

"I'm a valued member of the Chamber of Commerce. My shop brings in tons of tourists."

"I guess that nails it, then." He made a serious face even though his eyes were twinkling. Still dancing, he led her to the side of the dance floor. "Rules are rules, after all."

She swallowed as liquid heat flooded her system. Her fingers locked around the back of his neck. "I suppose after the reception…"

The heat in his blue eyes made her breath catch. He didn't have to say he wanted her. It was there and it scorched her through to her soul. She didn't want to wait. It had been too long since she'd held him, since her skin had brushed against his.

His smile grew cocky. "Why wait?"

Penny glanced around them. The music had shifted to a fast song again. Most everyone was on the dance floor. Amber was dancing with her parents. Sam was brooding in a corner with a glass of liquor. The older folks were on the other side of the dance floor gathered around a few tables. It looked as if they were shouting to talk above the music.

His hand closed firmly around hers and she met his eyes. Apparently they'd reached the same conclusion. No one would miss them if they ducked out at this moment. She doubted anyone would even think anything of it if they did disappear.

Luke started backing up, pulling her with him. Giddiness welled inside her, the same feeling she used to get in high school when Luke would pick her up for a date. Anticipation mixed with the knowledge that no one would know what they were doing. Something hidden that was hers alone.

"You know, I'm not this type of guy." He stopped and pulled her hard until she stumbled into his chest. His teasing smile made her heart skip a beat. "I usually require dinner and wine first."

She smiled up at him. "Good thing we came to a wedding, then. Dinner, check. Wine, check."

"I wouldn't want you to think less of me." He was joking around, but her heart wouldn't let her say something flippant. It demanded she let him know this much.

"Nothing would make me think less of you."

He glanced over her shoulder toward the rest of the party as they approached the exit. "Where should we go?"

When he turned back to her, she forgot to breathe, let alone think. She knew that in Luke's eyes, they were equals, but she'd always known she wasn't as good as he was. During sex was the only time she felt like his match.

"Follow me." She led him past the curtain and into the darkness behind it. The closet door opened easily and she slid in with Luke behind her.

"Classy," Luke muttered. The door closed and the small space seemed to close in on them. Even the music was muffled beyond recognition. The smell of lemon cleaner tinged the air.

"If you'd rather go out in the parking lot and risk causing Bitsy heart palpitations when she sees me straddling you in your brother's truck—"

"Stop thinking, Penny." In the darkness, he moved closer until she felt his whole body pressed against hers.

Her breath quickened as she waited. For his next move. For his touch. For his kiss.

She felt the brush of his arm next to her and caught her breath. The click of the lock could barely be heard over the sound of their breaths. The warm, clean scent of Luke filled her.

"You don't have to do this." Luke's whispered words caressed her earlobe. "Just because we're here at a wedding doesn't mean we have to have sex."

"Are you trying to give *me* an out, Luke Ward?" She laughed, releasing some of the tension that had been welling within her. "I must be pretty darned good if you think this is all your idea."

He chuckled and his knuckles brushed over her jaw, ending her own laughter. "I don't want you to think I only want sex."

"What else would you want?" She didn't bother trying to hide the breathiness of her voice.

His forehead pressed against hers and his hands ran up and down her arms. "I don't know."

Her heart beat with his quickened breath. Once, twice, three times.

She slid off her heels and lifted onto her toes. Pressing a kiss to his jaw, she could feel his heart beat in time with hers against her palm. "I want you."

His lips closed over hers. Sparks rippled through her as he pulled her in close. Relief spiraled out of her heart even as her pulse quickened. Her memories of his kisses collapsed under the weight of this one. It wasn't the technique that had her clutching at his dress shirt—though the technique was definitely good. It was the man.

In an instant, she knew if it were ten years from now,

even a hundred, and Luke kissed her, it would still feel like this. Explosive, powerful, soul shattering.

Desire pulsed within her, and that little piece of her that would always belong to Luke throbbed with satisfaction. He was kissing her as if they had only moments to live. Maybe they did. Maybe she felt alive only when Luke was here. Kissing her.

His hands clutched at the fabric around her hips, slowly easing the silky material up her calves and over her thighs. It was as if the silk were his fingers trailing ever higher, stealing her breath.

She unclenched her fingers and started undoing the buttons of his shirt. The need to feel his skin against hers was overwhelming. His warmth beckoned beneath the fabric. The cool air caressed her legs as her dress slipped up over her hips. The crisp fabric of his tux pants brushed against her skin.

Pulling his shirt free of his pants, she opened it. His fingers brushed under the edge of her panties at her hips. She leaned back against the door as his lips left her mouth and trailed kisses along her jaw.

The warmth of his chest beckoned. She ran her fingers over the muscles, making a mental picture in the dark. Memorizing the contours. As her hand slid down his abs, he sucked in his breath and nipped at her neck.

Power coursed through her veins as she eased down his zipper and brushed the hardness underneath. He grabbed her hands and pushed them against the door, reclaiming her mouth.

The silk dress rushed down her thighs, but caught as his knee moved between her legs. The door and Luke had her captured, unable to escape. Not that she wanted freedom. If she could, she would spend eternity in this little closet with Luke.

This wasn't like a one-night stand or even a booty call. Luke wouldn't fill just her need for an orgasm. She craved relief, but she didn't want this to end.

She'd made a mistake.

Having Luke one more time wouldn't fulfill some need for closure. The sound of his pants dropping filled the space between them.

Even knowing this was a mistake, she wanted him. Even though it would only widen the hole he'd left behind. Even as her body hummed from his touch, she wanted to cry.

She'd take what she could from him and he'd leave. That would be the end of it. She'd survived before and she'd survive this time.

"Are you okay?" He kissed her next to her ear as his fingers teased the edge of her underwear.

She sucked in a breath as his hand slipped under the fabric and touched her skin. Wrapping her hands behind his head, she pulled his mouth to hers. She was beyond being okay. She needed to shut down her brain and feel. Brand him the way he branded her.

He slid off her underwear. Her dress remained bunched up around her waist. His bare skin brushed against hers. Rough against soft. She heard him open a condom packet.

After a moment, his hands returned to her hips and his mouth returned to hers. He lifted her against the door and she wrapped her legs around his waist. In the darkness all she could do was feel. The real world was far away. The fact that they were in a closet at a wedding didn't matter. All that mattered was that he was with her now.

"Say my name," he whispered against her ear. The darkness engulfed them. They could only feel and hear.

But she knew it meant more to him. It was his way of claiming her, of making sure she knew it was him and not any number of guys.

She wanted to please him, needed him to know that it was only him. That it had always been only him.

"Luke." Her world came unhinged as he entered her slowly. His hands held her hips. The tears she'd been holding back pressed forward. She repeated his name and muttered words she couldn't be held accountable for as he moved within her, the only thing she could allow herself from him.

The tears edged over her eyes and trailed down her cheeks as her body rejoiced. It felt like coming home and like nothing she'd ever felt before. Dangerous and tempting. Something she never should have messed with. He lifted her higher and higher until she fell over the edge into bliss. He joined her with her name on his lips.

She choked back a sob and held him tighter, never wanting to let go.

Chapter Four

Luke fought to steady his breathing in the dark room. Penny fit against his body perfectly. He wanted to continue to hold her, but the noise of the party beyond the door told him that they needed to get back. Her breath shuddered in and out. Lowering her gently to the floor, he stepped back. In the dark he couldn't see her, but it sounded as if she was crying. "Did I hurt you?"

"No."

Suddenly the dark that had wrapped them in an intimate fog pissed him off. He could tell she was lying but couldn't prove it.

"Something's wrong." Luke felt the wall next to the door for a light switch.

"Nothing's wrong." She reached past him and the light blinked on. For a moment he was blind as his eyes adjusted to the brightness.

Penny had bent down and retrieved her underwear. "We need to get back out there."

"Nothing's wrong, my ass." Luke pulled up his boxers and pants.

"What do you want me to say?" She turned her back to him as she fixed her clothing. "It was fantastic, wonderful, the best thing ever."

"What's gotten into you?" The lightness in his chest grew heavy. Trying to recapture the mood, he dropped a kiss on the nape of her neck.

Her shoulders tensed but then relaxed. When she turned around, the plastic smile was in place. He closed his eyes for a moment and took a deep breath. Whatever had made her upset, she wasn't going to tell him.

"I'm fine. Really. We just need to get back." Her flirtatious smile returned. "I had a really good time."

She moved to open the door, but he grabbed the knob to hold it closed.

"Fine? You are far from fine. You can act all you want for the revolving door of men you have, but I know you." The anger raging within was tempered by the orgasm he'd just had. After he'd left all those years ago, he'd heard about her escapades from classmates and folks around town. They had acted as if he should step in and do something. He didn't tell them that he'd heard the rumors of her with other guys the entire time they'd dated.

She didn't even bristle. She reached up to fix his collar as if they were discussing the weather. "Is that what you are worried about? That I'm comparing you to other lovers?"

"What I'm worried about is the fact that you don't seem to feel anything anymore." Luke brushed her hair away from her face. "Does anything matter to you?"

Her smile didn't show even a hint of anger, which just made him more determined to break through that wall. To what end? He didn't know.

"You're leaving tomorrow?" Her brown eyes lifted to his.

He nodded, not really wanting to be reminded of that at this moment.

"Let's go out to the party and afterward…" She held on to his shoulders as she slipped her feet into her shoes.

His imagination could do a lot of things with *afterward.*

She kissed his jaw. "Afterward."

The background noise changed. It had been so subtle he hadn't even noticed the music and laughing beyond the door, but the sudden lack of it gained his attention. He thought he heard someone call his name.

"Something's happening." Luke opened the door and found his way out from behind the curtain. The overhead lights were on and everyone was hovering near the dance floor.

Luke's heart pounded against his chest as he saw someone lying on the floor beyond the crowd. His training kicked in as he rushed forward.

Breaking through the crowd, he froze when he saw Sam unconscious on the ground, his face ashen. Luke's world lurched. "What happened?"

"He just fell over," an old man who looked familiar said.

"Everyone back up and give him some space," Luke ordered. "Has anyone called 911?"

"Yes. The ambulance is on the way."

Luke checked Sam's pulse. He was still breathing, but his pulse was faint. "Bring over a chair."

Luke pulled Sam's bow tie off and unbuttoned his

collar. When Amber dragged over a chair, Luke lifted Sam's feet up onto the seat.

"Where are Brady and Maggie?" Luke asked the nearest woman.

"They just left."

"Is he going to be okay?" Tears ran freely down Amber's cheeks. Penny kneeled next to Amber and held out her arms. Amber collapsed against her but kept her big blue eyes on Luke and Sam.

"We need to get him checked at the hospital." Luke met Penny's eyes and saw the worry there.

He tried not to think about it as he worked on evaluating Sam's condition.

"The ambulance is here," someone said.

The paramedics came in and Luke gave them a rundown of what he knew, which wasn't much. Sam had fainted and hadn't regained consciousness.

"Should I call Brady and Maggie?" Penny asked as Luke stepped out of the way to let the paramedics work.

"Not yet." Luke ran a hand over his face. "They just left for their wedding night, and we have nothing to tell them. They'd just worry or, worse, spend their wedding night in the hospital waiting room."

She nodded, still holding on to Amber. "Maybe I should take Amber home."

"No." Amber shook her head. "I'm going with Uncle Sam."

"It's late. We can go wait at my house with Flicker, and your uncle Luke will call with any news." Penny's gaze met Luke's, looking for his support.

He nodded, but that wasn't enough for Amber.

"I'm supposed to stay with Uncle Sam tonight," Amber said. If Luke knew anything about his family, it was that stubbornness definitely ran in it. But he had only just met his niece.

"What if—" Penny looked up at Luke "—we go to the hospital and see that Uncle Sam is taken care of, then you and I will go get Flicker and drive out to check on the farm?"

Luke nodded in agreement. What else could he do until he knew what was going on with Sam?

"I wanna ride in the ambulance." Amber turned her stubborn little chin up at Luke.

"No," Penny said, her voice more firm than he'd ever heard it before. "You ride with me or the deal is off, kiddo."

"Okay." Amber pouted but went to grab her flowers and sweater from their table.

"Did you want to ride with us or with the ambulance?" Penny's presence actually calmed his racing heart for a moment.

"I'll drive Sam's truck and meet you there." Luke watched as the paramedics wheeled Sam out the door. He felt lost, as if he could have prevented whatever was happening.

Penny wrapped her arms around him in a hug that had nothing to do with sex. "He'll be all right."

He returned her hug and breathed in her floral scent. The knot in his stomach loosened slightly.

She released him before he wanted to let go, but things had to get done. "We'll be there in a few minutes. I'm going to talk to the wedding coordinator and make sure everything is taken care of before we head to the hospital."

Amber came back over with tears in her big blue eyes. "Can I ride with Uncle Luke? Please?"

Penny gave him a questioning look, leaving it up to

him. He looked around at the people waiting and the chaos beyond. It might take Penny a half hour or more to finish up here and Amber would be left sitting alone. He remembered how that felt when his father had been rushed to the hospital. No one had taken the time to tell him what was happening. He was just left waiting.

Luke held out his hand to Amber. "Sure. Let's go."

An hour later, Luke sat in the waiting room of the hospital in Owen with his niece fast asleep against his side. Sam had woken during the ambulance ride and had been cranky as ever. When he arrived at the hospital, the doctor ordered several tests to make sure he hadn't had a heart attack or wasn't on the verge of having one. The doctor had insisted Luke go to the waiting area since Sam didn't look to be in any eminent danger.

A flicker of gold caught Luke's attention. He lifted his head in the direction of the hallway. Penny sauntered toward him with her heels in one hand and a soft smile on her lips. It had been only an hour or so since he'd held her in his arms, but it felt as if an eternity had passed.

Careful not to wake Amber, she sat gently on his other side and whispered, "How's Sam?"

Luke took a deep breath and released it. "No word yet. Apparently a few months ago, he had an X-ray that showed an enlarged heart, but he skipped his follow-up with the cardiologist. The fainting could mean a number of things, from cardiomyopathy to hypothyroidism to hemo—"

Penny took his hand between hers. "Lots of doctor mumbo jumbo. Is he going to be okay?"

"I hope so." He ran his other hand through his hair. Their family history of heart disease was the reason Luke had gone to med school and why he'd specialized in cardiology. If Luke had known at fourteen what he knew now, maybe he could have prevented the heart attack that killed his father. The warning signs had all been there. No one had pushed Dad to get checked out. Not that his father could have been pushed. A trait Sam inherited.

"I guess I should take Amber home and get her into bed." Penny didn't move and he felt her eyes on him. "Unless you want me to stay."

Luke didn't know what he wanted. Earlier it had been easy to just pull Penny into his arms and forget the past and future. He would definitely prefer to argue more with Penny instead of sitting in a waiting room with months-old magazines and a news channel on a muted TV. If his niece weren't here, he might even flirt, if only for the distraction.

As if sensing his hesitation, Penny leaned forward to look around him at Amber. "If I wake Amber now, she'll be a bear to get back to sleep. Why don't I just keep you company while we wait to hear about Sam?"

"Why are you being like this?" Luke stared at the television in the corner. There was no reason for Penny to be here for him now. Not even after what happened in the closet. They weren't anything more than exes thrown together at a wedding. She didn't have to be nice to him.

She settled next to him, pulling her feet up under her and leaning her head against his shoulder. "Being like what?"

He looked down at the top of her auburn head. "It doesn't matter."

She shrugged. "When should we call Maggie and Brady?" A yawn followed as she squirmed herself into a more comfortable spot.

"It's late. We'll wait until morning and give them a call. No reason to disrupt their wedding night. As long as Sam remains stable, there's nothing they could do but worry anyway." Sam was only thirty and relatively healthy, but fainting was serious…especially with an unknown heart condition. Luke needed to get up and do something, but he couldn't without disturbing Amber. His leg started to bounce.

Penny kept hold of his hand in her lap. He should ask to look over Sam's chart and figure out if they were doing all the necessary testing. EKG, echocardiogram, CBC. Maybe he should talk to the doctor about a transfer to the nearest medical school hospital. He wondered if they could Life Flight him to his hospital in St. Louis.

"I hear you got into one of the better programs for med school," Penny said.

"What?" He pulled his gaze from the doors the doctor had vanished behind recently.

"Med school. Good program?" Penny repeated and looked up at him.

"Yeah. It took a lot of cramming, but I got the grades to get in." If he could figure out a way to slide out from under Amber without waking her, he would go through those doors that said "Authorized Personnel Only." Surely they missed something on the chart. Most hospitals generally had rules against working on family. But they probably didn't have a cardiologist on staff.

"I was glad to graduate high school with a C average," Penny scoffed. "You always were the smarter of the two of us."

"That's not true. You were just a misguided youth." He smiled at the memory.

"Remember when we were studying for my final

in Geometry? If it hadn't been for you, I wouldn't still have the useless phrase SOH CAH TOA in my head."

Luke chuckled. "Do you even remember what it means?"

Penny screwed up her nose. "Of course not. If it had been useful, then I definitely would have remembered it. I bet I haven't used half of what they forced us to learn in high school."

"You probably use more than you think." Luke sank farther into his chair. His legs relaxed out in front of him. "If we'd been together longer, I bet you would have received straight As."

"You definitely made studying fun." She rubbed her thumb across the back of his hand. "Do you remember that one night we walked all the way to Owen to The Morning Rooster to have breakfast at 2:00 a.m.?"

"I remember heading back and having to carry you piggyback half the way."

"I didn't know we were going to walk eight miles each way when I decided on my shoe choice for the evening. Most nights I didn't even need my shoes."

"I remember talking about everything that night. Philosophy, love, family, sex, shoes." He squeezed her hand. "We were quite the rebels."

"More like trendsetters. Apparently it's a new dare among the kids in Tawnee Valley. How far are you willing to walk to breakfast?"

Luke laughed. "Not like there was much else to do on Saturday nights. Especially when Sam would take away my car privileges."

"And my car was in the shop. You know, I kept that old beater until it finally coughed its final gas fumes into the air about five years ago."

"I'm surprised it made it that long." This was the part

of Penny he'd missed the most. The quiet times when it was just the two of them talking. That piece of her that only he got to see.

The doors swung open. Dr. Sanchez came into the waiting area and walked their way. "Don't get up."

Luke had automatically started to rise without thinking about Amber and Penny leaning on him. She smiled down at the three of them. Penny released his hand and he missed her warmth.

"So far the test results have been promising. It doesn't look like he suffered from cardiac arrest, but we can't rule out a future one. We'd like to keep him overnight for observation."

Luke breathed out as if he'd been holding his breath for days. No cardiac arrest was good, but Sam wasn't out of the woods yet. "What's the plan once he's released?"

"Until we have a few more test results, we won't know for sure the type and extent of damage. I can't give you any more information until tomorrow."

"But he's going to be okay?" Penny asked, straightening in the chair.

"We'll know more tomorrow." Dr. Sanchez smiled that doctor smile Luke was all too familiar with. The one that said we don't know all that much and all we can do is hope for the best. "For tonight, I suggest you go home and get a good night's sleep. We've already given Mr. Ward something to help him sleep."

"Thank you," Luke said. Because of privacy laws, the doctor wouldn't tell Luke much more, so he didn't push. Besides, until the tests were completed, the doctor wouldn't know any more than he did.

Dr. Sanchez disappeared behind the doors again.

"Why don't I drive us all out to the farm?" Penny

stretched like a cat. "It's closer to the hospital and Amber won't pitch a fit if she wakes up there. I asked Bitsy to look in on my dog when she left the reception."

Luke hesitated. It felt odd to invite Penny back to Sam's house. "It's not that I don't appreciate the offer—"

"I wasn't doing it just for you." She stood and looked down her nose at him. "Maggie is family to me. That makes Brady family and Sam by extension. I need to take care of Amber and make sure things go smoothly so those two can take their daughter to Disney World on their honeymoon and make me more babies to take care of. I'm tired and I just want to crash and be there when Amber and Maggie need me in the morning."

Luke stood and picked up Amber. Thinking of Penny with babies did something strange to his heart. "I just didn't want you to think that I needed you—"

"Trust me. I know you don't need me." He saw a flash of hurt in Penny's eyes. "Maggie and Amber need me."

"I'm sorry, Penny. I didn't mean..." Oh, hell, what did he mean? If it meant avoiding a fight and not disappointing Amber, who was he to care whether they stayed here or went to the farm? They could work out the details when they arrived. Right now, he just wanted to look at something besides these four walls. "Look, we're both tired. Why don't *I* drive us out to the farm and we'll work on it from there? It doesn't look like I'll be flying out tomorrow."

"If you are talking about staying for Sam, maybe I can help."

Help? She was the reason he hadn't been out there to help Sam in the first place. His brother might have been showing signs that he could have picked up on if he hadn't been too busy making eyes at the pretty woman in front of him. "He's my family. For now, let's go home."

"He'll be okay." Penny rested her hand above his heart.

Penny's touch comforted him in a way he'd almost forgotten. For a long moment, he searched her eyes. With Sam's condition unknown, Luke couldn't just leave. Depending on what was wrong, he might need surgery or just bed rest. His mind shuffled through all the possible diagnoses, but he didn't have the chart to see what they'd uncovered when they'd examined him today. He trusted the doctor to make the right call regarding Sam's treatment.

Regardless, his brother might be here longer than a night. What happened after tonight with Penny? They hadn't promised more than tonight because that wasn't an option. Maybe it still wasn't an option. He didn't know Penny that well anymore, but from what he heard she rarely made a habit of any man.

He needed to get out of his head. There was plenty to worry about tomorrow. First he had to get through tonight. "Let's go."

Chapter Five

Penny shut the door of the bedroom. Amber had taken very little coaxing to fall back to sleep in Brady's old bedroom. Reassuring her that Sam would be okay and they'd see him in the morning was all it had taken. The old wooden stairs creaked under her feet as she returned to the first floor. It was past two in the morning, the lights were all still on and she didn't feel tired at all.

The sound of a chair scraping across the linoleum in the kitchen drew her that way. She stopped in the doorway and leaned against the doorjamb. Luke sat at the kitchen table, his head in his hands. If she had stayed with him after high school, would things have turned out differently? Would he have made it through med school with her dragging him down? Where would she have been when he left her? Stuck in some city where she wouldn't know a soul and Maggie would have been

here all alone dealing with her mother's illness and raising Amber.

She could play the what-if game, but she had decided
a long time ago to live in the present. And presently,
the weight of the world was on Luke's shoulders. He'd
always taken on too much. All she'd ever wanted to do
was take some of that weight off him. In high school,
it had been easy. Nothing takes a man's mind off his
problems like sex. Now they were adults with a complicated history. She had no idea of the problems he was
facing in his day-to-day life, but Sam's collapse was
one more thing to deal with.

Even though it had been years since they'd been together as a couple, she'd known at the hospital that he
needed her to be there with him. To keep him out of
his head.

"Hey," she said and shoved off the wall to join him
in the kitchen.

He lifted his head and gave her a weary smile. "Hey."

"Not exactly how I thought this night would end."
She flashed him a smile and leaned against the counter,
putting one bare foot on top of the other. She'd ditched
her killer high heels next to the door as soon as they'd
walked in. They looked a little obscene next to the work
boots and sneakers stacked there.

Her feet felt only half as weary as Luke looked. She
wanted to go over and pull him into her arms and just
hold him, but she needed to let him dictate what he
needed. Whether it was just to talk or…

He rubbed his hand over his hair. "You want some
coffee?"

"Nah, I should sleep at some point tonight, so I can
wake up when Amber gets up." A knot formed in her
stomach. He probably thought she was pushing for him

to invite her to sleep with him. For once she felt awkward. This was one of those situations she avoided for just this reason. She didn't sleep over and she didn't let anyone near her bed. She was all for sex, but cuddling wasn't her style.

He started to rise from his chair. "I can set up the guest bed—"

"Is that really necessary?" She put on her best brazen-it-out smile. Typically she didn't "sleep" with anyone except her puppy, but the last thing Luke needed to do tonight was worry about making her comfortable in his family home. She'd be fine whether he wanted her in his bed or on the couch. "I can crash wherever."

When she shrugged so that he would know it wasn't a big deal, the strap from her gown slid down her arm, drawing Luke's gaze. She felt it like a physical caress. The air in the room was suddenly charged.

"You always liked to finish what you started." His gaze met hers and his eyes flamed with desire.

Her body responded with all the repressed heat she'd sidelined since their closet interlude. Her body always would react to his. But she didn't want to push him, not with everything else weighing on his mind. "You know me. I'm always game. But I leave the decision up to you. I know you have a lot on your mind right now—"

"I'd rather not think at all." Luke crossed the kitchen floor and pulled her into his arms. Her toes brushed against the warm, soft fabric of his socks. "I'd rather forget everything outside of these walls for the rest of the night. Stop my mind from circling around what I'll need to do to be able to stay here with Sam. Stop from worrying that he might not be getting sufficient care. Stop trying to figure out—"

"Just stop," she whispered and drew his head down to hers. "I won't ask you for anything."

"I know," he said before claiming her mouth.

The creak of the bed woke Luke from a deep sleep. He automatically reached for his phone on the night-stand but hit only air where his nightstand should be. He blinked into the darkness and squinted at the dim light coming through the window. Instead of city lights, he saw the moon lighting up the fields rolling into the distance. The crops swayed slightly in the breeze.

The night came rushing back to him. The wedding. Sam's collapse. Inviting Penny into his bed. A shadow moved in front of the window.

"What are you doing?" Luke sat up and rubbed his face.

She flinched and turned around to face him. He couldn't see her features, but his eyes were quickly ad-justing to the darkness. Her light skin glowed in the moonlight that managed to sneak through the curtains. Standing only in her underwear, she held the rest of her dress at her waist like a shield in front of her. "I was… going to get a drink of water. Do you want some?"

"No, I don't want some water."

"More for me, then." She started to move away.

"Enough bull. What is really going on, Penny?"

She glanced at the door to the hallway and then back to the side of the bed that was still warm from her body. "I just thought…" She shrugged.

"That there isn't enough room? I snore too loudly?" He shifted off the bed and flicked on the lamp, casting the room in soft light.

She blinked but didn't move to cover herself. "What does it matter?"

"Just get back into bed, Penny. I swear we'll only sleep."

"Isn't it the woman's job to be needy and clingy?"

"Far be it from me to stop you." He stepped away from the bed and held his hand out. "I just thought you might want to be comfortable for the night. The last thing I'd want to do is make you feel needed."

Penny's shoulders pushed back and her chin tipped up. "Contrary to popular belief, a woman does not need a man to need her to feel complete."

Though her words and actions were angry, saying them nearly naked was having the opposite effect on his body. "I made you feel complete at least three times if my count is correct."

She threw her dress at him. He caught it and dropped it to the floor.

He strode across the room and grabbed her elbows, pulling her flush against his chest. "Unless you plan to traipse around the farmhouse in your underwear." At the devilish glint in her eyes, he added, "Remembering that my niece could wake up at any moment, I suggest you come back to bed."

Her body was tense against his and fire crackled in her eyes. "Maybe I don't want to sleep with you."

His hands rubbed her back. "If you don't want to sleep with me, I'm sure I could be convinced to stay awake."

Apparently he was starting to speak her language because she softened. Her curves molded into his and the heat that had pooled in his stomach flooded his system. "I've never been good at sleepovers."

"I doubt there are many people who would accuse you of being good at all." He lifted her into his arms. Penny was a puzzle. One he would be better off not trying to solve. One he should be pushing away instead of carrying back to his bed.

He lowered her onto the mattress, never releasing his hold on her body.

"Good is overrated." Penny pulled him down to her. "When has being good ever gotten you what you wanted?"

At one point, the thing he'd wanted most had been her. He'd been willing to do anything to keep her, except share her with anyone else. He lowered his head to hers. "Being good has gotten me nothing."

Chapter Six

Waiting rooms weren't nearly as bad as sitting in a patient's room, especially when the patient was Sam. Luke had taken the recliner, whereas Amber had chosen to sit at the end of Sam's bed. Apparently Sam was confident that he wasn't staying there because he'd been dressed in his tux, minus the jacket and tie, and ready to go as soon as they'd come in. When Luke had given Sam a bag with some of his clothes from home, he'd grunted a thank-you and immediately changed.

"I made sure to give the baby calves their bottles." Amber had been listing all the chores she'd insisted on helping with this morning. "I'll walk the fences this afternoon to make sure there aren't any breaks."

"I knew I could count on you." Sam smiled at his niece, if you could call the slight curve to his lips a smile.

Luke still couldn't understand Amber's loyal devotion to hardheaded Sam. This morning at the breakfast table, she'd run off a list of all the chores that she did when she stayed at the farm. While Luke had been amused with the list, he'd barely been able to keep his eyes from the woman who had kept him up all night.

Penny had moved around the kitchen with ease, as if she made breakfast there frequently. For all he knew she did. She had said she and Sam had had nothing more than that kiss years ago, but how could he believe a word that slipped past those wicked lips?

Wearing one of his T-shirts and not a whole lot more, she'd slipped out of his room. He'd assumed she'd join him after using the bathroom, but when he woke a few hours later from little feet creaking down the stairs, Penny was not in his bed.

He'd found her on the couch with an afghan pulled over her, fast asleep.

"Can I name the new piglets? Please?" Amber brought his attention back to the present. They were waiting for the doctor to talk to them and discharge Sam. Penny had excused herself as soon as they got to the hospital to go check on her puppy and to change out of Luke's oversize T-shirt and sweats.

"We can just call them Pork Chop, Ham and Bacon." Sam rested against the elevated back of the hospital bed. Luke couldn't remember the last time he'd heard Sam tease someone. Maybe when Luke had been Amber's age. Before Dad… Before Mom…

"That's not very nice, Uncle Sam." Amber gave him a look that reminded Luke of their mother when she'd scolded them even though she wanted to laugh at their antics. Sam just chuckled lightly, drawing Luke's questioning gaze to him. Sam shrugged.

"When am I getting out of this place?" Sam looked

toward the door as if willing the doctor to appear with his release instructions.

"I'm sure the staff is just as anxious for you to go," Luke said before standing. "I'm going to go find a cup of coffee. Do you want anything?" He looked at Amber.

She turned her bright blue eyes up to him and shook her head no. "I'm going to take care of Uncle Sam."

He believed her. He didn't know why she was so attached, but somehow Sam had become her hero. Or maybe Amber would be his savior. Either way, Sam must have done at least one good deed in his life to deserve her devotion.

The hallway was bustling with energy. Nurses darted in and out of rooms. The high-school-aged candy stripers were unloading the breakfast trays. The various beeping and swishing sounds of equipment blended into a discordant symphony. The smell of antiseptics filled his nose. It invigorated him. Hospitals had been his home for the past few years.

He wasn't used to being a visitor, though. Instead of part of the natural flow, he felt as if he was in the way as he walked to the coffee machine in the waiting area. As his coffee finished brewing, he caught Penny's voice behind him.

His pulse surged like a teenager in heat. Last night had to be the end of it. She laughed deep and throaty, and he twitched. Grabbing his cup of coffee, he turned, ready to do battle, and found her walking with Maggie and Brady.

"How's Sam?" Brady searched Luke's eyes.

"We're waiting for the doctor to come in and let us know the test results." Luke glanced at Penny. She stood there as if nothing had happened between them.

Nothing had changed. That was how he had wanted it, after all.

"Amber's with him?" Maggie shook her head and smiled. "That girl… I'm amazed you were able to tear her away from his side last night. Penny said it was a good thing you were there for Sam."

"I'm glad I was there, too." Luke felt the collar on his black T-shirt tighten around his throat. "Sam never told me he was having heart problems or I would have been more diligent." And not been having sex in the closet.

"You know Sam," Penny said. "The strong, silent types rarely give you a clue into their hearts."

He narrowed his eyes on her. This wasn't the first time she'd referenced Sam as if she knew him better than just another person in the small town where they grew up. Everyone he kept in touch with had alluded to the fact that Penny got around. Hopping from one bed to another. Was Sam's one of those beds?

It wasn't inconceivable. The number of eligible men in Tawnee Valley, and even in Owen, dropped off after high school. Although the farmhouse looked as if a monk lived there, Sam might have had a booty call or two.

"Which room is he in?" Brady drew Luke's attention away from Penny, who had started to give him a strange look.

"I was just heading back there." Luke turned and walked with Brady down the hallway. Penny and Maggie chatted lightly behind them.

"You could have called me last night," Brady said.

"Ha! And interrupted your wedding night? No way." Luke took in a breath. "There wasn't much you could have done. Sam wasn't in immediate danger. They just wanted to monitor him overnight and run tests in the morning. Besides, they won't tell us anything unless Sam lets them."

"I'm glad you were here to take care of things." Brady stopped him. "What do you know about his heart?"

"He said you knew about the X-ray." At Brady's nod, Luke continued, "Glad to be in the loop. His problems could be caused by a number of possibilities. Until the test results are back, they won't be able to determine a course of treatment."

"How bad could it be?" Brady glanced back at Maggie and Penny, who had stopped discreetly a little farther down the hall.

The fainting had him most alarmed. Heart failure. Structural issues. But it could be just dehydration.

Luke took in a deep breath and released it. "Honestly, it could be as simple as monitoring and as complicated as a heart transplant."

"Damn."

"We won't know anything until the doctor comes in."

"Right." Brady ran a hand over his dark hair. "Right. Let's go, then."

When Luke glanced at her, Penny's insides turned molten. Luke had definitely improved with age and had gone about proving that to her with a fierce determination that had kept her up all night. If it weren't for his glances that seemed to be trying to dissect her, she would be afraid of falling for him again and begging him not to leave her. As if that would happen.

"Earth to Penny." Maggie waved a hand in front of Penny's eyes, breaking her view of Luke's butt in denim.

"Sorry. Did I miss something?" Penny blinked and tried to maintain an air of innocence.

"You aren't fooling me for one minute, Penny Montgomery." Maggie took her arm as the men started to move again. "I've known you practically all my life and I know when you've done the naughty."

"The naughty?" Penny laughed. "Good lord, woman, just call it what it is. Sex. S-e-x. Sex. Down-and-dirty, in-and-out sex. Which you should know because everyone is assuming you had sex last night, too."

"Shh. We're in a hospital, for goodness' sake." Maggie looked around as if a group of avenging nuns would descend on them.

"Yes, and it was good." Penny smirked. Damn good, if truth be told. She'd known that Luke had ruined her from falling in love ever again, but she'd hate it if he ruined her for sex, too.

"Hey." Maggie pulled her to a stop. Her hazel eyes searched Penny's. "He's not seeing anyone…."

Penny laughed. "You sound like Bitsy. You do know that I have a shop to run and he has a medical thingy hundreds of miles away, right? How's that supposed to work without the capability of time travel?"

"If you are in love, there are ways."

"Spoken like a true romantic." Penny tugged Maggie forward. "I'll just have to reserve myself for my weekly Winchester brothers viewing and let you stay the hopeless romantic."

"You know *Supernatural* won't be on the air forever." Maggie turned into the room.

"That's why I own the DVDs." She wiggled her eyebrows. "More Sam and Dean all to myself."

Penny couldn't make Maggie believe that she was determined to stay alone for the rest of her life. Okay, maybe not alone. She had Maggie and Amber, and she had Brady by marriage and any little ones that would come along. She'd be happy with that as long as they stayed right around the block.

Her heart pinched. Brady could have to move with his job. Even though he claimed he wanted to settle down in Tawnee Valley, how long would he be happy with small-town life? If Maggie left, where would Penny be?

God, she never got this emotional, even with lack of sleep. She'd deal with them moving if it happened. She turned the corner into the almost-full hospital room. Sam and Amber sat on the bed, and Luke and Brady stood beside Dr. Sanchez. Maggie joined Brady, who wrapped his arm around her.

There was no place for her. She glanced once at Luke, who had his head down over the chart the doctor had given him. She didn't belong with him. Taking a deep breath and ignoring the choking tears in the back of her throat, she left the room and the only family she had.

Dr. Sanchez was good at her job.

Luke didn't question that, even as he reviewed all her notes and the test results and cardiologist reports from St. Mercy in Springfield from last night and this morning. He wasn't looking for errors, just making sure that what she was saying was correct. Maggie had taken Amber to find some ice cream for Uncle Sam, while Brady and Luke stayed to listen to the doctor.

Luke checked the picture from the echocardiogram they had performed this morning. The still images had the measurements marked, showing the aortic valve. This wasn't what Luke had been expecting. His hand quaked as he turned to the next page. "Why didn't you mention the murmur last night?"

"Dr. Ward, you are well aware of HIPAA." Dr. Sanchez waited for his acknowledging nod before continuing. She couldn't release any information without Sam's consent, which he obviously hadn't given. "Everything points to severe aortic stenosis. We'd like to get Sam on the schedule in the next few days for surgery at St. Mercy Hospital in Springfield."

"Is this because of the enlargement of his heart?" Brady leaned against the windowsill with his arms crossed. His brow furrowed as he assessed the situation.

"Most likely the doctor who examined the X-ray couldn't tell that only the left side was enlarged from too much blood." Dr. Sanchez started writing on her chart. "That's why they strongly suggested that Sam go to a cardiologist, but I'm sure they told him not to worry. Some athletic men have slightly larger hearts, and for them it's nothing to worry about."

Sam had remained silent while the doctor spoke in her no-nonsense manner. Luke wanted to berate Sam for not following up, for not calling him to talk about his medical problems. Luke was training to be a cardiologist. The one person Luke had never understood—besides Penny—was Sam. Hell, maybe Sam and Penny were meant for each other. They both drove him nuts.

"I guess we'll cancel the trip." Brady looked at his phone. "I've already got the time off work, so I should be able to help out around the farm while Sam's recovering."

Before Luke could speak up, Sam said, "Who says I'm having the surgery?"

Dr. Sanchez held the chart to her chest and stared at Sam with dark, serious eyes. "If you were asymptomatic, we might be able to treat with drugs or even wait awhile, but your heart valve has already started to calcify. The fainting was only the beginning of your problems. If you don't have the surgery, you could go into heart failure."

Sam kept his lips together tightly. Not a single word. Just as he'd done all those times the principal had called him to the school for Luke's misconduct. Just as he had when he'd had to come to the police station to pick up Luke after a fight off campus. It was as if Sam just stopped caring at some point.

"I'm staying here." Luke stared into Sam's eyes, daring him to contradict him. Wanting him to. "I'll take family emergency leave to help out at the farm and help Sam out after his surgery."

"You need to get back to being a fancy doctor." Sam pushed up out of the chair.

"Brady deserves to go on his honeymoon and you need surgery."

"I'm fine. I don't even need to be here now."

"Bull." Luke saw red. "Of all the stupid, arrogant things you could do…. Do you think you are invincible? That you won't die if you don't have this surgery?"

Sam went lockjaw again. His face was stone.

"I'll let you discuss this in private." Dr. Sanchez backed out of the conversation. "I'll have the nurse call St. Mercy's to set up the necessary procedures."

The door shut behind her, leaving the cold silence. Luke didn't drop his gaze from Sam's eyes. If Sam could be stubborn, so could Luke. Sam was the tallest of the three, but he didn't have much height over Luke. They were practically eye to eye. Backing down wasn't an option. He wasn't a child who Sam could order around anymore.

Brady sighed and sank into the chair. "Are you guys going to stare at each other all day? Because I'd like to go have lunch with my wife and daughter."

"I'd be happy to leave now——" Luke brushed his hand over his hair "——but I'm not going to let another stubborn Ward die because he didn't listen to what the doctor was saying. I know the statistics. I know the symptoms. The doctor wasn't being completely honest."

Sam narrowed his eyes. The muscle in his jaw twitched.

"You will die if you don't have the surgery." Luke kept his expression flat and emotionless. "Within a year or two. Maybe sooner. This isn't something you can brush off…unless you have a death wish."

"What do you know about running a farm?" Sam said quietly. "The time and effort? The brute strength required? The long hours——"

"I'm a freaking doctor, Sam. I've spent twenty hours on shift before, followed by being on call. I know all about long hours and sacrifice." Cold seeped through him, taking the heat out of his words. Luke sat on the edge of the bed and rubbed his hand over his chin. He was not giving up, but he needed another tactic. "You need the surgery, Sam. I'm not ready to dig any more six-feet-deep holes."

Sam turned to Brady, who dropped his gaze to his hands. "Luke's right, Sam. I'm not ready to bury any more family. If it will save your life, I don't know why we are even having this discussion."

"They want to cut into my body and mess with my heart." Sam's face screwed up as if he'd eaten something bad. "While they are in there, they are going to take out part of my heart and replace it with a fake valve."

"And you'll feel better and live longer," Luke said. "I don't see what the problem is."

Sam shook his head and leaned against the end table. His gaze fell to the floor. "What if I don't make it?"

Luke took in a deep breath. He'd gone through this with patients before. The fear of the unknown. He hadn't expected Sam to be afraid. Not the Sam who had taken on Brady and him as a young man. Who'd stood at their mother's and father's gravesites without tears in his eyes.

In Luke's world growing up, Sam was brave and uncompromising. He was stern and unyielding. But he was never afraid.

"This surgery is less invasive than open-heart surgery." Luke stopped acting like a younger brother and became the doctor. "Every surgery has risks, but the benefits of this surgery far outweigh them. You'll be down for a few weeks and then able to do some light work. Before you know it, you'll be full Sam again. Except you'll feel better."

Sam grunted. "I have been feeling a little sick lately."

Luke wanted to exclaim disbelief but he held it back. Most likely Sam had felt like hell for weeks before this collapse. But pushing Sam would get him nowhere. Luke always got so frustrated with Sam that he forgot and blew up, even now as an adult.

Luke placed his hand on Sam's shoulder. "We'll get through this, Sam. Together."

Chapter Seven

"Hey, there you are."

Penny turned toward Maggie's voice. She'd found a magazine in the waiting room with a semi-interesting article on Chris Hemsworth and had decided to read instead of mope. She didn't need to mope. No one to love meant no one to leave you when you least expected it, when you really needed them, when you were starting to trust them again.

"I looked all over for you." Maggie sat down next to Penny and glanced at the article and the picture of Chris without his shirt on. "Nice." She smiled. "They are finishing up Sam's paperwork now, so we should be out of here soon. Then we're going to stop and grab some lunch before heading to the farm."

"What's the verdict?" Penny's stomach clenched. If Sam was okay, Luke would go back to his life in St. Louis.

If Sam wasn't, then Luke would hang around for a while. She wasn't sure which she wanted.

"Sam needs heart valve surgery." Maggie took in a deep breath. "Luke is insisting on staying and handling everything and that Brady and I go on our vacation after the surgery, while Sam is recovering. But I don't know. Sam and Brady were just starting to get to know each other again and if something happens to Sam…"

Penny took Maggie's hand. "We've gotten through worse before."

Maggie nodded and looked up at the ceiling as if to stop tears from forming. "But Sam's young and strong and we didn't even know he was sick."

"Sometimes it's like that." Penny could see her mother's drawn face twisted and ravaged from the years of abuse. For all she knew, her mother was dead. She shook off the image. "He's otherwise healthy. He'll get through this."

"Brady and Luke are talking the logistics." Maggie brushed her hair behind her ear. "I don't know what's going to happen, but would you be willing to help out while we are out of town? I can't imagine Luke being able to do everything by himself."

"He's perfectly capable." Penny shifted in her seat. "But I'll do what I can."

Maggie stared out the window into the blue sky. Some thought must have made her happy because she smiled softly. "It wouldn't be so bad."

"What's that?"

"Getting back together with Luke."

Penny laughed sharply as her heart ached. "I don't do relationships. I keep my options open. You never know when a hottie like Thor here will roll up into town. It'd be a shame to have to waste the eye candy because I'm *with* someone."

"You don't fool me for a minute, Penny." Maggie glanced down the hallway before returning her hazel gaze to Penny. "You talk a good game, but I know you. I know how much you loved Luke in high school. I don't know all of what happened between you two, but it couldn't have been too bad if he was willing to sleep with you last night."

"We didn't sleep." Penny winked, trying to throw off Maggie's speech. She was hitting a little too close to Penny's heart.

"You know what I mean." Maggie tightened her hold on Penny's hand. "I know you aren't happy with the way things are. You may enjoy other men, but I've never seen you light up the way you do when Luke is nearby. I know you've been hurt, but maybe it's time to heal a little. Maybe this is the second chance you need."

"Second chances like that are pretty rare." Penny looked out the window as a small brown bird flew by. If she let Luke in, he'd hurt her because she actually could love him. "And you got the only second chance we're going to see. Don't worry about me. I've got all the men I need in my life right now."

Maggie looked skeptical and opened her mouth.

"I swear, Maggie. I'm happy the way things are. I don't need anything more."

"Weren't you the one who said it wasn't about need?"

"That was to get you laid." Penny stood and brushed the wrinkles out of her slacks. "I'm doing just fine on that part."

Maggie stood. "This discussion isn't over."

"Yeah, it is. I don't need Luke and he doesn't need

me. We had a good time together. It's all good. Now, what's the plan? Is there food to be had?"

Maggie shook her head. "Come on."

When they got to the room, Penny's gaze met Luke's. He gave a hint of a smile, but the wrinkles on his forehead betrayed his worry. She hoped that Sam pulled through. Losing both his parents had devastated Luke. He couldn't lose Sam, too.

"I take it you guys have this all sorted?" Maggie asked as she touched Amber's dark hair.

Amber pouted. "We're going to Disney."

"You were excited for this trip, Squirt," Penny said.

"But who's going to take care of Uncle Sam after his surgery?" Amber turned to Penny. "You'll take care of him, won't you, Penny?"

Penny glanced around the room. Sam didn't make eye contact. Luke was intensely watching for her answer. Brady and Maggie just smiled indulgently.

"You always take real good care of me when I'm sick." Amber reached out and took both of Penny's hands. "If I know you'll be there, I might be able to have fun while I'm gone."

Amber's face was hopeful. Penny knew that no matter what she said Amber would have fun at Disney, but if it helped to get her on the plane without causing Maggie too much grief…

"You know I'll do whatever I can." Penny squeezed Amber's hands. "But you have to promise to have fun."

"Only if you call every night with an update."

"You drive a hard bargain." Penny bit out a laugh. Amber narrowed her eyes as if Penny weren't taking her seriously. "Sure. I'll check in with Luke every day and then call you."

"Check on Uncle Sam," Amber clarified.

Penny glanced over to Luke. "Your uncle Luke will be there—"

"I want you to."

"That's enough, young lady," Brady finally spoke up. "Penny has promised. Now let's go get something to eat and then get Sam set up at home. We have a lot to do to prepare for Sam's surgery and while we're on our trip."

Luke's eyes never left Penny's. Her pulse throbbed. She didn't know what he was searching for, but she didn't have anything left to hide. She wasn't Luke's girl anymore. He was just another notch on her lipstick case. Even though she'd have to talk to him and maybe even see him, nothing else was going to happen. A few weeks and he'd be gone and out of her life again.

Maybe she was the one with a heart condition. She rubbed the ache in her chest.

The surgery was set for Wednesday. Frankly it couldn't come soon enough. Keeping Sam indoors was proving to be a feat even for both Brady and Luke combined.

"You need to stay off your feet and rest." Brady shoved Sam toward the living room. "Play Xbox or watch a movie."

"I'm not an infant. I can do more than sit on my butt."

Brady headed back to the kitchen to talk to Maggie.

"Not if you want to live." Luke stood in the doorway. "We all grew up on this farm and each of us has done these chores a million times. I'm not sure why you think we're going to mess something up."

Sam grumbled something under his breath as he plopped in the worn-out recliner and grabbed the remote. Hopefully killing zombies on the Xbox would make Sam content to stay inside. He could pretend they were Brady and Luke if he really wanted to take out his anger. Lord knew that Luke had pretended they were Sam when he was younger. Luke turned and nearly ran over Penny.

"Sorry," he said. His breath caught in his throat as she looked up at him, startled.

"It was my fault," she muttered.

They'd barely spoken since the morning at the hospital. Apparently where Maggie and Amber went, Penny wasn't far behind. The three ladies worked on scrubbing the house, while he and Brady worked on straightening up the outside. Mom would have been thrilled that her house was being put back in order. They needed to get ahead on the farm chores for the days that Sam would be in the hospital for his surgery and recovery.

The unfortunate side effect was that Luke kept running into Penny, both figuratively and literally. Every touch caused his pulse to kick into overdrive. The house wasn't that big, which meant everyone was in everyone's way. It also meant that he hadn't been alone with Penny since the night of the wedding.

Penny still stood in front of him, looking at him with her brown eyes that always carried a hint of a devilish glint in them.

They weren't going to have sex again, he reminded himself for the tenth time that day. The night of the wedding was a one-time deal, but his body clearly had misread the memo.

"Did you need something?" Penny asked. A hint of a smile tugged at her lips.

Did he need something? How 'bout a convenient closet or bed for an hour or two? "No, I'm just heading out to work on the fence."

"Sounds exciting." She stretched her arms over her

head, which pushed her breasts against her tight black T-shirt.

His pants tightened and he had to restrain from adjusting himself.

"I get to clean the living room," she said in a fake excited voice. "Maybe afterward we can go beat laundry down on the rocks in the creek? Won't that be fun?"

Luke chuckled. "Better than gathering up the pigs for market."

"At least when Maggie and Brady leave, we can slack off once in a while." She leaned in conspiratorially. "I hid a package of ice cream bars in the back of the freezer behind a bag of frozen broccoli."

"Always thinking ahead—that's what I like about you, Montgomery." Luke relaxed.

"Someone has to." Penny took a deep breath and looked around. "Back to dusting. Yay?"

As she passed by him, he grabbed her hand. She looked at him with a question in her eyes.

"Thanks." Luke released her hand and flexed his still tingling fingers.

Penny winked. "Anytime."

Things with Penny were less complicated right now than his relationship with Sam. He really did appreciate that she got it. He knew, even though she didn't say it, that she did.

Penny's relationship with her grandma had always been similarly tense. They'd called her Grandma Tilly the Battle Ax.

She'd been old and alone when Penny's mother had dropped Penny off at her doorstep. Penny was more rambunctious than most kids and everyone knew that Tilly wasn't happy about having to raise her granddaughter. The stricter Tilly got, the wilder Penny got.

They were opposites in everything. Luke remembered the endless nights on a blanket staring up at the stars with Penny lying beside him. They'd talk about her grandma and Sam—the people who had gotten stuck with caring for Penny and Luke. They vowed that they'd never make anyone feel the way their caregivers made them feel. Like inconveniences instead of kids hurting from the loss of their parents.

He shook his head. Such thoughts didn't help anyone. He needed to focus on the farm and on getting Sam better. Not on Penny.

Chapter Eight

The days passed quickly, and before Luke knew it, it was Wednesday. Luke had driven Sam and Brady the hour to the hospital in Springfield. Everything ran smoothly. Checking Sam in. The staff preparing him for surgery. Watching them take him away.

Luke found himself once more in the hospital waiting room, this time with Brady. They talked for a little bit, but there wasn't much new to say because they'd spent the past few days working together.

Luke missed Penny's presence. She'd wished them the best last night before leaving and said she'd check in. He wished she were here now. She could always distract him, whether it was through flirting, having sex or just sitting and talking.

Now all he could do was run through the surgery in his mind's eye. Noting all the things that needed to happen. Everything that could go wrong. The steps to fix the mistakes. When he'd run through the procedures three times, he rubbed his face and turned to look to see what Brady was doing.

Brady had his laptop out and was working on some spreadsheet with numbers and formulas that Luke would need a business degree to understand. Luke pulled out his iPhone and scrolled through the emails he'd missed over the past few days. The signal out at the farm was questionable. Sometimes he received his emails, and other times, the battery drained from trying to connect to the server.

"Dr. Ward?"

Luke looked up at the nurse in scrubs. "Yes?"

"Sam is in recovery. The doctor would like to talk to you and your brother."

Luke glanced over to where Brady had been. His laptop was back in its case, but Brady wasn't there.

"Sorry, had to use the bathroom." Brady came down the hall toward them. "Everything okay?"

"Sam's out and in recovery." Luke took a deep breath. A lot of things still could go wrong, but the worst part was over.

After another hour, Luke had all the post-op information and had talked to Sam briefly. On the way home, he and Brady talked about the surgery and what they needed to do to prepare for Sam's homecoming in a few days.

When Luke pulled the car up to Maggie and Brady's house, Brady turned to him.

"Do you want to come in for a little bit? Maybe for some dinner? Maggie's a great cook."

Luke looked past Brady to the lights in the old Victorian's windows. He could see Maggie and Amber heading to the door to greet Brady. "Nah, you go ahead.

It's been a long day. You'll need to start packing for your trip."

"You sure?" Brady wasn't just being nice. He was sincere, but Luke wasn't in the mood for company.

"Yeah, we'll see each other tomorrow."

"'Night." Brady got out and without a backward glance walked into his family's arms.

Luke remembered what that felt like. To hug someone who cared more about what you were feeling than their own agenda.

It had been a long time since he'd felt that way. Dating in med school had been hard. He'd dated other med students mostly and everyone was mainly concerned about their grades and their shifts. No one really worried about anyone except themselves.

He didn't have what Brady had. Someone who would welcome him with open arms. His gaze went to the direction of Penny's house. It was only a block away.

Penny stared at the inventory screen of the online auction. It had a few good pieces that would look wonderful in What Goes Around Comes Around. A pair of gilded-and-silvered metal vases from nineteenth-century France and a seventeenth-century Italian writing desk had captured her attention. Although they were a bit ornate for her local customers, the tourists loved finding these types of treasures in her little shop.

Most of her inventory consisted of American furniture, artwork and tableware. But she loved to have a few older pieces from across the ocean for interest. People would come in to look at the vases and notice a set of silver or glassware that their grandma had and buy that instead.

She put in her bids and stretched. Flicker perked up

at her feet and looked at her hopefully with his giant brown eyes.

"No, I'm not taking you for a walk, you overgrown mop."

Flicker wagged his tail, knocking it against the table leg.

"If I'd known you were going to weigh almost as much as me, I would have let Brady take you back to the farm." When Brady had shown up with a surprise dog for Amber, Maggie had blown a gasket. Penny had stepped in and offered to keep the puppy. At the time, it had seemed easy and Amber loved the dog. Having never had a puppy before, Penny had been in for a treat.

The dog looked up at her with utter devotion. Penny couldn't resist an answering smile.

"Go back to sleep and maybe later we'll get a quick walk."

Flicker jumped up and headed to the door.

"Not now." Why did she say the word *walk?* "Flicker."

The dog growled and then barked.

"What's—"

Someone knocked on the door. Most likely Amber or Maggie. They'd spent the afternoon together working on a new scrapbook for Amber. Penny shut her laptop.

When she opened the door, she didn't see anyone for a moment.

"Hey."

She jumped and looked to her right. Luke stood in the shadows. "You startled me."

"Sorry about that."

Flicker rushed out the door and sniffed at Luke. Luke rubbed the dog's head, and the poor thing turned to putty in his hand. Penny was way too intimately familiar with the feeling.

"This must be the legendary Flicker." Luke didn't look up at her as Flicker put his front paws on Luke's chest in an effort to lick his face. His jeans, slung low on his hips, drew her attention. He filled them out nicely. She forced her gaze up to his button-down white shirt.

She ran her suddenly damp palms over her pink cotton shorts. Expecting to be alone this evening, she'd already changed into her pajamas. She hadn't thought to grab her sweater before answering the door since it was probably Maggie or Amber, and her comfy pink cotton tank didn't help against the cool evening air.

"Did you want to come in?" Penny grabbed Flicker's collar and tugged him off Luke. "It's a bit chilly out here."

Luke's eyes caught on her breasts before lifting to meet her eyes. "Sure."

He followed her into the house.

"Have a seat. I'll put Flicker out in the backyard." She motioned to the living room and hauled the dog out through the kitchen door. When she got back, Luke was staring at the pictures on the wall.

Her heart stopped. Most of the pictures were of Maggie, Amber and her, but the one he was focused on was the one of Luke and her. The night hadn't mattered and hadn't been anything special. It could have been any night or every night, but that picture showed how much in love they had been.

"Can I get you something to drink?" She wanted to ask why he was here. What had happened with Sam? Did he feel this intense, almost-drunk feeling when she was near, as she did? It made her feel comfortable and on edge in the same moment. "I have a beer or I could make some tea."

"No." He reached out and stroked a finger down the picture.

She shuddered as if he'd touched her. Goose bumps rose on her arms. It wasn't the chill in the air affecting her. It was the electric current running between them that had her body humming like a live wire.

He turned toward her. His blue eyes glowed in the dim light the lamp offered. "Are you expecting someone?"

"No. I was just working some before going to bed." She didn't normally have anyone over during the week. Before last weekend, it had been quite a while since she'd hooked up with someone. She was busy with work and helping with Maggie's wedding. It definitely didn't have anything to do with the fact that Luke would be coming home.

He glanced over her shoulder, down the hallway. A thrill shot through her. He knew exactly where her bedroom was. They hadn't had the chance to use it very often as teenagers, but he'd snuck in a few times. He was the only guy who had made it to her bedroom.

Suddenly she felt vulnerable and naked.

It had nothing to do with her state of dress. She wouldn't care if she were literally naked in front of Luke, but he'd been inside her head and heart as a teenager. Maggie knew her, but not as Luke did...or, rather, had.

"Sorry I interrupted you." Luke sank into the worn recliner.

"I had just finished up when you knocked." She hesitated in the doorway for a moment before she shook herself. She wasn't shy when it came to men, but something about Luke threw her off her game. She walked into the room and sat across from Luke with her legs tucked up under her. "What's up?"

"Sam's surgery went well." He combed his hand through his hair.

"It must have been a long day for you." Her heart beat mercilessly against her rib cage. Why was he here? To talk? To vent? To have sex?

"I just dropped off Brady."

To not be alone? She'd been there many times.

His fingers stroked sensually down the ruby-red glass of the Egermann Bohemian perfume bottle on the end table next to him. It didn't take much for her to remember those fingers tracing the vein in her neck.

"And since you were in the neighborhood, you thought you'd pass along the news of Sam?" Not bloody likely. This whole week had been an exercise in chastity. Something she wasn't entirely comfortable or familiar with. They'd never had a moment alone, which was probably good. If they had, she would have dragged him somewhere and to hell with her promises to her heart to keep him at arm's length for the duration of his stay. Besides, all promises were meant to be broken.

"Something like that." He seemed way too fascinated with the glass. It was as if he was trying to put her on edge. Draw her attention to the fingers that had provided her with hours of pleasure.

Keeping up this conversation was pointless. If he were here to drive her mad with desire, it was working. And since he hadn't touched her, she'd be on her own tonight. He'd hardly acknowledged the fact that she was barely dressed. If they weren't going to get busy, she would have to work through her desires by herself. She started to stand up.

"Wait." He held up his hand, still looking at the bottle.

She returned to her seat, not because he'd ordered her to, but because she was curious.

"Tell me about this." His words were so quiet and his voice so deep she almost didn't hear him.

"It's a ruby perfume bottle made by Egermann after 1860 in Bohemia."

Luke lifted his gaze to hers. "Penny?"

"Yes?"

"Give me its story."

She drew in a deep breath. When she was younger, she'd been fascinated with the antiques in her grandma's store. She'd spent countless hours there, wondering where everything came from, making up their stories to make them so much more than they were: things left behind by people who were either gone or no longer wanted them. "The real one?"

"Give me your story."

She hadn't thought up stories in years. Something in his lost look made her want to draw him into her embrace and just hold him for hours until whatever haunted him went away. He hadn't asked for that, but she could give him a story. "The year was 1867. There was a man who desired a woman very much."

He watched her with an intensity that took her breath away. "Go on."

She licked her lips and continued, "She was everything to him, but she didn't see him. Not as a man. Not as a person. One day he saw her standing in a store. In her hands she held that very perfume bottle. She stroked it with longing and smelled deeply of the perfume, which had the rich scent of jasmine in it. He could tell she wanted it very much."

Luke stood and crossed the room. He hunkered down

in front of her. His knuckles brushed her bare leg. "Tell me more."

She swallowed. "The woman put it back because she didn't have enough money for it. After she left the store, he went to the bottle and spent every last coin he had in his pocket on it, confident that with it, he would finally have her love. That night he went to her house and presented her with the bottle."

"What did she do?" He brushed her hair behind her ear and cradled her head in his hand.

Her breath whispered past her lips. "She invited him inside."

"Will you?" He pulled her head down toward his. She didn't resist.

"Will I what?"

He stopped before their lips touched. "Let me in."

Penny closed the distance between their mouths, answering him the only way she knew how. Their lips met and clung together. Sparks flew behind her eyes. Her skin tingled with the longing to be touched. Liquid heat flowed through her and pooled in the center of her.

Without breaking the kiss, he rose and took her into his arms. This was crazy. Foolish. The future was an unknown. The past was gone. This was perhaps the worst mistake she could make. But right now, Luke was the only thing that mattered to her. This connection. His mouth, his body, his essence…the fuel for this raging passion within her.

Chapter Nine

Luke hadn't known what to expect when he knocked on Penny's door. He wouldn't fool himself into believing his intentions had been any less than kissing Penny until he managed to release the devil that had been riding him since their night together.

He pulled away from the kiss. Her body was flush against his, her chest rising and falling with every breath. He ran a finger under the strap of her tank top.

"I never figured you for a pink-cotton girl." He rested his forehead against hers.

"My black and red lace teddies are all in the wash." Her fingers tangled in his hair.

"Liar." He pulled her from her chair and sat back on the floor with her on his lap.

"You've discovered my secret." She ran her fingers along the neckline of his shirt until she reached the top button. With a flick of her finger, she released it. "I have an all-encompassing passion for cotton pajamas. Shorts, pants, T-shirts, tank tops. I can't get enough of them."

He ran his hands up her bare legs until he brushed the cotton of her shorts.

"I can't let you leave here," she said. Her expression was serious, but the glint in her eyes ruined the effect.

He cupped her bottom and pulled her tight against his hardness. "Why is that?"

"Because you know at least one of my secrets." She dipped her head to kiss his neck. A pulse of pure heat went straight through his body. She pushed him back until he lay flat on the carpet. "I have to find out what else you know."

Her fingers wove with his and pressed his hands into the floor. He could easily overpower her if he wanted to. She took his mouth with hers. Her tongue danced with his. His blood ran hot through his veins and his brain began to short-circuit. His fingers twitched with the desire to explore her lush body. She released his mouth and stared down into his eyes.

"What if I'm not willing to talk?" Luke leaned up and nipped her chin.

She smiled wickedly. "We'll see about that."

Penny took her time removing his clothes, button by button, kissing every inch of skin she uncovered until Luke couldn't think straight. By the time she had him fully naked, he was sensitive everywhere. The slightest breeze from the open window made him stiffen with desire. He allowed her to do what she wanted, enjoying her attentions more than he probably should.

When he couldn't take any more, he lifted her top over her head and helped her out of her shorts and underwear. Having her naked skin against his was the most enticing feeling in the world. She was intoxicating. So sure and aware of herself as a sexual creature.

He wanted too much from her. He knew that. He wanted everything, every piece of her down to her very soul. But it was impossible. He'd learned that lesson years ago as a boy. As a man, he would take what she offered and enjoy her without reading too much into her moans of delight and her desire to please him.

After covering him with a condom, she hovered above him. Aphrodite herself. Her flesh pressed intimately with his. He had so many things he wanted to say, needed to tell her. Things she should know. She was one of a kind. In nine years, he hadn't been able to replace her in his mind or in his heart. No one compared to her.

"So beautiful." He reached up and stroked the side of her face.

Her passion-glazed eyes met his. She took his hand, pressed her lips against his fingertips. "I want to come apart with you."

She came down on him. They both gasped in air as if they were starving for it. She set a slow rhythm, but he couldn't take it. He grabbed her hips and set a new pace. He watched her every expression until she tightened all around him, taking him over the edge with her.

She collapsed on his chest. Both of them worked to catch their breaths.

A laugh escaped Penny.

"Not something a guy likes to hear after sex," he grumbled and kissed the top of her hair.

She rested her chin on her hands on his chest to look at him. Her brown eyes sparkled. "Trust me when I say that laugh *wasn't* about your performance. And may I say, 'bravo'?"

"You can applaud if you like." He smiled and pushed her hair from her face. "But I think you did most of the work."

"I wouldn't call it work." She squirmed against him and raised an eyebrow. "But you know, if you have some pent-up energy you need to expend—"

She squealed as he flipped her onto her back.

He leaned over her, his hand tracing along the side of her breast. "Since you seem in the mood to laugh, let's see if I can remember where your tickle spots are."

Penny hummed as she dusted the shelves of her shop the next morning. She still wasn't entirely sure why Luke had come over last night, but she definitely wasn't complaining after the christening of her living room rug.

"Penny dear, did you get bit by a mosquito?" Bitsy Clemons was making her morning rounds. With only a few shops on Main Street, Bitsy could spend a lot of time in each and still make it home for lunch.

Penny reached up and touched her neck. "Uh, yeah, nasty little buggers."

"We need to spray for them before they get bad this summer." Bitsy wandered down the aisle to the jewelry trays.

Penny glanced in one of the antique mirrors on the wall. Sure enough, she had a huge hickey from Luke as a greeting card this morning. Damn.

Luke had left sometime during the night and she'd crawled into bed exhausted. This morning, she'd overslept and managed to roll into the shower and pull on some clothes just in time to get to the shop for opening. She'd forgotten to look for collateral damage.

The bell above the door rang—hopefully announcing Bitsy's departure.

Some damage Penny had noticed—thankfully. The rug burns on her knees were discreetly hidden by her slacks. Bitsy would have a heart attack if she'd seen exactly how Penny had gotten those puppies. She chuckled.

"Someone's in a happy mood," Luke's voice slipped over her like a satin nightie, causing her knees to turn to gelatin.

She grabbed a shelf to hold herself steady before turning to face him. "Well, I did get lucky last night."

He moved in, drawing her closer with the crisp scent of his cologne. "Maybe you are on a winning streak."

"God, I hope so." She smiled up at him.

He leaned toward her as if to kiss her. The tinkling of jewelry being sorted alerted him that they weren't alone. He stiffened and took a step back. "Maggie, Brady and Amber went next door to grab something for their trip. They should be here in a minute. I'm driving them to the airport and they insisted on saying goodbye. Afterward I'm heading to the hospital to sit with Sam for a while."

"Cool." What power did Luke have that he always made her feel awkward when he was near? She didn't know what to do with her hands or how to stand. Which was ridiculous because this was Luke. He'd seen and touched every inch of her body.

"Is that Luke Ward?" Bitsy came hurrying down the aisle as if Luke might take off at the sight of her. Her blue floral skirt billowed out behind her like a cape.

Luke gave Penny a help-me look.

Penny just smiled and returned to dusting.

"My goodness, you've grown into quite the man. I remember when you were knee high to a grasshopper."

Bitsy eyed Luke as if he was the prize pig at the county fair. If he weren't careful, she might start poking and testing his muscles. Penny covered a laugh with a cough. "And a doctor, too."

"It's a pleasure to see you again, Mrs. Clemons."

"Oh, stop." Bitsy blushed to the roots of her silver hair and waved her hand. "We're all adults here. You can call me Bitsy."

Luke smiled. "What are you looking for today, Bitsy?"

"I just come to browse and help Penny in her quest for true love." Bitsy placed her hand on Luke's arm. "I know you two were involved once upon a time, but really she needs to settle down with someone before she's too old to have children."

Penny stopped her dusting. "True love? Kids? And here I thought you were just setting me up with men for the fun of it."

"What's wrong with kids?" Luke had a mischievous look in his eyes, as if he was enjoying her torture.

"Nothing's *wrong* with kids as long as they are someone else's." Penny raised her eyebrow, daring him to contradict her.

"Now, now, Penny. Take it from an old lady who never had kids of her own. One day you'll want kids and it will be too late." Bitsy nodded her head sagely. She'd married late in life and never had any children. She'd been friends with Penny's grandma and had always slipped Penny sweets when she came by to talk with Grandma Tilly.

"Don't worry, Bitsy. I have a few good years left if I want to push out a brat or two."

"Ticktock," Bitsy scolded. She glanced to the clock on the wall. "Oh, time to go see Mr. Martin. It was good seeing you, Luke, and if you have any single doctor friends, make sure to send them Penny's way."

They watched her scurry out of the store. Alone once again with Luke, Penny's heart fluttered. Talking about kids and men in front of Luke had been extremely awkward. But now that they were alone, they didn't have to talk at all.

He closed in on her, forcing her to look up to meet his eyes or stare at his chest. Hmm, decisions, decisions. It was such a fine chest. She sighed and met his eyes.

"Ticktock." He grinned down at her.

"Not you, too." She took a deep breath and her breasts grazed his chest. "I've got years before I even need to worry about that damned clock."

His fingers stroked a strand of hair that had escaped her messy bun. "Do you want children?"

"You offering?" She intended to throw him off. With him standing so near, her insides were pooling into liquid warmth that flowed through her whole body.

"Stop trying to distract me, Penny." He dipped his head slightly and she swore he was going to kiss her. Talk about distracting. "What are your future plans? What happens after right now?"

"I get lucky?" She flashed him a grin. She certainly hoped she would.

"What do you want?" he whispered close to her ear, stealing any breath she had left. His voice was rich and soothing. She swore she could listen to him read a dictionary and be turned on.

He pulled back. His blue eyes were dark pools, begging her to strip naked and dive in. He was close enough that his heat made her want to sway forward and rub against his warmth. She wanted him. 24/7.

"Do you want kids?" he asked.

Kids? A baby? With Luke's blue eyes and her red hair? Someone she could love and who would love her in return. Who would rely on her for everything. Who she would disappoint.

A shard of cold went through her.

"I—" She swallowed and stepped back against the shelf. Straightening, she slid away from him down the aisle. She didn't want these thoughts. She knew what she could and couldn't have, and a child was a *couldn't*. "I need to get back to work."

"I want children," Luke said as if she hadn't walked away from the conversation. "I want a wife and home and children. Someday."

Her chest ached. She didn't look back at him. Thinking of Luke with his future wife and their perfect house and perfect children was enough to make her want to lose her breakfast.

"That's great," Penny choked out and blinked back the burning tears in her eyes. "You'll make a great dad."

His hands rested on her shoulders. His touch brought on another surge of tears. "Penny—"

The bell on the door jingled and Brady's, Maggie's and Amber's voices broke their solitude. She heard his sigh before his hands slipped away. She rushed to the back into the storeroom and shut the door behind her. She took a great shuddering breath in and scolded herself.

Luke wasn't hers. In no universe would he be hers. She'd made sure of that years ago. So why did the thought of him with someone else burn through her stomach like a branding iron? She set down the duster and grabbed a tissue. After a few deep breaths, she pulled herself together.

Just because they were having some fun didn't give

her any hold over Luke. Just because she'd loved him once didn't mean she was in danger of being in love with him again. Just because the thought of a child, his child, made her clench up inside with longing didn't mean she wanted one.

She picked up the present she'd wrapped for Amber and opened the storeroom door, prepared to do battle.

Chapter Ten

Luke stepped out from behind the shelving and into the open part of the store, where the front desk and cash register were.

"Where's Penny?" Amber asked.

"She went into the back for something." Most likely to get away from him. She was upset and she had every reason to be. He didn't know why he'd pushed so hard. Maybe it was because Bitsy hadn't thought he'd be the right guy for Penny. If he had any single friends... Not in this lifetime. "I'm sure she'll be right out."

"Everything okay?" Maggie asked.

"Yeah." No, it wasn't. "Did you guys get what you needed?"

"We're all set," Brady said as he picked up a little blue bottle, which looked as if it might have once had medicine in it, off a shelf.

"I hear someone is going to Disney World." Penny

appeared. It was as if nothing strange had passed between them. She smiled at Amber and held out a little box, gift-wrapped and tied with a bow.

"For me?" Amber took the box and opened it very carefully.

Penny glanced up at him before returning her gaze to Amber. He saw how much she loved being around Amber. Why wouldn't she want that for herself? His heart beat a little harder with the thought of Penny with a baby in her arms. Would they already have a few kids if she'd come with him to university? He could imagine lying in bed with her on a Sunday morning with kids climbing onto the bed with them. One happy family.

He startled. He could have been happy with her, but not if he couldn't even be sure if the kids were his. What was so fundamentally broken with her that she couldn't be with just him? Hadn't he been enough? Lord knew he couldn't get enough of her. Even now.

"O.M.G. It's a Mickey necklace. Mom, it's a Mickey necklace." Amber brought him back to the here and now.

"I see that," Maggie said.

"Oh, thank you, thank you, thank you. I've always wanted one." Amber threw her arms around Penny and Penny squeezed her tight.

As soon as Amber released her to go show Brady, Penny looked at Luke. It was there in her eyes, that longing for something she couldn't have. Whether she told him she wanted children or not, that look told him everything. She wanted a child, but she was content holding her best friend's daughter as her own.

He kept his gaze on Penny as they all said their goodbyes. Brady's family would be gone for ten days and then they'd be back to help out again. After that, Luke could leave at that time if he wanted to. As they exited the shop, Penny met his gaze. He knew the only thing he wanted right now was her. And although she seemed to want him now, who's to say that tomorrow, she wouldn't want someone else?

"'Bout time you showed up." Sam lay in his hospital bed in a robe and hospital gown, looking distinctly uncomfortable. "When do I get out of this place?"

"You only had surgery two days ago," Luke sat in the chair next to the bed. "They want you to stay one more night."

"How am I supposed to get better with all these tubes in me?" Sam held up his IV with disdain. "This sucks."

"I'm sure it does." Luke looked out the window. Springfield wasn't nearly as big as St. Louis, but it was a decent size for the middle-of-nowhere Illinois. The surrounding buildings seemed dreary and worn-out.

"How's the farm?" Sam picked up the remote and flipped the channel on the TV. A news channel played in the background with the sound on mute.

"The animals are tended. The Baxter boys have been by to help with the fields."

John Baxter was a neighboring farmer who helped Sam out in the spring and fall during seeding and harvesting. His two sons went to the local community college and helped out year-round. Sam returned the favor by giving them bales of hay at baling time.

"That's good." Sam rubbed at the stubble on his chin. After a few minutes, he said, "I made an appointment with the cardiologist. His office is around the corner from the hospital."

"There isn't anyone closer?" An hour's drive both ways every day to the hospital to check up on Sam was annoying, especially because Luke kept going to Penny's before going home. Last night they'd barely spoken when he'd shown up at her door. He hadn't said a word, just took her in his arms. She'd pulled him into her dining room, where they'd made good use of the table and chairs. He had yet to see the inside of her bedroom. He barely managed any sleep before waking for the morning chores. "What about Dr. Patterson?"

"He retired. Tawnee Valley hasn't had a doctor in years, and Owen only has a handful of specialists. No cardiologists." Sam fluffed a pillow and shoved it behind his head.

Luke leaned forward, thinking of the ramifications of sick people having to go an hour just to get to their doctor. Most people would either just not go to the doctor at all or go to the emergency room rather than make the trip. Filling up the emergency room with people best seen in an office made it hard for the true emergencies to get in. The hospital in Owen must be a nightmare of never-ending patients.

"You get the tractor running?" Sam asked, interrupting Luke's thoughts.

"What? Yeah, it only needed a new fuse."

Sam nodded and continued to watch the TV.

Luke returned to his thoughts. It was bad enough that a lot of patients came from miles away to see specialists in the hospital he worked at in St. Louis, but those patients usually had a doctor close by who they could follow up with.

The population of Tawnee Valley and even Owen was skewed to an older than average age. Those people shouldn't have to sit in a car for an hour just to get some medical advice. Especially just for checkups to make sure nothing has changed or whether a new medicine was working or not.

"Anything new?" Sam said.

"What?" Luke turned to look at Sam.

Sam rarely spoke outside of direct questions and answers. He looked highly uncomfortable. "I'm stuck in a hospital bed watching bad TV. I'm bored."

Luke smiled. "You want me to bring you my laptop next time? It has solitaire on it."

"I better be going home tomorrow. If you won't take me, I'll hitch a ride." Sam shoved the remote away. "Or maybe Penny would come get me."

If Luke were a rooster, his feathers would be rustled. "Why would Penny do that?"

"She and I are a lot alike. Both alone." Sam closed his eyes and put his arm behind his head.

The idea of Sam and Penny together burned Luke deeper than thinking of her with any other man. Sam was his brother, his guardian. He was supposed to watch out for Luke, not steal his girl. Even if his girl had been a willing participant. "You won't have to call Penny because I'll be here."

"Good."

Luke sat for an hour more with Sam, answering his random questions and silently fuming. He couldn't get the image of Sam kissing Penny out of his head. The night of his graduation, he'd been outside with his friends when he went back into the house to get a drink. Through the kitchen door, he could see Penny with her hands around Sam's neck, her body tight against his. Her lips pressed against Sam's. Sam's hands had been on her hips.

He hadn't needed to see more. All that locker room talk. All the times Penny had talked him down from kicking some guy's ass for saying he was nailing her. It had all been true. What he had thought was love had been a lie.

All those hours they'd spent, dreaming and planning, had been for nothing. He was just another one of her guys. He just hadn't realized it.

The drive home didn't help his dark mood. If Sam and Penny did end up together, she'd be his sister-in-law. He'd have to see her with him at every family get-together. Participate in her and Sam's wedding as if he were happy to be there.

By the time he drove into Tawnee Valley, it was late. He could have gone straight to the farm and just skipped seeing Penny tonight, but that wasn't going to happen.

He parked his car in front of her house and stared at the dark street ahead of him. It was all in the past. He'd moved on. She'd moved on. What they were doing now…that was just for fun. Something to keep the boredom away.

It had taken him a year to get over the betrayal. But he'd never truly let it go. Maybe that was because he'd been so sure that they had been in love. He slammed his hand against the steering wheel. This was stupid.

The past shouldn't matter. Penny wasn't the same girl. She had solid roots in the community. A sensitive side that she rarely showed. So she enjoyed sex. Since when had that been a crime?

If she and Sam were involved, they didn't act like it. Even if they were just having sex, it would be a while before Sam was up to anything. This was ridiculous. Luke was here for only another week or so. He didn't have any hold over Penny or control over who she spent her time with.

But he'd make damned sure who she would spend her time with tonight.

Penny was just about to give up on Luke coming over when she heard a knock on the door. The fluttering in her stomach made her want to not answer. He was getting to her, and that could be very bad.

Sex didn't equal love in her world. But Luke...Luke was an intensity she couldn't deny.

She crossed the room to the door and pulled it open. Their eyes met. No matter if it was the first time or the thousandth time, when Luke came near her she melted.

She moved out of the doorway to let him in, as if she had a choice. In her heart she knew that anytime Luke wanted her, she would let him in. Into her home. Into her body. Into her heart.

He moved past her into the living room.

"Who are you sleeping with?" Luke asked as he sat on her couch. His long legs spread out before him.

His question took her aback, but she wasn't intimidated by it. It didn't prevent the pain that gouged her heart at his question. She remembered how easy it was for him to believe the worst in her. Did he worry that she was sleeping with someone else now? Was he afraid she couldn't juggle the workload? She curled up in the corner of the couch next to, but not touching, him. She let him stew a few minutes before meeting his gaze.

"Honey, I'm not sleeping with anyone." It was the God's honest truth. They hadn't slept together. They had mind-blowing sex and then he left to go out to the farm so he could rise with the roosters.

"You know what I mean."

"Someone's a little testy this evening." She stretched back and put her legs across his lap.

He met her eyes and held them. Every bit as serious as he sounded. "Are you having sex?"

"With you? Not yet." She gave him a wink. What was he after? If she played this game long enough, he'd get to his point sooner or later or give up entirely and get to the good part of the evening.

"I'm serious."

"I know you are." Penny sighed and put her arms behind her head. "What do you want from me, Luke? An oath of fidelity? My declaration of love?"

His eyes narrowed, but then he took in a deep breath and pulled her by her legs toward him. She went willingly. When he had her straddling his lap, he took both her hands and placed them on his shoulders. "This isn't normal for me."

"This position or this situation?" She cocked a grin at him. Her core pulsed.

"I'm supposed to be working right now."

"I know and I wish you'd get on with it already." She ran her hands down his T-shirt, feeling the hard muscles twitch beneath it.

"Penny, stop."

"Killjoy."

"I want to have a conversation with you."

"Why?" Penny traced the bottom edge of his shirt with her fingernail. "Why do we have to talk at all? What is there to say that would make any difference?"

"How about 'I care about you'?"

She held her breath, waiting for the *but*.

"I want to know that you take care of yourself. It seems like we skipped some of the important conversations to have before having sex." Luke placed his hands on her hips lightly.

"What kind of conversations?" she asked suspiciously.

"How many people have you been with?"

Her heart hitched. This seemed like a huge trap. "I don't want to play this game."

She moved to get off him, but his hands held her tightly.

"Okay, no numbers," he said. He clearly wasn't happy about it, though.

She stopped trying to move off him. The real number probably wasn't as high as he imagined it was. She had no reason to be ashamed of the amount of men she'd been with, but this was Luke. Her first and her latest.

"Have you always been safe?" His eyes delved into hers.

"Is this the doctor asking?" she teased, trying to ease the tension growing inside her.

"No, it's the man who's having sex with you and plans on doing it again. I know we are using condoms, but have you always?"

"Yes, always." She met his gaze head-on. If he wanted to know the details, why the hell not? "You?"

He nodded and his fingers relaxed their grip of her hips. "Do you get tested?"

She nodded and raised her eyebrow at him as if to say, *Do you?*

"Of course." He shifted slightly beneath her. "When was the last time you had sex?"

"You should know. You were there. Was I that forgettable?" She fake pouted and then winked, not able to resist trying to lighten this conversation. Why was he suddenly being so serious?

He pulled her in tightly against him. He was solid everywhere and it made her want him more. "With someone else."

She threaded her fingers through his hair. "Well, Doctor, let's see…. It was before the wedding, before planning the wedding, before Maggie and Brady got back together…. Was it spring last year or winter? Damn, it's been a while. Good thing you're here."

Leaning into him, she placed a kiss on his lips. His arms wrapped around her, holding her, and he opened his mouth beneath hers. Pleasure raced down her spine as his tongue brushed against hers. It was as if he were rewarding her for her answer. If those were the types of rewards he was doling out, he could ask away. He pulled back and she whimpered. His satisfied smile made her want to key him up and then leave him hanging as he was doing to her. The most sensual torture.

"I'm not done asking questions," he said.

"What if I'm done answering questions?"

"Fine. Ask me a question, then."

She sat back and thought for a moment. "When was your last serious relationship?"

For a moment, hurt flashed in his eyes. Was he remembering them? His smile didn't reach his eyes. "I haven't had time for serious."

That one hurt. This great guy hadn't had anyone in his life. What was the point of breaking it off if he didn't find that special someone who would be the woman he needed? She asked, "Semi-serious?"

He shook his head. This crazy feeling started in her chest, like a boa constrictor releasing its prey. She shouldn't feel this way about Luke. It was dangerous to even consider anything past tonight. She'd just end up more ruined.

"You?" he asked.

"Not even kind of serious." She met his eyes and could see the relief in them, but there was still some reserve. Something he was holding back.

"Have you loved anyone?" he asked.

Since you? She couldn't make her voice work, so she shook her head.

"Me neither." He relaxed against the couch and pulled her hips forward. "Do you think we are broken?"

"How do you mean?"

"Like the reason we can't love someone is because of the stuff we went through as kids?" Luke leaned his head back and looked up at the ceiling. "I was a mess after Mom and Dad died."

"You weren't that bad," she said softly and cradled his face in her hand.

"I was a walking disaster. I almost had to repeat a year in high school because my grades were so low. I picked fights with anyone who looked at me the wrong way—"

"You were hurt. You were lashing out."

He'd been a wounded animal. She'd recognized him as a kindred spirit right away.

"You were, too." He brushed her hair off her cheek and cradled the back of her head. "We should have self-destructed. Instead we came together."

"You needed someone. I needed someone." She shrugged. "We made sense."

"What about now?" He pulled her in close but held back from kissing her. His breath was warm against her lips. Tantalizing, teasing. "Do we make sense now, Penny?"

Heaven help her. Her eyes fluttered closed, waiting for him to take her. "Didn't we self-destruct back then?"

"I want you." He brushed his lips across hers. "I can't get you out of my head. When I'm sitting alone, I wish you were there to talk to. When I'm working on the farm, I want you there beside me."

"So you can push me in the mud?" She tried to inch forward, but he held her back.

"Can't you be serious for one minute?" He tsked and leaned down to nip at her neck.

She released a low moan as he hit a spot that made her whole body quake with desire. "I want you, Luke. Any way you want me. Anytime. I want you now. I'll want you tomorrow and the next day. I crave your touch and covet your time."

He pulled back and rested his forehead against hers. Their eyes locked. "What's happening?"

"Do we have to pick it apart?" she whispered. The ache in her core was driving her insane. "Do we have to analyze this? Can't it just be what it is?"

"But what is it?" Luke brushed his thumb over her bottom lip. "Is this just a sex thing? Or is more going on?"

Her hands started to shake, and deep in her chest that boa wrapped tightly around her heart again. She wanted to scream that she was unlovable. That even if he thought he was in love with her, it wouldn't last.

"Are you willing to admit that we have more than sex between us?" Luke brushed his lips against hers again.

"Do you want me to admit that I need you? Because that's not going to happen. I don't need anyone. I have my house, my business, my dog—"

"I'm not asking you to need me, Penny." Luke lifted her to her feet and stood before her.

"Then what do you want?"

"A chance. A date. To get to know the woman you

are and not the girl I knew." He stroked his knuckles down the side of her face. "I don't know where any of this is going. Or what's going to happen in a week. But I know I want to spend time with you."

"So you want to hang out without having sex?" She looked up at him through her eyelashes.

"Yes."

She smiled and raised her eyebrow. "No sex?"

"I'm sorry, but sex is definitely on the table...or the floor, if you prefer." Luke grabbed her hips and pulled her close. "Or even a bed. You do own one, right?"

"Of course I have a bed."

He wiggled his eyebrows wickedly. "Point the way."

She put her hand to his chest to stop him. "My bedroom is off-limits."

Wrinkles formed on his forehead. "You do live alone, right?"

"Yes, I live alone. My rules." She didn't want to tell him that it was her personal space and that to invite someone in was too scary.

"I'll go out with you and have sex with you, but not in my bedroom."

Luke held her hand against his heart. "Someday you'll have to let someone in."

She smiled sadly. Not today. Never again.

"Can I offer you a drink?" She took his hand in hers and led him through the dining room. With her other hand, she started unbuttoning her blouse. "There's a lovely view out of the kitchen."

"I don't think the view could get much lovelier."

"Keep up lines like that and I might let you take me to dinner."

"I can keep it up all night if you like."

Chapter Eleven

"I can walk myself." Sam shoved Luke away for the third time.

Luke ran his hand through his hair. "I'm not trying to hold your hand, you ninny. The gravel drive isn't a stable surface and you have steps up the porch."

"That I've been climbing since I was one." Sam gave him a menacing look when Luke stepped closer. "I'll be fine, but *you* won't if you keep trying to touch me."

"Fine." Luke held his hands up. "Just don't take one step past the downstairs bedroom."

Sam made a rude gesture and continued to plod his way to the house.

The screen door opened and Penny came out. Her ginger hair shone in the sunlight. She wore a pink tank top and a pair of cutoff jeans with sandals. Even though the days were warming up, the nights were still cool.

"I just finished putting away the groceries," she said as Sam shuffled past without even a look.

Clearly, Luke had misread the few times either of them had brought up the other. Seeing that kiss had colored his view. They barely acknowledged each other even when they were in the same room.

"Thanks, Penny." Luke leaned over and kissed her before going into the house. His chest felt warm; being able to claim her in public put him in a great mood. Before he'd left to pick up Sam, they'd had breakfast at The Rooster Café in Tawnee Valley. She'd even held his hand across the table. It was ridiculous how good that made him feel when hours before he'd been in heaven in her arms.

"I'll get dinner ready, but then I need to go into town." Penny shut the screen door and moved to the stove.

"You aren't going to eat with us?" Luke set down Sam's hospital bag and came up behind Penny. He pulled her back against him while she lit the stove under a pot with water and potatoes in it.

"I have to get some work done and put Flicker out."

He bit down lightly on the place where her shoulder and neck met. "What about later?"

"Sam's here. You are going to have your hands full. I've got a big day tomorrow at the store." She turned in his arms to face him. Her smile didn't quite reach her eyes. "We can see each other the following day."

Sam's here. Did that have anything to do with her not wanting to be with him? God, he *was* clingy.

"That's fine." He returned to Sam's bag and lifted it. "I'm going to make sure Sam is settled in."

"Yup." She turned back to the potatoes.

Something was up, but after pushing her so hard last

night, he didn't know if pushing her today would be a good idea. Penny had always bottled her emotions. It'd been difficult for her to be honest about her feelings. He wanted to respect that, but at times it drove him crazy.

"Your room is all set up and you can easily get to the family room from here." Luke paused in the doorway. Sam sat on the bed, holding his side. His face was crumpled in pain.

"What happened?" Luke dropped the bag and moved forward. He automatically reached for Sam's pulse.

"I just got winded." Sam took a shaky breath in. "You don't think they gave me a bum heart valve, do you?"

His pulse was fine. A little higher than Luke would like, but not in a danger zone. "You need to lie down for a bit and rest."

Luke kneeled and undid Sam's sneakers.

"I'm not a baby." Sam coughed and groaned.

"No, but you just had surgery, so lay off." Tossing the sneakers to the side, Luke helped lift Sam's legs onto the bed. "You have water on your nightstand and also a bell."

"A bell?" Sam looked over as if Luke had said a snake was over there.

"To ring when you need something."

"I can take care of myself."

"No. You can't. When you ring the bell, I'll come help you. Trust me, it's only temporary. Don't get used to it." Luke stood and put the curtains down to block some of the sunlight. "Rest."

"Whatever." Sam punched the pillow. He laid back and closed his eyes.

Luke started out of the room.

"Luke?"

"Do you need something?"

Sam didn't open his eyes. "Thanks."

Luke didn't hide his shock. "You're welcome."

Sam grunted and rolled to face away from the door.

Luke stared at his back. How long had it been since he'd had a conversation with Sam that wasn't just a status update? How long since they'd been honest with each other? Luke had never brought up Sam's betrayal, but it had eaten away at what had been left of their relationship.

Shaking his head, Luke left the door open a crack before returning to the kitchen. Perfectly at home, Penny moved around the kitchen to make dinner for him and Sam.

"Are you sure you won't eat with us?"

Penny stopped midreach for the salt in the cupboard. Her mouth opened as if she was going to say something, but then she closed it as if she'd changed her mind. She shook her head instead and grabbed the salt.

"No salt for Sam." Luke leaned on the counter next to the stove.

"Oh, right." She set the salt on the counter and stirred the pot. "That's about as spicy as I get with cooking, I'm afraid."

Luke crossed to the cabinet and pulled down a few dried herbs, which had probably been in there since his mother died. "Try these."

"Thank you."

He wanted to say more. He wanted to talk about Sam, but she seemed so distant. Was she already starting to push him away? Why, after letting him closer last night? It was a vicious cycle with Penny. Even in high school, one day she'd be warm and caring. The next she'd be cold and distant. He'd thought it was the birth control she'd been on, but maybe it'd been more her than he'd wanted to believe.

"Are you going to stare at me while I cook? Aren't there chores or something to be done?" Penny glanced over and flashed him a wicked smile. "Don't make me get inventive with this wooden spoon."

His chest loosened and he held up his hands in surrender. "I don't know what you have in mind, but something tells me I wouldn't like it. I'll go see if the pigs could use some cuddling."

Penny hadn't exactly lied about having work to do this morning, but she could have stayed longer last night if she wanted to. The problem was every time she was near Sam she felt sick to her stomach. She may not be overly discriminating with whom she went out with these days, but back then...

She picked up the small tea sets and placed them on her cart. Once a month she did a full cleaning of the store. Everything came off the shelf. She cleaned each and every piece and did an inventory. It took her about a week to get through the entire store, but it made the store smell less like old stuff and more clean and fresh, with just a hint of old-stuff smell for atmosphere.

The door jangled as someone entered. She set down her rag and wiped her hands on the towel.

"Hello?" she called out as she walked to the front of the store.

"Hello?" returned a male voice that seemed familiar.

"Can I help you?" She stopped when she saw him. Jasper Ballard stood at her door. All six-foot, well-built, hunky goodness of him. Dark hair and brown eyes and a dimple on his right cheek.

"Hey, I was passing through town..." He smiled that

lopsided smile of his that had always gotten her motor revving. But not this time.

She shook herself out of her shocked stillness and headed for the cash register and the desk that would separate her from him. "How long are you in town?"

Her actions seemed to confuse him. She was usually overly friendly when he made his jaunts through Tawnee Valley. The local eligible male population was sadly lacking and most of them didn't hold a candle to Jasper. Jasper wasn't exactly a migrant worker, but he went from place to place looking for farming work. She rarely saw him in the winter, but when he was in town, he definitely liked to hook up. Normally she was all for it, but this time, it was complicated.

"For a few weeks. Looking for some easy money." He leaned his hands against her desk.

"Easy? Right. Because working on a farm is a piece of cake."

"For me it is." He flexed his arms, showing her their strength. If possible he'd developed more muscle since the last time he'd been in town. "Can I see you while I'm in town?"

"Uh…" Penny didn't want to burn this particular bridge. He was easy on the eyes and good in bed. But right now, she didn't want anyone but Luke. But Luke wouldn't be around forever, and eventually she'd have an itch.

The bell above the door saved her from having to come up with some excuse without blowing him off entirely.

Her eyes went to the door. Her heart froze in her chest. Luke.

His gaze took in Jasper's form and his casual stance.

Then those blue eyes flowed over her. He noticed every detail, making her want to squirm under his scrutiny.

"Penny." He closed the distance between them and the air around her grew heavy. Luke stuck out his hand to Jasper. "Luke Ward, and you are?"

"Jasper Ballard." Jasper's gaze flicked to hers for a moment before returning to Luke. "You part of the Ward farm?"

"Yeah, my brother owns it."

"I was heading out there this afternoon." Jasper stood with his feet apart and his arms crossed. "Sam usually has some odds and ends this time of year that he uses my help on."

"Sam's sick," Penny interjected, though neither man looked her way.

"I'd be willing to come out and help. My next job is in a week or so, but I work hard and don't mess around," Jasper said. "You can ask Sam about me if you want his approval. Here's my card."

Luke took the card and flipped it over in his hand. "I'll have to check with Sam about the finances, but we could use some more manpower."

"Great. I'll come out later this afternoon to see if we can make this work." Jasper winked at Penny. "I'll see you later, gorgeous."

Before she could get out a not-right-now-thank-you, Jasper was out the door, leaving her alone with Luke. She busied herself with the little knickknacks on the counter as if her life depended on getting them exactly in line.

"We going to talk about this?" Luke placed his hand over hers.

Her gaze bounced up to his and then back down. "Talk about what?"

Ignorance would save her. From what...she didn't know. She hadn't done anything wrong. She hadn't even encouraged Jasper. She just hadn't gotten the chance to say she was taken for now. And now she'd have to find Jasper to let him know that it wasn't going to happen this time.

Luke placed the card in her line of sight. "Is this why you were busy last night?"

"No." She met his gaze square on. "Of course not. I haven't seen him in over a year until this morning. Here in the shop, where we most definitely did not have sex."

"But he was the last guy you had sex with?"

"If it's any of your business, yeah. So what?" She pulled her hand back and crossed her arms.

"Do you even know him?"

"What does it matter?"

"It matters who you sleep with."

"For the last time, I didn't sleep with him. We had sex and it was good sex. There's nothing wrong with that."

"Is that all we are?" Luke flipped the card over and put it in the back pocket of his jeans. "Sex?"

"Why?" Penny threw her hands up. "What does it matter whether what I feel for you is more than sex? What is it going to change? You hate me for what I did. You know that I sleep around. That my standards are pretty low, except when it comes to you."

She felt as if she were ripping her heart open and spilling it all over the counter, but she didn't care. "We were fine apart. I got to do my thing and you got to do yours. You were only supposed to be here for the weekend."

"I'm here and I'm glad that I am." He came around

the counter and rested his hands on her shoulders. "We left some things unfinished, unsaid."

She braced herself, waiting for the anger and the accusations. Even though she felt strong on the outside, her heart felt like a brutalized piece of meat.

"I don't know where we go from here. I don't even know where here is." His hands squeezed her shoulders. "You promised me you'd try. I promise you I'll try to trust you."

Her eyes widened. She put her hands on his chest. "Trust?"

How could he say that after what she'd done to him? Kissing his own brother. Betraying every ounce of trust they had in their relationship. Making him feel like an idiot for ever believing her over all those guys.

"Yeah." His smile softened. "If you say you aren't having sex with that guy, I'll believe you. Just promise me if you decide to sleep—have sex with that guy or anyone else, you'll give me a heads-up. That way I can convince you not to."

He brushed his lips against hers, and that little fizzle of warmth spread throughout her chilled body. "Why?"

"Why would I convince you? Because you're hot and I'm horny."

She pushed on his chest. "You know what I mean."

"Because, Penny…" He kissed her and hugged her close.

Giving in to her desire, she rested her head against his chest and breathed in the freshness of him. His arms could make anything better. The day a little brighter. She wished she could stay here all the time and never let him go. "Because?"

"Because you make me feel alive. I like the way I feel

with you. I tried to forget how you made me feel by putting hundreds of miles between us. Let me be enough for you. For as long as this lasts…let me be enough."

Chapter Twelve

The next few days flew by in a haze. Penny kept busy at the store during the day and Luke showed up every night, though only for a short period before he went back out to be with Sam. Their time together wasn't just about sex anymore. They talked about everything. Her store. His medical career. The crappy stuff he had to do out at the farm. The crazy tourist with the yappy dog she'd insisted on bringing into Penny's shop.

What they didn't talk about was the past. Or their feelings. Which was fine with Penny.

Today was her day off, so she decided to drive out to the farm to check on Sam, as she promised Amber. She also planned to clean the house because the men likely hadn't had time to with everything that had to be done on the farm.

Jasper and Luke waved from the field as she passed by to turn down the driveway. Jasper hadn't shown up at her doorstep yet. Maybe Luke had told him that she was unavailable. Or maybe Jasper had noticed Luke's car in her driveway. Either way she was glad it was a nonissue.

She parked and grabbed the bags of groceries out of the back. As she walked into the kitchen, the screen door slammed behind her. Someone had tightened the spring again.

She set the bags on the counter and started to unload them. It hadn't taken her long to figure out the kitchen setup when she'd been out here with Luke and Amber.

"Oh, it's you." Sam stood in the doorway with his perma-scowl on.

"Sorry to disappoint." Penny didn't look up from unloading groceries.

Sam walked into the kitchen and sat on one of the wooden chairs.

"Shouldn't you be in a comfy chair or your bed?"

Sam rested his head on his hands. "Not you, too. How many reruns and episodes of *Judge Judy* do you people think I can take?"

Penny shrugged and grabbed the empty bags to store in the closet. When she turned back, Sam was looking at her expectantly, so she asked him, "Did you need something to eat?"

"Sure." Sam brushed his hand over his jaw. "I'd do it myself, but I'm too feeble apparently."

Penny shook her head and smiled. "Dr. Luke has you on lockdown?"

Sam nodded miserably.

"One grilled cheese sandwich coming up." She got out the bread, cheese and margarine and started heating up a skillet. She wasn't used to being alone with Sam.

His silence had always been somewhat off-putting to her; she liked to talk.

"Amber called me yesterday." Sam's voice shattered the silence.

"How's she doing?" Penny buttered the bread and unwrapped the cheese. Sam must be really bored if he was willing to talk to her.

"She's having the time of her life and trying not to sound like it."

Penny glanced back in time to catch Sam's smile. Weird.

He pulled out a farm magazine and flipped through the pages.

"I've talked to her every day, and she's always excited about all the rides. So…" Penny crossed her arms over her chest. "What's your secret?"

"What?" He stopped flipping and looked up at her.

"Before you came along, I was Amber's favorite person to hang out with. We'd order pizza, do our nails and watch romantic tween movies together." She waved the spatula at him. "Did you bribe her with chocolate? Or is it the dogs? Because I got her one of those, too."

Sam scratched his chin. "I don't know. I give her chores and she asks for more. Maybe it's because I don't treat her like a kid."

Penny narrowed her eyes. "Are you sure it isn't chocolate? Because I can totally hook her up with chocolate."

"She likes the animals." Sam shrugged.

"I'm not about to install a circus in my backyard." She turned and put his sandwich in the skillet.

"Guess you won't win, then."

She spun around, but he had his head buried in the magazine again. "I wouldn't taunt the woman making your meal, Sam Ward."

"It can't taste any worse than my cooking, no matter what you do to it."

Penny laughed and turned back to the stove. "Luke used to always try to eat at my place or we'd go out somewhere. He said he'd starve to death if he had to live on what you prepared."

"I haven't starved yet."

She finished his sandwich and put it on a plate. She grabbed a diet pop and some carrots from the fridge and placed it all in front of Sam.

"Thanks."

"No problem." Penny washed the pan and the spatula and put them in the drying rack. She scrubbed down the counters and the rest of the kitchen while Sam ate his lunch and read the magazines.

"How was the sandwich?" she asked as she took his empty plate.

"Pretty good." Sam glanced up at her. "But we already know I have the taste buds of a dog."

"True." Penny smiled.

The screen door creaked as it was pulled open. They both looked toward the door as Luke came in. He stopped and the door slammed shut behind him.

His mouth opened and closed. Penny realized how close she was standing to Sam's chair and stepped back. Jasper followed Luke in.

"Penny! Long time no see." Jasper winked, completely oblivious to the tension in the room. The door slammed behind him. "What's for lunch?"

"I think I'm going to go lie down." Sam rose from his chair and headed back toward his bedroom.

Penny went to the sink and washed the plate in the water she had left from doing the pan. She'd done nothing wrong, but her stomach rolled and pitched like a boat caught in a storm.

"Guess I'll get my own lunch. You want anything, Luke?" Jasper said.

"Nah, I'm good. I think I'll go wash up some."

She knew the moment he left the room. Some of the warmth left with him.

"So you and Luke, eh?" Jasper said as he sat at the table. "I guess that means I'll have to find another lovely companion to spend my time with in Tawnee Valley."

She set the dish in the drying rack and faced Jasper. "I'm sure you'll have no trouble securing a 'companion.'"

"I don't know about that." He took a drink from his pop can. "Most of the women are looking for someone to marry them so they can pop out a few brats. Or someone to take care of the brats they already have."

"That sounds pretty bitter." She leaned against the counter and crossed her arms. "Harboring some resentment there?"

"Hardly. I just know the lay of the land. The young ones are looking for a way to get out of town. The older ones are looking for someone to hold on to." Jasper smiled. "You are definitely one of a kind."

"How so?"

"You don't want anything from guys except sex. No strings. No attachment. No having to fake I care. You get yours and I get mine and we go on our separate ways."

The way he described it, sex with her was a transaction. She'd never put much thought into it. It was a basic need like eating and sleeping. Lots of people attached significance to the act that she just didn't.

Luke walked in and she met his gaze.

Except with Luke. It was more than sex with him. Her breath caught in her throat and her knees felt as if they were going to give out from underneath her. She'd tried to keep that distance she needed, but somehow she'd fallen for him.

She loved him. It hit her like a punch to the gut. Her heart had always belonged to him, but part of her had always held itself apart. The part that knew no matter how hard she tried to stay with him, it wouldn't last. Love? She fought against the realization…and the need to breathe.

He was going to leave soon and she wouldn't be able to do anything about it. Her heart collapsed in her chest.

"Are you okay?" Concern filled Luke's blue eyes as he crossed the kitchen. He rubbed her arms.

Her head felt light and darkness surrounded her.

"Penny. Breathe."

She gasped in air.

The world spun as Luke swept her up in his arms. She linked her hands behind his head, more by instinct than by conscious thought.

"Keep breathing," he said quietly as he carried her up the stairs and into his bedroom. He kicked the door shut behind him and laid her on the bed. Sitting next to her, he brushed his hand over her forehead and her hair. "Tell me what's wrong."

I love you—that's what's wrong. Heat rushed to her cheeks. "I just got faint, is all."

"Has this happened before?" He took her wrist in his hand and watched his watch as he took her pulse.

"No." Only once. Even though she'd done it intentionally…. When she'd realized what she'd done with Sam. When she realized that everything she'd wanted was never to be hers. Because the only thing she had ever really wanted was Luke.

She'd never questioned her decision. It had been for the best. They couldn't possibly last because love didn't last. At least not for her. At some point everyone she loved went away.

Taking deep breaths, she tried to slow down her racing heart. "I'm feeling better now."

When she tried to sit, Luke gently pushed her shoulder back to the bed. "I shouldn't come over every night. You have work. You need rest."

She shook her head. She'd never needed much sleep, and having Luke was worth needing to down an extra cup of coffee in the morning. "I get plenty of sleep."

"Maybe we should cool it for a night."

She grabbed his hand. She didn't want to miss a single day with him. All too soon he'd be gone and she'd be alone. He might not have moved on yet, but he would. Luke was built for happily ever after. Just not with her.

"Luke, we don't need to cool it. I'm getting enough sleep. It was probably just the heat in the kitchen." She grasped at straws.

He brushed the hair off her forehead and smiled. "It's okay. Tonight you get some sleep and tomorrow night we'll go out on a real date. With dinner and a movie and all that crap."

She relaxed into the bed and grabbed his hand. Tracing his fingers with her fingertip, she said, "That sounds great, but you should still come over tonight."

Time alone was something she didn't need. She would have plenty of time alone after he left. She wanted the oblivion making love with him gave her. She needed it.

He leaned down and kissed her. Slow and steady. It

wasn't earth-shattering, but it was everything to her. It was the pleasure she would remember when winter came and she had to cuddle with the dog to keep warm.

Luke lifted his head. "Maybe if you are good, I'll try to make it by."

She gave a dramatic sigh and held her arm over her eyes. "Then I'm doomed because I'm never good."

"You're always good to me, Penny."

She peeked out from behind her arm. "You're the good one."

He stood and pulled her up gently, checking her eyes closely while he pulled her to sitting and then to standing. She squinted back at him.

"I'm fine, Luke." Just terminally in love.

Chapter Thirteen

Penny pulled the blanket around herself, and Flicker snuggled closer to her. The television volume was low enough that she would hear Luke's knock on her door. When she'd left the farm earlier, he'd given her a scorching kiss that felt more like a promise than a good-night kiss.

Fortunately, *My Best Friend's Wedding* was on cable to keep her occupied while she waited. Sleep was the last thing on her mind. She had to deal with the fact that she was in love with Luke, but she had pushed him away long ago by kissing Sam. Seeing that had been brutal enough to keep Luke away for years.

It hadn't hurt only Luke, though. He'd left her without asking for an explanation. Just assumed the worst and left, as she'd known he would. Luke had never been the jealous type. At least not when they were teenagers.

He had been so confident in their love. And he had

every reason to be. She had loved him with everything she had. But the thought of trying to make it in the real world—outside of the bubble of Tawnee Valley—had brought back memories of her mother.

She glanced at the time. If he didn't show up in the next thirty minutes, she would text him. She'd make up some excuse, like she was feeling faint and needed a doctor. He would show up and take her in his arms and make her feel alive.

But for how long? Could she really let him go again? Even if it would be better for both of them? He had his job at the hospital and she had her store. Three hundred miles apart. This was the one time that their lives had intersected in almost nine years. That definitely didn't boost her confidence that this could actually work.

She tried to concentrate on the story line of the movie. The future would come quickly enough without her worrying over it.

Just as she was dozing off, there was a knock at the door. Flicker lifted his head and then lay back down.

"My ferocious guard dog." Penny shook her head as she walked to the front door. Maybe she should make Luke a key. That way even if she did fall asleep he could come in and wake her up. That put a smile on her face.

"I was beginning to think you wouldn't show up." She yanked open the door and her heart plummeted. Instead of Luke on her porch, a woman about her height stood in the shadows.

Apprehension filled her as Penny flicked on the porch light. A ghost would have made more sense than what she was seeing.

"Hi, baby," Cheryl Montgomery said. Her auburn hair was streaked with silver. Her familiar brown eyes were so light they were almost tan. Her build was similar to Penny's, but her clothes were loose around her small frame. Even though it had been over fifteen years since Penny had last seen her, she would always recognize her mother.

That didn't mean that she could handle it. Her brain went completely blank trying to process this unexpected arrival. She couldn't think, let alone speak. Her chest burned as if she'd run for miles without stopping. Her hands were cold and clammy.

"Are you going to invite me in?" Cheryl looked around Penny into the house and smiled hesitantly. "From what I see you've changed some things since Mom died."

"You didn't come to the funeral." It was her voice, but Penny hadn't realized she'd said anything. She'd had seventeen years to come up with something to say when her mother finally showed up, but she'd never believed it would actually happen.

Cheryl looked down at her feet before lifting her gaze to Penny. "Do we have to talk about this on the porch? It's kind of chilly."

She didn't want her mother in this house. It was hers now. Anything she'd had as a child, her mother had destroyed, whether she'd sold it so she could buy more liquor or she'd broken it during one of her alcohol-induced rampages. Penny had never had anything until her grandma took her in. The few treasures her grandma had given her were on the dresser in her bedroom.

"I swear I'm sober." Cheryl held up a coin. "One year."

Penny wanted to scream and slam the door in Cheryl's face. Instead she stepped aside and let her in. Blood thundered in her ears as she followed her mother into her living room.

"This is so much better than my mother's decorations. She never did like much color." Cheryl moved to the wall of photos. "Is this your daughter?"

"No, I don't have any children." Penny stood next to the door frame with her arms crossed in front of her.

"That's a shame. She's a pretty girl. I'd love to be a grandma."

Don't hold your breath on that one, Mom. Cheryl would likely be the worst grandma in the world. She had definitely never received a Number One Mom mug from Penny.

Cheryl sat in the recliner and looked at Penny expectantly.

There was no way Penny was going to sit down and talk as if nothing had happened with the woman who had abandoned her. As if this was some kind of happy reunion between mother and daughter. As if she hadn't waited for her for seventeen years. "Why weren't you at Grandma's funeral?"

Cheryl sighed and clasped her hands in her lap. "I got into some trouble and had to go into rehab."

"The funeral was four years ago. You just said you've only been sober a year." It was hard to keep the accusation out of her voice. Penny didn't want her mother to matter to her. She didn't want anything to do with Cheryl at all.

"I relapsed, but I went into the program myself afterward."

"Who'd you end up in bed with?" Penny tried to keep the venom from her voice.

Cheryl lowered her eyes and took a deep breath. "You have every right to be mad at me, Penny—"

"Really? For what, *Cheryl?* Making me clean up your vomit after you'd partied all night? Or how about

how I'd have to skip school to take care of you when
you were hungover? Or how about the sleazy men you
brought into my life? Thank God you had the decency to
give me a bolt on my bedroom door. The handle rattled
enough to make me fear going to the bathroom at night
because you'd be too passed out to actually help me."

"I wasn't a good mom. I wasn't a good anything."
Cheryl lifted her gaze to Penny. "I want to make this
right. I want to start fresh. I want to be a family."

Penny recoiled as if her mother had asked her to join
a cult that worshiped goats and sacrificed bunnies for
fun. "What about what I wanted, Cheryl?"

She'd begged her mother not to leave her behind.
When they'd lived together, she'd reached out for help
for her mother's addiction and every now and then,
Cheryl would clean up and they'd be happy. Until
Cheryl let another man into her life, and it wasn't long
after that the drinking would begin again. Even though
Penny had hated cleaning up her mother's mess, she
hadn't wanted to leave her. And she'd never thought
that Cheryl would leave her behind.

*I love you, Penny. We'll be together soon. I just need
to fix myself right now.* The words had echoed in her
head for years while she waited for her mother to come
get her and for them to be a family again.

"I..." Cheryl looked confused. She flipped the coin
over in her hand and closed her eyes. Taking a deep
breath, she raised her gaze to Penny. "I can't take back
the past. All I can do is apologize and try to make you
believe that I never wanted to leave you."

Penny's lips tightened to a thin line. That was the one
thing she would never believe. She stared at Cheryl and
wondered what lies would come out of her mouth next.

Cheryl frowned and put the coin in her pocket. "I

don't know what else I can say. I'm late, but Alan says better late than never. So here I am."

"Alan," Penny spit out the name. "Is that the most recent in your train wreck of boyfriends?"

She shook her head. "He's my sponsor. He's been sober for fifteen years. He's happily remarried with kids."

"Good for him." Everything inside Penny wanted to explode. This wasn't happening. It was some sort of sick joke. Why was *she* here after everything? Where had *she* been when Penny had needed her?

They stared at each other, and Cheryl's eyes pleaded with her to understand. To forgive. But that wasn't in Penny. She couldn't just forget. Not when it had cost her everything.

The knock on the door broke their gazes. Penny took a deep breath and released it as she turned to go answer the door.

"Hey, I brought you—" Luke looked up from the bag he held. "What's wrong?"

She could feel the sob pressing on her throat. She wanted to hug him and let go of everything, but she didn't. Luke would save her because that's what he did.

"My mom is here." The words came out flat. She couldn't put any emotion behind them or she wouldn't make it through the next few minutes. *Just hold it together for a few more minutes.* That's all she needed.

Luke closed her door and set the bag down on the table. Then he took her hand in his. It was all things good and warm. She drew strength from him. He would be here for her and that meant the world to her.

She led him back to the living room. Cheryl looked expectantly at Penny and then over to Luke.

"Hello, Ms. Montgomery. I'm Luke Ward." He didn't

release Penny's hand to offer to shake Cheryl's. He stood with her as a united front.

Penny wanted to lean into him, let him take care of this situation, but she hadn't grown into a wet mop at the sight of her mother. She wasn't going to start acting like one now because Luke was here.

"It's nice to meet you, Luke." Cheryl stood. "I didn't realize Penny was expecting company."

Penny couldn't think of anything to say. She wanted her mother to leave, but that part of her that had taken care of her mother reared up. "Do you have some place to go?"

For a moment, she thought her mother was going to ask to stay with her. Luke squeezed her hand and she realized she had him in a death grip and loosened it slightly.

"I've got a room in Owen. I didn't want to assume that you would forgive me right away." She laughed awkwardly. "I hoped, but…"

Penny's heart felt as if it had been through a blender today. She shook her head as the tears pressed against the back of her eyes.

"I didn't think so." Cheryl took in a deep breath and held her head up. "I hope that you'll let me come and see you."

Penny didn't say anything but stepped out of the way so that Cheryl could leave.

Cheryl sighed and walked to the door. Once there, she stopped and turned back. "I know you don't believe me, but I love you, Penny."

Penny had never doubted that. She just wasn't enough for her mother.

"Good night, Luke."

"Good night, Ms. Montgomery."

"You can call me Cheryl." She smiled wearily. "Penny does."

With that she was gone. As soon as the door closed, Penny collapsed against Luke.

Chapter Fourteen

It had to be a cosmic joke. Penny could take only so much. Luke folded her in his arms against his chest, and she allowed the first choking sob to escape.

Her whole world had just been shaken. The pain she'd felt when her mother had left her resurfaced. How many nights had she cried herself to sleep in her bedroom? How many times had she sworn her mother would come tomorrow? How many nights had she re-packed her suitcase?

Until one day she just knew. Her mother would never come back for her. Just as her father had never wanted her. What had made her believe her mother was any different than him? Just because she was the one who got stuck with Penny? Sure, she'd said she loved Penny. But love was a deception.

"Do you want to go sit down?" Luke ran his hands over her back and brushed her hair away from her face.

"Why are you so good to me?" Penny looked up at him through the tears gathering in her eyes.

He smiled softly and kissed her forehead. "Because someone has to be good to you. It might as well be me."

Penny backed away out of his arms. She needed to give him something. Something important to her. Taking his hand, she pulled him behind her up the stairs and down the hallway. At the door to her bedroom, she stopped and turned to face him.

"This doesn't mean anything." She said the words but knew they weren't true. This was the one rule she'd held close all these years. If no one came into her bedroom, she'd be safe. She wouldn't have memories, except of herself, attached to the one place in her world that was hers. If she let Luke in, every time she entered her bedroom she'd think of him in it. Somehow forever seemed bearable when it came to Luke.

She searched his eyes for a long minute. It wouldn't matter if she looked into them for hours; she wouldn't know how to find what she was looking for, because she didn't know what it looked like. At least not as other people did. Love.

Pushing the door open behind her, she pulled him into her bedroom. As he closed the door, her heart shuddered. This was as close as she might ever come to telling Luke she loved him. The words weren't possible. Not when this all would end. She couldn't reopen that wound, but she could show him how she felt.

Her room wasn't much. Bed, dresser, lamp, nightstand. But her treasures sat arranged on a white doily on her dresser. Everything in here was hers and hers alone. No one could take them from her.

She dropped his hand and walked to her queen-size bed. Sitting down with her back against the headrest, she propped up a few pillows beside her and patted the bed. Not saying a word, Luke kicked off his shoes and joined her. Side by side.

Deep breaths. She took his hand in hers, leaned against his shoulder and let out a long sigh.

"You want to talk about it?" Luke rubbed his thumb across her knuckles.

Penny shook her head. "You don't want to hear about it."

"Don't hide yourself from me, Penny." Luke tipped her chin up and gazed into her eyes. "I care about you, and I know that had to have been painful."

She wanted to deny it. To press her body against his and take his mouth with hers until they both forgot about Cheryl's visit. But she couldn't. Her mother's visit had unlocked a dam that had been ready to burst for years.

"She left me when I was ten."

Years ago, she'd told Luke some of the story, but she wanted to get it all out now. As he listened, he held her hand in his and kept rubbing his thumb across her knuckles. His touch gave her comfort and courage.

"Sometimes it was good. It would be me and her against the world. She was fun and a little crazy. We moved a lot. Wherever she could find work. When she first started a job, we'd have a little extra money. She'd buy me gifts and ice cream. I'd go to school like a normal kid."

She closed her eyes as she rested against his shoulder. Remembering the good times was almost more painful than remembering the bad. Without the good, she would have never known that the other times were that bad.

"We'd spend the weekends like a normal family. I'd join the basketball team at school. Then mom would find a guy. She never really stopped drinking, just drank less during the good times. Things would start to get rough and she'd start drinking more. He'd get sick of her and she'd find herself at the bottom of a bottle."

"That couldn't have been easy for you." Luke put his arm around her and took her hand with his other.

"She'd start getting sick. I'd have to clean up after her just so I could use the bathroom. I'd miss school to stay home to take care of her and make sure she ate and was hydrated. She'd always go right back to the bottle, though, and bring home any guy who would have her."

A shudder ran through her. "I'd lock myself in my room those nights. But I'd always be there in the morning to help her. I thought that's what love was. Always being there. No matter what."

She shook her head. "She'd lose her job and then she'd start selling things to get more alcohol. Everything she'd bought me would be gone within a few days. I'd use any spare money I could find to get us food. Sometimes we only had ramen noodles all week. I cooked. I cleaned. When I was exhausted, I'd reach out for help."

"You were brave."

"Not brave. Scared." She struggled to form the next part into words. "It wasn't that I couldn't take care of her anymore. It was that I couldn't control her anymore. When we had no money left to buy food, I worried that she'd have to start selling herself to maintain her addiction. When she drank heavily, she wasn't my mom anymore. She didn't care about me. When she'd sober up, she'd apologize. She'd swear she wouldn't drink anymore. She'd go out to find a job and then come home drunk."

She swiped at the tear that had escaped down her cheek. "But I could handle it. I knew she loved me and I was there for her. It was us against everything. I looked into rehab, but every place wanted her to stay for a long time to get clean. How was I supposed to survive without my mom? They would have thrown me into foster care."

"What about your grandma?"

Penny scoffed. "Grandma threw out Mom when she found out she was pregnant. You remember how strict Grandma had been with me?"

She felt his nod against her head.

"She was that way because Mom had run wild. Not that I didn't, but Mom had started drinking at fourteen. Grandma had told Mom never to come to her for anything. She'd broken the rules and that was that. Grandma didn't care what Mom had to do to survive.

"So we had no one but each other. For years we made it work. I don't know what changed. I thought about it for a long time. Had she gotten sick of me? Had I done something wrong? I was always helpful. I might have talked back a few times, but that wasn't anything new."

Penny struggled to sit up straight and put a little distance between her and Luke, but she didn't let go of his hand. "When she brought me to my grandma, I begged her not to leave me. What would she do without me to take care of her? How would she remember to eat?"

Luke squeezed her hand. "Maybe she just wanted you to have someone to look out for you for a change."

"By leaving me with Grandma? By taking away everything I'd ever known?" Penny blinked away the tears. "She was supposed to come back. She promised. She said—"

Tears choked her and she couldn't hold them back anymore. Luke pulled her toward him and she fell against his chest, soaking his blue T-shirt with her tears. He gently stroked her hair and made soothing noises.

For seventeen years she'd held it inside. Pushed it down deep so that it wouldn't consume her. Forced everyone in her life away. Grandma had been easy. She had always kept Penny at arm's length. Penny had been just another thing she had to take care of, not a grandchild to be loved and cherished. It had probably been better that way. Penny would have pushed back hard if her grandma had wanted any sort of real relationship with her.

"She left me with my grandma. All alone. Maggie and I got to be friends, but for years I could never really make it real because I thought that someday Mom would come back for me. And we'd leave Tawnee Valley and start our lives together. But she never came...."

His warmth penetrated the coldness that had engulfed her when she'd seen her mother. But she still shook as the tears streamed down her cheeks.

"How could she leave me if she loved me?"

Chapter Fifteen

Luke held Penny as she released what had to be years of pent-up emotion. As the sobs diminished, he could feel her body relaxing against his, until her breath became even and slow. He grabbed a tissue from the nightstand and patted her face dry as she slept.

Everyone knew that Cheryl Montgomery had dropped her daughter at her mother's and run off. A few people remembered she'd had issues with alcohol in high school. Before Penny had been at school a month, most of their classmates had labeled her a lost cause. Probably because their parents didn't want a bad influence around them. But Penny hadn't been bad. Not at first.

After a while she seemed to become whatever they thought she should become. He wished he'd been strong enough to turn the tide. To make his classmates and the people they grew up with forget their prejudice. But he hadn't.

Of course, at the time he had a mom and dad who loved their children and who would do anything for them.

Luke slipped his cell phone out of his jeans. He texted Jasper that he'd be back later than he'd planned and asked him to look in on Sam. Jasper texted back, No problem. Luke set the phone on the nightstand and settled down further on the bed, keeping Penny close.

She was the puzzle he could spend the rest of his life solving. Even Jasper made sense once Luke got over his initial jealousy. It still bugged him that Penny had used Jasper to scratch an itch, but part of him was glad it had been Jasper, a loner without an attachment to anywhere or anyone. He would never have tried to settle down and be the man that Penny needed in her life.

Maybe *needed* wasn't the right term. Luke stroked her hair. Because any man who loved Penny would have to love her unconditionally and forgive her, knowing that something truly wild would never be true to one person.

Perhaps he should turn in his man card because of all the gushy stuff going through his mind. The thing was, as much as he wanted to be that man for Penny, he wasn't sure he could forgive her for Sam. Anyone else, yes…but Sam?

"Don't you need to go home?" Penny's voice was sleepy. She didn't even open her eyes, just stayed where she was across his chest.

"I'm good here." Because home had always been with Penny. Over the years, he'd thought of her and what she would say about what he was doing. She wasn't his moral compass—she'd always had a skewed perspective for whatever she wanted. But sometimes being a little selfish instead of selfless was just what the doctor ordered.

And right now, he wanted to be in this bed with this woman. Until she kicked him out. He closed his eyes and focused on the rhythm of her breathing.

Her eyes felt like grit paper when Penny tried to open them. They felt swollen and her chest still ached slightly. Even opening her eyes didn't help much; the room was dark. Her alarm clock read 4:24 a.m.

Luke's warm body was the only thing keeping the chill of the room from making her shiver and dive under the covers. She pressed in closer and breathed him in.

"You keep doing that and I won't be responsible for my actions." Luke's voice was low and rough.

"Thank you for listening to me," she whispered. With the darkness surrounding them, it felt safe to admit she'd needed him.

"Thank you for letting me in." He hugged her to him.

She slid off him and onto the mattress. He turned on his side to face her. Just enough light from the streetlights peeked through the curtain to let her make out his features. Her heart swelled in her chest. She wanted to tell him everything, from how stupid she had been to push him away to how much she was falling for him again.

Instead she leaned in and kissed him. Gently, exploring with just a hint of the raw passion that normally devoured them. He followed her lead, seeming to know that this time wasn't so much about fulfilling a desire but exploring the connection they shared.

His hand settled on her waist and sent intense waves of longing through her. Longing to stay in his arms forever. To be one with him. Things she'd never have, but tonight she'd cling to them and let herself dream of a future where they could be together.

"You're shaking," Luke said as he trailed kisses from her mouth to her throat. "We should get you under the covers."

"I'm not cold." Her eyes fluttered shut as his hand trailed across her belly.

"Good." He plucked the bottom button of her shirt undone.

Her breath caught and he flicked another button open. When she opened her eyes, he was watching her face. Another button and his knuckles brushed against her bare skin. Her stomach tightened and a burst of heat sparked through her system.

She reached up and ran her hand along his scruffy jaw. His cheek twitched under her fingertips. One more button loosened. She ran her fingers through his hair and brought his mouth down to hers. Kissing Luke was like Christmas and her birthday rolled into one. Excitement, anticipation, joy.

His fingertips grazed the underside of her breast and she gasped. Even though they had been more intimate previously, tonight felt like the start of something new. Or maybe it was the end of everything they had. She brushed off the dark thought and let herself be in this moment, no matter the consequence.

Her heart was already his. It always had been. It always would be. But it wasn't just her heart she was giving to him. As he undid the remaining buttons and opened her shirt, he gazed down at her silhouette. His fingers were rough from helping out at the farm as they trailed down over her white lace bra and across her stomach down to the waistband of her dark slacks.

Normally she'd be helping him remove her clothes

and his, but something about the quiet house, her bedroom and the darkness, this man, made her want to take things slowly. Luke kissed along the lace edge of her bra, making her nipples harden and beg for his touch.

He lifted his head and kissed her mouth as his hand traced along the band of her bra, then unhooked it in the back.

"I've never met anyone who ties me up in knots the way you do," he said before pushing her shirt off her shoulders. He nipped at every inch of her skin he exposed until her breath and pulse pounded.

She wanted to come back with something to take away the seriousness. But when he pulled off her shirt and slowly eased off her bra, her mouth went dry. His lips closed around her nipple. Any thought she might have had was gone in the flash fire of desire that seared through her.

Helpless to the heat flooding her, she held on to him as he took his time to explore one breast and then the other. If she bound him in ropes, he held her in chains. Surely ropes would break, whereas her chains would hold her to him forever.

Love wasn't a blessing to Penny. It was a curse that bound her to a mother who easily cast her off when she became too much of a burden and to a man who had been easily dissuaded from his pursuit. It didn't stop her from loving him or wanting to be loved by him.

When his mouth found hers again, she wished she could be more aloof and brush him off. But she couldn't. Luke had been her rock and stability in high school. They'd turned each other away from self-destruction.

His touch had always wiped away the bad. She hadn't been looking for a relationship the night at the dance when she'd approached him. With her reputation and his, she thought maybe they could raise a little hell. Instead they'd made each other better. Sure they'd done some crazy things, but he'd stopped picking fights and getting in trouble at school and she'd stopped trying to become her mother with booze and guys.

"Luke?" she said when he lifted his head.

He brushed the hair away from her face and brushed his thumb across her bottom lip. "Yeah?"

Tears pressed against her eyes. "Do you think I'm a bad person?"

"Never in a million years." He rested his head against his hand and looked down at her. "How can you think you're bad? You helped your best friend through her mother's death and helped her with her child. You took care of your mother when she needed you most. You helped your grandma and improved on her dream after she passed."

A tear slid free.

"But most of all you turned around a screwed-up teenager. Showed him what it was to be loved and how to fix his life instead of wreck it. You might want people to stay away and think that you are bad, but you are incredible." His hand reached down to her slacks and slowly undid the button and zipper.

"I never deserved you," she whispered. Her fingers played with the ends of his hair, caressing the softness.

He smiled and finished undressing her. His gaze followed her body from head to toe. The attention made her want to stretch like a cat and let him pet her until she purred.

He stood to take off his clothes. She tried to fill her head with memories for when he was gone. Tried to imagine what her life would be like once he was back in St. Louis. She couldn't begin to picture it without feeling her gut roll in protest.

Instead she held out her arms to him and drew him down to the bed. Sex would never be the same with anyone else. Just the feel of his skin against hers made her shiver with need. His kiss could steal her breath and bring her life. His hands kindled fire inside her everywhere they touched. His mouth on her skin made her melt.

No one had ever had the ability to make her burn with desire the way Luke did. She couldn't deny that what they were doing was making love. It was too intense, too emotional to be sex. He made her his and she couldn't resist.

When he entered her, she was so beyond herself that she raked her nails over his shoulders, trying to draw him closer.

He brushed her lips with his and whispered next to her ear, "Let go, Penny. Just let us be."

He moved slowly in her, building the already-raging fire into a blaze until he started to lose control and his breathing grew more ragged and his motions more intentional. Their bodies moved together, striving for release.

The edge was so near. Penny opened her eyes. Luke's face was twisted in pleasurable agony. She never wanted this to end, but she couldn't hold back any longer. Her release pulsed through her and it pushed him over.

I love you so much and you'll never know. The words rang through her mind as she slipped back into sleep.

Chapter Sixteen

Luke tried to concentrate on moving the bales of hay in the barn, but it didn't actually require brainpower, so his mind kept drifting back to Penny. How desperately she'd clung to his hand when introducing him to her mother. How vulnerable she'd been when she'd led him back to her room. How sensual she'd been lying beneath him.

"Watch out."

A bale of hay came flying down to land beside Luke. He looked up at Jasper in the rafter.

"What the hell?" Luke grabbed the bale by the strings and stacked it with the others. "You're lucky that didn't bust my head open."

"At least Penny would be available." Jasper smiled.

Luke grunted in response. The fact that Jasper still had a job out here meant Luke knew the man was teasing, but it didn't help that when he went back to

St. Louis in a few days Penny would be free to resume all her extracurricular activities.

He had no hold over Penny. She was as free as when he'd first seen her at the wedding. When he left, he would have no right to expect her to wait for him. When he left...

"Hey, I don't mind babysitting your brother so you can get some, but could you keep working so I can get out of here and hit the bars? Since you took the only hottie in town, I'm going to have to go trolling." Jasper swung down from the loft and landed a few feet from Luke.

This wasn't the first time Luke had the urge to knock the guy's smile in. Sam had insisted that Jasper would be an asset. But he'd also been an asset to Penny, which rubbed Luke the wrong way. If Penny had feelings for this guy, though, she would have said something. Wouldn't she have?

"Don't worry. You'll have plenty of time to get to the bar." Luke wiped the sweat from his forehead with a rag.

Besides, it hadn't been Jasper at her door last night and there for her when she needed someone to hold on to. She'd made a big fuss over never having anyone in her bed and never "sleeping" with anyone. Last night he'd been privy to both.

That had to count for something.

Luke climbed out of the barn and took off his work gloves. The sun was almost to midday. His skin itched from the hay and dust that clung to his sweat. He'd give his left nut for a shower, but that meant dealing with Sam.

He squinted up at the sun. It was starting to get too hot to do much, but staying outside seemed like the best defense against Sam, who couldn't seem to accept the fact that he needed to sit down and relax.

Even the dogs were napping in the shade. A drop of sweat rolled down his spine. It couldn't be helped. Luke needed a shower and everything else would have to wait until it got cooler.

"I'm heading to the house," Luke shouted back to Jasper.

"I'll take lunch after I finish this."

Taking a deep breath, Luke headed to the porch. The door creaked open and banged shut behind him. He swore.

Yesterday, Luke had readjusted the tension on the door so that it wouldn't bang shut anymore. Apparently Sam was using it as a way to know when someone was in the house and had reset it when Luke wasn't looking. Luke didn't know whether to be mad that Sam had adjusted the door or mad that he'd obviously not been sitting while he did it.

"Hey." Sam appeared in the doorway as Luke took off his shoes.

"Go lie down." Luke hung up the hat he'd been wearing. It hadn't helped to keep the hay from making his head itch.

"You guys got the bales out of the rafters?"

"Yeah." Luke had dusted off what he could outside, but hay clung stubbornly to his jeans. His dad would have dumped his jeans at the door; otherwise Mom would have yelled at him. The memory of his parents brought a bittersweet smile to his face.

"It's time to change the oil in the tractor," Sam said.

"I know." Luke glared at Sam. "You told me this morning and yesterday evening and yesterday morning."

"If it doesn't get done, you won't be able to get to the fields this afternoon." Sam's mouth was set in a stubborn line.

"I don't need to be micromanaged, Sam. I've got it covered." Luke brushed past Sam into the dining room. "Right now I need to get the hay off my skin. Unless you want to tell me how to do that, too."

"I'm sure you can handle that." Sam shuffled toward the living room.

Luke bit back anything he might have said. Sam was just trying to control a situation he felt was out of his control. It was one of the reasons he and Sam had butted heads as teenagers. It hadn't made sense to him that Sam had the right to give him punishments, but no one had been punishing Sam when he screwed up.

Sam had always been his father's favorite and got most of his attention. First Sam, then Brady, then Luke. Luke had been their mother's favorite, though. She'd always sneak him an extra cookie...for him to grow on.

He blinked back tears as he went into the bathroom. Penny's relationship with her mother was complicated—to put it mildly. But if Luke could see his mother one more time...he'd do whatever it would take.

He stripped and showered quickly before changing into fresh jeans and a T-shirt. It had been a while since he'd done so much manual labor, and sitting on his bed even long enough to pull socks on made him want to shut his eyes for a little while.

Maybe sleep would help him figure out what to do about Penny and Sam. She couldn't be trusted before. Had she really changed any? Sam hadn't changed. He was just as controlling. Just as stubborn.

Just a few minutes of sleep...

* * *

The bell above the door startled Penny into almost dropping the glass perfume bottle. Her head whipped around to see who had come in.

"Don't worry, dear. It's just me."

Penny didn't think she'd ever be relieved to see Bitsy Clemons coming through the door, but she was grateful it wasn't Cheryl, who was somewhere out there, lurking, and wanted a relationship with her. That had her on edge. That and Luke…. God, she'd been stupid last night. Wanting to cling to him as if he could ever love her again after what she did to him. She wouldn't blame him for never trusting her. But she'd wanted to believe for a few seconds that he could love her. Even if nothing came of it.

"I heard that your mother is staying in Owen." Bitsy's voice had a hint of a question at the end.

Penny decided to take it as a comment and not a question. She didn't want to acknowledge her mother's presence. She didn't want any part of the woman.

Bitsy rounded the corner and picked up a trinket off the shelf. "You wouldn't know anything about that, would you?"

Penny took in a deep breath and released it. "Yes. She came by the house last night."

Bitsy tsked and placed her hand on Penny's arm. "How are you holding up, dear?"

"I'm fine." Penny walked farther down the aisle.

"It's okay if you don't like the woman. After all, she all but left you with your grandmother—God rest her soul. You know we'll stand behind you. No matter what your decision regarding your mother."

Penny turned and looked into the serene face of Bitsy Clemons. "What do you mean?"

Bitsy smiled slightly, as if she had a secret to pass on. "Well, you didn't hear it from me, but word is Cheryl is looking at a few houses today in Tawnee Valley. Not to buy, of course, but to rent. A full-year lease."

Penny's heart clattered to a stop. "A year?"

"The Brindells' place over on First Street and the Adams' place over on Oak." Bitsy pretended to be interested in the shelf, but Penny could tell she was watching her like a hawk for the slightest reaction.

"What she does doesn't concern me." Penny straightened. "If she wants to be in our town, that's fine."

But it wasn't fine. It was terrifying, but if Bitsy saw even a hint of that, she'd tell everyone. Better to hold it in than to let the whole town know.

Cheryl destroyed everything she touched. When she was young, Penny had thought she'd been immune. That she was the one thing Cheryl had wanted to keep. Boy, had she been wrong. As she got older, Penny realized that she had just been in the way. More trouble than she'd been worth. Even though yesterday her mother had assured her that she loved her, how was that possible when she'd left her like discarded trash all those years ago?

"That's real mature of you, Penny." Bitsy glanced at her watch. "Oh, I have to run. Things to do, you know."

Most likely Bitsy wanted to go from store to store to tell everyone about their conversation. The bell rang as Bitsy went out the door, throwing a goodbye behind her as she went.

A year? Cheryl never committed to anything longer than month to month. How would she ever fit in in this small town? The nearest bar was over in Owen. Did she even have a car? A license? How did she have money to pay the security deposit on a house?

Cheryl had been pretty hard up for money when she'd dropped Penny off years ago. Hadn't she said she'd wound up in rehab because of being arrested? Or had Penny filled in that part herself?

The door rang again. Penny held her breath as she peeked around the corner. A couple, probably from out of town, walked in.

"If you need any help with anything, just holler," she said and turned back to the shelf she was reorganizing.

"Thanks," the man said.

When minutes went by and the door jingled again, she figured the couple had left. She didn't like to police her store by hovering over customers. It made people feel uncomfortable if she stood up front and stared at them while they browsed.

She went back to her register and looked over the monthly receipts.

"I love what you've done with the shop."

Penny froze, then lifted her gaze to her mother's. Her eyes darted to the back, where the couple was looking at furniture.

"Thanks." Penny didn't want her mother here. This was hers. Her safety net. Her roots. Everything her mother had never given her. It was Penny's and she didn't want her mother to destroy that. But she couldn't exactly throw a fit with customers in the back.

"I'm sorry I came over unannounced last night."

"You mean like you are doing now?"

Cheryl grinned sheepishly. "I had a feeling you wouldn't want to meet up for lunch or dinner after last night. If the only way to see you is to just pop up, then that's what I'm going to do."

"Gee, aren't I lucky?" Penny's voice might have been deadpan, but her heart was racing as if the devil himself was chasing her. The antiques store's high ceilings and large rooms seemed to close in around her. If she didn't get some air soon, she might pass out.

"Breathe, Penny," her mother said calmly.

Penny pulled in a breath and then another.

Her mother had the gall to look hurt. "I swear I didn't come back to upset you."

"You don't upset me. You don't do anything to me." She wasn't fooling Cheryl and she knew it.

"I promised to come back."

"Excuse me, but what is the price of this plate?" the woman said.

Penny pulled her gaze away from Cheryl and focused on the costumer. She put on her best smile and glanced at the plate. "That one is a 1938 Wedgwood nonhunting dog plate with poodles called March Winds. It runs around one hundred and fifty online, but I'd be willing to bargain if you are interested."

The woman glanced back at the man with a pleading look on her face.

The man shook his head but got out his wallet. "Would you take one-thirty for it?"

"For you two? Of course." Penny held out her hand for the plate.

The woman beamed. Cheryl slipped away from the counter as Penny conducted the sales transaction. Penny tried to ignore her mother's wanderings, but the back of her neck prickled.

"There you go. I added a care instruction sheet in there. Have a safe trip." Penny handed the bag to the woman, who hadn't stopped grinning.

The man put his hand on the woman's back and led her to the door as if he were afraid she might find something else.

"Thank you," he called out.

"Come again," Penny said. As soon as the door closed, the smile fell off her face.

She found Cheryl in the toy aisle. Penny kept her inventory low on these items because they weren't big sellers around here, but occasionally someone wanted something that they'd had as a child. Penny herself didn't have good memories associated with her childhood toys.

"You know, I don't think Mom would have thought of toys as antiques," Cheryl said as she picked up an old spinning top. "She always wanted this to be a classy store with only antiques from overseas."

"Classy stores don't do well in the country." Penny looked around to make sure Cheryl hadn't pocketed anything.

"She never understood that." She set down the top and faced Penny. "I know she wasn't the easiest person to live with, but she was good to you, wasn't she?"

Penny crossed her arms over her chest. "If you had cared, maybe you should have checked up on us. But then again, you just didn't care enough about me."

"I deserve that." Cheryl put her hands in her back pockets and looked down at the floor. "I wanted to come back, but I knew you were better off without me."

"How would you know?" Penny dropped her arms, walked behind the front counter and pretended to study a list of recent transactions. Her mother could run off with the whole inventory for all she cared, as long as she left.

Penny was done. This wasn't supposed to happen. Her mother had been long gone. She had no right to show up now. Penny didn't need her anymore.

"Mother wrote me."

Penny didn't look up from the figures, but they blurred before her eyes.

"She told me all about you and school and your friend Maggie." Cheryl sighed. "How could I come back and ask you to come live with me when you were clearly happier without me? How could I take care of you when I couldn't even take care of myself?"

"I could take care of myself."

"Exactly. What type of mother was I that my daughter took better care of me than I did of her? Everything you said last night was true. The men, the drinking. I couldn't control myself. I didn't want my addiction to hurt you any more than it already had." Cheryl brushed tears from her cheeks.

"Do you know how hard it was to call my mother, let alone drive back to this godforsaken town and give you to her?" Cheryl laughed bitterly. "I couldn't put you in the foster system. I was afraid I'd never get you back out of it. Plus I've heard about what happens to some kids in the system and you were already starting to develop…"

Penny pushed away from the counter. Her mother's "dates" had definitely begun to notice her development. She could still feel their hot gazes and subtle remarks.

Crossing her arms over her chest, Penny glared at Cheryl. "What do you want from me? Money?"

"No. No," she said firmly. "It took me a year of sobriety to get here because I wanted to be able to stay. I worked hard and saved every cent I made. I knew it wouldn't be easy coming back, but the only person's approval I need is yours."

Penny pressed her lips together tightly.

"I swear to you, I'm not out for anything except you. I know you don't believe it, but I love you, Penny. I've already applied for a waitressing job at The Rooster Café. I'm going to rent one of the houses in town. I'm staying—"

"Until you fall off the wagon."

"No, baby." Cheryl looked her in the eyes. "I'm staying for good."

Chapter Seventeen

"I promised you dinner and a movie." Luke held up a bag of groceries and a DVD.

"I hope you aren't looking for homemade from me because I'm no Betty Crocker." Penny stepped aside to let him in.

"I'll have you know that not only did I attend medical school, but I also learned to cook decent-tasting food on a small allowance every week." Luke started pulling out the ingredients. "Besides, if it really sucks, I've got a twenty in my wallet for pizza."

Penny smiled. "I suppose I can risk food poisoning as long as there's a backup plan."

He leaned in and kissed her. "That's my girl."

She flushed with warmth and sat at the kitchen table. This was just what she needed. No strings, no future commitment, just here and now with Luke. He wasn't pressing her to be family with him or to let him back into her life. No, it was just casual sex with the bonus of spending time together.

So what if she was head over heels in love with him? It wasn't as if that would make a difference, and it shouldn't. They could just keep having sex until he left for St. Louis.

She rubbed at the sudden ache in her chest. She needed a distraction from her crazy thoughts. "Okay, what are you going to make me?"

He wiggled his eyebrows mischievously. "Let's see if you can guess from the ingredients."

She raised her eyebrow in retaliation. "What part of 'I'm no Betty Crocker' did you not understand?"

"That's okay—I just want the saucy part of you."

"Good answer."

"I was a straight-A student."

"Mostly."

"Hey, everyone has an off year." He tweaked her nose for that one.

"I had twelve of them."

"I know for a fact you did much better your senior year." He sorted his groceries on her counter. "You can't tell me you didn't do well in kindergarten. I've seen you color. You *mostly* get it inside the lines."

Her mouth dropped open in mock indignity. "Mostly?"

"You've always been a little bit of a rebel." He winked at her.

She chuckled. "You've got me there."

He started opening and closing her drawers, pulling out a knife and then a cutting board. "I bet you would have done awesome if you'd had a fair shot at school."

Some of her lightheartedness fled at the reminder of her mother. "Probably not. Like you said, I was always a rebel."

"You know if you want to talk about it, I'm here." He glanced up at her as he cut a tomato.

"I didn't think you'd know that much about being a rebel." She touched her finger to her lip in mock surprise. "Oh, wait, you did have that one year.... How many fights did you get in? Five or six?"

"Seven." Luke set aside the diced tomato and started cutting a garlic clove. "All but two were off school property."

"And what did those boys do to deserve your anger?" She reached over and plucked a chunk of tomato off the cutting board and popped it in her mouth.

"Is it bad if I say I don't remember?" He glanced at her sheepishly, then sliced a green pepper.

She laughed. "I wouldn't believe you. That giant brain of yours won't let you forget anything."

It was what she'd counted on when she decided to kiss Sam. Luke would remember every time some guy had implied he'd banged her.

"Yeah, well," he said, "some things I wish I could forget and others I wish I remembered better."

"What do you wish you remembered?"

Luke rinsed his hands and pulled out a saucepan and a stockpot. "My childhood. My parents. Sam and Brady before our parents died. Every now and then I catch a memory, but they are few and far between. I can't remember much before I became angry all the time."

She watched him as he added his chopped ingredients to the saucepan and set a pot of water to boil. "And here I keep wishing I could forget my childhood, but that's not going to happen now that Cheryl is in town."

"Do you want wine or something else to drink?" He held up a bottle of red.

"It's definitely a wine night." When he raised his eyebrow, she added, "In moderation."

He poured them both a glass. When he brought her glass to her, he leaned down and kissed her. Sparks sizzled through her at the contact.

"I don't think I could ever forget you." Luke straightened and winked before turning back to the stove.

"I hope not," she said softly, more to herself than to him. She hoped she was as scorched into his memory as he was in hers. After the past week and a half with him she was fairly certain that he'd ruined her for casual sex. It didn't help that she'd already been losing interest in it before he arrived. She still wanted sex, just not from some random guy. Actually only one guy would do now....

"So have you guessed what I'm making you yet?" Luke glanced over his shoulder.

"Hamburgers?"

"I don't even have ground meat."

"That's probably a good thing."

"Guess again."

"Hmm...tomatoes, garlic, pepper and some stuff in a jar.... Haggis?"

Luke turned and gave her the stink eye. "Haggis?"

"You mean I guessed right?" She grinned.

"If I didn't have to make sure the food didn't burn, I'd show you what I think of your guesses." He stirred the sauce and then added pasta to the boiling water.

"I'm just surprised you don't have garlic bread. After all, everyone knows garlic bread goes well with haggis."

He very carefully laid down his spoon, then turned and headed for her.

She tried not to giggle, but a few laughs slipped out. "Spaghetti! Spaghetti!"

"Too late." He yanked her up to standing and kissed her soundly. Without breaking the kiss, he lifted her against him and walked her back toward the stove.

She squealed when he lifted her higher and set her on the counter next to the cooking food. Without a word, he walked back to the kitchen table and grabbed her wine. He handed her the glass before resuming his stirring.

She crossed her legs, glad that she'd worn shorts today. Luke's gaze dropped to her calves. Everything felt wonderful. It was so easy to forget that Cheryl was in town and that Luke was leaving. This moment could last forever for all she cared.

"Isn't using the jar sauce cheating?" She lifted the empty jar off the counter behind her.

"Rather than spend hours waiting for the sauce to get ready, I'd rather spend the extra time making love with you."

Tingles coursed through Penny at the words *making love*. It meant nothing. Loads of people used that term for sex. Just because she was in love with him didn't make him in love with her.

"I add a few things to make their sauce a little richer. You'll notice I used store-bought pasta, too. Think of all the time I saved not doing that from scratch." His eyes raked her body from head to toe and back again.

"You better watch it, or dinner will burn and we'll be stuck with pizza."

"Thirty minutes for delivery time…." He looked as if he was contemplating it.

She laughed. "Forget it. You promised me a home-cooked meal, so you're stuck now."

"Good thing this is quick to prepare. The pasta only needs a few more minutes."

When he returned to stirring, she took in a deep

breath and filled her senses with rich garlicky tomato sauce and just a hint of Luke.

"I hope you are a fast eater." Luke lifted the pot and took it to the sink, careful not to lose any noodles as he poured out the water.

"Why is that?"

He put the pot down and lifted her from the counter. The kiss he gave her was less teasing and more ravenous. It lit an answering hunger from deep inside her that had nothing to do with food. His lips tasted of the red wine they'd been sharing.

When he released her, she leaned against the counter to regain her balance. "Good answer."

He grinned. "I can't wait to ace the final."

She pulled out two plates. He loaded their plates with pasta, sauce and garlic bread—which he'd waited to unpack from the sack. She refilled their glasses and they sat at the kitchen table.

"To healthy appetites." Luke lifted his glass.

She flushed with warmth from the look in his blue eyes. "To healthy appetites."

They made it about halfway through their dinner before he moved in for a kiss. They rose from the table as one and worked their way down the hall and up the stairs to her bedroom, chucking clothes as they went.

Right beside her bedroom door, he pinned her to the wall and pressed his naked body against hers. Her breath caught in her throat as he kissed his way down her neck and along her shoulder. His hands held hers against the wall as he dipped his head to take her breast into his mouth. She was helpless against the rising tide of passion that engulfed her. When she thought she could take no more, he pushed her just a little further over the edge until she forgot where he ended and she began.

He pulled her through the doorway to her bedroom. They fell together on the bed, consuming each other with hands and mouths, finding the spots that made her moan and him gasp. When he finally lifted above her and slowly entered her, she felt as if the fire in her had always been and would never find release.

Luke made the flames burn hotter with every stroke, every touch of his hands. Finally she reached the highest point and turned to ashes, floating back down into her body. He came down with her.

With the gentlest touch, he brushed her hair away from her face. Still joined, he lightly touched his lips against hers. She'd never felt more fulfilled, more cherished. More loved.

"This isn't just about sex anymore, Penny." Luke lay beside her with his shoulder touching hers and her hand in his. She wanted this and it was terrifying.

She stared up at the ceiling, willing her body to return to normal. Fighting to hold back from proclaiming her love. She didn't say anything. She couldn't. The one person she'd never wanted to lie to... The one person she always wanted to tell everything... But she couldn't ruin his future.

"Even as teenagers, I felt it. That this could be so much more."

"This is all we'll have, though," Penny whispered because if she said it too loud it would break her heart.

"Why?" He leaned up on his elbow and looked down at her.

It was harder to hide this way, lying naked with him. It wasn't the lack of clothing, but being in her bedroom,

having him make love to her, having him care for her.
It was all too much.

"You can never trust me." The words barely made
any sound, yet they rang loud through the room.

"Have you had sex with anyone else since I arrived?"
His hand trailed over the side of her breast, down over
the dip in her waist and over her hip.

"No, bu—"

"Have you wanted to have sex with someone else
since I arrived?"

She stared up at the ceiling. Everything in her
screamed at her to tell him the truth. To stop playing
the game. She shook her head no.

"All I ever wanted was you." He leaned down and
kissed her lips.

"You shouldn't." Penny shook her head.

"Why not?" Luke's voice was seductive. "You're intelligent. Independent. Beautiful."

She rolled away from him. "You shouldn't want me.
There are better women out there for you. Ones who
aren't so…broken."

"Let me fix you." He stroked his hand down her
back.

"I can't." She wanted nothing more than to sink back
into his arms, but she knew if she did, she'd never have
the strength to let go. "You know the type of woman
I am."

"What type is that?"

Steeling herself, she sat up and turned to face him.
"The kind who kisses your brother."

She saw the light go out of his eyes. She kept her head
up, but inside her world was crumbling. Her stomach
knotted and her throat seized closed. He turned from
her and sat on the edge of the bed. Her eyes burned.

"So *you* kissed him?" His tone was even, not betraying one ounce of feeling.

"Yeah." She'd been strong enough to do it before, and she could do it again. She could push Luke away one last time and make this one stick. And she could just tell the truth.

"Why?" He turned and lifted his gaze to hers. His question held no accusation in it, just curiosity.

In all her lonely nights, she'd wondered the same damned question. Had she just been a scared little girl? Or had there been more to it? But for him, she'd brazen it out. Be the stronger of the two of them because she knew that Luke deserved better than her. "Maybe I wanted to know if he kissed like you."

"Did he?"

No one kissed like Luke. But admitting that wouldn't help him to leave her.

"Maybe I wanted to kiss every guy in Tawnee Valley and just needed to add Sam to my list." It felt as if there was a freight train rattling down the tracks toward her and she couldn't step out of the way. "Maybe all the rumors were true. Maybe I was the town slut."

He looked away from her, and she felt the hole beginning to form in her heart. This is where he'd walk away. It didn't matter how many days he had left before he went back to St. Louis. This would be when he walked away from her again.

She should be glad. This is what she wanted. What he needed.

"Bull."

"Excuse me?" she said. Her slowing heart picked up its tempo.

"You heard me," he said as he stood. He came around the bed and stood in front of her. "Bull."

"What the hell is that supposed to mean?" She tried to recapture her breath, but when he was near, the air disappeared.

"That was years ago. If you wanted to be the town slut, you could have been. Instead you were with me. You never once looked at another guy while we were together. I knew it. I saw it. You were mine and always have been."

"You don't know that." God, she wanted him to believe that. But she couldn't let him. If he'd said this to her after she'd kissed Sam, she would have lost her resolve to push him away.

He lowered his head until his lips were barely brushing against hers. "Yes, I do. Just like I know that you are mine now."

She wanted to shake her head no and go down swinging. Instead she got lost in his eyes, picking out the flecks of dark and light blue. His mouth captured hers and she gave up. Only for tonight.

She'd start the fight over in the morning, make him see that she wasn't what he wanted. That they wouldn't have a happily ever after because she wasn't built that way.

He pressed her back down onto the bed and into the mattress. Tomorrow was definitely soon enough.

Chapter Eighteen

"Sam?" Luke came in through the screen door followed by the bang. "Sam!"

"What?" Sam came out of the bathroom, drying his hair with a towel. He looked as he always did in jeans and a black T-shirt with the faded Metallica logo. It was hard to believe he had surgery less than a week ago.

"What happened that night?" Luke came to a halt in front of Sam and searched his face for clues. It was time to learn the truth, and he knew Penny wouldn't be the one to tell him. She was afraid of something. Getting to the bottom of his graduation night seemed like his best shot at convincing her they belonged together.

"What night?" Sam threw the towel back into the bathroom. His dark wet hair stood haphazardly around his head. He slicked a hand over it and headed to the living room.

Luke followed in his wake. "The night of my graduation. I saw you kissing Penny."

Sam sighed as he sat in his recliner. "I'm surprised
you didn't bring it up before."

"Why would I?"

"Because I saw you walking off when I pushed her
away." Sam rubbed a hand down his face.

That answered one question. Sam knew he'd seen
him. "What happened?"

"You want a blow-by-blow?" Sam lifted his eyebrow
as if to say, *Are you sure?*

Luke took in a deep breath and sat on the couch. "It's
been years, but I need to know."

Something about the way she reacted when her
mother had come back into her life unexpectedly had
reminded him of right before graduation. They'd been
talking about the coming year and how he'd be at University of Illinois and she'd come with him. Or more
to the point, *he'd* talked about it. Now that he thought
about it, the more he'd talked about it, the quieter and
more distant she'd become.

"I went into the house to get a beer." Sam reached
over and grabbed his glass of water. "I was surprised to
find Penny in the room when I closed the refrigerator.
She glanced out the door and then kissed me."

Luke remembered that part way too well. "You
kissed her back."

The tips of Sam's ears turned red. "I'd had a couple
of drinks and it'd been a while.... I pushed her away
as soon as I realized what was happening. She looked
out the door and I followed her gaze to see you walking
away. She seemed satisfied with whatever she wanted to
happen, but then she just collapsed. Sank to the ground
like a stone."

Luke leaned forward, concentrating on every detail.

"I grabbed her elbow to help her up. She'd gone pale and was shaking all over. She kept repeating, 'He can't know, he can't know.' I had no idea what her problem was. She was your girlfriend, after all."

Sam shook his head. "I told her you saw us and she just nodded like she was numb. I told her I'd talk to you, but she grabbed my hand and said no."

"What happened next?" Luke's mind was spinning around the details.

"She got up, said she was sorry and went out the door. I didn't see her again that night." Sam shrugged. "I couldn't find you, and you left before breakfast the next morning. That was the day Brady told me he was going to London and I lost it."

"That was a rough day." Luke remembered when he got home that afternoon. He'd still been upset at Sam and Penny, but Brady had pulled him aside. Luke said to Sam, "Brady told me to watch over you. He said you acted like you didn't need anyone, but you did."

"Leave it to Brady to make it sound like a Hallmark card." Sam shook his head and rubbed his chest.

"Do you need a pain pill?" Luke started to get up, but Sam waved him off.

"I don't need to be babied." Sam leaned his recliner back. "I just need to take it easy, like you've told me a hundred times."

Luke searched Sam's face for signs of pain or distress from his heart surgery. He'd have enough time to think about what he'd learned when he was outside working. "Why didn't you ever bring the kiss up?"

"I didn't want to deal with it. You'd broken up with Penny. Brady had left. It seemed better to just leave well enough alone."

Luke's brow furrowed. "But I barely spoke to you when I came home."

Sam closed his eyes and smiled. "But you came home."

"He's fine. I'm not sure why you still call me when I know you call him every night, too." Penny put the TV on mute and leaned back on the couch.

"Uncle Sam's not good on the phone," Amber said.

"Don't his grunts come through okay?" Penny glanced at her nails. She should paint them. It would give her something to do tonight. Who knew who would show up at her door this time? Her mother? Luke? The Easter Bunny?

"That's not funny. Uncle Sam doesn't just grunt."

"But he does grunt a lot." Penny smiled.

"Okay, he does." Amber called something out that was muffled. "Mom says we're coming home in a couple days, so I shouldn't have to call you every night...."

"You can still call if you want." Penny stared at the image of the Winchesters driving down a dark road.

"Penny says I can call if I want," Amber yelled. After a pause, Amber said, "Okay, I have to go, but Mom wants to talk to you."

"Bye, sweetie." Penny picked up the remote and pressed pause. Talking with Maggie would take more than half her attention.

Penny could almost picture her friend in a sundress in a fancy hotel room, waiting to go out with her new family. God, she missed her.

"How are things going?" Maggie said.

"Fine." Penny couldn't disguise the strain in her voice. "You're on your honeymoon. You should be having fun, not talking on the phone."

"I have a few minutes. Brady took Amber down to the pool. Now spill."

"There's nothing to tell." She was dealing with everything the best she could on her own. Maggie needed to focus on having a good time.

"Please. I know your 'fine' is never fine. Is it Luke? Sam?"

That was the issue with being best friends. They were always in each other's business. It was the best and only relationship Penny had kept.

"You asked for it." Penny looked up at the ceiling. "Cheryl is in town."

"Your mother came back! And all you said was fine. This is big. Huge. What did she say? What did you say? Is she still there? Did she leave again?"

Penny sighed. "She's here. Not here, here. But she's looking for a place to rent in Tawnee Valley. She wants us to try to get to know each other again." The last sentence left a bad taste in her mouth. No matter how many times she thought about it, her mother being here was bad. How long before she fell off the wagon? How long before she made Penny believe she was here for good and then leave?

"Is she sober?"

"Yeah, for a year apparently." Penny rubbed the bridge of her nose.

"Wow. So you guys are talking?"

"Not exactly." Penny winced because this had always been a sticking point with her and Maggie. Maggie had begged her to track down her mother. Life was short and you never knew how much time was left. But Penny didn't want to let her mother back into her life just to watch her walk away again.

"Seriously?" Maggie took a deep breath—probably

preparing for her lecture. "How many people do you have in your life?"

"Counting you and Amber?"

"Exactly—me and Amber. I know you had something with Luke and I know you still feel something for your mother. You can't keep doing this, Penny."

"Doing what?"

"Pushing everyone away. I love you. I have always been there and I'm not planning on going anywhere, but…"

"But?"

"I can't be your everything." Maggie sighed. "I wish I could be there every minute of the day, but I can't. You need more than me. You need someone who you love and who loves you and supports you in ways I can't."

Penny rolled her eyes. "That's the honeymoon and too much Disney talking."

"Weren't you the one who encouraged me to try with Brady?"

"Yeah, but that was different."

"How is that differ—"

"Because you deserve happiness. You deserve love and devotion and a great guy and a great family."

Maggie's voice was soft when she spoke after a heartbeat. "And you don't?"

"No. I don't. I deserve to grow old and die alone."

"You don't mean that."

"What else do you want me to say?"

"I want you to say that you'll try. That you'll give your mother a chance to explain. That you'll give Luke a chance to love you. Not the you who was eighteen and impulsive, but this woman you've become. What's the worst that could happen?"

Penny shook her head, pressed her lips together and

clutched at the lump in her stomach threatening to come up. If Maggie were here in front of her, she would have pulled Penny into her arms and talked her down. But she wasn't here.

"I can't," Penny pushed past her lips.

"You know I'd kick your ass if I were there, don't you?" Maggie's voice was hard, but she could hear the frustrated love behind the hardness. "You are not less deserving than I am, Penny. You deserve love. You deserve happiness. You deserve to live a full life."

Penny swallowed.

"If *you* don't think you're worth it, remember that *I* believe you are. Just promise me you'll try."

Maggie's faith in her left Penny shaken.

"I'll try."

"Now, about Luke…"

Penny could hear the smile in Maggie's voice. "We don't have enough time to talk about Luke. You need to get back to your husband and daughter."

"You're no fun." Maggie's pout came through loud and clear over the telephone.

"Well, I could tell you about the sex toys—"

"Okay, you win. I love you, Penny."

"I love you, too."

Maggie hung up the phone, leaving Penny with a lot to think about. Her mother showing up in her life upset everything. She'd broken her rule about letting guys into her bedroom for Luke. She could sit and think all night or…she could continue to watch *Supernatural*.

Hmm…life decisions or the Winchester brothers. No contest.

She punched the play button. Just when she was getting into it and Sam and Dean, the main characters, were about to face the demon, the doorbell rang. It was only six and she wasn't expecting anyone. She stopped her DVR and went to the door.

"This better be good. You're interrupting Sam and—" Pulling open the door, she met Luke's shocked face. "Hey."

"Since I just left my brother at the farm, I'm assuming you mean another Sam?" Luke came in and she shut the door behind him.

"Why would I talk about your Sam?" Taking a deep breath in, Penny turned and faced him. "Why do you care what Sam I'm talking about?"

The phone rang before Luke could say anything. She held up a finger and walked back into her living room to pick up the phone. The number was unknown, but she'd rather deal with whoever was on the other end than talk with Luke about "where they were going."

"Hello?"

"Penny?" Cheryl's voice hit her hard. It would take a while for the shock of her mother's appearance to become part of her normal. Of course, that could change at any time. Her mother was prone to leaving.

Maggie told her to try. Penny straightened. "Yeah."

"I was wondering if you'd like to get lunch tomorrow. I just signed my lease on my house and wanted to celebrate with you."

As much as her head screamed, *It's a trap to lull you into believing she'll stay,* Penny ignored it. "Sure, lunch sounds good."

Luke moved into the room behind her and her heart ratcheted up a beat.

"Oh, that's great. I can't wait. I'll come by the store at noon."

"See you then." Penny cut off the call and set the

phone down. She put her hand over her racing heart. Her hands shook and the world shifted beneath her feet.

Luke's arms went around her from behind. "Are you okay?"

She leaned back into his warmth and tried to breathe normally, but the world wouldn't stand still even with Luke holding her.

"Let's sit down." Luke helped her to sit on the couch and then released her. He pressed Play on the TV and left the room.

As the Winchesters began their fight, Penny started to relax. Her heart managed to find a normal pace again. Nothing in the room spun. She took in a breath and then another.

Luke came in and handed her a glass of water before joining her on the couch.

"Thank you," she murmured.

"No problem." He didn't take his eyes off the screen. "Sam and Dean, huh?"

She flushed. "Yeah."

"Mind if I change the channel?" Luke picked up the remote.

"Afraid of a little competition?" She relaxed into his side. Her mother and Luke were just too much to take at the same time. She was glad he was here.

"I'm here. They aren't. No competition there." Luke stopped the recording and flipped to a movie.

If he didn't want to bring up the what's-happening-with-us talk, she was more than willing to let it go. She'd made a few strides forward with one relationship today. She didn't need to fix this thing with Luke at the same time.

She settled into the crook of his arm and stared blankly at the television. Tomorrow would be soon enough to talk.

Chapter Nineteen

Penny sorted her silverware and placed the napkin in her lap. Cheryl sat across from her, looking at her expectantly. At least Cheryl hadn't tried to hug her when she'd stopped by the shop to get her for lunch at the diner. Penny was fairly certain a panic attack would have devoured her whole if Cheryl tried to touch her.

"I don't know where to start." Cheryl laughed nervously.

Penny smiled tightly but didn't offer any suggestions. She'd promised Maggie she'd try, but she didn't have to like it.

"I know you work at the shop, but did you do anything before that? Did you go to college? How was high school? Did you have any serious boyfriends? Who was the guy who came over that night?"

"Whoa." Penny held up her hands. "One question

at a time and I have the right to refuse to answer any or all of them."

Cheryl nodded. But before she could ask anything, their waitress, Rachel Thompson, came over to take their order. When she left, Cheryl folded her hands on the table.

"Okay, let's start with something easy. Did you go to college?"

"No," Penny said and looked out the window, wishing she could be anywhere else but here.

"Why not? You were always such a smart girl." Cheryl's brow furrowed.

"I didn't have the best grades going into high school and apparently all that crap they taught us in elementary school really was the basis for everything we learned later. You don't get into college taking remedial courses." Penny stopped herself from adding that her mother was why she hadn't done well in elementary school. If Cheryl didn't know that, then they were going to have more than a rocky start.

"What about the community college?"

"Grandma needed help at the store." Penny shrugged. To be honest, every time she'd thought about taking classes, she'd thought of Luke. He'd been the best tutor she could have had, and taking classes would have only reopened that wound.

"I can't change the past, Penny." Cheryl looked down at her hands and had the decency to look remorseful. "If I could have controlled the addiction, I would have. It took me a long time to realize that the addiction was in control of me and not the other way around."

"Do you still want to drink?"

"Every day," Cheryl admitted. "It's easier now than

when I first went to rehab, but little setbacks in life have a way of triggering the desire to drink."

"At any moment you could disappear or, worse, stay around and be drunk off your ass all the time?" Penny didn't hide her bitterness.

"No. That's why I go to group and have a sponsor. Someone who can talk me down when I think I need a drink." Cheryl reached her hand out, but Penny pulled hers into her lap before Cheryl could touch her. Cheryl clasped her hands back together. "I swear I'm here to stay and I know you won't believe it until you see it, but I promise you—"

"Just like you promised to come back." Penny's head was starting to hurt. It didn't take much for the pain to resurface from all those years ago. "I waited for you. I didn't even unpack my bag for a year. I was always ready for when you'd come back and get me and we'd be a family again."

"I'm sorry—"

"That's not enough." Penny glanced around the diner and lowered her voice. "Sorry isn't worth anything. You not being there meant everything was wrong. Grandma kept telling me that I'd seen the last of you and I kept telling her she'd see in the morning. You would be here then and I'd be gone. Do you know what that does to someone? To constantly be waiting for someone who never comes back?"

"No, I don't know what it was like for you." Cheryl didn't move.

"It hurts. I cried every day. I didn't make friends because I wouldn't be here long enough. Maggie was the only one who understood me. I didn't build a relationship with my grandma. I kept everyone away because I would leave as soon as you came back for me."

Cheryl pressed her lips together, but her eyes looked as if she wanted to say she was sorry.

"Do you know how hard it is to let someone in when you've kept everyone away for so long?"

"Yes, I do." Cheryl's words stopped Penny cold.

"What?"

"I know what it's like to shut down and not trust anyone. I trusted your father. He'd been my first love. Sure, my mom called me wild in high school, but I'd only been with him. When I got pregnant and Mom kicked me out, I went to him."

Penny leaned forward. Her mother had never talked about her father before. She hadn't even been aware that he'd lived in Tawnee Valley.

"We were so stupid. Or at least I was. He came with me to start a new life. We didn't get married right away, but we talked about it. We didn't have much money and I'd already started showing. We needed to save up for you, so we put it off. I was working one night and got sick, so I came home early and found him with someone else."

Cheryl stopped and took a drink of her Diet Coke. Her eyes were glazed from remembering the past.

"I tore into him. He had become my world. The only person I could trust, and he was sleeping with anyone who made eyes at him. I blew up and told him to leave and never come back."

Penny swallowed the lump that had formed. She'd never thought her father might have been bad for them. She thought he'd left because of her.

"I wasn't thinking. All these feelings had been going through me. How could he do that to me? To us? I didn't think he'd stay away. We'd had fights before, but this was different. I wasn't even sure I would have taken him back if he'd showed up." Cheryl's eyes were filled with regrets.

"Did he ever contact you?" Penny couldn't help the hope in her voice. Her father hadn't left because of her. He'd left because he was two-timing her mother. Yet he hadn't come back to be with his daughter. But it hadn't just been her.

"No. After you were born, I was sure he'd come back, but he didn't. At some point I realized he wasn't coming back and tried to date, but the only thing that made me feel like dating was the numbness of alcohol. I knew it was bad and that I was letting you down, and that made me feel worse so I'd drink more."

"You tried...." Try as she might, Penny couldn't forget the good times with her mother. When she'd get a job and drink only in the evenings. Things always seemed better then.

"I did, but it never stuck. I'd meet a guy and start thinking he'd cheat on me or leave me or both and I'd drink." Tears filled her eyes. "I wanted so badly to stop for you. But I couldn't go to rehab and take you with me. I was lucky that Child Protective Services didn't step in earlier."

Cheryl reached across the table. "I left you so that I could get help to deserve you."

Penny stared at Cheryl's open, grasping hand. How easy would it be to just accept what she was offering? Put her hand in hers and have a mom again? How much heartbreak could she stand if she opened herself up to Cheryl and she left again?

She clasped her hands to keep from reaching out and shook her head to remind herself that this wasn't real.

Rachel stopped by with their food. Penny stared down at the burger and fries. She'd been hungry before, but now with all this new information swimming in her brain, she felt too overloaded.

"Aren't you going to eat?" Cheryl asked.

"Yeah." Penny shook herself out of it. "Of course."

She took a big bite of the burger and chewed. It tasted like sawdust in her mouth.

"Did you go to your prom?"

Penny blushed and finished swallowing the burger. That night she and Luke had had every intention of attending prom, but one thing had led to another... Technically they had gone to their prom. They just never made it into the gym, where the dance was being held. "Yes."

"Was there someone special?" Cheryl looked more relaxed now that they were talking about little stuff.

Penny wished she could relax, too, but Luke was a sticking point for her. She'd loved him forever and thinking back to high school... It all had been simple until graduation.

"Yeah, I had someone." She wiped her mouth with the napkin and flagged down Rachel. "Can we get the check?"

"Sure thing."

Penny placed the napkin on the table. "I really need to get back to the shop."

Her mother set down her fork. "Of course. I wouldn't want to keep you from your business. It seems important to you."

"It is." It was the only constant in her life. Even now when everything else was spiraling out of control, the shop was still there. All her antiques were on their shelves, exactly where they belonged. And when she was in there, she could try to forget about Luke and Cheryl. It didn't always work, but she could try.

"I'm glad you have something." Cheryl smiled. "Could we try to get together again this week?"

The world hadn't opened up and swallowed her whole from this lunch. Maybe she could rebuild a relationship with her mother. Or maybe she'd be better off cutting her losses now and telling Cheryl to find someone else to make amends to. "I'll check my schedule."

Luke checked his watch. It was only nine o'clock, but all the lights were off at Penny's house. He knew he should just go home. Sam was doing fine. Instead he parked his car and walked up to the front door.

He pressed the doorbell and Flicker barked from somewhere in the house. A light flicked on in the hallway and Penny emerged in her light blue cotton pajamas. He drank in the sight of her as she made her way to the door. Her ginger hair was tousled as if he'd woken her.

A moment of worry went through him. What if she was sick? What if she was with someone else?

She opened the door after checking to make sure it was him. "Hey."

"Are you okay? Are you sick?" Luke pressed his hand to her forehead.

She scowled at him and swatted his hand away. "I'm fine. I don't need you to play doctor."

"But that's my best role." He winked.

She just rolled her eyes. "Come on in. You can watch me sleep if you want."

"I didn't mean to wake you." Luke closed and locked the door behind them. "Usually you don't go to bed until later."

"*Usually,* I don't have a man keeping me up all hours

of the night." She raised an eyebrow and quirked the side of her mouth up in a little smile.

"I can go...." He put his thumb out to point to the door.

She smiled. "Don't be silly. You're better than an electric blanket and the dog combined."

She grabbed the waistband of his jeans and pulled him down the hallway to her bedroom. "Beat it, Flicker. I've got someone who won't hog the covers."

Flicker whined and looked at her from the bed with the most pathetic look Luke had ever seen a dog give.

"You had your chance, cover hog. Get!" Penny pointed to the door and the dog huffed his way off the bed and out of the bedroom. She closed the door behind him. "Now, where were we?"

"You were comparing me to heating devices?" Luke leaned against the wall next to her dresser.

"Ah, yes. You are definitely my favorite toy. And to think you don't even need batteries, and you're water-proof." Her pajama shorts revealed her long legs and hung low on her hips. Her top barely covered her breasts.

His body twitched in reaction. "I'd like to think I'm more than just a walking heated toy."

She advanced on him like a predator. "Mmm...you are so much better than any toy I've owned."

She stopped a hair's breadth away from him. As he inhaled her sweet scent, her breasts touched his chest. Something was off, though, and it wasn't just that she'd been sleeping.

"Maybe we should check to see if you need fresh batteries." She grinned as she cupped him.

He hardened against her hand. It had never taken much for Penny to get him going, but the past few days, she'd been different. More open. More emotional. Now it seemed as if she'd bottled that back up and was using the sexpot angle again. He shouldn't mind. They had only a few days left together.

Maggie and Brady would be home the day after tomorrow, and he'd need to get back to St. Louis. And this thing between them would end. But should it? Instead of stumbling through life numb, he could have Penny to come home to. It had been almost a decade since high school, and even though they'd changed, the chemistry between them hadn't.

They were combustible when mixed. He didn't want to leave her, but would she be willing to come with him? One thing had to be cleared up first.

Penny pressed her body against his and pulled his head down to meet her lips. His arms went around her and lifted her against him for the perfect fit. Her mouth tasted of vanilla ice cream and he couldn't get enough.

Before he was completely gone, he lifted his head. "We need to talk."

"Ugh. I've talked already today." She wove her fingers through his hair and tugged his head down. "I just want to play with my toy."

She nipped at his bottom lip. As enticing as the offer was, he needed to sort this out. Their time together was closing fast.

"I'll make you a deal." He shifted his hands to more comfortably hold her against him.

"I'm listening." She stared at his lips as if waiting for the right moment to pounce.

He gritted his teeth as she moved against him. The importance of talking was slowly ebbing; his body had other things it needed at the moment. "Maybe we can do both."

"Talk and sex? How original." She rolled her eyes.

"Next you'll be showing me a new sandwich made with peanut butter *and* jelly."

Instead of answering, he kissed her. She murmured something against his lips, but then softened against him. He walked them back until they hit the bed and lowered them both to the mattress.

"Is this really what you sleep in?" He lifted his head and gazed down at her exposed stomach. He ran his palm across it and watched her quake in response. "No wonder you are cold."

"I suppose you have flannel pajamas instead." Penny pulled his T-shirt out of his jeans and inched it upward. "Mmm. Maybe you wear nothing at all."

He helped her get his shirt off, but when she reached for his pants, he stalled her hand. "Not yet."

She pouted and pressed her hand against his abs, making him tighten them in response. "I guess this is the talking part?"

"The kiss with Sam—"

"Again?" Penny flopped back against the bed and put her arm over her eyes. Her shirt rose, revealing the underside of her breast.

"I just want to understand what made you run before." He managed to keep his hand on her stomach.

"What makes you think I was running?" She lifted her arm slightly to meet his eyes.

"You went to Sam and kissed him. You knew I would see you."

She put her arm back over her eyes. "Maybe I was drunk. Why are we obsessing over something that happened almost ten years ago?"

"Because it changed us." He pried her arm off her eyes and held her hand. "I thought we were on the same page. That you were coming with me to college. That eventually we'd get married and start a family."

"Do I look like a fairy tale to you?" She raised her eyebrow.

"It doesn't have to be a fairy tale, if it's true." Luke rested his elbow on the bed and leaned his head on his hand. "Hindsight is twenty-twenty. I didn't realize then that I'd been the one doing all the planning. We were following my dream because I thought it was our dream. But the more I talked, the more you acted like this."

She pressed her lips together.

"You can't deny that you shut down your emotions." Luke ran his hand across her stomach to keep from exploring the soft skin under her shirt. "You bottle them up so tight that you practically implode. Like last night."

"I don't want to play this game anymore."

"It's not a game, Penny. It never was." Luke used his knuckle to turn her face so she'd look at him. "I love you. I always have. You're the reason I couldn't move on. Even after seeing you kiss Sam, I wanted you in my life, but it drove me crazy thinking of you with other guys."

"But that's who I am. It's who I was and it's who I became." She wouldn't look him in the eyes.

Every part of him knew she was lying. "I'd believe that if you hadn't collapsed after kissing Sam. I'd believe that if I didn't know that you never looked at anyone else but me when we were dating. I'd believe that if you were a better liar."

"You believed it then. You believed it all. That I kissed Sam because I wanted to. That everything everyone had said about me was true."

"I was stupid and afraid." Luke didn't stop looking in her eyes. "It was easier to think the worst of you than to admit that I loved you but you didn't want to be with me."

"I wanted to be with you. I've always wanted you."

"Then what happened?"

She looked away from him.

"Don't hide from me. Don't lie. I have to go in a couple days and I don't want to leave this unfinished with me always wondering and you going on the way you did after I left."

"What if the truth hurts too much?"

"Then we'll face it together."

"What if it doesn't change anything?"

"It doesn't have to. It won't change the way I feel about you." He kissed her briefly, and when she opened her eyes, he said, "I love you."

She shook her head, rejecting his declaration, but it didn't matter. It wouldn't change the way he felt about her. Or the fact that he wanted her in his life, but he knew they had to overcome the past to start building a future. He also knew that he had to go slowly with her. Something was holding her back even now.

"It doesn't matter how much you love me…you'll leave me." Her voice was even. She believed every word that passed her lips. "Everyone who loves me leaves me. My dad, my mom, you."

"I wouldn't have left you—"

"Yes, you would have." She propped herself up on her elbows. "We would have gone off to follow your dream and you would have decided I was not smart enough or not pretty enough or you just would have been done with me. And I would have been left alone in a strange town with no family and no friends."

"I wouldn't have—"

"Wouldn't you have?" Penny pushed up to sitting and

grabbed a pillow to hold in front of her. A tear trailed down her cheek. "How long did it take you to believe the worst in me after seeing me kiss Sam?"

His heart thundered in his chest. She was right. He'd made the connections quickly because she'd been distant.

"Exactly. You didn't even come to me and ask me to clear it up. You just left. You didn't even say goodbye."

"What can I say, Penny? I thought I'd lost you. I was terrified of ending up hurt and in that dark place I'd been in after my parents died." He didn't ever want to experience that again. The rage, the pain, the bleakness.

"But you didn't." Her smile was sad. "Because life without me was so much better than life with me. Admit it. You did better in school because I wasn't there to weigh you down."

"You never weighed me down. You lifted me up out of a bad situation. You always have. That night in the hospital, when you so easily could have gone home and not given me another thought, you stayed. You took my mind off what was happening with Sam. When I'm with you, I feel alive. I don't know how to explain it better."

He grabbed her hands and pressed them to his heart. "If I have to, I can *survive* without you in my life, but I can't *live* without you. I love you."

"It won't work," she said softly. "We are too different now. We both have our own lives. I have the shop and you work at a hospital. We have lives that don't intersect except for this one time. Can we just enjoy the time we have left?"

He wanted to press her. To insist that they could be more. That together they could solve any problem. But the harder he pushed her, the more closed off she'd get. He could see that now.

"Yeah, we can enjoy what time we have left, but I want you to know, I would never willingly leave you."

Chapter Twenty

Penny threw down the stack of papers she was organizing and stared out her shop window. Luke loved her. How was she supposed to process that information?

If it were any other guy, she'd have laughed at him or kicked him out of her bedroom last night. But with Luke, she'd curled up in his arms and slept. Well, she slept after he'd made love to her.

Maggie and Brady came back tomorrow. Sam was feeling better every day. Between Brady and Jasper, the farmwork would be taken care of, so Luke could go back to his big-city living and find that girl who was going to keep his house and give him two point five children.

That wasn't going to be her. The sharp pain in her chest wanted to say differently, but she wasn't going to listen to it. After everything her heart had been through, Luke wouldn't be the hardest thing to let go.

She'd done it once already. Next time should be a cakewalk because, although he said he loved her, she hadn't said it back. Admitting it out loud would have been her downfall. It was bad enough that she felt it.

The bell jingled above her door, bringing her back to today. She glanced at the middle-aged woman who came in.

"Let me know if I can help you find anything." Penny picked up her papers and tried to focus on the words again. In the past two weeks or so, she'd lost her focus. First Luke coming back, which would have been fine if it'd been confined to the wedding. But he'd been here longer and every time he came to her, she couldn't help but let him in.

Worse, she'd broken the rule of letting him into her bedroom. Now anywhere she went in her house, his ghost would haunt her long after he returned to St. Louis. Him leaning against the kitchen counter with his smile and telling her about the piglets on the farm. Him sitting next to her on the couch, quietly watching a movie together. Him sleeping next to her in her bed.

She sighed and set the papers down. There had to be something else she could work on.

The bell jingled. Her mother came in, glanced around and then focused on Penny.

"I swear I wasn't planning to stop by, but I got some terrific news." Cheryl set her purse down on top of the papers. Her hair was caught back in a ponytail and she wore the uniform of the waitstaff at The Rooster Café.

"Did you want me to guess?" Penny asked after a moment. She wasn't really interested, but apparently Cheryl had the best news in the world from the smile on her face.

"No, of course not. I mean how could you guess? I

know it's not the best timing, but when is it ever. I met someone."

Penny flinched as if Cheryl had slapped her across the face. She sank into the chair behind the register and waited for her heart to start beating again. This was how it always began. Cheryl was happy with a job and a place to live and then she met someone. It wouldn't be long before she started drinking again. And that's when things got rough.

"I just needed to share with someone." Cheryl hadn't noticed Penny's reaction yet. "I wanted to share with you. You are the reason I'm here, but…to have this opportunity, when I thought I was done with men."

That's when Cheryl turned around and noticed Penny. Penny couldn't breathe, let alone speak.

"Is something wrong?" Cheryl rushed around the counter and squatted next to Penny's chair. She reached out hesitantly, as if she was going to touch Penny's hand, but decided against it. "Are you okay?"

From the pit of Penny's stomach the old pain and longing rose to the surface. She looked Cheryl in the eyes. "You left me."

"I—"

"You left me alone and didn't come back. The one person in the world I had. The one person I loved. I trusted you and you left me all alone."

"It broke my heart to leave you. I did my best. I found you a home and somewhere you would be safe. I thought if I got help I could come back to you."

"But you didn't come back."

"No," Cheryl said slowly. "So many times I tried to get clean. I wanted to. I knew it was the only way to get you back. Mother made me promise. She made me—"

Cheryl covered her mouth as tears flowed down her

cheeks. "I had to prove to her that I was worthy of you. That was the only way she'd take you in. I told her about the men, the alcohol, selling your stuff. She knew that if she didn't take you in, I couldn't protect you. It was bad enough that I was with those type of men, but if they'd hurt you, I would have never forgiven myself."

Penny couldn't respond. What was there to say that hadn't already been said?

"Every time I thought I was getting close, something would happen. I was afraid I'd never make it back to you. So I drank."

"What's different about this time? Tell me so I can believe you. Make me understand why you are waltzing back into my life seventeen years later and expecting to have some sort of relationship with me, when all I can think about is when you are going to leave me again." Penny kept her voice down; inside she felt cold and hollow.

"Don't say that, Penny-pie. Please don't say that. I'm never going to leave again. I'm never going to drink again. If it means that I grow old alone but get to be with the one thing that I did that was ever worthwhile, I can do it. I can do it for you." Cheryl brushed a strand of hair out of Penny's eyes.

"Don't do it for me." Penny grabbed Cheryl's hands and held them still. "Don't do it for me. Do it for you because you want to. Because you need to. Because I won't be held responsible for the next time you fall down that rabbit hole. I won't be responsible when you pick up a drink because you've had a bad day or week or your boyfriend isn't treating you right. I won't be responsible for you."

Cheryl straightened. "You're right. It's my fault you took on so much when you were growing up. You don't need to be responsible for me anymore. I will stay clean for me and for you, but if I do stumble, please don't shut me out. I'm not perfect. I make mistakes."

Penny felt the beginnings of a smile. "I'm not going anywhere."

"Neither am I. And if you think I shouldn't date—"

"Please, I'm hardly the authority on dating." Penny laughed and stood. "Just don't let it get bad. Make sure to end it before it gets bad."

"Promise." Cheryl walked around to the other side of the counter and leaned across it. "So let me tell you about Paul."

Penny opened the screen door of the farmhouse as the car stopped in the driveway. The two farm dogs crowded around the car and barked. Luke was already coming down from the field. Sam was inside snoring on the recliner. She wouldn't be surprised if the dogs woke him up with their insistence that the household needed to be alerted to the arrival of outsiders.

The car doors opened, and Amber was the first to be greeted by the dogs. Maggie and Brady got out while they were distracted. Penny's chest felt lighter seeing her best friend. Penny and Maggie hugged as soon as they were close enough. They hadn't been apart much in the years since high school.

"You look wonderful," Penny said. Maggie wore a sundress with a white shrug over it. She looked more than wonderful; she looked relaxed and happy.

"You haven't been eating, have you?" Maggie put her hand on Penny's cheek.

"I've been eating fine, Maggie."

"How's Sam been?" Brady asked before hugging Penny, too.

"Besides bored out of his mind, he's been fine." Penny led them inside. Her pot of potatoes had started to boil, so she turned down the stove a little to keep it from boiling over.

"I'll go find Sam." Brady left the kitchen.

"So what's new?" Maggie sat at the kitchen table and grabbed a handful of M&M's from the candy dish.

"In this kitchen, not much." Penny used stirring to keep from meeting Maggie's gaze.

"You're lucky that I missed you and your quirky ways." Maggie popped an M&M in her mouth. "Tell me about your mother."

"Cheryl's fine. She's got a job, a house and a potential love interest."

"What about your relationship with her?"

"We're working on it. It won't fix itself overnight." Penny stirred the potatoes and set the lid over them.

Maggie hugged her from behind. "I'm glad you are trying."

"Me, too." She patted Maggie's arm.

Maggie sank back into her chair and Penny joined her at the table. The screen door opened, and Amber and Luke came in. Amber was talking his ear off about some ride at Disney. Luke glanced Penny's way.

She couldn't keep her smile down, but she dropped her gaze. She loved him, and just seeing him made her feel warm and gooey inside. But the time to deal with Luke was coming. She wanted to avoid it so she focused on living in this moment. This could end only one way.

Amber ran up and tackle-hugged Penny. "I missed you, Penny."

"I missed you, too, munchkin."

"Where's Uncle Sam?"

"I think he's in the living room with your dad." Luke

pointed in that direction and she was off. He stood there undecided for a moment.

"You can join us if you like. We're just catching up," Maggie said.

"I'd hate to be a third wheel. I'll go see what my brothers are talking about. I have to give Brady the grand tour of everything that is happening on the farm anyway and try to get Sam to sit it out."

"Good luck," Penny said.

He nodded and rubbed the back of his neck as he headed out of the room.

"So…" Maggie pointedly glanced at the door that Luke had disappeared through.

"So what?" Penny grabbed an M&M. How could she begin to talk about Luke when she didn't know what was going on herself?

"Penny?" Maggie put her hand over hers on the table. "Oh, sweetie, you've fallen for him again, haven't you?"

That's the thing that sucked about a best friend. They could see through any of the bull you put up for everyone else.

"Have you guys talked about the future?" Maggie asked with her concerned face on.

"What's there to talk about? I can't just leave What Goes Around Comes Around. I'm only just making a name for it. He's not going to give up his job at the hospital in St. Louis to come here…for what? To work in the hospital in Owen or drive all the way to Springfield for work every day."

"But you've thought about it."

"Of course I've thought about it. It's the only thing I can think about. That or my mother, and neither of them are very conducive to sleeping, eating or working."

Maggie squeezed her hand. "I bet if we put our heads together we could figure out something."

"It won't matter. What we have won't last."

"Why not?" Their heads both turned to see Luke standing in the doorway. "Why won't we last, Penny?"

Penny swallowed hard.

"Oh, I think someone is calling me." Maggie started to get up, but Penny gripped her hand tighter and gave her the please-don't-leave-me look. Maggie yanked her hand away and mouthed, "You'll be fine."

She hoped Maggie could read faces because hers was screaming, *Traitor!*

Maggie patted Luke's shoulder as she passed him. And to think Penny actually encouraged Maggie to go after Brady.

Luke took Maggie's seat at the table and continued to look at Penny, waiting for her explanation.

She opened her mouth and closed it. "We… I mean… There's just no… Can't we talk about this later?"

"When, Penny?" Luke leaned back in the chair and folded his hands behind his head. "Later today, tonight, tomorrow, or is later when I'm gone and you don't have to deal with what's going on between us?"

Heat rushed to her face. "We're just having fun while you are here."

The words sounded false to even her ears. Maybe if she hadn't said them like a question…

Luke nodded solemnly. "Sure."

The word cut into her heart. Even though she knew that's what they'd been doing, it had seemed more real than that to her. Maybe it had meant more to her than to him. It didn't matter. It had to end, and if she wanted to save her sanity, maybe now was the time to end it.

"After all—" she got up and checked on the pots on

the stove "—we were just teenage sweethearts. It's not like we could have ever made it work. Our relationship was built on rampaging hormones."

"Is that what you really believe?" Luke didn't move and his inflection didn't change to show any emotions.

"Every night we spend together is just about chemistry." She tried to make it sound believable.

"It wasn't just about sex." Luke stood up and looked out the window above the sink.

"So we had a few laughs. I cried on your shoulder. That's what friends do, right?" She walked across the room to stand as far away from him as possible when she faced him. "We're just friends."

"If you believed that, you wouldn't need to put so much distance between us. And I'm not talking about physical distance."

"I do believe it. What do you want from me?"

"In truth?"

"Yes, please tell me. I'm dying to know." She crossed her arms over her chest.

"The truth is I want you, Penny." He turned and slowly closed the distance between them. "I want you when you are laughing at a game of cards. I want you when you are mad at me for something little I did. I want you when you go sexpot on me to hide how you really feel. I want you when you cry in my arms."

He stopped in front of her and put his hands on her arms. "I want you with me. Morning, noon and night. I love you and nothing is going to change that."

Her insides felt heavy. She wanted to throw herself into his arms and say yes, but what if it all went wrong? "I can't. My shop, my house, my life…it's here."

"And no one can take those away from you."

She shook her head and pulled away. "I can't just leave. Maggie—"

"Has Brady now. You won't be gone forever."

"No." Tears flowed down her face. "No. I can't. I can't."

She stumbled to the door and jerked it open. The warm air hit her in the chest and stopped her breathing. *Turn around. Go back.*

She couldn't. She stood in the driveway with no purse and no keys. She'd have to go back in to get them, but that meant facing Luke. If he hadn't already followed her out....

The screen door screeched on its hinge and banged shut like a gun. She didn't turn. She didn't want to know. Luke had just handed her his heart on a platter and she'd shoved it back at him. How could she claim she loved him when she couldn't even accept his words?

"Hey," Maggie said.

Penny spun around and swiped at the tears on her cheeks. "Hey."

"I thought you might want these." She held out Penny's purse and keys.

"Thank you." Penny stepped closer to claim them, but Maggie held them back.

"Think about it." Maggie gave her her things. "Just think about what you really want and need. I know you're scared. I was scared, too, but this isn't just kids playing at being in love. I know Luke loves you. I've seen it in his eyes when he looks at you. And I know you love him, too."

Penny shook her head.

"Don't deny it. You might be able to hide from everyone else, but you can't hide from me." Maggie wrapped her arms around Penny.

She leaned into the hug, wishing she knew what to do.

"Whatever you decide," Maggie said, "I'll support you. You aren't alone."

Chapter Twenty-One

Luke sat on the couch and watched a show he hadn't caught the name of with Sam.

"Aren't you going out?" Sam asked.

"Not tonight." He'd considered going over to Penny's, but with the way things ended only a few hours ago, he thought it was best to let her have her space. For now.

"Penny's a good person." Sam leaned farther back in his recliner.

"I know that." Luke picked up his beer and took a swig from it.

"She's actually really responsible. I never picked up on that when you two were going out."

"I know that, too."

"She's brought in people from all over to visit her shop."

"Dammit, Sam, what's your point?"

"I can see why you like her, is all."

"Really? Wow, thanks. I was just about to ask your permission to court her." Luke rolled his eyes and stared at the cops trying to solve a case.

"No need to bite my head off. If you want to leave, I won't stop you."

"I think I'll stay right here."

"What, so she can get it in her mind that you really don't care that much about her? Can you blame the girl for being a little leery of you? After all, she kissed me once and you assumed she'd banged the entire student population. Trust is a two-way street."

"Big words from the guy who for eight years withheld the fact that Brady knocked up Maggie."

Sam held his hands up. "I have my own devils to deal with."

"Penny's just not ready." Luke shook his head.

"Will she ever be?"

"I hope so."

He was leaving tomorrow. Maggie had told her at the shop that afternoon. For the rest of the afternoon, Penny had been out of it. She caught herself staring at the door as if waiting for someone to come in.

Home alone that evening, she couldn't get settled. Not even watching *Supernatural* appealed to her. When she started to pace, Flicker barked at her.

"Screw it." She went to the bedroom and changed from her pajamas into a pair of cutoffs and a pink tank top. She let Flicker out one last time before grabbing her keys.

The drive out to the farm took ten minutes flat. A new record. She sat in her car in the driveway, wondering what her move should be. She didn't want to give Luke the idea that she was coming with him, but she wanted to be with him one more time before he left. That was all this was.

Maybe it was stupid. Maybe she should leave well enough alone.

The driver's-side door opened.

"Are you going to sit in there all night or come inside?" Luke looked down at her with the same smile in his eyes, as if nothing had changed. As if he hadn't asked her to give up everything and go with him.

He held out his hand and she took it. He kept her hand as they walked to the house and through the stupid, creaky, bangy screen door. Her heart beat in time with their footsteps as she followed him to his bedroom.

When he closed the door, she turned to face him. "This doesn't mean anything."

"Of course not." Luke sat on the edge of the bed and pulled off his shoes. He wore a pair of flannel pajama pants and no shirt.

Her mouth went dry. "I'm not coming with you to St. Louis."

"That's okay." He stood and moved toward her.

She pressed back into the wall. "I haven't said I love you."

"I know." His tone sounded as if he was trying to calm down a wild animal. He put his hands beside her head on the wall.

"I don't need you. I'm happy with my life the way it is." Her heart pounded harder with every word, knowing that he should be kicking her out.

"And I love you more for it." He leaned in.

She put a hand on his chest to hold him away, knowing he could ignore it if he wanted, but he didn't. "I don't want your love."

"But you have it." He brought his lips to hers and she gave in.

Gave in to the whirlwind of feelings only Luke inspired in her. Gave in to the fact that she wouldn't feel this way with anyone else. Gave in to the press of his lips against hers, his tongue sliding along hers, his heartbeat in time with hers.

She did need him. Her fingers wove in his hair and she pressed her body against his. The warmth of his skin penetrated through her thin layer of clothes. She wanted this night to last forever, but she knew it would end and he'd be gone. Just one last time for closure.

But in truth, she wanted to mark him as hers. Claim him one more time so he'd never forget her. Make him as insane about her as she was about him.

He lifted her shirt, trailing his fingertips across her ribs and along the sides of her breasts. She held her arms up to help him. He pressed his bare chest against hers as her shirt came off. Heat flooded her system and pooled at her core.

His hands rested on her hips as he drew her to him for another kiss. The friction of his skin against hers was setting her system on fire. His fingers stroked along the waistband of her cutoffs until he found the button.

When he rested his forehead against hers, she opened her eyes and met his blue gaze.

"I want you, Luke." *For today, for a month from now, for the rest of my life.* The love she felt for him wouldn't die when he left. She'd probably end up a bitter old woman with just her dog for company.

"There's no one I want more than you." His lips closed over hers. She let his words flow through her. It should be enough that he loved her and wanted her. But something held her back. Even as she gave her body to him fully, she still couldn't give him what he wanted. Trust. Her trust that he wouldn't leave when things got bad. His trust that she wouldn't sleep around.

She shoved the thoughts from her head. Tonight was about saying goodbye. Tomorrow would be soon enough for regrets. He pushed down her cutoffs and slid off his pajama bottoms. With their clothes in a puddle on the floor, he carried her to the bed.

It didn't matter that they'd been together so many times recently. It felt like the first time and the last combined. A hint of discovery as she found a new spot that made him moan and he found a spot that made her hold her breath. And a hint of finality when he entered her. She focused on his eyes, wanting to remember every ounce of pleasure they could wring from each other. And when she came, she cried out his name. Always his and only his. His arms wrapped around her, holding her close to his heart afterward.

Her skin still tingled and her breathing was erratic. She'd never felt more relaxed and at peace than she did in his arms. Her hand rested over his heart. The beating of his corresponded with her own. He pulled her tightly against him and tugged the covers over them.

She shouldn't sleep with him. It was another rule she'd broken for him. She loved to feel him next to her in bed, but she had to give him up in the morning. He'd become a habit that made sleeping without him impossible. She shouldn't let him have that control over her. Wouldn't it be easier to slip out now and avoid the whole scene in the morning anyway?

When she started to rise, his arms pulled her back to him. "Not yet, Penny. I just want to hold you for a little while longer."

Tears gathered in her eyes. She blinked them back. She wanted that, too. "Okay."

"Tell me you won't forget me." Luke's voice was on the edge of sleep.

"Never." Penny could feel the energy draining from her. She just needed a little sleep and then she'd drive back to her place and climb into her cold bed....

"Promise me something." He kissed the top of her head.

"Hmm?" She was so close to sleep. There was nowhere she slept better than in his arms.

"Don't shut me out."

"You're going to be gone," she murmured.

"Not forever. I'll be back." He pulled her against his body until she forgot where she ended and he began. "Promise?"

"Promise."

Luke woke with Penny still in his arms. He smiled at the ceiling. Someday this would be his every day. Penny could take only so much pushing before she closed up entirely. She needed time. He was willing to let her go for now. He could wait for as long as she needed.

She pressed on his chest and propped her head on her hand. "Morning?"

"Yeah." He brushed his knuckles across her cheek.

"I didn't mean to sleep all night." Her smile filled him with relief. Her brown eyes blinked at him, but she wasn't stumbling to get out of bed and away from him.

"I'm glad you did." He scrubbed a hand over his face. "I'd have hated not being able to say goodbye today."

Her brow wrinkled and her fingers curled into him. "I don't like goodbyes."

"How about see-you-soons?"

She pushed up to sitting and brushed her hair from her face. "It'd be better if it weren't a lie."

"It doesn't have to be a lie." He couldn't help the little push; after all, he'd already told her he wanted her to come with him.

"I can't leave here." Penny looked over her shoulder at him. "That's not why I came to see you last night."

He put his hands behind his head. "I know."

If she'd been gearing up for a fight, he didn't have one ready for her. She turned her head away from him. Her slender back was pale with a few freckles. He reached out and followed the trail of freckles with his fingertip.

"If I didn't have to get packed and do chores, I'd spend my last few hours here making love with you."

Her body shuddered beneath his fingers. He breathed in deeply of that scent that was uniquely Penny and smiled. This wasn't goodbye. Things that felt this good didn't end. He would make sure it didn't.

"Do you want me to make breakfast while you do chores?" Penny looked back at him.

In that moment she seemed so vulnerable. He wanted to reassure her that nothing had to change, but she would close up if he did.

"Breakfast would be great." He opened his arms and she snuggled into them. He hugged her to him and kissed her forehead. "Time to start the day."

She nodded against his chest and he could feel the wetness of her tears.

"I love you," he said. "I'm never giving up on you."

She pulled away and searched his eyes. When she opened her mouth—most likely to tell him to stop talking that way—he shoved off the bed and grabbed a pair of underwear.

"Breakfast in twenty?" He pulled on his jeans and a T-shirt.

"Yeah." She still sat on his bed, completely naked except for the sheet she held up.

He brushed her lips with his and left the room. As soon as he reached the kitchen, he took a deep breath in and pushed it out. As much as he wanted to keep her with him, she needed to come to terms with them as a couple first. He might be able to bully her into it with sweet kisses and long nights in his bed, but that wouldn't last.

Something was holding her back. Whether it was because he hadn't trusted her when she tried to manipulate him or whether it went much deeper, she needed to face her fears. He could only let her know that he'd be there when the dust settled.

By the time Luke finished with chores, Brady had arrived. They walked around the farmyard where they'd grown up and talked about what had been taken care of and what still needed to be done.

"So...you and Penny?" Brady pulled a weed from the field and tossed it to the side.

"Hopefully." Luke wasn't used to having his brothers around for advice. Although Brady had been the one to set him straight the summer before senior year.

"Penny's not the same girl she was in high school," Brady said.

Luke couldn't help but smile. "Nope, she's even more magnificent."

"Do you love her?"

Luke stopped and stared at the farmhouse in the distance. Inside, Penny was probably making him breakfast and trying to figure out how to leave without saying goodbye. "Yeah, I love her."

"Maggie said her mother just came back."

"It has messed with her head pretty badly. But she's been dealing with it."

"And you offered to have her come with you?"

Luke started walking toward the farmhouse. "Of course. I love her."

"And what are you giving up for her?"

He stopped dead in his tracks and turned to face Brady. "What do you mean?"

"Love isn't about follow me or don't. It's about finding a happy medium ground. It's about talking through what is best for both your futures. Because it's not just your dreams anymore. It's what you can achieve together."

"I have to finish my rotation—"

"But what about after that? You can't expect her to blindly follow you. I almost lost Maggie by doing that. I thought the only way things would work out was if she and Amber came to New York with me. But the worst thing was going back alone and knowing I'd only get to see them some of the time."

Brady clapped him on the shoulder. "She's got her shop, her best friend and her mother in this town. What are you offering her?"

Brady strode toward the farmhouse, but Luke couldn't move yet. He had done the same thing he did back in high school—made plans for them without realizing that maybe she had plans, too. How stupid could he get? He might as well have drawn a line in the sand and said either come over here with me or stay over there.

Dammit. He needed to fix this now before he lost Penny.

Chapter Twenty-Two

Bacon and eggs and toast. The day was just starting to warm up as Penny stood over the stove. She'd pulled her hair back with a rubber band and used the toothbrush she kept in her purse. She tried her best to cover up the redness around her eyes but kept the rest of her makeup to a minimum.

Luke was leaving again. This time she'd get to say goodbye and good luck. She hoped whoever he ended up with would make him happy. She felt hollow on the inside, but maybe that was for the best. No emotions meant no one could hurt her.

"Morning." Sam came into the kitchen and sat in his chair as if they did this every day.

She plated the over-easy eggs, a couple strips of turkey bacon and two slices of toast. She put it in front of him with a cup of coffee. He grunted.

She was tempted to watch his face when he bit into

the turkey bacon to see if he'd notice the difference, but Brady walked in.

"Hi, Penny." He came over and gave her a one-armed hug, which she shrugged off. "How are things?"

Brady wasn't normally the cuddly type. Because the only thing happening today was Luke leaving, he must be trying to comfort her. Which she didn't need or want.

"Fine." She grabbed a plate and loaded it up for him and shoved it at his chest. "Go eat."

He chuckled and sat at the table.

She finished making two more plates and was about to set them on the table when the door opened. Luke looked out of sorts as he headed for her. She put the plates down and opened her mouth. He grabbed her hand and tugged her after him.

"Breakfast will get cold." She followed after him as he pulled her into his room and shut the door.

"Let it."

"Cold eggs? Not the breakfast of champions." Penny wrinkled her nose.

"Please sit down. I'll make you more eggs." He raked his hand through his hair and paced the room.

She sat on the edge of the bed and waited for whatever he needed to say. What if he was going to try to convince her to go with him? "If you are going to try to convince me to go with you—"

"I'm stupid." He sat next to her.

"Okay. Is that it? We can still make those eggs work...."

"Why do we do this? Every time?" He put his head in his hands.

She rubbed his back. "Whatever is eating you, let it out. I can take it."

He met her eyes. "You can, can't you? Here I was

thinking you needed time to change your mind, but you are the strong one. I get so one-track that I can't see all the other options."

"What are you talking about, Luke?" Her hands trembled as she clasped them in front of her.

"We need to work this out together if it's ever going to work. I can't demand you come to St. Louis with me. We need to make that decision together." He put a hand over hers.

She stood and walked across the room, holding herself tight. "What are you saying?"

"I want us to be together. We can figure out a way to make this work if we really want it."

"Is that what you want?" she said, nervous of what his answer would be and what that would mean to her.

"More than anything."

When she looked into his eyes, she could tell he was being honest, but was it enough?

"I kissed your brother because I knew you'd leave without me." The truth burst out of her before she could stop it. "I knew the rumors of me with other guys bothered you and I hoped you'd believe them if I kissed him. I tore us apart because you will leave me. Everyone I love leaves me."

"I'm not going any—"

"For how long?" She couldn't stop the tears flowing down her cheeks. "A month? A year? Until one of your colleagues gets handsy at the Christmas party? Would you believe me if I said it wasn't my fault? Or would you blame me because I flirt too much?"

"I love—"

"Love isn't enough. You need to trust me."

He grabbed her shoulders and forced her to look up at him. "I trust you. I will believe you always."

"How can I know that?" she whispered.

"I'll spend the rest of my life proving that I trust you, if you'll let me."

She searched those blue eyes she'd always loved. She wanted to believe him. To forget her fears. To not end up alone.

She shook her head. "I can't."

She turned and walked out of his room. She grabbed her purse and said goodbye to Sam and Brady before heading out the door. It closed with a final bang.

Maggie had tried to talk to her about Luke for the past few days, but Penny walked away every time. She just needed to get over him. A few months and she'd be back to her old self and out at the bars, dancing and flirting. Maybe not picking up men....

As she stared out the door of her antiques shop, she rubbed the ache in her chest that had been her constant companion since Luke had left. He'd left himself everywhere she looked. Leaning against the counter while she worked. Teasing her down the aisle while she dusted. Asking her for the story of an old glass bottle.

It wasn't any better at home. Her couch, her kitchen, her dining room, her bedroom. He was everywhere she turned. Every night she'd wait for the doorbell to ring to let her know he was there. But it never did. She lay awake in her bed for hours, trying to ignore the cold spot beside her that still smelled like him.

Penny sighed. It wouldn't be so bad if business weren't so slow. All she had were her thoughts to spin constantly back to Luke.

When the bell over the door rang, she stood and walked around the counter, ready for any distraction.

"I hadn't heard from you in a while." Cheryl walked

over to the counter, all smiles. "I thought I'd pop in and check up on you."

"I'm here." Which was part of the problem. She sank down into a chair.

"What's going on?" Cheryl sat in the chair next to her. "I know I'm not your most favorite person, but I've got a world of experience to share. You can talk to me."

"I don't know what I'm doing." Penny stared out the door at the cars going down Main Street. "I don't know why I can't get over him."

"Man troubles. Was this that handsome man from the other night?" Cheryl leaned back in the chair and crossed her legs.

"Yes." Penny was not at all certain she wanted to talk to Cheryl about this, but maybe she was the best to understand. "I made him leave."

"Why?"

"I hate to blame my messed-up childhood but..." She waved her hand as if she had presented something to her audience.

"It has to be more than that." Cheryl sat quietly for a moment.

Penny wasn't ready to fill in all the blanks.

"Do you love him?"

"Yes." With every fiber of her being.

"Then what's the problem? Doesn't he love you?"

"Yes." Penny stood. "Don't you get it? He loves me and I love him. When he leaves me, I'll be crushed. Alone."

"How is that different than now?" Cheryl said softly.

"I left him! So he couldn't leave me. The first time I made him leave, and this time I left him." She buried her face in her hands.

"If you love him, why did you leave? Was he bad for you? Into drugs? Gambling? Alcohol?"

Penny shook her head. "He would leave me."

"Why, Penny?" her mother pressed.

Penny spun around. "Because you did. Because everyone I ever loved and who claimed to love me leaves and they don't come back."

Cheryl looked down at her hands and took a deep breath. "I'm back now."

"But how can I trust that you won't leave me again? He left me before, so how can I trust he won't do it again?"

"Oh, baby." Tears welled in Cheryl's eyes and trailed down her face. "You have to have faith and let go of your fear. If you don't, you'll just shut everyone out. Wouldn't you rather have a year more with him if it meant you were happy for that year?"

Fear? Faith? "What if he doesn't want me?"

"That's just fear talking." Cheryl stood and put her arm around Penny. "You can't let fear speak for you. Wouldn't it be worse to never see him again? I know I hurt you, Penny. I can't make up for the past, but don't let my problems and my regrets make you not live your life."

"But how do I know?"

Cheryl smiled at her. "You already know. You wouldn't be miserable if you thought you'd done the right thing."

Her mother was making sense. Luke had been pressing her to reveal more of herself, and every fear she'd shown him, he'd held her through. "What do I do?"

"Call him, go to him, get him to come back here or go be with him." Her mother smiled. "I'll be here when you come around."

"But my shop—"

"Won't die without you."

"You won't leave?" The ten-year-old girl inside her needed to hear the words.

"I'm never leaving your life again. No matter what you throw at me. I'm here to support you and need to be part of your life. Even if we aren't in the same town." Cheryl hugged her again, and this time Penny opened her arms and returned the hug.

"Well, then," Penny said, wiping the tears from her eyes, "I need to call Maggie."

Chapter Twenty-Three

Luke finished up his notes in his patient's file. It was quarter past one in the morning, but he knew sleep wouldn't come easily. He'd been back at the hospital for a week, and in that time he'd worked more fiercely than ever to keep his mind from dwelling on Penny.

His first days off weren't for another week, so he couldn't do anything until then. He'd already made plans to go back to Tawnee Valley for that weekend. He wanted to check up on Sam, but mostly he wanted to convince Penny that they belonged together whether it was here or there or anywhere in between.

He scrubbed his hand down his face and stared at the hospital-green walls. He should go home and try to sleep. He was supposed to scrub in on a surgery in the morning.

Stacking his paperwork, he scooted back in his chair,

then grabbed his keys. As he headed to the elevator, a nurse called out to him.

"Doctor Ward?"

Luke walked toward the nurse. "What is it?"

"Someone's here to see you." The nurse glanced down the hallway.

"At this hour?"

She nodded. "I put her in room twenty."

"Thanks." Luke grabbed a cup of coffee from the nurse's station and went to the room she'd indicated. "How can I hel—"

Sitting on the bed was Penny. "Hi."

Luke closed the door and crossed the room to stand before her, but he didn't touch her, afraid she wouldn't be real. "What are you— When did you—"

"Cat got your tongue?" Penny swung her crossed leg. "Never thought I'd make Luke Ward speechless. Where are your color-coded index cards when you need them?"

"I missed you." Luke's pulse raced. She'd come to him.

"I missed you, too." She pushed her hair behind her ear. "So, *Doctor,* I've been having these pains right here." She pressed her hand to her chest.

"Is that so?" He wanted to reach out and touch her so badly, but he held himself back. If he touched her, he wouldn't stop until they were both naked.

"It started before you left." Her brown eyes held his gaze. "I don't think I ever stopped loving you. I was so scared that you would leave me that I didn't want to give you that power over my heart. You left so easily the last time—"

"Because I was scared, too. I loved you so much it hurt and seeing you with Sam did a number on me.

But I think you knew that. Otherwise you would have picked any other guy to kiss."

"I'm sorry."

"I don't need you to be sorry. I need you to have a little faith in me and trust that I won't ever intentionally try to hurt you."

"I couldn't help trying to drive you away this time, too...."

"It didn't work. I was planning on coming back to you every chance I got. Even if it was just to get inside your bedroom for a day or two, I knew eventually I'd win you over. You make my life fun and sexy. You remind me of the man I am when my logical side wants to take over. I want you with me for as long as you'll have me. If I thought you'd say yes to marrying me, I'd fly us to Vegas on the next flight out."

She smiled and reached out to hold his face. "Someday on the marriage thing. First, let's try to make this work. You make the fear worthwhile. You make it easy to forget to be afraid. Are you ready to trust me?"

He lowered his mouth until just a hair's breadth was between them. "With my life and with my heart. I love you, Penny."

"I love you, Luke." She pressed her lips to his, sealing their love with perfection.

* * * * *

THE BRIDESMAID'S BEST MAN

BARBARA HANNAY

Barbara Hannay has written over forty romance novels and has won the RITA® award, the Romantic Times Reviewer's Choice award, as well as Australia's Romantic Book of the Year.

A city bred girl with a yen for country life, Barbara lives with her husband on a misty hillside in beautiful Far North Queensland where they raise pigs and chickens and enjoy an untidy but productive garden.

CHAPTER ONE

As DUSK settled over the mustering camp, Mark Winchester stepped away from the circle of stockmen crouched around the open fire. He turned his back on them and stood very straight and still, staring across the plains of pale Mitchell grass to the distant red hills.

The men shrugged laconically and let him be. After all, Mark was the boss, the owner of Coolabah Waters, and everyone knew he was a man who kept his troubles to himself.

But as Mark shoved his hands deep in the pockets of his jeans he was grateful the men couldn't guess that his thoughts were centred on a woman. He couldn't quite believe it himself. It didn't seem possible that he was out here, in the middle of the first big muster on this newly acquired cattle property, and still haunted by memories of a girl he'd met in London six weeks ago.

The focus of his life was here—caring for his stock and his land, building an Outback empire. Until now, women had only ever been a pleasant diversion at parties or race meetings, or during occasional trips to the city. But, no matter how hard he'd tried to forget

Sophie Felsham, she had stayed in Mark's head for six long weeks.

Even now, at the end of a hard day's muster, he was staring at the fading sky, at the copper-tinted plains and burnt-ochre hills, but he was seeing Sophie as he'd seen her first in London. He could see her coming down the aisle in a floaty, pale pink bridesmaid's gown, her arms full of pink flowers, her grey eyes sparkling and her lips curved in an impossibly pretty smile. Her skin clear and pale as the moon. So soft.

The crazy thing was, they'd only spent one night together. When they'd parted, they'd agreed that was the end of it. And to Mark's eternal surprise he'd managed to sound as casual about that as Sophie had—as if one night of amazing passion with a beautiful stranger was nothing out of the ordinary.

The next day he'd flown back to Australia. There'd been no fond farewells, no promises to keep in touch. They'd both agreed there wasn't much sense.

Which was exactly how it should have been. It made no sense at all that he'd been tormented and restless ever since.

'Hey, boss!'

Mark swung around, jerked into the present by the excited cry of a young jackaroo, a newly apprenticed stockman.

'There's a long-distance phone call for you,' the boy shouted, waving the satellite phone above his head. 'It's a woman! And she's got an English accent!'

A jolt streaked through Mark like a bullet from an unseen sniper. A stir rippled through the entire camp.

The quiet chatter of the men around the fire stopped, and the ringer mending his saddle paused, his long iron needle suspended above the leather. Everyone's amused and curious glances swung to Mark.

He knew exactly what the men were thinking: why would an English woman be ringing the boss way out here?

He was asking himself the same question.

And he was struggling to breathe. He only had to hear the words 'English' and 'woman' in the same sentence and an avalanche of adrenaline flooded his body.

But this phone call couldn't possibly be from Sophie. The only person in England who knew the number of his sat phone was his mate Tim—and Tim knew that only very urgent calls should be made to this remote outpost.

If a woman with an English accent needed to contact him very urgently, she had to be Tim's new bride, Emma. Mark had flown to England to be best man at their wedding, and only last week he'd received an email from the happy couple reporting that they were home from their honeymoon and settling into wedded bliss with great enthusiasm. So what had gone wrong?

Keeping his face impassive, Mark hoped the men couldn't sense the alarm snaking through him as he watched the grinning jackaroo run from the horse truck, waving the phone high like an Olympic torch.

He knew that Emma would only ring him out here if something serious had happened, and his stomach pitched as he was handed the phone.

The boy's eyebrows waggled cheekily, and he muttered out of the side of his mouth, 'She's got a very pretty voice. A bit posh, though.'

A cold glance silenced him and Mark swept an equally stern glare over the knowing smirks on the faces around the fire. Then he turned his back on them again, looked out instead over the holding pens of crowded and dusty cattle, still restless after the day's muster.

An unearthly quiet settled over the camp. The only sounds were the lowing and snorting of the cattle, and the distant trumpets of the brolga cranes dancing out on the plain.

Holding the phone to his ear, Mark heard the line crackle. He swallowed, tasted the acid that always came with the anticipation of bad news, and squared his shoulders. 'Hello? Mark Winchester speaking.'

'Hello?'

The woman on the other end sounded nervous. And the line was bad. Was the blasted battery low?

'Is that Mark Winchester?'

'Yes, it's Mark here.' He fixed his gaze on the red backs of the cattle and lifted his voice. 'Is that you, Emma?'

'No, it's not Emma.'

He frowned.

'It's Sophie, Mark. Sophie Felsham.'

Mark almost dropped the phone.

He swallowed again, which did little to help the sudden tightness in his throat, the flare of excitement leaping in the centre of his chest.

'I don't suppose you expected to hear from me,' she said, still sounding very nervous.

He threw a wary glance over his shoulder, and the

men around the campfire quickly averted their eyes, but he knew damned well that their pesky ears were straining to catch every word. Gossip was scarce on an Outback mustering camp.

Fighting an urge to leap on a horse and take off for the distant hills, he strolled away from the camp. Small stones crunched beneath his riding boots, but the crackling on the line eased. He cleared his throat. Cautiously, he said, 'This is a nice surprise, Sophie.' And then, because she'd sounded so nervous, 'Is everything OK?'

'Not exactly.'

A vice-like clamp tightened around Mark's chest as he kept walking. 'Nothing's happened to Emma and Tim? They're all right, aren't they?'

'Oh, yes, they're fine. Fabulous, actually. But I'm afraid I have some rather bad news, Mark. At least, I don't think you'll like it.'

A fresh burst of alarm stirred his insides. How could Sophie's bad news involve him?

On the far horizon, the sun was melting behind the hills in a pool of tangerine. He pictured Sophie on the other side of the world, her pretty heart-shaped face framed by a glossy tangle of black curls, her clear, grey eyes uncharacteristically troubled, her determined little chin beginning to tremble as her slim, pale fingers tightly gripped the telephone receiver.

'What is it?' he asked. 'What's happened?'

'I'm going to have a baby.'

He came to an abrupt halt. Went cold all over.

This wasn't real.

'Mark, I'm so sorry.' There were tears in her voice.

He dragged in a desperate breath, tried to stem the rising cloud of dismay. He couldn't think what to say.

Behind him the cook yelled, 'Dinner's up!' The ringers began to move about. Chatter resumed. Boots shuffled, and cutlery clinked against enamel plates. Someone laughed a deep belly chuckle.

Around Mark, the red and gold plains of the Outback stretched all the way to the semicircle of the blazing sun fast slipping out of sight. A rogue breeze stirred the grass and rattled the tin roof on the cook's shelter. A flock of white cockatoos flapped heavy wings as they headed for home.

The rest of the world continued on its merry way, while a girl in England began to cry, and Mark felt as if he'd stepped into an alternate reality.

'I—I don't understand,' he said, and then, hurrying further from the camp, he lowered his voice. 'We took precautions.'

'I know.' Sophie sniffed. 'But it—*something* mustn't have worked.'

He closed his eyes.

The very thought that he and the gorgeous English bridesmaid had created a new life sent him into a tailspin. He couldn't take it in, was too stunned to think.

'You're absolutely certain? There's no chance of a mistake?'

'I'm dead certain, Mark. I went to a doctor yesterday.'

He wanted to ask Sophie how he could be sure that this baby was his, but couldn't bring himself to be so blunt when she sounded so very upset.

'How are you?' he asked instead. 'I mean, are—are you keeping well?'

'Fair to middling.'

'Have you had a chance to—' The line began to break up again, the crackling louder than before.

Sophie was saying something, but the words were impossible to make out.

'I'm sorry. I can't hear you.'

Again, another burst of static. He walked further away, fiddled with the setting and caught her in mid-sentence.

'...I was thinking that maybe I should come and see you. To talk.'

'Well...yes.' Mark looked about him again, dazed. Had he heard correctly? Sophie wanted to come here, to the Outback?

He raised his voice. 'I'm stuck out here, mustering for another week. But as soon as I get back to the homestead I'll ring you on a landline. We can make arrangements then.'

There was more static, and he wondered if she'd heard him. And then the line went dead.

Mark cursed. Who the hell had let the damned battery get flat? He felt rotten. Would Sophie think he was deliberately trying to wriggle out of this conversation?

It was almost dark.

A chorus of cicadas began to buzz in the trees down by the creek. The temperature dropped, as it always did with the coming of night in the Outback, but that wasn't why Mark shivered.

A baby.

He was going to be a father.

Again he saw pretty, flirtatious Sophie in her pink dress, remembered the flash of fun in her eyes, the sweet curve of her smile, the whiteness of her skin. The breathtaking eagerness of her kisses.

She was going to be a mother. It was the last thing she wanted, he was sure.

It's the bullet you don't hear that kills you.

He gave a helpless shake of his head, kicked at a stone and sent it spinning across the parched earth. Being haunted by memories of a lovely girl on the other side of the world was one thing, but discovering that he'd made her pregnant felt like a bad joke.

Was she really planning to come out here?

Sophie, the elegant daughter of Sir Kenneth and Lady Eliza Felsham of London, and a rough-riding cattleman from Coolabah Waters, via Wandabilla in Outback Australia were going to be parents? It was crazy. Impossible.

Sophie hugged a glass of warming champagne and hoped no one at her mother's soirée noticed that she wasn't drinking. She couldn't face questions tonight.

She couldn't allow herself to think about her parents' reaction when they learned that their grandchild was on the way. No grandchild of Sir Kenneth and Lady Eliza should have the temerity to be born out of wedlock. And it was so much worse that the baby's father was a man their daughter barely knew, a man who lived with a few thousand cattle at the bottom of the world.

Sophie shuddered as she pictured her parents' faces.

Some time soon they would have to know the worst, but not tonight. It was too soon. She was feeling too fragile.

Fortunately, her father was busy in the far corner, deep in animated conversation with a Viennese conductor. Her mother was equally occupied, relaxed on a sofa, surrounded by a gaggle of young opera hopefuls listening in wide-eyed awe as she recounted highly coloured stories of life backstage at Covent Garden and La Scala.

All around Sophie, corks popped and glasses clinked, and well-bred voices made clever remarks while others laughed. The large room was awash with elegant, brilliant musicians in party mode, and Sophie wished wholeheartedly that she hadn't come.

But her mother had insisted. 'It will be so good for your business, darling. You know you always get a rash of new clients after one of my soirées.'

Sophie couldn't deny that. Besides, this week had been dire enough without getting her mother offside. So she'd come. But already she was regretting her decision.

She was feeling ill and tired, and more than a tad miserable, and Freddie Halverson, a dead bore, was heading her way. Without question, it was time to make a hasty exit.

Slipping out of the room, Sophie hurried up the darkened back stairs to the second floor, and then down the passage to the far end of the house to the little room that had been her bedroom until she was nineteen.

She set the champagne flute on a dresser and flopped onto the window seat, pressed her flushed cheek against the cool pane, and looked out at the faint silhouettes of the rooftops of London, and at the street below that glistened with rain. For the hundredth time, she tried to imagine where Mark Winchester had been when she'd telephoned him this morning.

What was a mustering camp, anyway? Cowboy films had never been her thing.

Twelve long hours had passed since her phone call, but she still felt wiped out and exhausted. Their conversation had been so very unsatisfactory, even though she'd been reassured to hear Mark's voice.

She'd almost forgotten how deep and warm and rumbly it was. It had reverberated inside her, resounding so deeply she could almost imagine it reaching his baby, curled like a tiny bean in her womb.

But then static had got in the way just when they'd reached the important part, and she'd started to blub! *How pathetic*. After she'd got off the phone, she'd wept solidly for ten minutes, and had washed her face three times.

Now Sophie turned from the window and threw her shoulders back, determined there would be no more crying. She wasn't the first woman in history to find herself in this dilemma.

Problem was, she didn't only feel sorry for herself, she felt sorry for landing this shock on Mark. And she felt sorry for the baby, too. Poor little dot. It hadn't asked to be conceived by a dizzy, reckless girl and a rugged, long-legged stranger with a slow, charming smile. It wouldn't want parents who lived worlds apart, who could never offer it the snug, secure family it deserved.

Just the same, she couldn't contemplate an abortion. She had wanted to explain that to Mark, and would have felt better if she'd been able to—but in the end the phone call hadn't helped at all. She felt worse than before she'd picked up the receiver.

Ever since, she'd been wondering if she'd expected too much of Mark Winchester. After all, they hardly knew each other, and they'd said their goodbyes six weeks ago, had gone their separate ways. She'd tried to forget him, and it had almost worked.

Liar.

Sophie hugged her knees and sighed into the darkness. She could still picture Mark in perfect detail, could see his eyes—dark, rich brown and curiously penetrating. She remembered exactly how tall and broad-shouldered he was, could picture his bronzed skin, the sheen on his dark-brown hair, his slightly crooked nose, the no-nonsense squareness of his jaw.

She remembered the way he'd looked at her when they'd been dancing at the wedding, the quiet hunger that had sent fierce chills chasing through her.

And, of course, she remembered everything that had happened later…the warm touch of his fingers, the heady magic of his lips on her bare skin. She felt a flash of heat flooding her, trembled all over, inside and out— just as she had on that fateful night when they'd been best man and bridesmaid.

There was a soft knock outside. 'Are you in there, Sophie?'

Her best friend's slim silhouette appeared at the doorway.

'Oh, Emma, thank goodness it's you.'

Emma was the only other person she'd told about the baby. Jumping to her feet, Sophie kissed her. 'I didn't expect you to come here tonight. Haven't you and Tim got better things to do?'

'Not when my best friend's in trouble,' Emma said, giving her a hug.

Sophie turned on a lamp, and its glow illuminated the neat orderliness of the room, so different now that it was a guest room. Luckily none of the guests downstairs was using it this evening, and she closed the door.

Cautiously, Emma asked, 'Have you called Mark?'

'Yes.' Sophie let out a sigh. 'But it was pretty disappointing. The line was bad, and we didn't really get to discuss anything important.'

'But how did he take the news?'

'I'm not really sure. He was rather stunned, of course.'

'Of course,' Emma agreed with a small smile. She sat on the edge of the single bed, kicked off her shoes and tucked her legs up, just as she had when they'd been children. 'It would have been a bolt from the blue, poor man.'

'Yes.' Sophie slumped back into the window seat, reliving her dog-awful shock yesterday when the doctor had told her that the tightness in her breasts and the tiredness that had haunted her for the past fortnight had been caused by pregnancy. She'd known she'd missed a period, but she'd been so sure there had to be another explanation, and had been embarrassed beyond belief.

In the twenty-first century, an educated girl was expected to avoid this kind of pitfall. She cringed inwardly, could hear her father's lecture already.

Oh, help.

'Cheer up, Sox.'

Hearing her childhood nickname, Sophie smiled and quickly shoved thoughts of her parents aside. She would deal with them later. *Much* later.

She sighed again, heavily. 'I suppose I was crazy to insist on talking to Mark while he's out in the middle of nowhere, and now I'm going to have to wait another whole week until he gets home and I can speak to him. But I can't think, can't work out what to do about…about *anything* until I've had a chance to talk to him properly.'

'What are you hoping for?'

Unable to give a straight answer, Sophie twisted the locket Emma had given her as a bridesmaid's present.

'That he'll ask you to marry him?' Emma suggested gently.

'Good heavens, no.' She might have been silly enough to get pregnant, but she wasn't so naïve that she believed in fairy tales.

'It's not the easiest option, is it?'

'To marry a man I've known for less than twenty-four hours?' Sophie regarded her friend with a sharply raised eyebrow. 'It wouldn't be very smart, would it?' She gave an annoyed little shrug, and tried to ignore a stab of jealousy. Emma was newly married and blissfully happy with Tim, and *not* pregnant.

'Just the same,' she added quickly. 'I need to know how Mark feels about—well—about *everything*.' Her lower lip trembled as she remembered just how deeply she'd been smitten by him that night. *Stop it*.

'For example,' she said quickly, 'if Mark's going to

demand visitation rights there'll be steep air-fares to negotiate.'

Emma slipped from the bed and squeezed onto the window seat, wrapping an arm around Sophie's hunched shoulders. 'It'll work out. You'll feel better once you're able to have a proper talk with Mark, when he gets back from this—' She frowned. 'What did you say he was doing exactly?'

Sophie rolled her eyes. 'Rounding up cattle. But apparently they call it "mustering" in Australia. He seems to be way out in the very centre of the Outback somewhere.'

Emma's upper lip curled with poorly restrained amusement. 'It's hard to imagine Mark Winchester doing the whole cowboy thing in all that heat and dust, isn't it? I mean, he was so wonderfully dashing when he was best man at the wedding. Even I managed to drag my eyes away from Tim long enough to notice how tall, dark and handsome Mark was. And beautifully groomed.'

'Yes,' Sophie agreed with another sigh. 'That was the problem. He was far *too* dashing and handsome. He had such a presence. I wouldn't be in this pickle now if he hadn't been quite so eye-catching.'

'Or if Oliver wasn't such a pig,' Emma added darkly.

Sophie's jaw dropped as she stared at her friend. 'Did you guess?'

'That you started flirting madly with Mark to show Oliver Pembleton that he hadn't hurt you?'

Miserably, Sophie nodded.

'It wasn't hard to figure out, Sox. I know you're not normally a flirt. But I can't blame you for giving it a go at the wedding. Mark was attractive enough to make any girl flutter her eyelashes. And the way Oliver pranced around in front of you with his ghastly new fiancée was insufferable.'

Sophie nodded and felt a momentary sense of comfort that a good friend like Emma understood just how humiliated she'd felt when Oliver had turned up, with his glamorous heiress wearing the sapphire-and-diamond ring originally intended for her.

Practically everyone at the wedding had known she was Oliver's reject. Most had tried not to look sorry for her, but she'd felt their sympathy. It had been smothering. Suffocating. Had sent her a little crazy.

Her good friend let out a huff of annoyance. 'I'm still furious with my mother for letting Oliver come to the wedding. When he broke off with you he should have been axed from the invitation list, but somehow he wangled his way in, plus a fresh invite for *her*, as well.'

'The thing is,' said Sophie, not wanting to dwell on what might have been, 'getting back at Oliver isn't exactly a suitable excuse for getting pregnant. I mean, it's not something I can explain to my parents, is it? Or to my child in the future, for that matter.'

She wasn't sure she could explain to anyone exactly how getting back at Oliver had morphed into getting pregnant with Mark.

But, deep inside, she knew. Her heart could pinpoint the precise moment she'd looked into Mark Winchester's dark eyes and the chatter in her head about Oliver had stopped, and she'd been drawn radically into the present. She'd been suddenly and completely captivated by the magnetic allure of the tall, rangy Australian. It had been like coming out of a deep sleep to find her senses truly awakened for the very first time.

As she'd danced with Mark, her entire body had tensed with an excitement beyond anything she'd ever experienced. Her fingers had longed to touch the sun-tanned skin on his jaw and, as they'd danced, she'd kept thinking about how his lips would feel on hers.

'So you're definitely going to keep the baby?' asked Emma.

Sophie blinked, then nodded. 'Yes.'

'That's wonderful.'

Was it? Sophie wished she could feel more excited about the fact that she was going to be a *mother*. It was still so hard to believe.

A heavy sigh escaped her. 'I think I did something silly when I was talking to Mark. I suggested I might come out to see him, so we could talk through what we're going to do about the baby.'

'But that's a fabulous idea. It's exactly what I was hoping you'd do. I told Tim last night—'

'You told Tim about it?'

'Sophie, he's my husband, and he's your friend as well as Mark's best mate. He's worried about both of you. You're so far apart, it's almost like being on another planet. He said last night that if only you two could get together again you'd be able to sort this all out. And I agree.'

'So you think I should go?'

'Absolutely. It's going to be horrendous to try to

talk about everything from the opposite ends of the earth.'

That was true. But it would be horrendously extravagant to go all that way for a conversation she could have over the phone.

Except…she would see Mark again. And she might feel stronger about facing her family after she'd spoken to Mark.

And there was always a chance—a tiny, tiny chance admittedly—that when she and Mark got together again, they might…

Be careful, Sophie. Remember what happened with Oliver. Don't get carried away dreaming of a happy-ever-after with Mark.

'Sophie,' insisted Emma. 'It's your future that's at stake. And the baby's and Mark's. This is a big deal. It's not something you can do long-distance.'

'You're probably right,' Sophie said. 'I'll think about it.'

Emma wriggled off the seat, slipped her feet back into her black and silver sandals, then patted the top of Sophie's head. 'Listen to Aunt Emma, darling. If there's a single event when a man and a woman need to sit down and look into each other's eyes while they talk something through, it's a shared pregnancy.'

'I suppose so.'

'I know Marion Bradley's on the lookout for work. She'd take care of your agency for a week or two. Actually, Marion would probably take your business over if she had half a chance.'

'I'll bear her in mind.'

'It'll all work out beautifully.' Emma looked at her watch. 'I promised Tim I'd only be five minutes.'

'You'd better go and rescue him. Thanks so much for coming.'

'I'll be in touch.'

CHAPTER TWO

THE three-quarter moon drifted out from behind a patch of cloud and cast a cool, white glow over the mustering camp. Mark tried to take comfort from his surroundings.

He saw the silvered silhouettes of the sleeping ringers, the last of the tough breed of Outback cowboys who still worked in the saddle, and who were essential help on big musters like this. He stared above at the night sky, at the familiar stars and constellations he'd known all his life. Everything was in the right place, just as it was at this time every year…the saucepan-shaped Orion…the Southern Cross with its two bright pointers…the dusty spill of the Milky Way…

A long sigh escaped him. He'd had twenty-four hours to digest Sophie's news, but he still looked about him with a sense of bewilderment, still felt as if the whole world should have changed to match the sudden turmoil inside him.

He'd made her pregnant.

It was impossible. Astonishing.

He felt so damn guilty.

What the hell was he going to do about it? And what

did Sophie intend to do? He didn't even know if she wanted to keep the baby.

It would be her decision, of course, but he hoped that she would keep it. He would support her, would do the right thing.

He sighed heavily. If only they could have finished their conversation. He blamed himself that the phone's battery had run down. He hadn't realised that the cook he'd hired had a gambling problem. The damn fellow had been using the phone on the sly to place bets with his bookmaker in Melbourne and hadn't bothered to recharge it.

Now, lying in his sleeping swag on the hard, red earth, Mark couldn't stop thinking about Sophie. Kept remembering her gut-punching loveliness. Everything about her had set him on fire—the happy sparkle in her eyes, the musical laughter in her voice, the astonishing smoothness and whiteness of her skin, the seductive tease of her slender body brushing against him as they'd danced.

And then in bed…

He rolled uneasily in his swag. What was the point in tormenting himself with such memories? Sophie wasn't happy now. He'd seduced her and wrecked her life.

When he got back, he would have to bite the bullet and make her understand that there was no point in her coming all the way down here.

Under other circumstances, it would have been different—fantastic, actually—if she'd been coming here. He could think of nothing better than having Sophie arrive for a brief holiday, so that they could take up where they left off. But if she was pregnant? Hell! She might be thinking of something more permanent, and that would be crazy.

His lifestyle was too hard, his world too alien and remote for a pregnant city girl from England. He had a property to run, which meant he was away from the homestead for long stretches. And Sophie would hate it here on her own. Apart from the heat and the dust, everything else was so far away—doctors, hospitals, shops, restaurants. There were no other women handy for girly chats.

It would be much more sensible if they simply worked everything out over the phone. He could send her money and arrange to see the child from time to time.

When he or she was old enough, they would be able to come out here for holidays.

That was the only way to handle this. He would do everything he could to support her, but Sophie shouldn't leave London.

The coffee table in Sophie's lounge was strewn with travel brochures, flight schedules and maps of Australia, as well as flyers advertising her sisters' next concerts.

Sophie stared at an elegant black and white head-shot of her eldest sister, Alicia, and sighed. Both her sisters were musically gifted, like their parents, and both had launched brilliant careers. Neither of them would have landed in a mess like Sophie's.

As the youngest Felsham daughter, Sophie had often been told she was pretty, but she'd been too given to daydreaming and too impulsive to ever be called brilliant. She'd never been able to stick at music practice the way Alicia and Elspeth had, had never felt driven to be a high achiever like her famous parents.

Emma had suggested once that Sophie had stopped competing with her sisters because she was afraid of failure, and Emma was probably right, but Sophie figured she'd failed often enough to justify her choice.

Oliver's rejection—her most recent and spectacular failure—had been one too many.

Now her unplanned pregnancy would cement her position as the family's very, very black lamb.

Sophie shook her head to clear her mind of that thought. Somehow she had to turn this latest negative into a shining positive. She owed it to her baby.

Of course, she was scared—she'd never had much to do with babies—but she was strangely excited, too. She wanted to be really good at motherhood, was determined to be a perfect mum. Her own mother had always been so terribly busy, especially by the time her third daughter had arrived.

Sophie would be loving and patient, happy to let her baby grow into a little individual, free from the pressures of great expectations.

And for the first time in her life Sophie would be doing something that Alicia and Elspeth hadn't done already and done better than she ever could. She would care for her baby so brilliantly that no one in her family would dare to utter a single 'tut tut'.

Cheered by that thought, she picked up a brochure about the Australian Outback. Her instincts had urged her to go straight to Mark as soon as she'd found out about the baby.

OK, OK, so maybe her instincts had also nudged her clear away from her parents. But, family aside, surely she owed Mark a visit?

Or was she crazy to even think of going all the way Down Under, to face the possibility of being rejected and hurt yet again?

Closing her eyes, she pictured Mark—remembered his hard, lean body, the tan of his skin, the crinkles at the corners of his eyes, his unhurried smile—and she felt a sudden, thudding catch in her heart. In every way, Mark was very different from Oliver.

Her fingers traced a light circle over her tummy, and she couldn't help smiling. She was carrying a little boy or girl who might look like its daddy, who might walk like him, or smile like him. A whole little person whose future happiness rested in her hands.

And Mark's.

Was Emma right? Did she owe it to her baby to go to Australia, to find Mark in the Outback? But, if she did, what then? What if she fell deeply in love with Mark, only to have him reject her and send her packing? It would be like Oliver all over again only a hundred— no, a thousand—times worse.

Sophie doubted she was brave enough to sacrifice her dignity on that particular altar. But would she be any safer if she stayed here in London to endure the dismayed gaze of her family while she grew fat with this pregnancy?

Wouldn't it be better to take a gamble on Mark?

CHAPTER THREE

THERE was nobody home.

Sophie stared in consternation at the peeling paint and tarnished brass knocker on the front door of the sprawling timber homestead. She read the name plate again: Coolabah Waters. This was definitely Mark Winchester's home.

But no one answered her knock. Where was he?

It had never occurred to her that Mark wouldn't be here. He'd said he would be back before now. Would phone. When she'd called his caretaker to tell him of her plan to fly out here, he had confirmed that Mark was due home any day. But now there was no sign of either of them.

She knocked again, called anxiously, 'Hello!' and 'Anybody home?'

She waited.

There was no answer, no sound from within the big house. All she could hear was the buzz of insects in the grass and the distant call of a lone crow.

She sent a desperate glance behind her, squinting in the harsh Outback sunlight. The mail truck that had brought her from Wandabilla was already a cloud of dust on the distant horizon. Even if she ran after it, jumping and waving madly, the driver wouldn't see her.

She was alone. Alone in the middle of Australia, surrounded by nothing but miles and miles and *miles* of treeless plains and bare, rocky ridges.

Why wasn't Mark here?

She'd thought about him constantly through the long, long flight from England, another flight halfway across Australia to Mount Isa, and then a scary journey in a light aircraft no bigger than a paper plane over endless flat, dry grassland to Wandabilla, near the Northern Territory border. Finally, after getting advice from a helpful woman in the Wandabilla Post Office, she'd cadged a lift to Coolabah Waters on the mail truck.

Now she didn't know what to do. She was exhausted to the point of dropping, and her decision to come all this way to talk to Mark felt like a really, really bad idea—even crazier than inviting him back to her flat on the night of the wedding.

It had been Tim, Emma's husband, who had finally convinced her that she must make the trip Down Under.

'Of course you need to talk to Mark face to face,' he'd insisted. 'He's that kind of guy. A straight shooter. He won't muck you about. And you'll love it in Australia. There's no place like it in the world.'

Well, that was certainly true, Sophie thought dispiritedly, looking about her. But she didn't think she could share Tim's enthusiasm for endless dry and dusty spaces.

She hadn't expected Mark's home to be so very isolated. She'd understood that the Australian Outback would be vast and scantily populated, but she'd thought there'd be some kind of a village nearby at least.

Fighting down the nausea that had been troubling her more frequently over the past fortnight, she tiptoed to a window and tried to peer inside the house. But the glass was covered by an ageing lace curtain, and she could only make out the shape of an armchair.

The window was the sash kind that had to be lifted up. Feeling like a criminal, Sophie tried it, but it wouldn't budge.

Another glance at the road behind her showed that the mail truck had completely disappeared. She was surrounded by absolute stillness, no background noise at all. No comforting hum of traffic, no aircraft, no voices. Nothing.

If she wasn't careful, the silence would rattle her completely.

I mustn't panic.

Sophie sat on her suitcase and tried to think.

Was this her biggest mistake yet?

The family failure strikes again?

Mark could be anywhere on this vast property. She knew there'd been a muster, but she had no idea what other kinds of work cattlemen did. She supposed they kept busy doing *something*. They couldn't simply lounge about the house all day with their feet up, while their cattle ate grass and grew fat.

But, if Mark was off working somewhere on his vast cattle station, where was his caretaker? When she'd spoken to him on the phone, he'd sounded rather nice, with a warm Scottish brogue that had made her feel very welcome.

The abandoned house, however, didn't look particularly welcoming. The veranda was swept, but the floorboards were unpainted and faded to a silvery grey, and the ferns in the big pottery urns were brown-tipped and drooping. The house in general needed a coat of paint, and the garden—well, you couldn't really call it a garden—was a mere strip of straggling vegetation around the house, full of weeds and dried clumps of grass.

Sophie looked at her watch and sighed. It was only ten in the morning, and Mark might be away all day. It was midnight at home. No wonder she felt so exhausted and ill.

Leaving her bags near the front door, she went down the front steps and tottered over the uneven, stubbly grass in her high heels.

Back in London, high heels and a two-piece suit had seemed like a smart idea. She'd wanted to impress Mark. Huh! Now, twenty-six hours and twelve thousand miles later, she felt positively ridiculous. No wonder the fellow in the mail truck had looked amused. She'd probably been his week's entertainment.

She reached the back of the house and found a huge shed with tractors, but no sign of anyone. The house had a back veranda with a partly enclosed laundry at one end. A large glass panel in the back door offered her a view down a long central passage, and an uncurtained window revealed a big, old-fashioned kitchen with an ancient dresser and an enormous scrubbed pine table set squarely in the middle. It was all very neat and tidy, if a bit drab and Spartan.

A large brown teapot on the dresser had a piece of paper propped against it, and Sophie could see that there was a handwritten note on it. A message?

She chewed her lip. She felt wretchedly hot and nauseous. If she didn't get inside soon, she might faint.

She rattled the back-door knob and shoved at it with her hip, but it held firm.

Desperate, she pulled out her mobile phone and stared at it, thinking. The only person she knew in Australia was Mark, but his satellite phone wasn't being answered. If she'd had a phone book, she could have rung the helpful woman in the Post Office in Wandabilla. If only she'd thought to take down her number.

She tried Mark's phone again, with little hope, and of course there was no answer.

She was stuck here, on the outside of this enormous, old shambles of a house, and her stomach warned her that she was going to be ill very soon.

There was only one option, really. She would have to find a way to break in, and she would simply have to explain to Mark later—*if* he turned up.

The louvres beside the back door were promising. She studied them for about five seconds, and then carefully pulled at one. To her utter amazement, it slid out, leaving her a gap to slip her hand through. Straining, with her body pressed hard against the wall, she could just reach the key on the other side of the door. It turned easily, and the door opened.

As Sophie stepped inside, she felt a twinge of guilt

and then dismissed it. At least now she could make a cup of tea and find somewhere to lie down. And hope that Mark would understand.

Sundown.

Low rays of the setting sun lit the pink feathery tops of the grass as Mark's stock horse galloped towards the home paddock, with two blue-heeler cattle dogs loping close behind.

Man, horse and dogs were tired to the bone, glad to be home.

At last.

The past fortnight had been damned frustrating, and quite possibly the worst weeks of Mark's life. He'd been preoccupied and worried the whole time, and desperate to get back early, but then the young jackaroo had thrown a spanner in the works.

A week ago, on a pitch-black, still night before the moon was up, the boy had been standing near the cattle in the holding yard when he'd lit a cigarette. The fool hadn't covered the flare of the match with his hat, and the cleanskins had panicked. In no time their fear had spread through the herd. Six hundred head of cattle had broken away, following the wild bulls back into the scrub, into rough gullies and ravines, the worst country on Coolabah.

It had taken almost a week to retrieve them—time Mark hadn't really been able to spare—but with the bank breathing down his neck for the first repayment on this property he'd needed to get those cattle trucked away.

During the whole exasperating process, he hadn't

been able to stop thinking about Sophie and about his promise to ring her. Hadn't been able to hide his frustration, and had been too hard on the men, which was why he'd encouraged the mustering team and plant to travel straight on to Wandabilla now. The men had earned the right to a few nights in town before they headed off to their next job.

Mark had left them at the crossroads because he needed the solitude. Thinking time.

And, now he was almost home, his guts clenched. He had an important phone call to make, possibly the most important phone call of his life.

At last he saw his homestead, crouched low against the red and khaki landscape. It was good to be back. After almost three weeks in the saddle, sleeping in swags on the hard ground, showering beneath a bucket and hose nozzle tied to a tree branch, bathing and washing clothes in rocky creeks, he was looking forward to one thing.

Make that three things—a long, hot soak in a tub, clean clothes and clean sheets. Oh, yeah, and a mattress.

Luxury.

But he attended to his hard working, loyal animals first, washing the dust from them and rubbing his horse down, giving the dogs and the horse water to drink, and food.

He entered the homestead by the back, pulling off his elastic-sided riding boots and leaving them on the top step. He dumped his pack on the laundry floor beside the washing machine, drew off his dusty shirt and tossed it into one of the concrete tubs. Looking down, he saw the dried mud caked around the bottom of his jeans, and decided his clothes were so dirty he'd be better to strip off here and head straight for the bathroom.

He smiled as he anticipated the hot, sudsy bath-water lapping over him, easing his tired muscles. After a good long soak, he'd find his elderly caretaker, irreverently nicknamed Haggis. The two of them would crack open a couple of cold beers and sit on the veranda, while Mark told Haggis about the muster.

After dinner, he would ring Sophie.

His insides jumped again at the thought. He'd gone over what he had to say a thousand times in his head, but no amount of rehearsing had made the task any easier.

The worst of it was, he would have to ring Tim first to get Sophie's number, and he could just imagine Emma's curiosity.

Hell.

Mark reached the bathroom, and frowned. The door was locked.

Splashing sounds came from inside.

Who in the name of fortune…?

'Is that you in there, Haggis?' he called through the door. 'You'd better hurry up, man.'

He heard a startled exclamation and a loud splash, followed by coughing and spluttering. The person inside shouted something, but the words were indistinct. One thing was certain though—the voice was not Haggis's. It was distinctly, unmistakably feminine.

'Who is it?' Mark shouted, his voice extra loud with shock. 'Who's in there?'

Sophie spluttered and gasped as she struggled out of

the slippery bath, her shocked heart pounding so wildly she feared it might collapse with fright.

She'd been asleep for most of the day, had woken feeling much better, and hadn't been able to resist the chance to relax in warm water scented with the lavender oil that she'd found in the bottom of the bathroom cupboard. But now her relief that it was Mark Winchester's deep voice booming through the door, and not some stranger's, was short lived. Mark sounded so angry.

She grabbed at a big yellow towel on the rail behind the door. 'It's me, Mark! Sophie Felsham.'

'Sophie?'

She could hear the stunned disbelief in his voice.

'When did you get here?' he cried.

Oh, help. He was annoyed. And he sounded impatient.

So many times she'd pictured her first meeting with Mark in Australia, and she'd been wrong on every occasion!

With frantic fingers, she wrapped the towel around her and managed a fumbling knot. 'I'm so sorry, Mark! There was no one home, and I didn't know what to do.'

When there was no response from the other side of the door, she called again, hoping desperately that he would understand. 'I've come out here to see you. So we can talk.'

Then, because it was ridiculous to communicate through a locked door, she opened it.

Oh, gosh.

Bad idea.

Her heart stopped beating.

Mark was…

Totally, totally naked.

Her face burst into flames. 'I—I'm s-sorry,' she stammered. 'I d-didn't realise.'

Mark didn't flinch. There was something almost godlike in the way he stood very still, and with unmistakable dignity, but his silence and his very stillness betrayed his shock. And then a dark stain flooded his cheekbones.

An anguished, apologetic cry burst from Sophie and she slammed the door shut again.

Sagging against it, she covered her hot face with her hands. She hadn't seen a skerrick of warmth in Mark's eyes.

Could she blame him? She wished she could drop through a hole and arrive back in London on the other side of the globe.

She'd never been so embarrassed.

And yet, as Sophie cringed, a part of her heart marvelled at how fabulous Mark had looked. In those scant, brief seconds, her senses had taken in particulars of his tall, dark, handsome gorgeousness—the hard planes of his chest, the breathtaking breadth of his shoulders, the powerful muscles in his thighs.

Although she'd tried to keep her eyes averted, she hadn't been able to avoid seeing the rest of him—and how very *male* Mark was.

But alien, too, with his dark, stubbled jaw, and suntanned limbs, with the red dust of the Outback clinging to him.

Mark cursed and his heart thundered as he flung open wardrobe doors, grabbed clean clothes and dragged them over his dusty body. It would be some time before he recovered from the sight of Sophie Felsham, in *his* bathroom, wearing nothing but a towel—and the equal shock of standing in front of her like a dumbstruck fool. Stark naked.

Then again, Sophie Felsham wearing *anything* at Coolabah Waters would have stunned Mark.

He swallowed. He'd never dreamed she would arrive here before they'd had a chance to talk.

Why had she come? What did she expect from him?

Leaving his shirt unbuttoned and hanging loose over his jeans, he hurried barefoot down the passage to the kitchen, expecting to find Haggis peeling spuds at the sink, or slicing onions.

He was going to demand answers.

But the kitchen was empty.

It smelled great, however. There was something cooking in the oven—beef and mushrooms, if Mark wasn't mistaken.

And then he saw a piece of paper propped against the teapot. Frowning, he snatched it up.

> *Mark,*
> *My only sister, Deirdre, is seriously ill in Adelaide and I need to visit her. I've tried to call you, but the sat phone doesn't seem to be working. Sorry, mate, but I know you'll understand. I've left frozen meals for you and I've left Deirdre's number beside the phone.*
> *Apologies for the haste,*
> *Angus.*

P.S. A young English woman called. She's coming to visit you. Good luck with that one.

The note was dated four days ago. Mark scratched the back of his neck and wondered when the surprises would stop. He crushed the sheet of paper and tossed it back onto the dresser. He was still trying to come to terms with the twist of fate that had allowed Haggis's trip south to coincide with Sophie's arrival when he heard light footsteps behind him.

'The bathroom's free.'

He swung around, and there was Sophie again. He inhaled sharply.

Her hair was still damp, as if she'd dried it hastily with a towel. Wispy, dark curls clung to her forehead and her soft, pale cheeks. She was dressed in a simple white T-shirt, a slim red skirt, and she wore sandals covered in white daisies.

'Hello again, Mark,' she said shyly.

She hadn't used any make-up, and she looked pale and wide eyed. Incredibly pretty. Impossibly young. Her figure was so slender it didn't seem feasible that it would expand and swell with pregnancy. With his baby.

Something hard and sharp jammed in Mark's throat, and he swallowed fiercely.

'I—I'm really sorry about—' Sophie's mouth twisted into an embarrassed pout, and her eyes widened as she flapped her hands helplessly out to her sides. 'You know—the bathroom and everything.'

'Forget it.' He spoke more gruffly than he meant to, and the back of his neck began to burn.

How should he handle this? Should he greet her formally with a handshake? Ask her if she was feeling well? Throw his arms around her? That would be smart, given the filthy state of him.

Stepping forward quickly, he dropped a quick peck on her soft cheek. She smelled sweet and clean, of shampoo and soap, with a hint of something else. Lavender? 'It's good to see you.'

Super-conscious of his open shirt and unwashed state, he stepped back again. He felt so uncertain. There were so many questions he should ask. *How was your journey? How are you keeping?*

Why have you come?

'I feel terrible about turning up like this,' she said. 'Moving into your home when you weren't even here. I—I thought you said you'd be back last week.'

He nodded slowly. 'I should have been back, but we ran into a spot of trouble.'

'Oh?'

'A big mob of cattle broke away. Took off for the most inaccessible country. Gave us no end of a headache.'

A little huff escaped her, and her shoulders relaxed. 'That sounds like hard work.'

'It was.' He picked up the crumpled note from Haggis. 'I'm sorry my caretaker wasn't here to greet you. He had to go away.'

'Yes, I couldn't help seeing that note.'

It suddenly occurred to Mark that she might have been here for days. 'When did you get here?'

'This morning. I came on the mail truck.'

'The mail truck?' His mouth tilted into an incredulous smile as he tried to imagine Sophie Felsham from London arriving in the dusty township of Wandabilla and asking for directions to Coolabah Waters.

'I hope you don't mind that I used your bathroom. I know there's another one.'

'No. No, of course not.' Mark avoided the unexpected shyness in her eyes. 'You're welcome to it. That's fine.' He ran his fingers through his dusty hair, and remembered that he was still in urgent need of a bath.

Sophie twisted a small, gold locket at her throat. 'I don't make a habit of breaking into people's houses.'

He managed a grin. 'No, you've got the wrong colour hair.' When she looked puzzled, he added, 'You're not Goldilocks.'

Her smile lit up her face, and she looked so incredibly pretty that Mark fought an urge to close his eyes in self-protection.

Sophie pointed to the stove. 'I took the liberty of putting one of your housekeeper's frozen meals in the oven.'

'Good thinking.'

There was an awkward pause while he wondered if he should demand that she explain her presence here. What did she want from him—his support to have an abortion? Money? Marriage?

'Look,' he said, and then he had to stop and take a breath. 'If—if you'll excuse me, I'll make use of the bathroom before I try to be sociable.' He offered her the briefest shadow of a smile. 'I've got half the Outback's dirt and dust on me.'

'Of course,' she said with a dismissive little wave, but her eyes were worried and her cheeks had turned bright pink.

CHAPTER FOUR

SHE shouldn't have come.

As Mark disappeared back down the passage to the bathroom, Sophie felt completely out of her depth.

In England Mark had been so different—so smooth, and almost passing for a city-dweller in his dark, formal suit—more familiar, less intimidating.

It seemed so silly now, but before she'd left London she'd imagined she would be able to book into a hotel or a motel in a village near Mark's place. She'd planned to call him from there, arrange to meet for a meal in a country tavern, have a nice, long talk. Take it from there...

What an idiot she'd been. She should have quizzed Tim more closely. He could have told her what to expect in the Australian Outback. But the sad truth was, she hadn't really wanted to know too much. She'd been pretty certain a heavy dose of reality would have frightened her off.

Which mightn't have been a bad thing.

But she was here now, so she couldn't back down just yet.

She looked about her, and decided she might as well make herself useful. Perhaps she could set the table for dinner. She crossed the kitchen to the ancient pine dresser to hunt for tablecloths and napkins, then wondered if Mark used the dining room for his evening meal.

It was directly across the passage from the kitchen and, like most of the rooms in this house, had French doors opening onto a timber veranda. This arrangement, Sophie had already discovered, was good for catching breezes and channelling them into the house.

The dining room, like all the other rooms, was a very generous size, but it was also ugly, with tongue-and-groove timber walls painted in a faded, murky green and without a single attractive, decorative touch. In fact, Mark's entire house was as plain and austere as a monk's cell.

It could do with a jolly good makeover—new paint, bright cushions, flowers, pretty fabrics, artwork.

A woman's touch.

Sophie's mind skidded away from that thought. *Not this woman's touch*. She knew for a fact that she couldn't live here.

She opened a door in the sideboard and found a pile of tablecloths—clean but un-ironed, and all of them ancient. Dull and boring. Depressing.

In a drawer, she found red tartan place mats with matching napkins and decided to use them. At least they were colourful. And the silver was clean and shining.

But despite the bright tartan the two place-settings looked rather austere on the huge dining table. She hunted about for a vase or candlesticks, anything to fill in the expanse of bare table-top.

There was nothing.

* * *

Showered and shaved, and neatly dressed in clean clothes, Mark stood in the middle of his bedroom and regarded his reflection in the mirror. He looked ridiculously nervous.

What did Sophie expect from him? Was she hoping for marriage? Surely not.

He'd never considered himself a family man, had more or less decided he was a habitual bachelor. His life was hard, and he worked long hours and took few holidays. He'd never really thought much about marriage, had never found a woman who would make a suitable wife—someone he really admired, who could take the hard life in the Outback.

Now, the irony was that just about any of the Australian girls he'd dated and parted with over the past decade would have fitted the bill better than this woman, with her milk-white English skin and high-flying, London-girl lifestyle.

Except…none of those other girls had been carrying his baby.

Mark glanced again at his reflection, saw concern and confusion, the downward slant of his mouth, and turned abruptly and marched from the room.

When Mark came into the kitchen wearing a crisp white shirt and casual chinos, with his jaw cleanly shaved, he looked so breathtaking that Sophie quickly became very busy, thrusting her hands into oven mitts and heading for the stove.

'This smells wonderful,' she said over her shoulder as she lifted out a pottery casserole dish. 'Your house-keeper must be a good cook.'

'He's a darn sight better than the fellow we had on

the mustering camp.' Mark looked down at the bare kitchen table. 'I'll grab some cutlery.'

'No need. I've set the table in the dining room.'

His eyebrows lifted with momentary surprise.

'Would you rather eat in the kitchen?'

'The dining room's fine.' He gave her a slow smile. 'I wouldn't have expected anything less from the daughter of Sir Kenneth Felsham.'

She gave a flustered little shrug.

'Perhaps I should open a bottle of wine and make it a proper occasion,' Mark suggested as he followed her, carrying the warmed plates through to the other room.

Sophie set the casserole dish down. 'I'm sure wine would be nice, but I'm afraid I can't join you.'

His eyes widened with surprise, and she pointed to her stomach. 'It's not good for the baby.'

'Oh, yes, of course. Sorry. I—I don't really care for wine anyway.'

She looked up quickly to see if Mark was joking, but suddenly it didn't matter if he was speaking the truth or lying through his teeth. Their gazes met and he smiled again, and his smile seemed to reach deep inside her. She had to sit down before her knees gave way.

Goodness. Surely she wasn't going to be all breathless and girly—just as she'd been at the wedding?

Mark sat, too, and indicated that she should help herself to the food. Her hand trembled ever so slightly as she lifted the serving spoon, and she was sure he noticed.

'You must be feeling rather jet-lagged,' he suggested.

She nodded, glad to hide behind this excuse, spooned beef and mushrooms onto her plate, and hoped Mark was the kind of man who liked to fill his stomach before he tackled difficult discussions. But when she looked up she found his dark eyes regarding her thoughtfully.

She pointed to the food. 'I'm sure you must be ravenous. Don't let this lovely dinner get cold.'

Without comment, he helped himself to the food and began to eat with some enthusiasm, but it wasn't long before he put his fork down. His throat worked, and he lifted his napkin from his lap and set it on the table.

'I can't help wondering why you've come all the way out here,' he said. 'I told you I'd telephone as soon as I got back.'

'I know, Mark.' Sophie felt as if a piece of meat had stuck in her throat. She swallowed. There was nothing there, but the feeling wouldn't go away. 'I—I thought it would be easier for us to talk face to face. I didn't like the idea of trying to discuss matters like child support and visiting rights over the phone. It—it seemed rather tacky.'

Her heart thumped madly, and she felt completely intimidated by his frowning silence.

At last he said, 'So you're planning to have the baby?'

Oh, heavens. Was he going to ask her to have an abortion?

She drew herself very straight. 'Yes. Absolutely.'

She fancied she saw a flash of relief in his eyes, but he didn't smile.

Under the table, she crossed her fingers. *So far, so good.*

Mark's gaze narrowed. 'And you're quite certain I'm the father?'

Sophie gasped. 'Of course. How can you ask that?'

He shrugged. 'I had to make certain. For all I know, you might do this kind of thing all the time.'

'What kind of thing?'

'Come on, Sophie. You know what I'm talking about.'

'No.'

His jaw tightened, and for the first time he looked uncomfortable. 'One-night stands. Casual sex with strangers.'

She flinched as if he'd physically hit her.

Casual sex with strangers.

She knew that was what their wonderful night had amounted to, but somehow she'd hoped that Mark might have looked on it with finer sentiments. Her baby's conception hadn't been sordid. But perhaps she'd romanticised it out of all proportion.

Mark must have seen the shock in her face. His expression softened immediately. 'I just think we should lay our cards on the table,' he said more gently.

'The baby's yours, Mark.' She lifted her chin high. 'I don't make a habit of casual flings. There's been no one else. Do you really think I would come all this way and single you out if it wasn't your child? Why would I bother?'

He nodded slowly. And then, as if he needed to hide his feelings, he looked down at the table cloth and cleared his throat. 'I'm prepared to help with any money you need.'

'Thanks. I might need to…to find a bigger flat. I'm not sure if I'll manage paying everything for the baby as well.'

'I wouldn't expect you to.' His long brown fingers folded a corner of the tartan table mat down then smoothed it out again, and a muscle in his jaw tightened into a hard little knot. 'I'm assuming you plan to have the baby in England? To be a single mother—at least for the time being?'

A hot, stinging sensation troubled Sophie's eyes. Oh, damn, she wasn't going to cry, was she? Mark's assumption was perfectly logical. Sensible.

She'd never really believed that she could come to Australia, get to know Mark better and start a relationship with him. But she hadn't been able to squash a tiny hope. Now she felt very foolish.

Mark cleared his throat. 'I assume you're not here to discuss marriage.'

'No! Of course not!' she cried with unnecessary passion, almost tearfully. She blinked away the wretched dampness. What was the matter with her? 'I'm certainly not expecting you to marry me. We hardly know each other.'

The tiniest hint of a smile glowed in Mark's dark eyes, and Sophie knew he was thinking about their night together. Her heart seemed to bounce inside her.

He dropped his gaze to the table. 'I guess the thing that still puzzles me is why you've come all this way,' he said quietly. 'All you said you want from me is child support, but you could have asked for that over the phone.'

He looked up quickly and his dark eyes probed her. 'So what's the deal, Sophie? Where do you want to take things from here?'

It was a very good question.

But, when Mark frowned at her like that, Sophie felt

so suddenly flustered and confused she couldn't remember the answer.

Her mouth went very dry. 'I suppose…' She swallowed. 'I suppose I wanted to be sure.'

His response was a look of intense bewilderment. "What about?"

Oh, help. Couldn't Mark guess how hard it was to explain the confusing, scary, almost intangible *something* that had pushed her here almost against her will? 'I—I think I wanted to be sure about—' Again she swallowed, and moistened her lips with her tongue. 'About us.'

She didn't look at him now, simply rushed on to explain. 'I've been feeling so confused. Everything happened so quickly. You've no idea how crazy it was to find myself pregnant after just one night.'

Her mouth trembled dangerously and she shoved a hand against her lips.

'And it was my fault entirely,' Mark said.

Not entirely, she thought, remembering how madly she'd flirted.

His face twisted into a complicated, fiercely gentle smile. 'At the very least, I should have stayed for one more night.'

Sophie wanted to smile back at him, but instead she spluttered tearfully, 'See? That's my point. I didn't even know you had a sense of humour.'

And then she burst into noisy tears.

She heard the scrape of Mark's chair on the timber floor, and next moment his deep voice was rumbling sexily beside her. 'Come here,' he said, taking her arms and pulling her gently out of her chair.

Holding her against his chest, he wrapped his arms around her, and she had no choice but to cling to him while her tears had their way.

'Hush,' he whispered, brushing a path of soft kisses over her brow and onto her cheeks.

'I'm so sorry, Mark.'

'Don't be,' he murmured, running a slow hand down her shaking spine.

'I don't want to cry like this.'

'Cry as much as you like. From where I'm standing, it feels great.'

That brought her to her senses. She pulled away, and immediately felt an awful sense of loss. Using the backs of her hands, she cleared tears from her eyes.

Mark was looking at her with a mixture of tenderness and concern that did all sorts of wicked things to her insides.

'There ought to be an instruction manual for this sort of thing,' he said as he shoved his hands into his trousers. 'But you will stay here for a while at least, won't you?'

Goodness! Was this the opening she'd hoped for?

Sophie wanted to hug him, but instead she said carefully, 'It would give us a chance to get to know each other better.'

And then, in case he changed his mind, she hurried to add, 'I can't stay here for very long. There's someone minding my business, and I have to see doctors, have antenatal checks and scans. That sort of thing.'

Mark smiled kindly. 'But, if you stayed for a couple of weeks, it would be an improvement on one night.'

She nodded. 'Indeed.'

'I guess we owe it to the baby, don't we?'

'Well, yes. I suppose it *would* be rather embarrassing to admit to our child that I know nothing about its father, apart from his name and the colour of his eyes.'

Mark's dark-brown eyes held hers. They shimmered with subtle innuendo, flooding Sophie with memories of their night together, sending a high-voltage flash scorching through her.

'You know a lot more about me than that,' he said.

Instinctively, in self-protection, she lowered her lashes. Her wanton behaviour on that night still bewildered her. To have been so suddenly carried away was completely out of character.

What if she fell deeply in love with Mark now, but he didn't love her back? She couldn't bear a repeat of what had happened with Oliver. Somehow, she knew that a break up after falling in love with Mark would be much, much worse.

'I'll stay for two weeks,' she said carefully. 'We should be able to sort out your paternity arrangements by then.'

Mark grinned, and his hands came out of his pockets as he reached for her again. She knew that he wanted her in his arms, wanted to kiss her.

But wasn't that crazy?

'What's the matter?' asked Mark.

'I—I—um—*don't* think we should get too intimate, do you?'

'Why ever not?' He smiled gorgeously as he reached for her. 'Isn't the harm done? We'd be shutting the stable door after the horse has bolted.'

Heavens! She had to be careful, had to remember that

staying here was risky. She had no idea if she and Mark could make a relationship work. And she had no idea how she could possibly be happy in the drab, monotonous Outback.

There were no shops around the corner. No little village nearby. No friendly faces. Nothing and no one for fifty miles at least.

Mark's big hands circled her waist, but Sophie planted her hands firmly over his to prevent his from moving. If she was to get through the next two weeks with her heart intact, she had to be clear headed and strong minded. Disciplined.

'We need to get to know each other as friends, not as lovers,' she said.

'Why not both?'

Mark looked deeply into her eyes, and her breath shivered in her throat. His hands were warm and strong beneath hers. Her blood fizzed in her veins.

His serious brown gaze studied her, as if he was trying to read how she really felt about this. 'You really mean it? You just want to be friends?'

No, she wanted to cry, but she forced herself to be sensible. 'I'll be leaving in two weeks' time, Mark. And—and I don't think we should make our situation any more complicated than it already is.'

'Friendship,' Mark murmured softly, but then, before Sophie knew quite what was happening, his hands were cupping her face and she was beginning to melt.

She tried to protest, but there was something too impossibly mesmerising about Mark Winchester when he was moving in for a kiss.

And yet incredibly, at the last moment, when his lips were a mere millimetre from hers, she managed a pathetic objection. 'Mark, we mustn't!'

'Shh,' he murmured against her mouth.

Valiantly, she ignored the delicious tremors dancing all over her skin and she tried again. 'But we've settled for friendship, right?'

'Whatever you say,' he replied lazily, and then he kissed her.

His lips were soft and warm, and his skin smelled clean and faintly of aftershave. His kiss was slow and dreamy, and Sophie's resistance melted like butter in summer. She leaned into him and gave herself up to the unhurried pressure of his lips, the sexy caress of his tongue, the rough, manly texture of his jaw against hers.

Ages later, when he pulled away and smiled into her eyes, every part of her was zinging and zapping with happiness, but she tried to tell him off.

'You weren't supposed to do that,' she said breathlessly.

'Neither were you.'

Well, yes, that was true. She'd kissed Mark with regrettable enthusiasm.

She wished she could think of a cutting remark to wipe the knowing smile from his face, but his kiss had made her woozy and warm and slow witted. Cutting remarks had never been her strong point anyway.

Just the same, as common sense returned she became very busy, gathering up their plates and marching to the kitchen to stack the dishwasher. And, using jet lag as her excuse, she went to bed early without any more kisses.

* * *

Mark stood at his bedroom window, staring out into the black, still night.

Friendship.

That was a rum deal.

All he could see was Sophie's lips, pink and trembling. He'd been desperate to taste her, and her kiss had sent him spinning. When her lovely body had melted against him, he could have sworn that her response was as eager as it had been in London.

But she wanted friendship.

At least, she'd *said* she wanted friendship. Her body had said something else.

He cursed softly.

What was a man to do? How was he supposed to live here alone, with a woman as alluring as Sophie, without wanting to hold her?

What a crazy situation.

He and Sophie should have been able to say goodbye in England and continue on their merry, separate ways. She could have done whatever it was that she did in London and marry some Brit—someone like Tim, or one of those other fellows he'd met at the wedding. Mark could have continued getting his property in order.

Instead, Sophie was going to be here on his turf, under his roof, for two weeks. For fourteen days and nights he would be seeing her, smelling her, wanting to make love to the most delectable, desirable woman he'd ever met.

Mark watched an owl fly across the path of the moon, and let out a heavy sigh. Sophie was probably wise to be wary of more complications. She'd already had more than her share of problems after their one night in

London, and when her two weeks were up she should be free to fly home without the burden of extra emotional baggage.

It might have been different if they'd been considering an ongoing relationship, but they both knew there wasn't much point. He could never get a decent job in London, and she was totally unsuited to life at Coolabah Waters.

Damn it. She was right. Friendship was their best option.

He let out a low curse. Why did making the right choice have to feel so wrong?

Sophie lay in bed, staring above her at the fan dangling from the ceiling. After the heat during the day, the night was surprisingly cool, so she hadn't turned it on. She'd left the curtains open so that silvery moonlight could stream through the window. In this light, the paintwork didn't look quite so bad.

But she couldn't sleep.

She was thinking about Mark's kiss and how easily she'd given in. And as she lay there in the moon-washed dark, she was remembering the night they'd met. She'd put up such little resistance that night it had been shameful.

Ever since, she'd been trying not to think too much about it, but perhaps it was important to remember. If she was going to be with Mark for a whole fortnight, that night should serve as a warning....

CHAPTER FIVE

'COME outside with me.'

That was how it had started—with words that had been ringing alarm bells for women since time began.

The wedding reception was almost over, and Emma and Tim had already left for their honeymoon.

'Everyone else will be leaving soon, so come on,' Mark urged. 'Let's take a walk in the garden.'

Sophie knew it was a line and, after the way she'd shamelessly flirted with Mark all evening, she couldn't really blame him for trying. But she was quite sure she would decline his invitation.

'I should help Emma's mother to pack up her wedding dress.'

Mark took Sophie's hand and sent a rush of thrills up her arm. 'There's a swarm of aunts to help her. She doesn't need you. Come on. It's a very important tradition—the best man and the bridesmaid—'

'Dance briefly, as part of the wedding waltz,' Sophie said very firmly as she tried to ignore the effect of his hand on her.

Mark's dark eyes gleamed, and he smiled at her. 'But then they briefly go outside together.'

Sophie laughed and rolled her eyes. 'Do you have much success using that kind of line with Australian girls?'

'Works like a dream every time.'

'I don't believe you. I've met Aussie girls. They're usually very savvy about men.'

'And how many Australian men have you met?'

She had to admit, 'Very few.'

He took her hand. 'Where I live in the Outback, we have almost all our parties outdoors. Under the stars.'

'What are you telling me, Mark? That you're feeling cooped up from being inside a building for too long?'

He grinned. Gorgeously. And Sophie knew she'd played right into his hands. But, strangely, she didn't mind. She'd been feeling miserable for weeks, and tonight, for the first time in ages, she was having a really good time.

In fact, 'good time' was something of an understatement. When she'd danced with Mark she'd been so entranced, so captivated and turned on she'd almost melted on the dance floor.

The look on Oliver's face had been very satisfying.

OK…so there was an undertone of gratitude in her smile as she stepped out into the June evening with Mark. But she felt inexplicably happy, too. The simple act of walking beside the Thames and holding hands had never been more exciting.

Sophie couldn't help but be flattered by all the curious glances they attracted. Mark looked unbelievably handsome in his dark formal evening-suit, and she felt like a film star in her dreamy bridesmaid's gown.

To Mark's disappointment, they couldn't see many stars. London was too brightly lit and the buildings were too tall. But they talked happily.

He told Sophie how he'd met Tim when Tim had gone to Australia in search of an Outback adventure during his gap year.

'Tim ended up working as a jackaroo on my family's property near Rockhampton,' Mark said. 'We became great mates, and we've been friends ever since.'

'That's rather unusual, considering how far apart you live,' Sophie remarked. 'There must have been a lot of phone calls and emails.'

He nodded. 'But we've travelled, too. We've met up at cricket test matches, and a couple of rugby grand finals.'

Sophie told him how she'd known Emma since kindergarten.

'And I organised the musicians for the wedding,' she said. 'I'm an agent for musicians. I hire bands, singers, string quartets, that sort of thing.'

'One of the wedding guests was telling me about all the musicians in your family. Oliver Pebble—no— Pemble-something…'

'Oliver Pembleton,' Sophie mumbled, not at all happy to have that name thrown into the conversation.

'That's it. He seemed to think it was his duty to fill me in about your famous connections.'

'Oh, yes,' she sighed. 'He *would*.'

'If I remember correctly, your father's an orchestral conductor, your mother's an opera singer and your sisters perform as soloists all over Europe?'

Sophie nodded.

'Very impressive. But I'm ashamed to confess I've never heard of any of them till tonight.'

'Bless you!' Sophie let out a hoot of laughter and clapped her hands. Linking her arm through Mark's, she gave it a squeeze. 'I usually have to spend hours listening to people rave on about my family. It gets very tedious explaining that I really don't have any musical talent and that's why I'm an agent and not a performer.'

'So what's your talent?' Mark asked her.

She held up her hands. 'Double-jointed thumbs.'

But then she felt silly and childish, even though Mark was kind enough to laugh.

'What else?' he prompted her.

'I make amazing desserts,' she offered, keen to atone for her gaffe.

'Really? Now, that's an impressive talent. My house-keeper doesn't know any fancy desserts. All I get is the plain stuff. Tinned fruit and ice cream.'

He looked down at her with a wistful, little-boy smile.

'Poor you,' she crooned, and then, unbelievably, she made a fateful mistake. 'I have three-quarters of a lemon-chiffon pie in my fridge.'

Mark grinned. 'And where's your fridge?'

'Don't be greedy. You've already eaten dessert tonight.'

'I know, but where's your fridge?'

She told him.

And before she knew what was happening he'd hailed a taxi.

OK, on the surface it *did* look as if she was very foolish and naïve. She'd normally never dream of taking a man she'd just met back to her flat. But, honestly, she did know she was leaping into dangerous waters. Mark was gorgeous and he'd been such good company, and she couldn't remember an evening when she'd felt so comfortable with a man she'd just met.

When they got back to her flat, she gave Mark a huge helping of lemon-chiffon pie and whipped cream, and a tiny helping for herself to be companionable.

'This is amazing,' he said, his face lit by a smile that seemed very close to rapture. 'It's by far the best dessert I've ever eaten.'

Sophie grinned. 'I told you I was talented.'

She put their bowls and spoons in the sink, and when she turned she found Mark standing close behind her.

That was when she made the *biggest* mistake of the night.

Perhaps she could blame Oliver for being a rat, or she could blame Emma for getting married. Sophie and Emma had been planning their weddings since they'd been nine years old, and she was feeling sentimental, wanted a little romance for herself.

Or maybe Mark was simply and utterly irresistible. Whatever…

'What's your talent, Mark?' she asked him breathlessly.

'I'll show you,' he murmured.

Later, she would cringe at the corniness of it. But at the time she didn't mind a jot, because Mark was already kissing her. His mouth was warm and deliciously seductive. And when he slipped his arms around her their bodies meshed perfectly, and sparks erupted in so many parts of Sophie that she desperately needed to discover every one of Mark's talents.

Her world had fallen apart as easily as that.

Now, as she lay in the back bedroom at Coolabah Waters, her hand pressed to her still-flat stomach, Sophie was miserably aware of the fallout from that one careless, blissfully romantic night.

To add to her mood of general gloom, the moon disappeared behind a bank of clouds, leaving her bedroom swathed in darkness. The fading paintwork, the ceiling fan and the cane chair in the corner disappeared into the suffocating black of the Outback night. She couldn't see a thing, and she couldn't remember where the light switch was. She felt panic stir.

From deep within the house there came a creaking sound, and hairs rose at the back of Sophie's neck. *What was that?*

A footstep?

It couldn't be Mark coming to her room, could it? He wouldn't do that, would he?

Alone in the dark, she was pitifully aware of how little she knew about the father of her baby. He'd seemed gentlemanly enough in London—when he hadn't been busily seducing her. This evening, although he'd kissed her, he'd kept his distance when she'd asked him to. But could she be sure she could trust him?

She heard another sound, another creak, and her ears strained for the soft fall of footsteps. Could he be moving about barefoot?

Her heart began to pound. If only it wasn't so dark.

If only she wasn't here all alone with him in the middle of the big, empty Outback! If only she wasn't such a trusting fool!

Good grief, she'd acted on some crazy impulses in her time, but surely coming here to Outback Australia was the worst, the craziest thing she'd ever done. She was alone out here with one man. A man she barely knew. A man who would much rather have sex with her than stay alone in his room down the hallway.

Again, she heard a creak.

Logic told her that it could be the iron roof, or the old house's timbers shifting in the cooling air. But in the pitch-black, all alone in a strange bed, Sophie's fear won out over logic.

Her heart thumped wildly and she leapt out of bed. Hands groping in front of her, she felt her way across the room to the door and kicked her foot on a chest of drawers, before she found the solid, old-fashioned key in the lock and turned it.

Mark slept badly, and as luck had it the phone rang shortly after dawn. He snatched it up quickly, afraid that its ringing would reach Sophie's room and disturb her.

Sinking groggily back onto his pillows, he mumbled, 'Good morning.' He blinked when he realised the caller was Tim.

'Apologies for calling so early, Mark, but Emma badgered me. Claims she can't rest till she knows if Sophie has reached your place in one piece.'

'Oh, sure,' Mark said, hefting onto one elbow and

squinting at his bedside clock—it had just gone five. 'Sophie got here yesterday. She's fine.'

'Thank God for that.'

Mark heard Tim relaying the news to his wife, and then Emma's voice issuing some kind of instruction. 'I'm not going to tell him that,' Tim hissed in a poorly disguised stage whisper. 'Of course he'll be nice to her.'

Mark sank back onto the pillow and rolled his eyes at the ceiling. 'Tell Emma I'll handle Sophie with kid gloves,' he said. 'I'm a very nice guy.' *Despite having made the poor girl pregnant.*

'I told Em she was worked up about nothing,' Tim said. 'But she's worried because of what happened last time.'

'Last time?' Mark frowned and scratched the back of his neck. 'What are you talking about? What last time? Surely Sophie hasn't been pregnant before?'

'No, mate. Nothing like that. But hasn't she told you about her ex?'

An uneasy pang circled Mark's heart. 'No. What about him?'

'Downright cad of a boyfriend. Dropped her cold a few months ago, just as they were about to announce their engagement.'

The pang in Mark's heart arrowed through his guts. 'Really?'

'Sophie was hurt rather badly,' Tim said. 'Understandable, of course, but she's a tender-hearted little thing. Was absolutely gutted when he turned up with a new fiancée just a few weeks later.'

Mark drew a sharp breath.

'That's why Emma and I are thrilled that the two of

you have hit it off,' Tim added. 'Bad luck about the un-planned pregnancy, of course, but I'm sure you'll work something out.'

Mark swallowed, couldn't bring himself to reply.

'At least we know we can rely on you to play it straight with Sophie,' Tim said.

'Yes,' Mark said faintly. 'Of course.'

When Tim said goodbye, Mark stared grimly at the receiver. Throwing his bed clothes aside, he launched himself out of bed and paced his room, aware of the anxious ache that had settled in the pit of his stomach.

Bloody hell. Poor Sophie. Dumped by one man, made pregnant by the next. Talk about leaping out of the frying pan into the furnace.

He sighed heavily, ploughed frantic fingers through his hair. He'd assured Tim that he would 'play it straight' with Sophie. And that was right. He had no in-tention of stringing her along with false promises. But was that enough?

Last night they'd both agreed that marriage wasn't really an option, but was Sophie secretly hoping for a proposal from him? Or was she extra wary of commit-ment, after her experience with this other jerk?

Last night she'd been nervous when he'd tried to kiss her. But then she'd liked it.

No doubt the poor girl was as confused as he was.

It was beginning to make sense now.

It made no sense at all.

Sophie slept in.

When she still hadn't emerged from her room at half-past ten, Mark made a pot of tea and toast with marmalade, piled everything onto a tray and knocked on her bedroom door.

There was no answer, and he told himself that it was to be expected. The woman was tired and jet-lagged.

Just the same, an unreasonable fear sent alarm creeping through him like spiders.

He set the tray on the floor and tried to open the door, and was surprised to discover that it was locked.

He knocked again carefully, and then called, 'Sophie? Are you all right?'

Still no sound.

He felt something close to panic, considered his options and was about to force the door with his shoulder when he heard a muffled sound.

A voice called faintly. Then silence again. His heart hammered as he imagined all sorts of dreadful possibilities. 'Sophie!' he cried. 'What's the matter?'

At last he heard footsteps on the bare-timber floor, the rattle of the key, and finally the door squeaking open on rusty hinges.

Sophie stood before him in a fine, white cotton nightgown rendered transparent by the morning sunlight pouring through the window behind her. Mark's breathing faltered. She was so exquisite—her lush curves and slenderness balanced in perfect proportion. He was grateful he'd already set the tray down or he might have dropped the lot.

Sweeping a tumble of dark curls out of her eyes, she smiled shyly.

'Good afternoon, Sleeping Beauty.' He was dismayed that his voice sound ragged and off-key, as if he'd run out of breath.

'What time is it?' she asked, blinking sleepily. 'Have I slept in?'

With commendable restraint, Mark kept his gaze strictly on her face. 'It's just gone half-past ten. I wasn't sure how long I should leave you.'

'Heavens, I'm glad you woke me.'

He retrieved the tray and Sophie's eyes widened.

'You've made breakfast, Mark? How kind.' But then she sagged against the door frame, groaned weakly, pressed a hand to her stomach and another against her mouth.

'What's the matter?' Mark cried, feeling helpless as he stood there with the tray.

She whispered, 'I need to use the bathroom.' Moaning softly, she pushed at him with a frantic hand.

He sprang back, giving her a clear path as she stumbled wretchedly down the hallway.

Hell. Last night he'd been fantasising about seducing this woman.

This was reality, he thought as he heard distressing sounds coming from the bathroom. This was Sophie Felsham's life for the next seven months—morning sickness, a baby growing inside her, stretching her body beyond recognition, and finally the frightening pain of giving birth. The responsibility of a new life, and the round-the-clock care of a baby.

And what was Mark's role—to watch from the side-lines?

What a damned crazy situation! Sophie had been

trying to recover from one disastrous relationship when she'd been landed with this. And Mark was totally implicated, utterly guilty, but unsure exactly what she wanted from him.

Suddenly, two weeks didn't seem nearly long enough for them to work out a solution.

Sophie felt much better when the dash to the bathroom was over and she'd washed her face, cleaned her teeth and combed her hair.

She came back into the bedroom and was surprised to find that Mark was still there, his eyes sympathetic. Worried.

'Does that happen every morning?'

'Just about.'

He shook his head, gave her a rueful smile. 'It's not fair, is it?'

'Oh, it could be worse. At least it's only first thing in the morning. Some poor women are sick all day long.' She sat on the edge of the bed and looked at the tray laden with tea and toast.

'I wasn't sure if you'd still want breakfast,' he said. 'But if you like, I'll make a fresh lot.'

'Don't bother. This will be fine, thanks.'

'It'll be cold.' He reached to take the tray. 'Let me make you some more. You hop back into bed. Put your feet up. This won't take a minute.'

'You're spoiling me,' Sophie protested, but she did exactly as she was told.

She remembered her middle-of-the-night fears about

Mark, and felt a twinge of guilt. He couldn't have been nicer or more caring if he'd been a loving husband.

It was irrational of her, but she found his kindness disconcerting. She couldn't shake off her fear that she might fall in love with him and get hurt. What if she got to the end of these two weeks and found that she wanted to stay with him, while Mark was more than happy to let her go?

Where's your stiff upper lip, Sophie? No need to throw in the towel just yet.

'Fresh tea and hot toast,' Mark said a little later, returning as promised in a jiffy, and setting the tray carefully on her bedside table.

'Mark, you're an angel. A knight in shining denim.'

He looked embarrassed and put his thumbs through the belt loops in his jeans. 'I'll leave you to have it in peace. Take as long as you like.'

Sophie enjoyed her breakfast immensely. She couldn't remember ever having eaten breakfast in bed before, not unless she'd made it for herself, and that didn't count. Afterwards, she dressed and took her tray to the kitchen, where she found Mark at the sink washing dishes.

For a moment she paused, rather stunned by the sight of this tall, mega-masculine cattleman dressed in battered jeans and a long-sleeved blue cotton shirt, engaged in such a domestic task. Her mind conjured a disturbing image of his strong, workmanlike hands tending to a little baby—bathing her, changing her nappy, laughing and blowing kisses while he chattered in baby talk.

Good grief. If she didn't get a grip on her imagination, she was going to find herself in no end of trouble.

Luckily the phone rang, providing a distraction.

Mark wiped his hands on a towel and grabbed the receiver from the wall. He frowned as he concentrated on the caller's message. 'OK. I'll come straight over,' was all he said, and then he hung up.

Sophie couldn't help wondering what this meant. Where was Mark going? Would she be involved?

His face was grim as he looked at her. 'That was my neighbour, Andrew Jackson. There's been an accident. A truck full of cattle has rolled coming out of a creek crossing.'

'That sounds bad. Is anyone hurt?'

'I don't think so. But it's on my boundary, so I'll have to head over there and see what I can do.'

'Oh.'

Sophie gulped.

At home there would be police, ambulances and the fire brigade all rushing to the scene of an accident. But the Outback was so remote that people had to depend on their neighbours to help them out. How scary was that?

'How will you be able to help, Mark?'

'Hard to say. I might be able to give them a hand to jack up the truck. Or I might have to use the winch on the four-wheel drive to pull them upright.' He shrugged. 'They might need assistance with injured cattle.'

'I—I see.' Sophie felt more than a little out of her depth. 'I don't suppose I'll be any use?'

He smiled. 'You'd be much better off resting here.'

That puts me in my place—the useless English girl.

Sophie hated the thought of being left alone again. Was this the fate of all Outback women? To be abandoned while their men ran around being heroes?

'What can I do, Mark?'

About to rush off, he paused, framed by the flyscreen door, then he came back into the room and touched her lightly on the elbow. 'You'll be OK here, won't you?'

No, she wouldn't be OK. She'd been looking forward to spending a whole day with Mark, but she couldn't bear him to think of her as a wimp. 'I'll be fine,' she assured him, holding her head high.

If this was the sort of thing that happened on Mark's property, then she was determined to try and fit in. No matter how scared she was, she had to make the best of it. 'Can I fix you a snack to take with you?'

Mark's eyes warmed in a way that made Sophie's blood sing. 'Some tea would be terrific. Can you put it in a flask? I'm going to load a few things into the ute.'

'All right.'

Sophie was glad she'd snooped in Mark's kitchen yesterday so she knew where things were. She flew to the kettle, and while the water was coming to the boil she collected bread, butter, cheese and pickles and began to make sandwiches. By the time Mark returned, the tea was in a flask, the sandwiches wrapped and in a paper bag along with oatmeal biscuits and an orange.

'This should keep you going,' she said, handing them to him.

He looked both surprised and delighted. 'Thanks.' With his free hand he drew her close, pressed a kiss to her forehead. It was only the lightest brush of his lips, but it sent a thrill from her breastbone to her toes.

A small gleam came into his eyes as he let her go and then he turned abruptly, snagged a wide-brimmed hat from a rack on the wall and set it on his head at a careless angle.

Sophie had trouble keeping up with his long-legged strides as he hurried across the yard to the parked truck.

Mark slanted her a crooked smile. 'Could you feed the dogs and give them water?'

'Oh, sure.'

She hoped she didn't sound as stunned and nervous as she felt. Her experience with dogs was limited to her mother's toy poodle.

'Come to think of it,' Mark said, frowning, 'I'd better take Monty with me. I might need his help to keep the cattle in check. But I'll unchain Blue Dog and leave him with you. I'll feel better about leaving you here, if you have a dog about the place.'

'Why? Am I in real danger here?'

'Not with one of my dogs to keep an eye on you.'

That's not what I wanted to hear.

Scant minutes later, Sophie stood with her hands on her hips and with a blue-speckled cattle dog sitting at her heels.

'He's a working dog, so don't try to pat him,' Mark warned as he swung into the driver's seat.

Sophie cast a wary glance at Blue Dog's teeth. *Oh, help.* She was scared—of the dog, of the empty Outback, of being alone. 'Are you sure I wouldn't be any use if I came with you, Mark?'

He didn't hear her. Already he was slamming his door shut and revving the engine. With an elbow on the window sill, he leaned out.

'Why don't you check out my collection of DVDs? There should be something there to keep you entertained.'

With a wave, and a grin that made his teeth flash white in his brown face, he took off in a flurry of dust.

Blue Dog sat quietly beside Sophie, his tongue lolling as he panted, and the raw heat of the sun stung the back of her bare neck as she watched Mark hurry off down the rutted track without a backwards glance.

Hard to believe that half an hour ago she was being spoiled with breakfast in bed.

Sophie lost count of the number of times she went to the front veranda to look out, her hand shielding her eyes from the glare as she scoured the sunburnt paddocks, hoping to see a cloud of dust that meant Mark was on his way home.

She told herself that there was no need to be scared—not with Blue Dog sprawled across the front steps, his ears alert, his eyes watchful as he kept guard.

She didn't want to feel sorry for herself today. This was what happened in Mark's Outback, and if she was going to spend two weeks here she might as well try her level best to fit in. But she would not watch DVDs like a spoilt teenager, she would keep busy.

She found dried dog-food and put it in a bowl for Blue Dog, and poured water into another bowl. He lapped thirstily and then sank back into his sprawling pose across the top of the steps. He was a very quiet dog, not at all yappy, unlike her mother's poodle. It didn't seem right that she shouldn't pat him, but she caught another glimpse of those teeth and was quite happy to obey Mark.

Even though Mark's housekeeper had left meals, Sophie decided that apart from watering the pot plants on the veranda the only useful thing she could do was to cook. She loved cooking, and it might help to calm her frazzled nerves.

She turned on the radio for company, and to try to block out the disturbing silence of the vast, empty plains outside. She hunted through the enormous deep freeze in Mark's kitchen and found minced beef, so she made a huge lasagna. And a search of the pantry produced all the necessary ingredients for a traditional English sherry-trifle, so she made one of those, too.

With enough food to throw a party, she abandoned the kitchen and wandered through the house, picturing ways it could be improved with paint, curtains and attractive furniture.

She took her afternoon cup of tea onto the front veranda, so she could keep a lookout for Mark. But instead of Mark she saw a flock of large, ugly emus straggling across the stretch of dry grass in front of the homestead. Sophie watched them warily. The dog took no notice of them, but they were quite scary, with long legs, scraggy necks and fat bodies covered in untidy, dark-grey feathers.

Their eyes were fierce and staring, and their beaks strong and too sharply pointed for Sophie's liking. She waved her hands at them, trying to shoo them away, but they kept coming closer. She tried to remember what she'd heard about them. Were they vicious?

Her heart thrashed. Could they climb the front stairs? Could their ghastly beaks peck her to death? Terrified, she raced back inside the house and watched them through a window.

I hate this place!

Everything in the Outback was ugly and scary. Sophie fought back tears. She felt unbearably homesick for lovely green England with its hills of emerald velvet and its gentle valleys, its bluebell woods and pretty, babbling brooks.

Why on earth had she thought it was a good idea to come here?

The emus hung around for ages, but at last they wandered away. Relieved, Sophie was about to take a shower when the hot, still silence of the afternoon was broken by the shrill ring of the telephone.

Please let it be Mark. She tore through the house, and was a little breathless as she answered it.

'Hello, Sophie,' said a friendly voice. 'I'm Jill Jackson, Mark's neighbour.'

'Oh, hello!'

'I thought I'd ring to let you know that Mark is on his way home.'

Sinking thankfully onto a kitchen stool, Sophie said, 'That's good news, Jill. Thanks so much for letting me know.'

'Mark saved the day,' Jill said. 'The men would never have righted the truck without his help.'

'Really?' Sophie found that she was absurdly pleased. 'Then he's earned the nice dinner I've prepared for him.'

Jill laughed. 'I dare say he has.'

'I'm glad you rang.'

'My pleasure. I was pretty sure Mark wouldn't think

to ring. The men were so preoccupied with a smashed-up road train and two hundred head of cattle that phone calls home wouldn't have scanned on their radar. But I know what it's like, waiting for news.'

'Thanks a lot. I appreciate it. Are you still there? At the crash?'

'Yes. I drove over at lunch time with extra provisions, but I'm heading home again now.'

Obviously, Jill was a proper Outback woman, the kind who pitched in with the men when necessary. Sophie squashed thoughts of inadequacy. She'd stayed back at the lonely homestead without a whimper, and that had been an act of courage as far as she was concerned.

'Andrew and I are hoping that you and Mark can come over for lunch,' Jill said. 'Actually, I've already mentioned it to Mark, and he suggested that Thursday would suit.'

'Oh? Well, yes, that would be lovely. Thank you.'

'I can't wait to meet you, Sophie.' Jill spoke with surprising warmth.

Sophie blinked. 'Really?'

'Mark's a wonderful neighbour. The nicest man I've ever known. Not counting Andrew, I suppose I should add.'

Sophie drew a shaky breath.

'We'll see you on Thursday, then?' enquired Jill.

'Yes,' Sophie assured her. 'I'm really looking forward to it.' But she couldn't help wondering what Mark had told his neighbours. What had he said that had caused the air of contained excitement in Jill's voice?

* * *

As soon as she heard the sound of a vehicle Sophie ran to the front veranda again, her eyes hungry for her first sight of Mark. She watched his truck roar up the track in a cloud of dust, saw the outline of his broad-brimmed hat and his wide shoulders, and her heart gave a very definite skip.

Mark waved, but kept driving around to the back of the house and came to a rattling stop under an enormous shade tree.

Blue Dog became a blurred streak, shooting down the steps and around the side of the house while Sophie followed at a more sedate pace. She watched Mark swing easily out of the truck and bend down to scratch the dog between his ears. 'Have you been a good guard dog?'

'He didn't move from the front steps,' Sophie announced as she drew near them.

Mark grinned at the dog, then looked up at her, and his face grew serious. 'How have you been?' he asked quietly.

'Fine.' She was determined that he mustn't guess how scared she'd been or how much she'd missed him.

'Good girl,' he said, in much the same tone that he might say 'good dog', and then he straightened, took off his hat and ran his fingers through his dark hair. 'It's been a big day.'

Dinner that evening was very pleasant. Mark ate with clear enjoyment, and complimented Sophie's cooking many times. He told her about his day and about his neighbours, the Jacksons. Sophie wanted to ask him what he'd told them about her, but she decided to hold her tongue. Perhaps she'd misread Jill, and was making Mount Everest out of a molehill.

But as they carried the plates back to the kitchen she was rather surprised to see that Mark was frowning at her.

'What's the matter?' she asked.

'Tim rang this morning,' he said. 'He rang quite early, while you were still asleep, but then you were sick, and I was in such a rush to get away I decided not to mention it then.'

Sophie smacked a hand to her forehead. 'I forgot to ring Emma last night.' She'd been so caught up in events here that her friend had slipped her mind. 'I promised I'd ring to tell her I'd arrived safely. I suppose Tim was checking up on me.'

'Well, yes, he was asking about you. He knows about the baby.'

'Emma told him. I had to confide in her, Mark. She's my best friend.'

He nodded. 'Tim gave me quite a lecture. Carried on about what a sweet little thing you are.'

'Naturally.' Sophie tossed a coy smile over her shoulder as she rinsed their plates at the sink.

Mark said quietly, but with a disturbing undertone, 'He mentioned your boyfriend.'

'Oliver?' Sophie's smile vanished. She still couldn't say that name without feeling sick. 'He's my ex,' she said stiffly. 'But I don't see why Tim needed to mention him.'

Leaning against a kitchen cupboard, Mark folded his arms and regarded her from beneath slightly hooded, unreadable eyes.

Sophie squirmed. 'I suppose Tim told you how we broke up?'

'He said you were about to announce your engagement when the boyfriend suddenly called it off.'

She nodded.

'Sounds like a nasty type.'

'Oliver's a rat,' she said vehemently.

'Oliver?' Mark's frown deepened. 'Wasn't there a guy called Oliver at the wedding—a tall, fair-haired fellow?'

'Yes.'

His eyes narrowed. 'He had a fiancée dangling on his arm, didn't he? I remember there were people making quite a fuss.'

Sophie's stomach lurched uncomfortably, and she gripped the edge of the sink. Mark would think she was such a loser.

'Don't tell me that Oliver guy at the wedding was your ex?'

Feeling sick, Sophie nodded. She turned to check Mark's expression. Too late, she realised where this conversation was heading.

'I don't suppose,' he said with menacing quiet, 'old Oliver was the reason you were so keen to dance with *me?*'

Sophie flinched, suddenly hypnotised by the dawning anger in Mark's eyes. She knew she had to defend herself, but her tongue was glued to the roof of her mouth.

'You might have warned me you were on the rebound,' he said.

'But I—'

'It might have been fair to let me know that I was ammunition for your counter attack. I would have appreciated knowing that you flirted with me and danced with me, and *slept* with me, simply because you needed to snub Oliver.'

She wanted to cry, '*No, no, no!*'

But what was the point of lying when Mark had already worked out the truth?

Except…except he only had half the truth.

Nevertheless, guilt flooded Sophie. She didn't dare to look at Mark. She stared at the floor while her heart began a panicky dance. With every moment that she spent with Mark, she liked him more—really liked him—in spite of his Outback. And she hoped that he liked her.

Deep down, she nursed a secret hope that they might find a way to make their relationship work. But if she couldn't allay Mark's doubts she might as well pack her bags and head straight back to London now.

Bravely, she lifted her head to meet his burning black gaze. 'I'll admit I started flirting with you to show Oliver that he hadn't hurt me.'

Mark remained very still with his arms tightly crossed over his chest, his face a dark, inscrutable mask. 'I need to check on the dogs,' he said quietly, and he turned to leave.

'But I haven't finished, Mark. You need to understand. My feelings were very mixed up that night, but when I—'

'Don't make it worse,' he snapped. 'I understand perfectly.' And then he shoved the flyscreen door open and strode out into the black of the night.

Sophie ran after him, batting blindly at the flyscreen door and letting it slam behind her, but when she got to the veranda she stopped. She desperately wanted to follow him, but beyond the house it was dark.

Already Mark had disappeared.

Oh, help. There were snakes and spiders out there that she wouldn't be able to see. And somewhere out in the dark paddocks there was a dreadful bird that kept making a blood-curdling, mournful cry like a distraught mother crying for a dead child.

'Mark, wait!'

His voice came out of the darkness. 'Do me a favour, Sophie. Stay inside.'

He spoke with such deep, quiet authority that she knew this was an order. It was not the time to confront Mark.

She had no choice but to stay in the safe, brightly lit kitchen and wait for him to come back inside.

Sick at heart, she stacked the dishwasher, then made a pot of tea and drank two cups. But Mark didn't come back.

Sophie knew he was avoiding her. He obviously had a stubborn streak and a great deal of pride, and she could hear him out in one of the sheds, tinkering with machinery. Eventually she understood there was no point in trying to talk this through tonight.

Feeling utterly miserable, she gave up waiting and went to bed. She could only hope that in the morning Mark would be prepared to listen.

CHAPTER SIX

THE phone rang again next morning, just as Mark came into the kitchen. He'd slept badly, and wasn't in the mood for phone calls, and he snatched it up angrily.

'Good morning.'

'Is that Coolabah Waters?'

The caller was a woman with a rich, mature and highly cultured English accent. Fine hairs lifted on the back of Mark's neck. Almost certainly the woman was calling Sophie, but, judging by the ominous sounds he'd heard when he'd passed the bathroom just now, she was in the grip of morning sickness.

'Yes,' he said carefully. 'This is Mark Winchester speaking.'

'Eliza Felsham here, Mark. I believe my daughter, Sophie, may have visited you recently.'

Something brick-shaped lodged in Mark's throat. He'd been mentally preparing himself for an awkward conversation with Sophie's father at some stage in the future, but her mother was another matter entirely. He swallowed. 'Sophie's still here, Lady Eliza. I—I imagine you'd like to speak to her?'

'Yes, please. But, before you go, there are a few questions I'd like to ask you.' The imperious voice made him squirm like a schoolboy summoned to the head-mistress's office.

'Certainly.' Mark hoped his grimace didn't show in his voice. He took a deep breath. 'What would you like to know?'

He braced himself for the worst.

Is it true that you've impregnated my precious daughter? Haven't you heard of safe sex in Australia?

'Where exactly in Australia do you live, Mark?'

The unexpected question caught him flat-footed, and he wished he could clear his throat. 'I have a cattle property in north-western Queensland.'

'What's the name of the nearest town?'

'Wandabilla.'

'Wanda *what*?' Lady Eliza demanded. 'How do you spell that?'

Patiently, Mark told her.

'Hmm…that doesn't show here. Could you tell me the nearest good-sized city?'

Mark suppressed an uneasy sigh. Lady Eliza's prima-donna qualities were certainly coming to the fore. 'The nearest town of note would be Mount Isa.' He heard the rustle of pages in the background, as if Sophie's mother was searching through an atlas.

'Ah, yes, I've found it,' she said. 'Good heavens.' There was an unnervingly long beat of silence. 'You must be very isolated.'

Mark forced a smile into his voice. 'Coolabah Waters is remote, but don't worry about your daughter's safety, Lady Eliza. She's—' he inhaled sharply '—in good hands.'

'I'm very pleased to hear that, Mark.' Her tone was surprisingly pleasant.

'I'll get Sophie.'

'Thank you.'

He hurried down the hallway to the bathroom and knocked on the door. 'Sophie?' he called carefully.

There was no reply. No doubt she was upset with him, after last night.

'Sophie!' Mark called more loudly, and his heart began an echoing knock against his ribs as he imagined the excuses he would have to offer Lady Eliza if her daughter wasn't well enough to come to the phone.

But to his relief the door opened and Sophie appeared, looking pale and tired, as if she hadn't slept.

'Your mother's on the phone,' he told her.

She groaned and closed her eyes, but almost immediately her eyes flashed open again. 'Does she know about the baby?'

Mark lifted his hands helplessly. 'She didn't mention it to me.'

'I begged Emma not to tell her.'

'I don't think she knows. She doesn't sound upset, but she's waiting. You can take the call in my study, if you like. I'll hang up the phone in the kitchen.'

Sophie felt several versions of rotten as she made her way to the study. The continuing effects of jet lag, morning sickness and Mark's horrible reaction after dinner last night had been a lethal combination.

Gingerly, she lifted the receiver. 'Hello, Mum. How are you?'

'I'm perfectly fine, darling. Just a little surprised, of course. I didn't expect to get back from Milan and find a garbled message on my phone telling me you've taken off for Australia on a holiday. That was a sudden decision, wasn't it?'

'Well, yes, it was a bit.'

'You left no information except this one telephone number, Sophie. Are you all right, dear? You sound a little…flat.'

'I'm fine, Mum.' Sophie injected extra brightness into her voice. 'Brilliant, actually.'

'That's good to hear.' After a pause, 'So how long are you staying at Mark Winchester's cattle property?'

After last night, she wasn't sure how she stood with Mark, but she said, 'About two weeks.'

This was greeted by unpromising silence. And then, 'When did you meet this young man, darling?'

'A couple of months ago.' Sophie tried to sound breezy and cool. 'At Emma and Tim's wedding. Mark was Tim's best man.'

'Oh, I see.' Her mother's tone was instantly lighter, and indicated that she saw much more than Sophie would have liked her to. 'So Mark's a good friend of Tim's, obviously.'

'That's right.'

There was a distinct sigh of relief. 'I'm sure he must be a fine young man, then.'

A coy chuckle on the other end of the line startled Sophie. She swallowed her gasp of surprise.

'I must say, Mark has the most marvellous voice, Sophie. A very rich baritone. Almost a bass.'

'Yes, it is deep.'

'I imagine he must be very tall?'

'Quite tall.'

'And dark?'

'Yes, Mum.'

To Sophie's alarm, her mother let out a sound that was suspiciously close to a dreamy sigh. 'It was such a pity that your father and I had to go to Sweden and miss the wedding. I must ring Emma and ask to see her photos.'

Sophie winced. Now her mother was getting disturbingly excited, almost as if she could hear another set of wedding bells in the air. 'Mum, Mark and I are—are just friends.'

'Yes, dear. Of course. And his Outback cattle property is so interesting that you don't want to bother with any of the sights in Australia—Sydney or Uluru or the Great Barrier Reef?'

'I—I don't have enough money to visit all those expensive tourist-spots.'

After a pause, Lady Eliza asked, 'Are there many people living on Coolabah Waters? I understand that some of those big properties have huge numbers of staff.'

'Umm.' Sophie's hand felt suddenly slick with sweat, and she almost dropped the telephone receiver. 'Mark has a caretaker, but—' She cast a frantic glance to the doorway, but Mark had disappeared. 'But he's had to go away.'

'How inconvenient.' Eliza's voice rippled with a

complicated blend of concern and innuendo. 'So you and Mark are spending two weeks alone?'

'More—more or less.'

'Sophie, darling, you are being sensible, aren't you?'

'Of course, Mum.'

'You're such a warm, impulsive little thing. I'd hate you to break your heart again.'

'Don't worry about me. I'm being super-sensible. And I'll be home again before you know it.'

To her surprise, her mother seemed willing to leave it at that. 'All right, then. I won't be a bore and make a fuss. So I suppose there's not much for me to say, except enjoy yourself, my dear.'

'I will. Thanks for calling, Mum. Give my love to Dad.'

'Yes, yes. Stay safe, darling.'

As soon as Sophie hung up, she slumped in the chair beside Mark's desk. Until this morning, she'd pushed her parents out of her mind. But now she could picture her mother's intelligent, beautiful face, could hear her relaying this phone conversation to her father. Sir Kenneth would not be so easily mollified, and he certainly wouldn't be won over by Mark's smooth, dark, baritone voice.

To make matters worse, Sophie knew that as soon as her mother saw photos of Mark, looking so handsome and splendid in his best man's suit, she would be convinced that her daughter had fallen head-over-heels in love with him. And she would quiz poor Emma.

And Emma knew about the baby.

Oh, help!

Sophie jumped from the chair in sudden panic and hurried down the hallway to the kitchen. 'Mark?'

He was doing something with a frying pan at the stove, and he turned as she hurried into the room. 'Everything all right?' he asked.

'On the surface,' she said with an uncertain shrug.

'Does your mother know—about the baby?'

'Not yet. But I'll have to ring Emma, to warn her to be ready for a call.'

'That's fine. Go ahead.'

Mark was polite enough, but he still spoke with an edge of reserve that chilled Sophie. As she returned to the study and dialled Emma's number, she wished she felt more confident about her chances of convincing him that she hadn't just used him to get back at Oliver.

But how hard would it be to convince him? She'd known from the start that there was something very strong and rock solid about Mark, a kind of unfailing inner strength, but that probably meant he was also very stubborn.

Emma's number was engaged. 'Damn,' Sophie said softly. 'I wonder if Mum's already called her.' After a panicky moment, she decided she would have to try Emma's mobile. You never knew, she might answer it even if she was taking another call.

She dialled, and chewed her lip as she waited.

Emma's voice said, 'Hello?'

Sophie let out a huff of relief. 'Emma, it's Sophie.'

'Sophie? What a coincidence. I'm in the middle of a phone conversation with your mother.'

'Oh, she beat me to it. I was hoping to warn you. Is she grilling you about Mark?'

'And how.'

Sophie nodded sympathetically. 'You won't tell her, will you? About the baby?'

'Trust me, Sox. I won't spill the beans. But I'd better hurry back. I'm in the middle of telling Lady E how dashing and gorgeous and marriageable your Mark is.'

'But why? There's no talk of us getting married!'

'Well, that's a jolly shame,' Emma remarked unhelpfully.

Sophie felt only marginally better as she hung up. She imagined Emma and her mother gossiping madly about her, and she pressed her hands over her mouth to hold back a groan. Very soon her father and sisters would all know about Mark. They would be certain Sophie was madly in love with him. Why else would she have dashed to the other side of the world to be with him?

And, after the fiasco with Oliver, they would be on tenterhooks, half expecting her to end up with a broken heart again. Another failure.

And, unless she could redress last night's misunderstanding, she knew that was exactly where she was heading.

Mark's sausages and tomatoes were almost burned black, but he stayed at the stove, wrestling with his thoughts.

He'd been rattled ever since last night's revelation. Until then, he'd assumed that Sophie had come all this way because she fancied him, because she hoped to make a go of their relationship. Poor fool that he was, he'd allowed himself to imagine that they'd both shared a similar instant attraction at the wedding.

He'd thought a lot about it last night, nursing his ego as he'd tinkered uselessly with the old tractor in the shed.

Now, he realised he hadn't a clue how Sophie really felt, and it disturbed him more than it probably should to know that he'd been part of a payback manoeuvre. A payback manoeuvre that had misfired.

And how it had misfired! Sophie's pregnancy had to be the worst possible result.

On top of that, Tim and Emma and Lady Eliza Felsham were all worried that she would be hurt again. Man, talk about pressure on him.

Problem was, he'd fallen halfway in love with a woman who probably had no interest in him apart from the child they'd accidentally conceived.

And yet, he couldn't help feeling sorry for Sophie, couldn't help wanting to protect her.

Getting this right was like walking a tightrope, and Mark was damn sure he didn't want to put a foot wrong. He had to make clear decisions with his head, not his heart. He had to set aside the romantic notion that he could woo Sophie over the next two weeks, had to ignore her tempting little mouth, her delectable body.

He had to remember that she wouldn't want to live here anyway. His mission had to be to take the best possible care of her and send her home in two weeks' time with a secure promise of regular contact and financial support.

Until then he would keep her safe.

They ate in uncomfortable silence.

Sophie waited until Mark had finished his breakfast

before she tried to take up where they'd left off last night. She'd had a lot of time to think about what she had to say, but she still wasn't sure that when she opened her mouth the right words would come out.

Butterflies fluttered in her stomach as she watched Mark drain the last of his coffee and set the cup down.

His expression was carefully blank as he looked at her. 'I thought you might like to take a tour over parts of the property today. If you're feeling up to it, that is.'

She took a deep breath, and spread her hands flat on the table. 'Before we talk about that, there's something else more important that I want to set straight.'

His throat worked. 'What is it?' He dropped his gaze, and began to gather up his breakfast things.

'Look at me, please, Mark.'

His hands stopped moving. Very slowly, he lifted his head, and Sophie's heart began to thump when she saw that all warmth had drained from his face.

I have to get this right. I can't make another mistake.

'You have to believe me,' she said. 'It's true that I started flirting with you at the wedding to get back at Oliver. But my decision to invite you back to my flat had nothing to do with Oliver. It was all about you.'

Nervously she reached out and touched the back of his hand with her fingertips. 'The only thing that influenced me to sleep with you was how I felt about you. I didn't give Oliver a single thought. It was all about you, Mark.'

When he didn't protest, she hurried on more confidently. 'You were far too dashing and handsome, Mark. I was totally smitten. A girl didn't stand a chance with you kitted out in your best-man's finery.'

He was looking deep into her eyes now.

Oh, please let him see that I'm telling the truth!

She held her breath.

Slowly, slowly, a faint glimmer stirred the darkness in his eyes. His upper lip curled as if he was fighting hard not to smile. At last, he said, 'So the expensive suit I hired did the trick?'

'I promise. You were a knockout, Mr Winchester.'

'Touché,' he said softly. 'You were far too lovely in your pretty bridesmaid's gown.'

'Really?'

'Oh, yeah.'

His smile came fully then, warming his whole face, making his eyes shine with a glow that caused a clutch in Sophie heart. She drew a deep breath of relief. Mark did the same.

Yesterday, they might have fallen into each other's arms. Today they were more cautious.

Mark simply stood, but his tread was lighter as he took his dishes to the sink. 'About this tour of the property,' he said. 'Are you interested?'

If Mark had asked that question when she'd first arrived, Sophie might have been content with a tame tour over Coolabah Waters. But ever since Jill's phone call, she'd been hoping to become more involved in the day-to-day life on his cattle property. She wanted to impress him, needed to prove that she could fit in.

'Are you sure you have time for a sightseeing tour?' she asked. 'What about your work? You've been away for a couple of weeks, and I'm sure you must have oodles to do.'

His eyebrows lifted in surprise. 'There are fences

that need fairly urgent attention,' he admitted. 'But a fencing job would take me most of the day. It would mean abandoning you again.'

'Why can't I come, too?'

Mark couldn't have looked more surprised if she'd announced that she wanted to walk across the Simpson Desert barefoot. 'It's too hot out there, Sophie. You'd hate it.'

'I've been outside. It's not that bad. I'd like to come.'

'But you're pregnant,' he protested.

'That doesn't mean I'm made of porcelain.'

'You were sick again this morning,' he added faintly. 'And I promised your mother I'd take good care of you.'

'I'm feeling fine now, Mark. I'd like to come.'

He sighed.

Hands on hips, Sophie eyed him levelly. 'I'm not a snowflake in the desert. I'm prepared to give your Outback a go.'

He cast a cautious glance over her clothes—denim shorts and a sleeveless cotton top.

'You couldn't go out dressed like that. That lovely skin of yours would be burned to a crisp in ten minutes out there. You'll have to cover up. Do you have jeans and a long-sleeved shirt?'

'I brought jeans, but none of my shirts have long sleeves.'

'You'll have to borrow one of mine, then. You can roll the sleeves up and wear it loose over the top—just to keep the sun off.'

Sophie was so pleased that Mark had stopped fighting her objections, she would have worn a tent.

He looked down at her dainty white sandals covered in daisies. 'Do you have anything sturdier to put on your feet?'

'Would sneakers do?'

'They'll have to. What about a hat?'

'I brought a sunhat with me.'

'A decent one with a wide brim?'

'Well, the brim's not terribly wide. I needed something I could squash into my suitcase. But if I unpick the daisies—'

Mark laughed. 'Forget it. You'd better wear one of my hats, too. It might not be pretty, but it will save your complexion.'

Half an hour later, she was grateful for Mark's big blue, double-pocket cotton shirt and his hat with a brim as wide as a veranda. She was standing in the middle of an enormous brown paddock with a fierce sun beating down, while she watched Mark pace out a line for metal fence-posts that he called star pickets.

To Sophie, the pickets looked rather thin and insubstantial—nothing like the old stone walls and strong timber fences on the farms she'd seen in England.

'Why don't you use timber?' she asked.

'The white ants would eat timber posts in no time,' he said as he pulled on leather gloves and began to lift heavy rolls of barbed wire from the back of the ute. 'We use timber from special termite-resistant trees for the gate posts and strainers, but otherwise these are best.'

'Do you have to look after all your fences?' There seemed to be thousands of miles of them.

'I use contract fencers for the big jobs. This is just a small maintenance job of a few hundred metres.'

'A bit like me changing a light bulb at home,' she joked.

Mark's white teeth flashed as he grinned.

'So, what can I do to help?'

She was pleased that he only hesitated briefly before he handed her a pair of gloves.

'You'd be a great help if you could hold the pickets steady, so I can ram them in. Keep your hands away from the top, and hold the picket about halfway down.'

'Right.'

She crouched to hold the slim black post in place, while Mark used a heavy-capped metal pipe with two handles that fitted over the picket.

He lifted the post driver a foot or so, then slammed the pipe down, forcing the picket into the ground with each blow.

'Much easier than driving it in with a sledgehammer,' he grunted.

Sophie thought it still looked like jolly hard work as she watched Mark's shirt stretch tightly over his broad shoulders, threatening to split.

His shirt tail lifted, exposing a glimpse of bare skin at his waist.

This is why he has such a great body, she thought, admiring his trim hips, strong thighs and wonderful biceps. He did this sort of hard work all the time. No need for a gym workout for this man.

He swung around and she quickly switched her gaze to the ute, but she knew he'd caught her checking him out.

'Ready with the next one?' he called.

'Sure.'

They worked their way along the fence line and, once the pickets were in place, Mark tensioned the wire with a metal lever, a bit like an old-fashioned tyre jack.

Sophie couldn't drag her eyes from him. His movements were so practised, so easy and fluid and unhurried, and yet he conveyed the capacity to be very quick indeed if it was necessary.

As the fence took shape, she felt a completely unwarranted sense of achievement. OK, so maybe her help had been minimal, but she thought they made a pretty good team.

They lunched in the shade of gum trees, enjoying sandwiches and tea from the flask. Mark found an old blanket in the ute and spread it on the grass.

'You should have a little rest before we head back,' he said.

In no mood to argue, she stretched out and looked up at the sky through the tree branches. It was astonishingly blue and clear. There wasn't a cloud anywhere.

'A granddad sky,' she said, speaking her thoughts aloud.

'I beg your pardon?' Mark was sitting with his back against a tree trunk and his long legs stretched in front of him, and he regarded her with quizzical amusement.

'Whenever I see a perfectly clear, blue sky without any clouds, I think of my grandfather. We don't get too many perfectly spotless blue skies in England. But when I was quite small I was out in the country walking with Grandad and we saw a perfect, clear sky.'

She pointed. 'Deep blue. Just like this. And he told

me if I ever saw another sky better than that I was to write and tell him.'

'And will you?'

'I can't. He died two years ago.'

Mark's eyes were sympathetic. 'He sounds like a nice fellow.'

'He was. The best.' She watched a flock of brightly coloured little birds swoop down to perch in a small tree to her right.

'I think Grandad and I were the odd ones out in our family,' she said. 'Whenever he came to my mother's Sunday lunch-parties, he got as bored as I did with all the music gossip, so we usually slipped away. Sometimes we'd just go into the garden to peak into birds' nests, or hunt for hedgehogs, but other times we'd sneak up to the High Street. He'd let me stuff myself silly with cream cakes and he'd never tell my mother.'

Mark chuckled, and Sophie rolled onto her side so she could see him better. 'The summer before Grandad died, I took him up to Scotland. I sat on a river bank for hours, reading novels, while he fished for trout to his heart's content.'

'Every man should be so lucky.'

A kind of shadow came over his face, and he sighed. 'My father died five years ago, fighting a bushfire. He worked hard all his life. I wish I'd thought to take him on a holiday.'

'Perhaps he was happy to be living in the bush on a beautiful property.'

'Yeah. Perhaps.' He sent her a grateful smile. 'Dad and Mum were very close. She died eighteen months later. They called it heart failure, but I think she missed him too much.'

'That's very sweet, really.' A painful lump filled Sophie's throat as she thought of Mark's parents living a self-contained, happy life in the Outback. Together and very much in love.

As she lay there, lost in a romantic fantasy where she was the next Mrs Winchester, she rubbed her tummy in an absentminded, careless kind of way.

Watching her, Mark said, 'I wonder if the baby's a boy or a girl.'

'Have you been thinking about that?' she asked, surprised.

'Sure. Haven't you?'

'I haven't dared,' she admitted.

'You mean you haven't been playing around, trying out names?'

'No.'

'I thought all women liked to do that.'

She closed her eyes. 'It would make being pregnant all too real.'

'But it is real, Sophie.'

Mark sounded shocked, and her eyes flashed open. She looked directly at him. His dark eyes were very serious, almost intimidating.

What she hadn't said was that thinking up names for the baby would have involved trusting the future, and Oliver had spoiled her ability to do that.

'I—I just think of it as my little bean,' she said.

'Bean?'

'Well, yes. Because it's just a little thing, a little blob, curled like a bean.'

His expression softened. 'A human bean?'

'Yes,' Sophie said, and her mouth began to twitch. 'A little human bean. Our little human bean.'

A helpless chuckle broke from her.

Next moment, Mark was grinning, too. Their gazes met, and Sophie felt quite overcome by the sense of connection she felt with him. After their morning working together, she dared to wonder for the first time if she and Mark might still be together when the baby was born.

It was a thought almost too big to take in. She pulled Mark's hat over her face, and tried to calm down by listening to the sun-drowsed stillness of the Outback.

The silence didn't disturb her as much today. She no longer missed the background hum of traffic and city sounds, and she was able to enjoy the peacefulness.

She lay very still and let her shoulders, then her whole body, relax. The only sound was the faint buzz of insects in the grass and her soft breathing. She was aware of the faint puffs of air passing from her nostrils and over her upper lip. And as she lay there, thinking about the sky and the tapering blue-green gum trees, her breath drifting slowly in and out, she felt for a fleeting moment connected to the entire universe.

She must have fallen asleep then, because she woke with a start when she heard Mark moving about, packing their things into the back of the ute.

She sat up stiffly. 'Have I been asleep long?'

He smiled. 'About an hour.'

'Heavens! Just as well I'm not being paid by the hour.'

He held up the flask. 'Would you like the last of the tea?'

'Thanks. It might help me to wake up.'

As Mark handed her the metal cup, she saw that he'd stowed everything away and that grey shadows had begun to stretch from the trees out across the newly mended fence and the yellowed grass.

They started back to the homestead in the cool of the afternoon, and as the shadows lengthened families of kangaroos came out to graze.

'If you like, I'll show you how to stalk right up to kangaroos,' he said. 'If you freeze every time they look up from feeding, you can almost get close enough to touch them.'

Sophie grinned. 'Sounds like fun.'

She couldn't believe how relaxed she felt. The bush wasn't nearly so scary with Mark beside her, his hands expertly guiding their vehicle around a huge anthill, then letting the wheel spin free as he corrected their direction and rushed on over the trackless ground.

She decided there was something almost infallible about Mark Winchester in this environment. His quiet competence put her completely at ease, and she knew she could trust him.

Until he said suddenly, 'If we're supposed to be getting to know each other better, why don't you tell me more about Oliver?'

CHAPTER SEVEN

SOPHIE'S sense of peace deserted her. Was she never to be free of the spectre of Oliver? 'What do you want to know?' she asked nervously.

Mark stared grimly ahead through the windscreen. 'You were going to marry the man. You must have loved him.'

She winced. She hated having to relive the humiliation of Oliver's rejection. But she supposed it was best to be completely honest with Mark. If she got this out in the open, she might with luck be able to leave it behind.

'I did love Oliver,' she admitted unhappily. 'At least, I thought I did. He's an accomplished musician, and I was flattered when he took an interest in me. And I suppose I thought my parents would be pleased.'

'Were they?'

'Not as pleased as I'd hoped.' Sophie fiddled nervously with her hair, winding a curl around her forefinger and then letting it spring free, before grabbing it again. 'I didn't realise he was a rat until it was too late.' She bit her lip.

Mark frowned at her. 'Too late?'

Sophie stopped fiddling with her hair and straightened her spine, summoned the dignity necessary to get through this confession. 'It wasn't until after I agreed to marry Oliver that I discovered he was only dating me because of my family.'

The shocked look on Mark's face was comforting. It reminded her of the night they'd met, when his refusal to be excessively impressed by her clever relations had endeared him to her.

'Oliver fancies himself as a concert master,' she explained. 'And a composer. Actually, minimalist opera is his big thing. He adored my mother.'

'Minimalist opera? What the hell is that?'

She rolled her eyes. 'Act one, a guy feels a sneeze coming on. Act two, he puts his hand in his pocket and pulls out a handkerchief. Act three, he sneezes.'

Mark's eyebrows rose high. 'Then dies?'

'No, dying only happens in grand opera.'

Chuckling, he shook his head, clearly bewildered by the entire concept.

'Oliver hoped that by marrying me he could convince my father to boost him into a brilliant career. But Dad wasn't very impressed with him, and, as soon as Oliver realised that his dreams were toast, he dumped me.'

Mark's hands tightened on the steering wheel. 'That must have been very rough.'

She lifted one shoulder in a carefully nonchalant shrug. 'For a time there, it wasn't pleasant.'

To her relief, Mark didn't press her for more details. They drove on in silence, while the sky in the west began to fade to the palest blue streaked with pink.

When she felt a little calmer, Sophie said, 'Should I be enquiring about your girlfriends, Mark? Is there anyone special?'

He smiled and shook his head. 'I've been so busy since I bought this place, I haven't had time for a social life.'

'I take it you haven't always lived here?'

'No. I grew up on Wynstead, a much prettier property near the coast, and after my father died I took over the running of it.'

'Why did you come out here, then?' She couldn't help asking this. A prettier property near the coast sounded so much more appealing.

'I wanted to expand. These days you either have to get big or get out. I didn't want to leave the cattle industry, so I hired a manager for Wynstead and came further west to more marginal country. The land's cheaper out here, but you need much more of it. I can run thousands of head of cattle, but it's a harder life.'

'How long have you been here?'

'A little over a year. I'm still in the process of knocking the property into shape.'

Sophie sank back into her seat as she digested this. It explained why Mark hadn't done anything about his dingy and depressing house. She found it interesting that he was something of a pioneer, prepared to put up with hardship in the short term while planning for a brighter future.

'I'm glad you let me come fencing today,' she said. 'But I still feel as if I have no idea about the things you normally do. I haven't seen any of your cowboy antics. I haven't seen you on a horse. I—I haven't even patted a cow.'

His eyes widened. 'You want to pat a cow?'

'Um—well—' Sophie imagined getting close to one of those enormous, multi-hoofed animals and made a quick adjustment. 'Maybe I could start with something less daunting—like one of your dogs?'

His lips twitched. 'I told you, my cattle dogs are working dogs. They might try to take off your fingers.'

'Oh.' *Well, that puts me in my place!*

'But they'd let you pat them if I told them it was OK.'

'That's big of them. I do find that a full set of fingers is rather useful.'

They came to a pair of metal gates between two paddocks. Mark stopped the vehicle, jumped out, opened the gates and then climbed back in.

Sophie shot him a thoughtful frown. 'If I was a proper Outback girl I'd open and close those gates for you, wouldn't I?'

He shrugged as he shoved the gear stick into first. 'Perhaps. But it's not necessary.'

'Let me close them,' she said, thrusting her door open.

'You don't have to, Sophie.'

'I want to!'

Didn't Mark understand? She didn't want to be treated like an English tourist. She would never fit into life in the Outback if she was constantly mollycoddled. Jumping to the ground, she gave him a jaunty wave, and he drove the truck through, then she swung the gate closed and hurried to lock it.

She'd seen Mark doing this before. It was dead easy. All she had to do was pull a chain through the gate and loop it over a bolt on the stout timber fence-post.

An impossibly big bolt.

No way could she stretch the metal chain to loop over it. Three times she tried and failed. *Darn.* Sophie refrained from stamping her foot, and she didn't dare to look back to Mark, couldn't bear to see his knowing smirk. If he made a wisecrack, so help her, she might box his ears. There had to be a trick to this. Perhaps she was trying too hard.

If she took this more slowly, lifted the chain higher and—

'Here.' Mark's deep voice sounded beside her. 'Let me show you.'

She looked up, her chin stubbornly proud. She didn't want his assistance. She'd helped him with fencing, so surely she could do something as simple as shut a gate!

But, although Mark was smiling, she saw to her relief that he was not making fun of her. His big hands closed over hers. 'There's a bit of a trick to it,' he said gently. 'You need to tilt the chain like so.'

Naturally, when he did it the chain slipped easily over the bolt.

'If you'd given me another minute, I would have worked that out,' she protested.

'Of course you would have.' Mark smiled again and let his knuckles gently graze the side of her cheek.

Her skin burned at his touch, and her heart skittered like a frisky colt. 'I'll be all right with the next gate.'

'Sure.'

Mark dropped his hand, and she let out a shaky breath as they climbed back into the ute.

They continued on in charged silence until Mark said, 'I didn't realise you wanted a really close encounter with Outback life.'

'But I'm supposed to be getting to know you better,' she said defensively. 'Shouldn't that involve getting to know about the everyday things you usually do? I mean, I don't even know what you do when you look after your cattle.'

He gave her a quick glance. 'I suppose you want a few details so you can tell our child about me when he's older?'

'Well…yes.' She felt suddenly, unaccountably depressed.

Ever since their conversation about the bean, she'd been toying with the romantic possibility that she could morph miraculously into a woman of the Outback, that she and Mark could really make a relationship work.

But it was jolly obvious that her thoughts were racing way ahead of Mark's. He was sticking to their original plan, and he fully expected her to go straight back to England at the end of next week to raise their child alone.

It was crazy to get carried away with dreams of something else. She'd known all along that there was no point in falling for Mark, or starting to weave dreams about living here. He wanted what was best for the baby, but today she'd learned that he was also struggling to get this property on its feet. An Englishwoman and a tiny baby were added burdens he could do without.

Unfortunately.

When they got back to the homestead, the blue-speckled cattle dogs barked a noisy greeting from their kennels beneath the shady mango tree. Mark climbed down from the ute and gave them a playful scuff about the ears, and then he looked back at Sophie. 'Would you like to say hello?'

Her enthusiasm for a close encounter with the Outback had dimmed somewhat on the journey back, but she put on a brave face and gave the dogs a self-conscious wave. 'Hi, guys.'

'Come and meet them properly,' Mark said, offering her a sideways grin.

Her hands had automatically clenched behind her back, and she kept them there as she took a couple of steps closer.

'Monty, Blue Dog, this is Sophie,' Mark announced rather grandly. 'I want you two to say hello to her very nicely.'

The dogs quieted immediately and stood looking up at Sophie, their intelligent eyes watchful, their pointy ears alert, tails wagging more sedately.

'You can pat them now,' Mark said, watching her with mild amusement.

Sophie tried to unclench her hands from behind her back. *Me and my big mouth.* Mark might have given permission, but the dogs still had frighteningly big teeth! And their short hair looked rather bristly.

'I'm actually more of a cat person,' she said, to show that she wasn't completely out of touch with the animal world.

But she took a tiny step towards Blue Dog—after all, he'd looked after her so beautifully yesterday.

Fortune favours the brave.

She held out her hand, preparing to deliver a swift pat

on his head, but to her amazement the dog sat and lifted a paw to her.

'He wants to shake hands?' She shot Mark a look of amazed delight, and her nervousness melted as she bent down and took the dog's paw. 'Hello, Blue Dog.'

She rather liked the feel of the soft pad of his paw, upholstered with work-toughened skin. And, when she patted the fur between his ears, she discovered that it was soft and quite pleasant to touch. Not bristly at all.

The introduction was repeated with Monty.

'They are so impressive, Mark.' Hands on hips, Sophie turned to him, beaming with unabashed admiration. 'How did you get them to do that?'

'Hand signals,' he replied airily. 'Now, show me *your* hand.'

Puzzled, she held it out to him, and her heart stumbled as he took her rather small, white hand and cradled it in his hands, which were by contrast very big and brown.

Sophie struggled to breathe as Mark examined her fingers. He turned her hand over gently and then back again, touching her knuckles, her fingertips, one by one. It was quite unfair of him, really. Didn't he know that electricity zapped through her whenever he touched her?

'W-what are you doing?' she stammered.

His face was close to hers, and when she looked up she found herself looking directly into his dark-brown eyes. 'I'm making sure you haven't lost a finger,' he said, and his slow smile made her insides roll like a tumbleweed.

'Now,' he said, letting her hand go, and apparently quite unaware that he'd reduced her to a puddle of melted hormones. 'Would you like to come with me while I take a look at the horses?'

Sophie gulped. 'I—I suppose it won't hurt to work my way up the animal kingdom.'

The horses weren't kept in stables, but in a long, skinny paddock that stretched from the stockyards beside the barn down to a string of trees lining an almost-dry creek bed. As they approached the fence line, Mark put his little fingers to the corners of his mouth and let out a shrill whistle. The horses were at the far end of the paddock, but they all turned together like choreographed dancers and began to canter gracefully over the yellow grass towards them.

One glance at Mark and Sophie could see that he was very fond and proud of these creatures, and she had to admit they were rather gorgeous in a scary, long-legged and horsy kind of way.

There were four of them in a mixture of colours— dappled grey, chestnut, piebald and black.

Mark went forward to greet them as they came up to the fence, but Sophie stood well back, her hands once more tightly clasped behind her back. Patting dogs was one thing, but horses were another matter entirely. To start with, they had much bigger teeth!

But she'd claimed that she wanted to know all about Outback life, and she couldn't exactly change her mind now.

Reaching up, Mark patted one horse's neck, and stroked the nose of another. He smiled at her again. 'This is Tilly. She's very gentle. Come and say hello.'

Tilly was the chestnut, rather pretty, with a white

blaze on her forehead and a silky black mane. But gentle? Sophie eyed the mare's arched neck, her raised tail and wrinkled lips revealing very large teeth. She didn't think gentleness was a possibility.

'Horses don't bite, do they, Mark?'

His eyes flashed as he grinned back at her. 'These are OK, but some stallions can be nasty. I'd rather be bitten by a dog than a horse any day.'

'I might say hello from here,' she said. But she could hear how wimpy and wet that sounded, and she forced herself to take a quick step forward. But, good grief, the closer she got to the horse the more enormous it seemed.

Mark had an arm looped around Tilly's neck and was practically embracing her.

A faint memory from Sophie's childhood tugged at her—a memory of her grandfather coaxing her to hold a baby hedgehog. She'd been frightened of the prickly quills, but, once Granddad had shown her how to hold the spiny little ball, she'd been totally charmed by its soft underbelly and the little purring sound it had made.

And meeting the dogs just now had been a breeze.

'What the heck?' Sophie's heart pounded and her hand shook as she reached up. She tried not to look at those huge horsy teeth. 'He-hello, Tilly.' Very quickly she patted the short hair on Tilly's nose, then snatched her hand away.

Done. And her fingers had survived. Phew. Not so bad after all.

'Which horse do you mostly ride?' she asked hastily, hoping that her question might serve to divert attention from her nervousness.

'Charcoal.' Mark pointed to the black horse.

Of course, Mark *would* ride the biggest and scariest horse of all.

'Have you ever fallen off?'

He grinned at her. 'Tons of times.'

Sophie winced. 'Have you been badly hurt?'

'Broken leg. Concussion. Torn ligaments in my shoulder.'

The very thought of his injuries made her blanch. 'How old were you when you learned to ride?'

'I can't remember.' Mark smiled and shook his head. 'It seems like I've been on a horse all my life.' Suddenly he was climbing the railings. 'Charcoal and I are old mates.'

Sophie started to protest that a demonstration wasn't necessary, but Mark had already reached the top rail. For a heart-stopping moment, he was poised on the thin slat of timber, then, in one swift, athletic leap, he was on Charcoal's back.

She gave a shriek of alarm. He had no saddle or reins. How on earth would he stay on? Her heart was in her mouth as she watched him nudge Charcoal with his knees, saw the huge black beast lift its head in a snort then take off, its hooves thundering across the hard ground, with Mark astride him.

'Be careful!' she called, her heart thudding as fast as the horse's hooves. But her words weren't heeded.

And she soon saw that they weren't necessary. By the time Charcoal had cantered to the far end of the field, she could see that Mark and the animal moved as one— both lean and muscular, superbly athletic. Magnificent creatures, perfectly attuned to each other, and in the prime of condition and fitness.

Near the line of trees that bordered the creek, Charcoal turned in a wide arc, then came racing back at breakneck speed, Mark leaning forward, head down and holding the horse's mane. And as they drew near Mark grinned broadly at Sophie, then sat upright and threw both arms triumphantly above his head, like an Olympian acknowledging the roar of the crowd.

'Crazy idiot,' she muttered, but she was smiling. She couldn't deny he was rather splendid. And incredibly sexy. She felt a burst of feminine longing so fierce she cried out. And was glad that he couldn't hear it.

As they walked back to the house, it occurred to her that she was gradually losing her fear of the Outback, which boded well for future visits. But she was caught in a new dilemma.

It was all very fine for her to feel more at home on Coolabah Waters, but wasn't it foolish to let herself fall in love with its gorgeous owner?

CHAPTER EIGHT

MARK'S neighbours, Sophie discovered next day, lived in a large homestead, not unlike the one on Coolabah Waters—low-set, with timber walls and an iron roof, and deep, shady verandas. But the difference was that their house was surrounded by lots of shade trees and, to Sophie's surprise, green lawns.

It was painted pristine-white, with a dark green roof. Green trims on the window sills and veranda railings made it look cool and thoroughly inviting.

Andrew and Jill Jackson were tall, slim and fair, in their late thirties, with wide, welcoming smiles that gave an impression of salt-of-the-earth wholesomeness. There were three children—two long-legged girls and a little boy of six, who was a pint-sized version of his father.

'The children love visitors,' Jill said with a laugh as she led Sophie and Mark to a grouping of cane chairs on a shaded veranda. 'You're a great excuse for them to get out of schoolwork.'

'Where do you go to school?' Sophie asked them.

'In our schoolroom here at home,' said the eldest, Katie.

'Long-distance education,' Jill explained as she

poured frosty glasses of home-made ginger beer. 'Their lessons are sent out by mail, and they each have thirty minutes on the phone every day with their teacher in Mount Isa. Some properties have governesses, but I'm home tutor for my three, and I really enjoy it.'

Sophie tried to imagine being tutored by her mother. *Impossible.* Lady Eliza had always been far too busy.

She was surprised that the children were encouraged to join in the conversation, and she listened while they chatted about their recent holiday on Magnetic Island.

Andrew asked Mark about the muster, and the men talked about a computer program that would allow them to monitor the condition of their paddocks via satellite photography. This interested Sophie immensely, but she kept quiet. She didn't want to give the impression that she was any more than an overseas visitor.

But when she went to the kitchen with Jill, to help carry salads to the table for lunch, she couldn't help asking, 'Were the children born out here?'

'Heavens, no,' Jill said, shaking her head. 'I went into Mount Isa Hospital.'

'But that's a long way to travel when you're in labour.'

'Oh, I wasn't in labour,' Jill assured her, as she drizzled vinaigrette onto rocket leaves. 'Pregnant women out here have to go into town when they reach thirty-six weeks. It's a requirement—to be on the safe side.'

'Oh, I see. That's sensible, I guess, but it's a bit of a nuisance, isn't it?'

Jill shrugged. 'It's just another thing you get used to when you live in the bush.'

'What about during your pregnancy? How did you manage doctor's visits?'

'A doctor comes out to Wandabilla from Mount Isa every week to conduct a clinic. He brings his ultra-sound machine, so it isn't too much of a drama.' Jill sent her a sharply curious glance and waited, almost as if she was expecting Sophie to explain her interest in Outback pregnancy.

But although this woman seemed very nice Sophie wasn't ready to confide. Instead, she asked, 'Have you always lived out here?'

Jill shook her head. 'I grew up in the city. In Adelaide, in the south. I trained to be a nurse with Andrew's sister, and I went home with her once for a holiday, set eyes on Andrew and…' She grinned. 'And that same afternoon I helped him to vaccinate a pen of steers. Wouldn't let the poor man out of my sight.' She winked. 'But he didn't seem to mind.'

Sophie wanted to ask if she had any regrets about leaving the city, but Jill was looking at her shrewdly again, as if she had questions of her own to ask. Luckily, Anna burst into the kitchen to announce that young John had already begun to help himself to the potato salad, so the questions were dropped.

Sophie enjoyed the lunch very much. Corned beef, she discovered, was very tasty, especially when accom-panied by home-made mango chutney. They ate in a large dining room, not unlike Mark's, but painted in a cool lemon and white, with pretty curtains framing a view of the lush and shady garden. When Sophie admired the garden, Jill offered her cuttings.

'Well…thank you,' Sophie said awkwardly.

'Sophie's only going to be here for another week or so,' Mark intervened. 'And that's hardly long enough to get a garden established, is it?'

This was met by puzzled silence. Across the table Jill's gaze met her husband's.

And Sophie's eyes met Mark's, but his expression was distinctly guarded.

Jill broke the awkward silence. 'Leave the plants till you come back, then, Sophie. In the meantime I'll pot up a few things for you. To get you started.'

Now it was Sophie's turn to feel confused. She wasn't coming back. What had Mark told the Jacksons about her? She shot him another searching glance, but he kept his eyes on his plate, as if those last slices of cucumber and carrot were the most important vegetables in the world.

If Jill noticed the tension, she didn't let on. 'Time for dessert,' she said. 'Who has room for lemon-chiffon pie?'

This time, when Sophie glanced Mark's way, she caught a small smile twitching the corners of his mouth. 'I'd love some, thanks,' he said, sending Sophie a slow wink that made her toes curl. 'Lemon-chiffon is my favourite.'

An embarassing heat warmed Sophie's face as she remembered what had happened the last time they'd eaten this dessert. In London after the wedding.

'Let me help you, Jill,' she said, jumping to her feet.

It was when everyone was tucking into their pie that Jill said, 'Mark's told us about your famous musical family, Sophie.'

Andrew chimed in. 'My grandfather was very musical, and we still have his grand piano, but it never gets used now. No one else in the family has ever shown any interest.'

'Except me,' piped up Anna, and then she pouted. 'But I can't have piano lessons until I go to boarding school.'

Sophie sent her a sympathetic smile.

'I'm sure you can play, can't you, Sophie?' prompted Jill. 'Maybe you could give Anna a few tips?'

Sophie was so used to denying any musical ability that she almost said no. She had too many painful memories of dire occasions in her childhood when she'd been forced to play for her parents' guests and had suffered the embarrassment of comparison with her brilliant sisters.

But this was a very different scene.

'I can play a little,' she admitted.

Anna clapped her hands. 'Will you play for us now?'

'Please do,' added Jill. 'It's an age since our piano was played properly, but I get it tuned every year just the same.'

'It would be a pleasant change to hear proper music and not the kids' tuneless thumping,' chimed in Andrew.

Everyone looked expectantly at Sophie.

'I don't have any music,' she said.

This was met by a chorus of groans.

And when Sophie saw Anna's crestfallen face she gave in. 'I can play simple things by ear,' she amended, but she didn't admit that she actually preferred playing by ear, improvising as the mood took her.

'Wonderful.' Jill leapt to her feet. 'The piano's in the lounge. Everyone go in there and I'll bring the coffee.'

* * *

It was three in the afternoon before Sophie and Mark reluctantly agreed that they should make their departure.

'You were a great hit,' Mark said as they drove back across the flat, sparsely treed plains, heading for Coolabah Waters. He shot Sophie a questioning glance. 'I thought you said you weren't musical.'

'Compared to the rest of the family, I'm not.'

'But you're fabulous. I bet your sisters can't play all those movie themes and pop songs by ear.'

'Well, no. I don't think they know many pop songs.'

'There you go,' he cried, giving the steering wheel a delighted thump. 'We don't need concert-standard performances at an old-fashioned Outback singalong.'

She smiled. 'It was fun, wasn't it?'

'It was terrific. The Jacksons loved you. I was very proud of you.' Mark looked suddenly embarrassed, as if he'd said too much.

But his praise sent a giddy thrill swirling through Sophie. 'Young Anna is very talented. She has an exceptional ear for a child. I felt bad when I had to explain that I wouldn't be able to teach her, that I'm going back to England.' She frowned at Mark. 'I don't understand why they think I'm staying on.'

His only reply was a throat-clearing sound and Sophie turned square on to him, crossing her arms over her chest. 'Is this confession time, Mark?'

'What are you talking about?' He flicked a quick look her way then speedily returned to staring at the track ahead.

'As if you don't know.' Sophie rolled her eyes even though he wasn't looking at her. 'Why do your neighbours think I'm here to stay?'

His jaw jutted stubbornly. 'They've just made an assumption.'

'Andrew and Jill don't strike me as the types who jump to conclusions on very little evidence. What did you tell them?'

'I simply told them you were a girl I met in England.'

'But they knew about my family. What else did you tell them?'

His shoulders lifted in an uneasy shrug. 'Not much at all. But word spreads quickly in the bush. And when your phone call came through on that mustering camp it caused quite a stir.'

'Really?' Sophie was faintly appalled. 'Why?'

'Well...it's not every day a man, out in the middle of a bush muster, gets a phone call from a girl in England.'

She frowned. 'Don't tell me all the men were listening in?'

'They weren't eavesdropping. They couldn't hear our conversation. But they knew you were calling from England, and they knew I'd been over there for the wedding. And now you've turned up here. I guess everyone has put two and two together.'

'And they've come up with five.'

After a beat, Mark said, 'When it should have been three.'

Sophie stared at him and gulped.

Three... The two of them plus their baby...

Unexpected sadness stung her throat, and she turned away and watched a mob of cattle moving quietly across the flat expanse of a golden paddock. She remembered how distraught she'd been when she'd rung Mark from

London, thought now about how embarrassed he must have been when he'd had to take her surprising call in front of a bunch of stockmen.

Now Mark's friends and neighbours had visions of a romance between them. They probably expected him to marry her.

If there was no wedding and she went back to England, they were going to be jolly disappointed for Mark. No doubt the gossip would start again, and Mark would be left with the awkward job of trying to shrug off her reasons for abandoning him.

And in England, she would be facing equally awkward questions from her parents. *Ouch*.

What a mess.

Sophie sagged against the car door and stared at the blur of pale-gold paddocks outside.

At the Jackson's today, she'd begun to sense that life in the Outback could be quite wonderful for a woman and a man who loved each other. The isolation of the bush demanded something special of a couple. Away from the hustle and bustle of city life, people focused on caring for each other and their children. She'd never met such a close-knit, happy family.

There had actually been a heady moment when Sophie had thought that perhaps she could live here and be a successful Outback wife, too. Jill was a wonderful inspiration—contented with her busy life, running the house as well as supervising her children's schooling and helping her husband with the business side of running their cattle property.

Sophie had begun to imagine living that kind of life with Mark. And during the fun of the singalong her eyes had caught Mark's and she'd seen such warmth and happiness in his face that she'd thought that perhaps marriage with him was more than possible.

But face it, she thought now as they sped over the dirt track, there were major differences between her and Jill Jackson.

For heaven's sake, on the very first afternoon Jill had arrived in the Outback she'd helped Andrew to vaccinate a pen of steers. For Sophie, the very thought of doing anything like that was laughable. But, beyond that, Jill and Andrew were a perfect love-match.

Love. That was the catch.

A pang settled around Sophie's heart. She doubted that Mark loved her. Oh, he was being very kind and patient with her, but she could never be the sort of girl he would really want to share his life with. He needed a very different breed of woman as his Outback wife.

No way could Sophie jump into a pen of steers. She was too frightened to give a horse's nose a decent pat, let alone climb aboard and ride one. She wore silly sandals with daisies instead of sensible elastic-sided boots. She could make fancy desserts, but she hadn't a clue how to cook corned beef.

Mark was all too aware of this. He knew she had little potential as a cattleman's wife.

And, unfortunately, there wasn't much she could do to change his mind.

Or was there?

* * *

At dinner that evening, Sophie paused with her fork midway between her plate and her mouth and asked, 'What happens when you go out mustering, Mark? Where do you sleep?'

Mark almost choked. Questions from Sophie about his sleeping habits had a bad effect on his table manners. She was looking incredibly lovely this evening. A flush of pink tinted her cheeks and pretty lights danced in her eyes. And she was wearing slim-fitting white jeans and a camisole top of pale-lavender silk with a fetching lace trim that skimmed the tops of her breasts.

And she wanted to talk about beds! *Have mercy, woman!*

'We sleep in a swag,' he told her quickly.

'In a *what*?' Her big grey eyes widened, looked lost.

'A swag. It's a lightweight mattress that rolls up inside waterproof canvas.'

'But you put these swags inside tents, don't you?'

Smiling at her worried frown, he shook his head. 'We sleep out in the open, under the stars.'

'Really?' Her eyes, if possible, grew wider. 'With nothing to protect you?'

'Tents are cumbersome.' He was struggling to concentrate on her questions and not on the thought of sleeping with her—in a swag, in a tent—her sweet curves snuggled close…

Whoa, boy! Heel.

Mark dragged in a hasty breath. 'Tents are too much trouble,' he said. 'We muster in the dry season, so there's hardly ever any rain. And you can always hang a tarpaulin between a couple of trees if it gets a bit wet.'

'So you just lie on—on the *ground*, out in the open?'

'Sure. But the swags are surprisingly comfortable. And there's nothing better than sleeping under the stars.'

Sophie looked worried, took a sip from her water glass. 'Do women like Jill Jackson sleep in swags, too?'

'Absolutely.' And then, because he couldn't help himself, Mark gave her a slow, teasing smile. 'You'd love it out there, curled in a swag and listening to the sounds of the bush at night.'

She looked paler than ever.

'So why don't we try it one night?'

What in the name of fortune had made him say that? No way would Sophie say yes.

She smiled shyly. 'I'd love to give it a go.'

Sophie stared up at the stars through the fine mosquito net suspended above her swag. She could hardly believe she was doing this. She was terrified and thrilled at once.

She told herself she was perfectly safe. Mark slept out in the open like this all the time. And, after all, they were only lying on the top of the creek bank, a few hundred metres from the house. Mark had kindly insisted that she must go back inside if it all got too much.

But, to her surprise, she discovered that he was right about the swag. It was actually quite comfy. She was safely cocooned in a flannelette-lined sleeping bag wrapped in canvas. There was a slim but adequate mattress beneath her, and the mosquito net to protect her from nasty creepy-crawlies, so there really wasn't anything to complain about.

And once she'd stopped fretting about the complete lack of electric lighting, and the fact that there were no walls around her, no roof above and no floor below, she was fine. If she could stop obsessing about Mark lying so close, she would really be able to appreciate this gorgeous evening.

The night air was cool and sweet, and the sky was crystal clear and studded with diamond-bright stars.

Actually, the sky was truly amazing…an astonishing dome arching over them.

Huge. Spectacular.

A miracle.

As for the moon! The quarter moon lay against the black velvet of the sky like a curled piece of hammered silver suspended within a faint circle, the promise of the full moon to come.

It reminded Sophie of her baby in her womb. Admittedly, it didn't take much to make her think about that these days. She slipped her hand under the waistband of her tracksuit, let it lie protectively over her tummy. Wondered about the little person she nurtured there.

One day in the future her child would come to visit Mark at Coolabah Waters. And he would bring the child out here at night to show off these glorious stars. This moon.

The two of them would be together here. And where would she be? Back in England, waiting jealously for her child's return? She blinked, and her vision grew misty as she turned to Mark's large, dark shape lying beside her in his separate swag.

As if he'd sensed her movement, he turned, too, and his deep, rumbly voice came out of the darkness. 'Everything OK?'

'Yes, thanks. Absolutely fine,' she said. She was glad of the darkness as she used a corner of the flannelette sheet to wipe her eye. 'But I'm sure I'll never actually get to sleep. I don't want to stop looking at the sky. It's so amazing. I knew there were lots of stars, but I had no idea there were as many as this.'

Mark chuckled softly. 'There are about two billion in the Milky Way alone. And what we see here is only the tip of the iceberg as far as the universe is concerned.'

'It takes my breath away. The stars are so bright! So beautiful.'

'That's because there's no artificial light out here, no glare from cities or towns to diminish the starlight.'

She remembered him looking for the stars in London and being disappointed.

Now they both lay very still, staring above at the sky, and listening to the occasional sounds that broke the silence—the spooky call of a bird that Mark called a mopoke, a low bellow from a distant cow, and the hoot of an owl that kept vigil over the starlit paddocks from a branch in a tree further down the creek.

'Do you know the names of any of those stars?' she asked.

'A few.'

'Which ones?'

'Well, the most famous constellation Down Under is the Southern Cross. Over there to the south you can see two bright stars in a vertical line above the horizon—they're the pointers—and if you follow them up you'll come to the cross. Four good-sized stars and a tiny one.'

'Yes, I see them.'

'Can you see the saucepan shape straight up above us?'

'Yes.'

'That's Orion. The handle of the saucepan is the hilt of his sword. And the V up there on the right?'

'Yup. Got it.'

'They're the horns of Taurus the bull.'

She laughed. 'Taurus is my star sign.'

As she stared at it, a streak of light seemed to come out of nowhere and shoot across the sky.

'Look!' she cried, making a dint in the mosquito net as she sat up quickly. 'Is that a falling star?'

The burning arc of fire zoomed downwards, heading for the horizon, and leaving a golden trail of sparks behind it like a skyrocket.

'We see a lot of them out here,' Mark said casually.

A lot of falling stars? How amazing! Sophie had been sure it was a once-in-a-lifetime experience.

'And there's a satellite,' he said, pointing.

'Where?'

'Directly above that tall ironbark tree. See it moving?'

Sophie caught it—a tiny, tiny light travelling bravely through the vast sea of stars.

Wow! She'd had no idea the night sky could be so absorbing. She lay down again, staring all about her, and felt again a strange sense of connection, just as she had on the day they'd gone fencing—an unexpected but deep connection with planet Earth, with the sky above and the ground beneath her, the creatures out there in the bush—the entire universe.

I feel different, she thought. *Out here I feel different about everything.*

Her life in London, her job, her friends and family, seemed so remote. She knew they were only a phone call or a plane trip away, but they belonged to another world, a world that seemed less real than this. Concerts and cafés, city buildings and crowds couldn't really compare with this simple, natural spectacle.

I can be myself here.

She could *find* herself here, find the real Sophie—not someone trying to pretend, forever trying to live up to the expectations of others.

Except, she thought with a heavy sigh, if she stayed here she would soon become just as busy trying to turn herself into the kind of woman that Mark needed, a perfect woman of the Outback.

'A penny for your thoughts.'

Mark's voice startled her.

In the darkness, Sophie blushed. 'I—I was wondering if anyone in my family has ever seen stars like this,' she said.

'Do you miss your family?'

'Not a lot,' she answered honestly. 'They're so busy, I hardly see them anyhow. I'm sure they're not missing me.' After a small silence, she asked shyly, 'What about you, Mark? What were you thinking about?'

At first he didn't answer, and then he released a long, heavy breath. 'I'm trying to come to terms with the fact that my child isn't going to see these stars at night, or hear the sounds of the bush.'

Sophie's throat tightened. 'Does that worry you?'

'To be honest, I hate the thought of him or her growing up without knowing the call of the curlews, or a kookaburra's laugh, even the howl of a distant dingo. It might sound strange to you, but these things give me comfort. I guess they're in my blood.'

The tightness in her throat became painful. 'But the baby, she or he, will…will come to visit you.'

There was no response.

She turned to him, felt her heart tumble when she saw his grim profile silvered by moonlight. She wanted to tell him that she could stay. She didn't have to go back to England. But surely it was his role to invite her?

She swallowed to relieve the ache in her throat. 'Mark, I promise I'll make it as easy as I can for you to have access.'

He grunted. 'That's all very easy to say.'

'I mean it.' She wished he were looking at her, wished he could see her face, wanted him to see her sincerity.

'I know you mean it now,' he said. 'But have you really thought ahead, Sophie? What about when you get married?'

'Married?' Her startled cry was close to a shriek.

'Don't sound so surprised. You know it's going to happen.'

But she didn't know anything of the sort. If Mark was talking about her marrying someone else, right now that seemed an impossible thought.

'You're a fabulous woman,' he went on. 'You're not going to be a single mum for the rest of your life. In weeks, months, maybe even years down the track, you're going to meet the man of your dreams. And how do you think your child's biological father will fit into the scheme of things then?'

'You'll…' The words died on Sophie's lips. She had no idea. Until tonight, she hadn't let herself think much further than telling her family about the baby.

She tried to see herself in the future Mark predicted—married to an Englishman, living in London—tried to imagine how a strange man would feel about taking Mark's child into his home. There was every chance he would be quite fine about it. Blended families were practically the norm these days.

Meanwhile, Mark would be back here in Australia, alone in the big, empty house, wishing he could be with his child. A glacial chill crept down her spine.

Mark had so much to offer as a father. He was a successful and confident man, at ease with himself and his surroundings, as steady as a rock, and interesting, too—a deep and passionate man with a vision for the future. And for him that future should include the raising of his child.

And… She really, really liked him.

She'd never met anyone like him before, and she'd never experienced anything remotely *close* to the wonderful night they'd spent together in London. She might never experience it again.

Again, she tried to picture herself back in England—happy, independent and getting on with her life—but the picture wouldn't hold, kept disintegrating before her eyes. Panic gripped her.

She'd stepped out on a limb by coming to Australia, but she'd felt safe, because she'd known she could always go back to England. Her family would be upset, it would be horrible for a bit, but then they'd settle down and adjust.

But now she felt as if that limb she'd stepped onto was beginning to crack under the weight of uncertainty. Going back to London felt much less appealing than staying here with Mark.

It would help if Mark loved her, if he hadn't merely let her stay because they had a baby's future to sort out.

For a fraught moment, Sophie had a terrible sense of not belonging *anywhere*. A deep loneliness took hold, wrapping its fingers around her throat, squeezing a miserable sob from her.

She heard a rustling sound in the swag beside her.

'Sophie, are you OK?'

'No.'

Mark sat up. 'Have you had enough of it out here? Would you like to go back inside?'

'No.' It was little more than a bleat, but quite definite.

He stared into the shadows where she lay. She could see his face, caught in the starlight, and he looked like something a master craftsman would sculpt in marble, all strong, masculine planes and angles.

'Is there anything you'd like?' he asked her.

'Yes.' Suddenly certain, she sat up, her heart thudding, her limbs trembling. 'I'd like you to hold me, Mark.'

There was an embarrassingly long stretch of silence during which the owl hooted again.

'You do realise what you're saying?' he said at last. 'Remember, you insisted I keep my dist—'

'I know,' Sophie interjected quickly, and she shoved the mosquito net roughly aside. 'It's OK, Mark.'

Mark tensed all over, was seized by a shuddering jolt of desire. *Oh, God.* He was aching with his need for this woman. The temptation she presented was agonising. He'd been crazy to think he could spend a night sleeping next to Sophie without needing to hold her.

But Sophie had known the danger of attachment when she'd first arrived here, and she was right—if they spent a night together, if they made love again, they would only make their problems worse. Parting again, sending her back to England where she belonged, would be so much harder.

Why couldn't she stick to her own damn rules?

'But you insisted that we mustn't,' he groaned. 'You made me promise.'

'I've changed my mind.'

Mark heard a choked cry, was aware of Sophie hurling herself across the short, dark chasm of night that separated them. Next moment his arms were full of her. Sweet smelling, sexy Sophie.

His heart thundered. All he wanted was to crush her to him, to taste her sweetness, kiss her senseless, to fling her down on his mattress and cover her with kisses from head to toe, to lose himself in her, to experience again that wild, wonderful, electrifying passion they'd shared in London.

Why was she tempting him?

Couldn't she remember that this was wrong? There

were a thousand reasons. She'd been so very certain that she didn't want any physical intimacy with him. She'd made that mistake once, and she was paying the highest price.

He held her carefully in his lap, as if she were fragile and might break into a thousand pieces, and tried to ignore the clamouring need rampaging through him. Against her ear, he whispered, 'Aren't you worried that this will complicate everything?'

She shook her head, and her silky hair brushed his cheek, eliciting a soft moan from him.

'Not any more, Mark.' Her voice was a sensuous, breathy whisper. 'I've realised now that this *simplifies* everything.'

She turned in his arms, and her soft, trembling lips brushed his jaw. Her subtle perfume surrounded him, and he felt the soft pressure of her lush, round breasts against his chest.

Mark knew he was a drowning man. How could he *not* kiss her?

And then, heaven help him, her arms twined around his neck. Her eager lips parted, and he dipped his mouth to taste her. Their tongues touched, tentatively at first, and then with familiar delight and building need.

At last.

At last.

Sweet shivers rippled over Sophie's skin, and her insides melted and tumbled as Mark clasped the sides of her head, as his fingers plunged roughly into her hair, and he showered her with kisses—over her face, over her throat, and into the dip of her collarbone.

He buried his face against her shoulder. 'You sweet thing,' he uttered between ragged breaths. 'Do you have any idea how wild you make me?'

'It's the same for me,' she whispered, pressing kisses to the hectic pulse in his neck.

She traced trembling fingers down the line of his jaw and he caught her fingers, kissed and nibbled them, sending rivers of pleasure coursing through her. Then, with a soft groan, his lips found hers again and he took her mouth urgently, deeply, with a forceful possession that thrilled her.

His hands slipped beneath her T-shirt and found her breasts. He stroked her gently, spreading wonderful heat spiralling outwards and downwards. His fingers squeezed, and she flinched momentarily.

He pulled his hand away. 'Sorry. Are you tender?'

'Just a little.'

'I don't want to hurt you.' He removed his hand completely, but Sophie clasped it in hers, took it shyly, impatiently, and pressed it against her.

'Don't worry, Mark.'

'I can be slow and gentle,' he breathed, tucking her head against his shoulder, and tracing feathery, soft circles over her with his fingertips.

'Yes,' she whispered. 'I remember. You have wonderfully slow hands.'

'I remember everything about making love to you, Sophie. Every touch, every kiss, is imprinted on me for all time.'

Gathering her close, he guided her gently backwards until she was lying on his mattress.

In a breathless daze, she looked up at him. 'Will there be enough room in one swag for both of us?'

A brief grin slashed the dark intensity in his face. 'I believe we'll manage.'

She reached up to him. He lowered his long body beside her and they were together at last.

Together. In the darkness, with only the stars as their witness, they shared achingly sweet kisses and heated caresses. Together they sought the intimacy they craved, confessed the need they'd not dared acknowledge with words.

CHAPTER NINE

SOPHIE hoped that the words might come afterwards when they lay wrapped in each other's arms, watching the glittering sky. But Mark was strangely silent.

He held her close, almost possessively, but he stared above at the stars as if he was lost in thought.

She snuggled into him, pressed a kiss into the musky shadows on his neck. 'Thank you,' she whispered.

'Thank *you*,' he said softly, and his arm tightened around her shoulders.

She waited for him to say something more, something about his feelings for her, wondered if she should lead the way. Should she tell him she'd never met a man who made her feel so happy, so appreciated and sexy?

His silence and the fact that she'd initiated this whole event stilled her tongue. She'd practically begged him to make love to her; she wasn't going to beg him for compliments afterwards.

And she wasn't going to get into a stew about his silence. She knew guys found it difficult to talk about their feelings, and she'd read in a magazine that they hated post-mortems about dates or parties or sex.

Especially sex. She would have to be patient. All would be revealed in the morning.

With no curtains or roof to hold back the daylight, Sophie woke at dawn for almost the first time in her life.

She lay with her head against the strong wall of Mark's chest and watched in a kind of hushed awe as the sun pushed ruddy fingers above the trees. Soon blue, red and gold streaks appeared in the clouds. The dawn was truly beautiful, more beautiful than any holiday sunset.

As the brilliance faded, light spread across the sky like a stain remover, sapping the heavens of darkness and casting a creamy warmth over the quiet, misty bush.

Sophie thought about the stars that had been so brilliant last night. They were still up there somewhere, invisible now.

She closed her eyes, overpowered by the memories of last night. She wondered if the amazing tenderness and intimacy she and Mark had shared would, like the stars, disappear with the arrival of the sun.

Turning, she looked at Mark. Feasted her eyes on him. From this angle she could see the underside of his jaw, the strong bones beneath his skin and the first signs of his beard's regrowth.

She pressed a wake-up kiss to his shoulder and he stirred, rolling sideways. He opened his eyes and smiled, and released a playful growl as he reached for her.

'I knew I was going to love waking up next to you.' He pressed his lips to the side of her brow. 'How are you this morning?'

'Wonderful.'

'No upset tummy?'

'No,' she said, surprised. *Fancy that.* She hadn't even thought about morning sickness. Perhaps it was over already.

Wriggling closer, she slipped an arm around his neck and nibbled his ear. 'If we were out on a muster, what would happen now?'

Mark chuckled. 'If we were on a muster, we'd have been up and gone from here long ago.'

'I'm glad we're not on a muster, then.'

'So am I,' he murmured, giving her neck a sleepy nuzzle.

'I could stay here all day.'

'No you couldn't.' He kissed her chin.

Sophie was certain she could camp right here in this swag with Mark for the rest of her life. 'Could, too,' she said smugly.

'No way.' He trailed his lips over hers. 'The sun would send you inside before eight o'clock.'

She sighed. 'I forgot about the sun.'

With the softest touch, Mark's fingers traced the line of her backbone. 'You must never forget about the sun in the Outback.' He looked at her through half-closed lashes. 'That's why we have a rule out here.' Cupping her bottom, he gathered her into him. 'You should never waste time in the morning.'

'That sounds like—' Sophie began, but Mark's lips cut her off in mid-sentence.

She didn't mind in the least. This was *exactly* what she wanted.

* * *

The sun had climbed quite high by the time they drove the ute the short distance back to the homestead. As Mark parked it beneath the mango tree and slipped the keys from the ignition, he turned to Sophie, and the light shining in his eyes made her heart leap high.

'Why don't you stay?' he said.

'Stay?' she repeated. There was nothing she wanted more than to stay here with this gorgeous, gorgeous man, but she was scared that she might misinterpret his meaning.

'Stay longer than two weeks.' He smiled, and the skin around his eyes crinkled. 'We seem to like each other, don't we?'

'Seems so,' she said breathlessly.

His slow smile climbed his cheeks. 'Is that a yes? You'll stay?'

Oh, man. Sophie couldn't breathe, she was so excited and scared. 'How—how long were you thinking?' *A month, three?* 'I'd have to arrange for someone to take care of my business. And there's a cut-off point when the airlines won't take pregnant women.'

'If you can sort out your business, couldn't you have the baby here?'

Her heart took off like a skyrocket.

Watching her, Mark's smile faded. 'Is that a bad idea, Sophie?'

She shook her head. 'No, it's not a bad idea.'

'Would you be worried about having the baby out here?'

'No. I've talked to Jill, and she told me about the

doctors and hospitals and everything. It seems to be perfectly safe to be pregnant in the Outback.'

Mark reached for her hands. 'I'll take care of you. We can fix up the house, choose somewhere to make a nursery.'

'Are you sure, Mark?'

His throat worked, and he looked down at their linked hands. 'I know we're still getting to know each other better. I'm not asking you to commit to anything permanent.' He lifted his gaze and smiled nervously. 'Down the track, if you realise that it's not going to work out, you should feel completely free to head back to England.'

Sophie gulped. It made perfect sense that Mark should offer her a way out if their relationship didn't work. He was being perfectly logical and reasonable, perfectly *perfect* actually.

So why was she feeling nervous?

Why couldn't she have more faith in herself? It was such a bore to be afraid of failure.

'Don't look like that, Sophie. What's the matter?'

Mark was frowning at her.

Her hands lifted in a gesture of helplessness. 'I'm just being a goose. Finding things to worry about that aren't really problems.'

'Are you worried about ringing your parents? Would you like me to speak to them?

'No, no. It's OK. I'll ring home tonight.'

To her surprise, having said that, she felt immediately better.

* * *

Sophie rang home before dinner that evening, and she was immensely relieved that it was her mother who answered.

'I just wanted to let you know there's been a slight change of plans,' she said, getting straight to the point with deceptive confidence. 'I've decided to stay on here.'

'How…nice,' her mother replied carefully. 'I assume that means you're staying on at Coolabah Waters with Mark?'

'Yes.' Sophie's heart began an anxious hammering. 'We…want more time to get to know each other better.'

'So you really like this young man, darling?'

'Yes,' Sophie said, wishing she didn't feel so nervous about the other news she had to deliver.

Her mother's voice sounded so close, as if she was in the same room, and Sophie wished she could see her face. Right now she could do with a motherly hug to smooth the way for this difficult conversation. Lady Eliza's busy life as an operatic diva hadn't spared much time for nurturing a close and easy intimacy with her youngest, most mystifying daughter.

Sophie's grandfather had filled the role of confidant, but even he hadn't been much help when it had come to boyfriends. They'd been Emma's territory.

Sophie took a deep breath. 'There's something else I should tell you, Mum.'

'Yes, dear?'

Instinctively she closed her eyes, and her face screwed up tightly as she dropped her bombshell. 'You're going to be a grandmother.'

'Good heavens!'

Silence followed.

Sophie felt sick. 'It happened in England, Mum. That's why I came down here, to see Mark. We're trying to sort things out.'

'You mean your wedding plans?'

'Well, no. We—we don't want to rush into marriage.' Sophie was so glad Mark wasn't listening.

'But you are planning to be married?'

'Nothing definite at this stage.'

There was an anguished sigh on the other end of the line.

Sophie chewed her lip. *The family failure strikes again!*

'Mum, don't worry about me. I'm fine.'

'Are you sure, dear? Are you keeping well?'

'Fit as the proverbial fiddle.'

'And—and Mark's taking good care of you?'

'He's being very sweet.'

'If I wasn't so busy, I'd come and visit you.'

'Oh, there's no need. Honestly.' Sophie blanched at the thought of Lady Eliza arriving in Wandabilla. Her mother would take one look at the place and want to cart Sophie back to London pronto.

'Mum, would you mind breaking the news gently to Dad? It might be better coming from you.'

'Of course, dear. It's always a matter of timing with your father. I'll wait for the right moment, and handle it so beautifully he'll slip into grandfather mode without realising it.'

'Thanks. You're a star.'

'You are happy, aren't you, Sophie? About the baby?'

'Oh, yes, I'm rapt,' she said. 'Don't worry, Mum, I really am excited. And Mark's excited, too.'

There was a distinct sigh of relief. 'Good. When all's said and done, if you're both happy nothing else matters, does it?'

'No,' said Sophie softly.

Fingers crossed, it really was as simple as that.

Telling her mum had certainly been a lot easier than she'd expected. And to think she'd been so stressed!

There's been a real turnaround in my life.

No doubt about it—after last night's love-making under the stars, and Marks' wonderful invitation to stay, she felt like a brand-new woman.

Flowers—where had they come from?

Mark stared at the kitchen table. They were eating in there tonight, had agreed it was cosier.

And it looked especially cosy with a simple jam-jar filled with deep red, purple and yellow flowers. There was no doubt the splashes of colour brightened the room. He looked more closely at the centrepiece and saw that the red flower was a rose.

A rose? Out here?

Sophie came from the stove, carrying a casserole dish wrapped in an oven cloth.

'Are these flowers real?' he asked her.

She laughed as she set the dish carefully down on a cane mat. 'Of course. Smell the rose. It's gorgeous.'

Mark dipped his nose low, and caught a sweet, almost forgotten perfume that took him straight back to his childhood. 'But how did it get here?' He gave the rose another sniff. 'It hasn't come all the way from England, has it?'

This roused another laugh, plus a jaunty toss of Sophie's glossy dark curls and a flash of pearly teeth. Mark felt at that moment that he could watch her for ever.

She lifted the lid of a casserole dish. 'I found the rose in *your* garden, Mark.'

With a shake of his head, he grinned. 'I didn't even know I had a garden.'

'Well, no self-respecting gardener would claim ownership.' She paused in the process of spooning rice onto their plates and smiled reproachfully. 'There are only a few poor straggling plants that aren't weeds.'

As they took their places, she said, 'I don't know how Jill Jackson managed to get such a lovely garden growing at Blue Hills.'

'You'd be surprised. Thanks to bore water, lots of homesteads have lovely gardens. My mother always had a fabulous garden at Wynstead.'

Just talking about his mother's garden brought back memories of his childhood. He and his sister had played endlessly, running over the long sweep of smooth, green lawn, climbing the enormous tamarind tree. Countless hours they'd spent, playing hide and seek beneath the huge, leafy hibiscus bushes, catching tadpoles in the fern-fringed lily pond.

And in his mother's house there'd always been flowers on the hall table, on the sideboard, on coffee tables and on the dining table, always lots of colour to please the eye and to make the house welcoming.

Just like this arrangement, he thought, staring at Sophie's flowers.

As they ate, Mark cast a critical eye over his kitchen. He knew it was drab, but now he tried to see it as an outsider might. No doubt about it, his house was in need of a paint job. The dining room and bedrooms were even worse than the kitchen. And women cared about things like that.

'My mother kept the inside of the house lovely, too,' he admitted. 'Lots of paintings and knick-knacks. Beautiful furniture. She'd be horrified if she could see the way I live out here.'

'What happened to all her things when you left Wynstead?'

'Tania, my sister, took all the decorative stuff.'

'Your sister?' Sophie's eyes widened. 'You never told me you had a sister. Where does she live?'

'In Melbourne. Married to a barrister.'

'Do you see much of her?'

Mark shrugged. 'Not a lot. Those two love the city life. They're opera buffs, actually.'

Afraid that talk of the city and opera might make Sophie homesick, he hurried on. 'I need to start a few home improvements, but I could do with some advice. Do you think you could help me to shop for the things I need? We could order them online from Mount Isa.'

She favoured him with a coy smile. 'When a man mentions shopping and home improvements in the same sentence, a girl can't help being a *tad* interested.' And then she confessed, 'Actually, I'm itching to get to this place with a paint brush. I have a secret hankering to be an interior designer.'

Mark's eyebrows lifted. 'What stopped you?'

'The usual,' she said, with an offhand shrug. 'Lack of self-confidence. Fear of failure.'

He found it difficult to believe that the lovely, effervescent Sophie Felsham had problems with self-confidence. But he couldn't deny that growing up with a family of overachievers must have taken its toll.

And that Oliver fellow had done quite a number on her.

To distract her further, he said, 'Tell me how I should redecorate this place. Where should I start?'

Her grin split her face. 'You're going to regret asking that.' With almost a skip of childish glee, Sophie hurried to the kitchen dresser, grabbed a note pad and pen and darted back to her chair.

Pushing her plate to one side, she sat with her legs crossed and pen poised, and smiled at him with such anticipation that Mark wanted to kiss her.

Heaven help him.

How was he supposed to think about interior decorating when he was assailed by visions of Sophie flat on her back on the kitchen table, smiling up at him with that same breathless eagerness?

'OK,' she said, blissfully unaware of his salacious thoughts. 'Give me an idea of what you'd like, Mark.'

'A-ah…'

'What's your favourite colour?'

He was looking into her eyes. 'Grey.'

'Grey?' Sophie frowned, but dutifully made note of this.

'What rooms are most important, do you think? Where do you spend most of your time?'

'In my bedroom.'

She went pink in the cheeks. 'Are you sure? Aren't there other rooms that have priority?'

'My bedroom's the most important room in my house,' he asserted. 'I spend almost a third of my life in bed.'

With a dignified straightening of her shoulders and an arch of her right eyebrow, Sophie made another note. 'OK. Bedroom heads the list. What other parts of the house would you like to fix?'

'Come on, I'll show you.' He held out his hand to her.

'Can't you just tell me? I'm making notes here.'

'Come on, Sophie. Interior decorating is a visual art form, and you'll find it immensely helpful if you can actually see what I'm talking about.'

She rolled her eyes, letting out a huff of exaggerated annoyance as she stood. 'Oh, all right.'

Sophie had a suspicion that she knew exactly where Mark was taking her. She was dead certain when he led her down the hallway. And straight to his bedroom.

For some reason that didn't quite make sense, she felt suddenly shy as she stepped into Mark's private domain.

She'd seen this room briefly on the first day she'd arrived, when she'd been searching for a bed to collapse onto, and she knew it had a lot of potential. Without leaving the doorway, she surveyed it again.

It was actually one of those rooms that interior designers dreamed about. A room with 'good bones'— generous proportions, a high ceiling and beautiful stained-glass windows framed by a graceful archway.

But interior decorating had obviously been a very low priority for generations of previous owners. The paint-work was dark and dingy like the rest of the house. The timber floors were covered by a ghastly, grey-and-maroon floral linoleum. The window frames were peeling, putty was falling out, and the bed was a very plain double mattress on a simple wooden base made up with white sheets and an old green blanket. No duvet or quilt.

Not the slightest bit romantic.

She could well understand why Mark wanted it decorated.

He was smiling his thousand-kilowatt smile as he stood, his thumbs hooked through the belt loops on his jeans, looking about him at the walls, the ceiling and the marvellous arch.

'You don't want grey in here,' she said.

Grey was totally wrong. The house was already as drab as a wet week in London. 'This room's shaded by the big mango tree outside, so it's already cool. You want a warmer colour. But I think it should be balanced by lots of white, or maybe soft beige.'

He nodded, but the tiny smile in his eyes made her wonder if he was really listening.

'I think this room calls for something quite luscious,' she said, looking again at the gold and rose, mauve and green glass in the beautiful windows. 'What about a pale primrose on the walls combined with a really deep, lush cream for the trims? And maybe rosy accents in some of the furnishings?'

'Rosy accents?' Mark looked amused, then doubtful. 'Do you really think so?'

She nodded. 'I know it doesn't sound very masculine, but it would be stunning.' Coming into the middle of the room, she looked about her and saw the changes already in her imagination, like 'before and after' shots in a magazine.

Mark pointed to an open set of French doors. 'What do you make of this over here?'

He gestured for her to go ahead of him into a much smaller adjoining room. When she did so, she saw that it was empty apart from a large leather saddle on the floor, some old text books stacked in a corner, and a pair of rowing oars propped against one wall. But there was the sweetest circular window that looked out across the front garden.

'I guess this must have been a dressing room,' she suggested, and then she smiled as she tried to imagine Mark bothering with a dressing room to pull on jeans, a work shirt and riding boots.

Her smile faded as she was hit by another idea. 'Oh, my.'

Mark frowned. 'What?'

Her answer was little more than a whisper. 'This little room would make an absolutely darling nursery.'

She could see it already: soft carpet on the floor. A baby's white cot and a change-table with jars of lotion and baby oil. A bright mobile dangling from the ceiling, a small bookshelf crowded with cuddly toys bought by adoring friends and family.

She looked up, and Mark's dark eyes were watching her with unnerving intensity.

'I thought it would make a great nursery, too,' he said.

'You did?'

He lifted his hand and touched the side of her face with his fingertips, sending a warm glow through her like a sunrise.

He dipped his head so that his mouth was close to her ear. 'I can see it all. This room with soft, filmy curtains and fresh paint. Lush carpet. You in bed beside me.'

His deep, low voice sent a fresh rash of thrills rippling under Sophie's skin.

'Our baby sound asleep close by,' he murmured.

She would have been happy in a swag with Mark, but she had to admit he painted a very tempting picture—this room transformed, and her curled close beside him with her head on his shoulder, her arm flung possessively across his broad, bare chest and their legs entwined.

And their sweet little baby, a plump cutie with pink cheeks and a soft cap of dark hair, asleep in this little room right next to them...

Mark's hands spanned her waist; his lips brushed her skin. He kissed her temple, kissed the crease at the corner of her eye, trailed warm, soft lips down her cheek. And her skin turned to fire wherever his mouth touched her.

His big, work-toughened hand covered her abdomen and he caressed it gently with slow, tantalising strokes. 'You're going to be a terrific mother.'

'And you'll be a wonderful dad.'

'Our baby's a lucky little guy or girl.'

He grinned at her from beneath lowered black lashes. 'How long will it be before we find out what sex it is?'

'I'm not sure. A few weeks yet.'

Wrapping his arms around her, he drew her hard against him, gently rubbing the side of her face with his chin. 'I'm starting to get quite excited about this parenthood caper.'

'Me, too.'

'I have a very good feeling that we're going to manage just fine, Sophie.'

Slipping an arm around her shoulders and another beneath her knees, he lifted her easily and carried her to his bed, and she wondered if it was possible to feel any happier than she did right at that moment.

CHAPTER TEN

As soon as Jill Jackson heard that Sophie was staying on, she began to make plans. 'Now listen,' she told Mark when he answered the phone a couple of days later. 'I know we're jumping the gun here, but you'd better warn Sophie to prepare for an invasion.'

'I hope that's a friendly invasion?'

'Of course.' Jill laughed. 'Sue Matthews and Carrie Roper and I want to come over for a girls-only lunch. We'll bring the food, so Sophie doesn't have to lift a finger. We think it's high time she got to know more of her neighbours.'

Mark relayed the message to Sophie.

'Oh, wow!' Her face was an instant snapshot of delight. 'How kind of them. That's fabulous.'

Covering the mouthpiece, he asked her quietly, 'Are you sure you're not too tired? I could put them off till another day.' He'd been worried when he'd woken this morning and seen how pale she looked. There were mauve shadows under her eyes.

'I'm fine, Mark.'

With some reluctance, he relayed this to Jill.

'Wonderful,' Jill said. 'Now, Mark, you'll oblige us by making yourself scarce, won't you? You can find a bore to mend, or something else useful. We girls are going to need plenty of time for a good old gossip.'

'What's this, secret women's business?'

'Exactly.'

'I can't believe they're going to so much trouble,' Sophie said after Mark hung up. 'They've got to travel so far!'

'Friendship's important out here.' He cupped her chin and looked into her face and felt a beat of fear, a dip in his pulse, like the shadow of a black crow's wing. 'I hope this lunch won't be too much for you.'

Sophie shook her head. 'If the women are bringing the food, I won't have to do much besides set the table.' She went to the stove, put the kettle on, then smiled back at him. 'Now this is why we need to do something about your dining room.'

'Point taken. Are you going to tell Jill and the girls about the baby?'

'I'd like to,' she said. 'Is it OK with you?'

'Sure. Women love to talk about babies, and if they know you're pregnant they'll understand that you should take things easy.'

'More importantly, they can tell me exactly what I need to know about the doctors and the hospital here.'

Whether it was presentiment, intuition, whatever... Mark felt a vague sense of unease as he kissed Sophie goodbye. He wished she didn't look quite so tired, but he wasn't planning on going too far today and he had no plausible excuse for hanging around. So he left her, taking a packed lunch and giving her his assurance that he would stay away until mid-afternoon so the women had plenty of time to chat.

It was about two o'clock, when he was in the middle of mending a leaky bore, that he heard the drone of an approaching plane. Looking up, he saw it dipping low as it came towards him. And then it waggled its wings, first port and then starboard.

He felt a shock of fright. It was the flying doctor's plane and it was never normally this low. It was a message. *Something was wrong!*

Instantly, he knew.

Sophie. Oh, God, Sophie.

His stomach turned to concrete.

Abandoning his task, he left his tools scattered as he ran two hundred metres to the truck. Why the hell had he left the phone in the truck? He should have had it with him.

As he ran, his mind threw up crazy possibilities. Sophie had sliced her hand with a kitchen knife. She'd been bitten by a snake. A red-back spider. Or maybe it was the food those women had brought. Food poisoning?

It couldn't be something to do with the baby. Fear clutched at his throat, strangled him.

Don't let anything happen to the baby. Please, no.

His hands shook as he reached for the phone. He didn't bother to listen to messages, but dialled straight to Coolabah Waters.

Jill Jackson answered.

'What's happened?' Mark yelled. 'Is Sophie all right?'

'Mark, the flying doctors have taken her to Mount Isa

hospital. She started having cramps. I knew you were out at the bore, but we couldn't get you on the phone so I asked the pilot to buzz you.'

She spoke quietly and calmly, but Mark wasn't deceived. Jill was a trained nurse and her calm manner was bluff.

'Cramps!' he cried. 'What's that mean? A miscarriage?'

'Not necessarily, but Sophie also started to bleed,' Jill said.

A cry of horror broke from Mark. 'I'm on my way.'

He careered across the plains at break-neck speed and he cursed at every gate. Cursed himself for leaving the sat phone in the truck and for leaving Sophie at home. He'd known this morning that something was wrong.

He even snapped at Monty, on the seat beside him. The cattle dog hunkered low and let out a whine.

It seemed to take for ever to reach the home paddock. Scorching across the final hundred metres, he pulled up in a cloud of red dust at the bottom of the back steps.

Jill Jackson was waiting for him, and the grim set of her face confirmed his worst fears. She hurried down the stairs as he leapt out of the truck.

'Don't panic, Mark,' she said, laying a cool hand on his arm.

Don't panic? How the hell could he *not* panic? Mark's head swam and his stomach pitched.

'Mark, sit down,' Jill said. 'You look like you're going to faint.'

Before he could deny this, he was dragged to the

steps. Two hands on his shoulders pushed him down until his butt came into contact with a timber slab.

'I'm OK,' he protested. 'I've never fainted in my life.'

Ignoring him, Jill set her hand on the back of his neck and gently but firmly held his head down between his knees.

'I know what you men are like. Andrew's just as bad. When you're dealing with men and cattle, you're the toughest guys in the west. But you should have seen Andrew trying to keep up a brave face when I was in labour.'

'I've got to go to her.' Mark jerked his head up, saw the paddocks swim before him, and Jill pushed him down again.

'You can't drive anywhere just yet, but you'll be all right in a minute. You just need to get over the shock and have a cup of tea.'

'For crying out loud!' This time Mark jumped to his feet. Dizziness threatened, but he ignored it. 'I don't need a tea party.'

If Sophie was in trouble, there was no way he would waste time sipping tea.

Looking up, he saw Sophie's other guests, Sue Matthews and Carrie Roper, peering anxiously from the back doorway.

'It's such a shame,' called Carrie. 'Such a shock for poor Sophie the way it happened. There we were, chatting away about hospitals and labour, when Sophie laughed and said she was having sympathy pains. No one dreamed…'

A warning glance from Jill stopped Carrie in mid-track.

'Thanks to all of you for looking after Sophie,' Mark said bleakly. 'I'll be off now.'

'What about taking a shower?' suggested Sue.

'And you might need some clean clothes,' said Carrie.

He brusquely waved these suggestions aside and ran to the shed where the Range Rover was parked. It would be quicker on the highway than the truck, and more comfortable for bringing Sophie home again.

'Take care, Mark,' Jill called after him. 'Don't be an idiot on the road. Sophie needs you in one piece.'

It was more than two hundred kilometres to Mount Isa, and Mark tore over the distance at a punishing pace. He was *burning* to get to Sophie.

He tried not to think about what might be happening to her, couldn't bear to think she might be losing the baby—or worse, that her own life was in danger.

Surely not? Sophie was young and strong, healthy and vibrant.

His mind was a turmoil of recriminations.

Hell. I shouldn't have let her take on so much.

But she'd seemed so well.

I shouldn't have made love to her. How could I have forgotten her delicate condition?

But she'd been so eager.

What could he do? He felt so useless, trapped in this vehicle, tormented by his imagination, angered beyond reason by the miles of bitumen that separated them.

He blinked as the road in front of him blurred. Damn. No sense in falling apart. He had to keep his head. But how was a guy supposed to stay calm in a situation like this? He'd rather face a stampede single-handed than see Sophie in a hospital bed.

At last, at the hospital, they directed Mark to Sophie's ward.

Uneasily aware of waxed linoleum and the smell of antiseptic, he stepped out of the lift onto her floor and made his way down a long hallway.

He caught a glimpse of his reflection in a glass door. Damn it, Sue and Carrie had been right. He should have showered and changed before dashing here straight from the dirty work of fixing a bore. Normally, he'd never think of coming to town in this condition.

When he stopped at a nurses' station and asked again for directions to Sophie Felsham, the nurse studied him over half-moon glasses. For the first time in his life, he felt his confidence draining. He was so out of place here, so not in control.

'Sophie Felsham,' the nurse repeated, and she studied her clipboard, looked up again and narrowed her pale eyes at him. 'Are you her next of kin?'

'I—I'm her baby's father.'

Her lips pursed as she considered this and she looked again at the clipboard.

'Her family are all in England,' he said, raising his voice as his patience frayed.

Why can't they just tell me where Sophie is?

Mark had always been slow to anger, but the longer the nurse took to tell him what he needed to know, the more impatient he grew.

'You've got to tell me where I can find her!' he commanded, bringing a clenched fist down on the counter and sending a pen flying. The pen was chained to the counter top, but Mark wouldn't have cared if it had flown out of the window.

From her seat behind the counter, the nurse glared up at him.

Mark scowled down at her.

She said finally in a tone of faint dismissal, 'Room twenty-two.'

'Thank you,' Mark replied, resuming his usual polite and gentlemanly charm. About to leave, he paused. 'How—how is she?'

Perhaps the nurse saw his fear. Her face softened and she said more gently, 'I'm afraid you'll have to ask Sister Hart.'

'OK. Where is she?'

'Busy with another patient at the moment.'

He spun away, cursed under his breath, went in search of room twenty-two.

From the doorway he saw her.

Sophie was the only patient in the room, and she lay perfectly still with her eyes shut. There was a white square of sticking plaster on the back of her hand, as if a drip had been inserted at some stage.

Mark's heart juddered.

He sucked in a deep breath. *Pull yourself together, man.*

She didn't stir when he tiptoed carefully into the room and pulled out a chair. He sat beside her bed and waited, unnerved to find her asleep. Somehow he hadn't expected that. What did it mean? Was she terribly ill?

His throat ached, and he couldn't swallow. He

watched the gentle rise and fall of her chest beneath the crisp white sheet, admired the sheen on her shiny dark hair as it caught the bright overhead lights, loved the way her eyelashes lay against her pale cheeks. He saw the delicate tracery of blue veins on her eyelids and the soft, pink lushness of her lips. He thought she'd never looked more beautiful.

But so alone.

Removed from him.

His gaze dropped to his dusty jeans and boots. There was a black grease-mark on his wrist and he rubbed it against his denim thigh, trying to clean it.

Perhaps the movement disturbed Sophie. She opened her eyes. 'Mark!'

He tried for a smile and missed. 'Hey there, beautiful girl.'

'How long have you been here?'

'Five minutes.' He leaned closer. 'How are you?'

Her face crumpled and she shook her head. She squashed three fingers against her quivering mouth, as if to stop herself from crying, but her lovely eyes glittered and tears spilled.

'Sweetheart.'

She gave a helpless shake of her head.

Mark didn't know what to say, what to ask, how to touch her. He patted her hand, fingered a strand of her hair. 'You sure know how to frighten a guy.'

This time he managed a weak smile.

But it didn't help Sophie. She began to sob and, no matter how hard she pressed her hand over her mouth, the sobs broke through.

Terrified and uncertain, conscious of his dusty clothes, Mark leaned close and tried to kiss her cheek.

Her arms encircled his neck. She clung to him, and her body shook violently with the force of her sobbing.

'You poor girl.' What could he say? What *should* he say? 'Don't worry.'

'I l-lost the b-baby!'

Mark's stomach dropped…and it kept falling and falling…

No baby.

He choked back an exclamation, a groan of despair. His job was to reassure Sophie, not to add to her anguish.

But the baby? Their little bean— Gone?

Another shock jolted through him and then an awful sense of loss pressed down, suffocating him, and he had to take huge gulps of air. *Hell.* If he felt this bad, how much worse must it be for poor Sophie?

She was weeping uncontrollably. He kissed her damp cheek and wished he could find the right words to comfort her. He held her, tried to soothe her, rocked her gently as he would a small child.

At last her storm of crying began to ease.

She sniffed noisily. 'I'm so sorry, Mark.'

'Shh.' It killed him that she felt a need to apologise. He lifted a box of tissues from the stand beside her bed. 'Here.'

Her eyes and nose were pink from crying. She took a handful of tissues, mopped at her face and blew her nose. 'Have they told you what happened?'

'Not a word. All I know is what Jill could tell me.'

Sophie gave a shaky sigh and sank back onto her pillow. 'As soon as I got here they did a scan,' she said.

'And they discovered that the baby—the—the foetus—had stopped developing.'

Her mouth pulled out of shape as she struggled to hold back another burst of tears. 'All this time I— I've been thinking about my little bean…our little baby growing into…' She stopped, closed her eyes and drew a deep, shuddering breath.

When she opened her eyes again, she said in a flat, exhausted voice, 'It was never going to happen. I've had what they call an inevitable miscarriage.'

Inevitable.

All this time, there'd been no chance of a baby.

'The doctor said it was just one of those things,' Sophie added. 'He said there's usually no explanation, but it's very common.'

Mark swallowed. 'Right.'

'And so that's that.' She sank miserably back onto her pillow and closed her eyes, and Mark saw again the blue-veined lids, the curling lashes. 'It's all over, Mark.'

It was like being cast adrift without a mooring rope.

Mark groped for words of reassurance, but could only find trite platitudes.

Grimly quiet, with her eyes still closed, Sophie said, 'It's "as you were" now. Everything's back to normal.'

Suddenly he sensed the direction of her thoughts. 'No!'

Sophie's eyes flashed open and she looked directly at him. 'I've been such a bother to you. I should never have rushed down here and thrown your life into chaos.'

'Have—have I ever complained?'

'No.' She laid her hand very lightly on his arm. 'You're a good man, Mark.'

'A good man'? Had any words been more dismissive? That was what people said at funerals—when they were saying goodbye. For ever.

Sophie's eyes were bright with a tough battle-light Mark had never seen before.

'You can go home to Coolabah Waters and get on with your life,' she said.

CHAPTER ELEVEN

THERE. She'd done it. The dreadful words that set Mark free had flowed from her in a painful rush, the way the baby had.

And she was left with the same desolate emptiness.

It was like ripping her heart out, but now, at the lowest point in her life, Sophie knew she had no choice. She had to face up to her most difficult challenge yet.

From the moment the mean, cramping pain had begun low in her abdomen, she'd known that she was losing the baby. And she'd known that meant losing Mark. She'd had plenty of time to think about it—in the plane on the way to the hospital, and later with tears rolling down her cheeks as the hospital staff had examined her and dealt with the miscarriage.

Afterwards, she'd wanted nothing more than to curl in a ball, to give in to her grief and the tumult of her hormones, to feel desperately sorry for herself. Yet again. But the funny thing about love was that it wouldn't let you be selfish. And, in the depths of her misery, she'd realised it was time to think about Mark for a change.

Poor Mark. She'd rushed down here and made a mess

of his life. She'd distracted him from important work by insisting that he show her his lifestyle.

She'd been so thoughtless. Even their love-making— Oh, *help,* how could she ever forget Mark's love-making? But even then, she'd been selfish. One minute she'd been holding him at bay, telling him that sex would complicate everything, next she was leaping into his swag.

She'd been too focused on her own problems for too long, too scared of failing yet again. But now it was time to grow up.

If she was brutally honest, she'd known from the start that Mark was a gentleman, too well-mannered to simply send her packing even though he'd probably wanted to. And Tim, Emma and her mum had all made their expectations clear to him. Everyone back in England was hoping Mark would 'do the right thing' and somehow save Sophie from yet another failure.

She'd failed anyhow. Life had taught her a huge and terrible lesson. She'd failed spectacularly. She'd lost the baby, the one thing that she and Mark had in common. The *only* thing tying him to her. And, after all the burdens she'd piled on the poor man, it was up to her to make things easier for him now.

It had to be done. Sophie knew she had no choice but to release Mark from any sense of obligation, had to be convincing for his sake.

If only he didn't look so ill. Beneath his tan, his skin had taken on a sickly pallor. His dark-brown eyes were glazed with shock.

And, although the muscles in his throat worked

overtime, he didn't speak. He wouldn't look at her, and simply stared at the foot of her bed.

Don't do this to me, Mark. Don't make it too hard.

Eventually, he said, 'Are you saying goodbye? You want to split?'

'Yes.' She was proud of how definite that one awful word sounded.

'But you'll come home with me first?'

Sophie, be brave.

'No, Mark. There's no need.'

'So—so after they let you out of here you plan to head straight back to England?'

'Of course.' She knew this sounded too harsh, so she added more gently, 'As soon as I can organise a flight.'

Mark's jaw clenched, and he shifted his point of focus to another part of her bed, but still he didn't look at her.

'It's a bit of a nuisance that I've left so much stuff at your place,' she said. 'Would it be too much to ask you to box it up and send it over?'

'I'll go home and get it tonight,' he said dully.

'But it's such a long way.'

His jaw clenched harder, and he spoke through gritted teeth. 'I'm used to long distances.'

Sophie felt sick at the thought of Mark driving back through the dark, over those long, lonely miles. Her throat burned with welling tears, but she didn't want to cry again. If she burst into tears, he'd never believe that she wanted to go. Besides, she'd cried too much already.

Mark said, 'Do you really think we can do this—just part as easily as we did in London, after the wedding?'

His voice was hard and cold, as if he'd chipped each word from a block of ice

She couldn't trust herself to speak, so she nodded, and she felt as if she might fall apart completely at any moment.

Mark leaned closer, his voice bitter-quiet. 'I can't believe you think we can say goodbye, as if nothing important has happened between us.'

Important?

Was that what he thought? What did he mean by that, was he just talking about sex?

Mark's hand gripped her shoulder. 'Tell me you don't mean it, Sophie.' His voice was too loud, almost angry.

'Is everything all right, Sophie?'

A woman's stern voice startled her. Through her tears, Sophie saw the nursing sister standing behind Mark.

Sophie nodded. 'Yes, I'm fine, thanks.' But her voice was squeaky and trembling. She groped for the ball of tissues under her pillow and dabbed at her face.

The nurse gave Mark a baleful look. 'She's obviously upset. I'll have to ask you to leave.'

'He's not upsetting me,' Sophie insisted.

'Just the same, I'll ask you step outside, sir. I need to check Sophie's progress. This will only take a moment.'

Outside, in the corridor, Mark wondered if he was losing his mind. He was free to go, but nothing about that felt right. What was wrong with him? Why did he feel so bad? Most bachelors in his position would have been relieved, wouldn't they?

He'd been let off the hook, and he was free to pick up his life where he'd left off when the young jackaroo had announced a long-distance phone call from a woman with an English accent.

Sophie Felsham was not going to make her home at Coolabah Waters after all. And he wasn't going to be a father. The burden of responsibility had rolled from his shoulders, and he was free to marry any girl he chose.

He should be pleased, shouldn't he? Wasn't this their lucky break—*his* lucky break?

There were unlimited Australian women who would slip into his lifestyle much more easily than Sophie could. Surely providence had intervened and had delivered them both from a life sentence?

But if that was the case why in blue blazes didn't he feel relieved?

The raw ache in the pit of his stomach, the numbness in his heart, didn't make sense. Shouldn't he feel the tiniest glimmer of hope about his future?

Hands plunged in pockets, he strode to the far end of the corridor, and glared out at the car park where windscreens flashed gold in the harsh blaze of the setting sun.

He didn't want an Australian girl. He didn't want anyone else.

That was the crazy truth of it. He wanted Sophie— bright, lovely, gutsy Sophie.

But fate had intervened and turned the clock back. They were just a man and woman again. There was no pregnancy. No possible son and heir. No cute baby girl. No chance that his bedroom would be decorated with rosy accents, whatever they were. No nursery…

Their lives had been stripped back to the basics. All that was left was how he and Sophie felt about each other.

And Sophie had already made her feelings crystal clear.

Turning from the window, he stared back down the long white corridor.

He couldn't believe how much it hurt that she wanted to rush back to England. It wasn't as if she had hated it at Coolabah. Already she'd made a terrific fist of settling into the Outback. She'd thrown everything she had into learning how to adapt, had shown the courageous spirit of the Englishwomen who'd pioneered this hard land.

And there'd been many times when he'd caught her looking at him, had seen in her eyes that she cared for him. *Really* cared. And she'd made love with heart-wrenching eagerness, with a depth of passion that couldn't be faked.

Damn it, there'd been every indication that they could have been happy together here.

You're fooling yourself, mate. If Sophie wanted to stay, she wouldn't hesitate to say so.

She's desperate to get back to England.

His hand balled into a fist. He wanted to smash something. But, damn it, if England was where Sophie truly wanted to be, he had no right to keep her here. He'd told her she was free to go if things didn't work out.

And, well…things hadn't worked out.

End of story.

She was the daughter of Sir Kenneth and Lady Eliza. She belonged in London with them, with Emma and Tim.

But how the hell could he let her go?

He couldn't.

It was as simple as that. Yes!

He couldn't let her go. He wasn't convinced that

Sophie really wanted to walk away from him. After everything they'd shared, it didn't make sense. He had questions to ask. He had to know for sure.

He set off down the corridor with a quickened step and a fiercely brave heart.

The nurse was just leaving the room.

'I've given Sophie a sedative to help her calm down,' she said, casting a dubious eye over Mark. 'I think it would be best if we leave her now. She mustn't be upset. She needs plenty of rest.'

'I'll just say goodbye,' he insisted.

But when he stepped through the doorway Sophie was lying curled on her side, with her back to him, and when he leaned over the bed she didn't move. Her eyes were shut, her eyelids red and swollen, and her hands were folded, clutching a bunch of damp tissues beneath her chin. She looked as if she might be praying.

She looked pale and exhausted, but the message was clear: she wasn't expecting or seeking any comfort from him.

In the car park he rang Jill.

'What a dreadful shame, Mark. Poor Sophie. Poor you.'

'I guess it's just one of those things that happen,' he said.

'Yes, of course. It happens a lot, actually. And I'm sure Sophie will have more babies.'

Mark cleared his throat. 'I—I guess so.'

'Just the same, it's a terrible disappointment for you both,' she said. 'And such a frightening experience for the poor girl.'

'I'm grateful you were there to help her.'

'Yes, so am I. Does she have enough things? I packed a small overnight bag for her.'

'I'm coming back to collect what she needs. I don't want to hang around in Mount Isa tonight, so I'll grab a hamburger and coffee at a service station and I can be home by ten.'

'You're coming back out here tonight?'

Jill was clearly puzzled by this, but Mark finished the conversation quickly and disconnected. He couldn't bring himself to tell her about Sophie's plans to return to London. He still couldn't believe them himself.

He tackled the task of gathering up Sophie's things as soon as he got back. 'Stressful' didn't go halfway to describing the ordeal. He was dog-tired, but too tense to sleep, so he went to the back bedroom, dragged out her suitcase from beneath the bed and began to pack.

He went about the task with grim thoroughness, taking care to put shoes and heavy things like jeans towards the bottom. He opened the drawer where Sophie kept her underwear. A hint of her scent still lingered, and his hands shook as he packed silken panties, lacy bras and her soft cotton nightdress. Every garment, each item, conjured memories that tore his heart to shreds.

On the little table in the corner of the room, he discovered pages torn from a notebook—a pen-and-ink sketch of his bedroom with notes about furniture and suggestions for colours, fabric and carpets. On the page beneath it, a sketch of the little nursery.

Sophie had drawn in details here: an old-fashioned timber cot, a patchwork quilt, a rug for the floor, a rocking chair and cupboard, shelves for stuffed toys, the small round window.

Mark stared at the simple drawings and wanted to hurl himself down on the floor and howl like a child.

He was losing her. Losing Sophie and her baby. Losing everything.

With an anguished groan, he tossed the pages of sketches on top of her folded clothes and fled her room.

But he knew that his bedroom couldn't offer him any peace either, not with memories of Sophie sharing it with him.

Tense as fencing wire, he flung open the door of the linen press, dragged out a blanket and pillow. He would make do with the sofa tonight.

He was hauling off his boots when the phone rang. Leaping up, he stumbled over them in his hurry to answer it.

Please, let it be Sophie!

'Hello. Is that Mark?'

He suppressed a groan. An English accent, but not Sophie's. Her mother's.

Hell! He was going to have to tell her the news.

'Hello, Lady Eliza.'

'I'm sorry to be ringing so late, Mark. I tried earlier, but you weren't home.'

'No worries. I wasn't asleep.' He dragged in a ragged breath. 'But I'm afraid Sophie's not here. She's—'

Damn. He was in danger of breaking down. He pinched the bridge of his nose as he struggled for control.

'Sophie's in hospital. I'm afraid she's had a miscarriage.'

'Oh, Mark.' Lady Eliza's voice trembled.

'She—she's OK. Just resting overnight.'

'My poor baby. I've had this dreadful feeling all day that something was wrong with her. That's why I've been trying to call.'

There was a tiny silence.

'I'm so sorry, Mark. When Sophie told me about the pregnancy, she sounded so happy. Confident and self-assured. I thought it was wonderful news. She said you were really happy about the baby, too.'

'Yeah.' Mark couldn't hold back a heavy sigh. He leaned a shoulder against the kitchen wall. 'But the doctors said it was inevitable. The foetus had stopped developing.'

'I see. Well, these things happen, of course. But it's very disappointing. Poor Sophie. She'll need some tender loving care when she gets back home with you.'

Mark swallowed. 'She's not coming back here.'

'I beg your pardon?'

'She's heading back to London.'

In the stunned silence that followed, Mark gritted his teeth, and squeezed his eyes tightly shut.

'Mark,' Lady Eliza said at last. 'I know it's none of my business, but are you happy with Sophie's decision?'

Oh God. His throat was so tight he didn't think he could speak.

'I know my daughter, Mark. She's very impulsive and inclined to overreact, and I don't suppose she's had much time to think this through.'

'Not really.'

'You're upset, aren't you?'

'This has been the worst day of my life.'

'Would it would help to talk?'

'I doubt it.'

But he knew it would happen anyway. There was something very kind and compelling about Sophie's mother. With another deep sigh, Mark lowered himself to the floor, sat with his back against the wall.

'OK,' he said, closing his eyes again as tears stung. 'What do you think we should do?'

The doctor was quite jovial when he saw Sophie on his rounds the next morning. 'Now, just remember, there is nothing wrong with your reproductive system,' he told her. 'You should put this behind you. I'm sure you'll be able to go full-term with your next pregnancy. And the other good news is you're fine to go home.'

Home. Her mind flashed to Coolabah Waters. But she had to scratch that thought. Home, of course, was her London flat. Sophie pictured it and waited for the appropriate rush of nostalgia.

Nothing happened.

Maybe she would feel more excited when she got back to England, when she saw her mother and Emma, when she was among her own things.

Maybe then she would be able to delete pictures of a tall, dark and handsome cattleman, and of wide, brown plains and a low house with an iron roof.

Once she was safely home she could put this episode behind her. In time, her memories of Mark Winchester and Coolabah Waters would fade like a bad dream.

Bad dream?

Who was she trying to kid?

Everything about Mark was perfect. She'd never forget him, never stop missing him. She'd fallen completely and totally in love with the man. In spite of his mysterious Outback.

Actually, there was every chance she was halfway in love with the Outback, too. After all, it was a part of Mark. And she'd known all along that Mark and his lifestyle were a package deal. Regrettably, now, it seemed that she loved them both.

As she threw her things into the overnight bag that Jill had packed for her, she wondered if there were enough words in the dictionary to describe how wretched she felt. She placed her hand over her stomach, over her *flat*, empty womb that had been denied the chance to finish its task.

She wanted it full to bursting, longed for her little bean, fat and healthy, growing into a naughty, lively, little boy or girl.

Her knees buckled and she sank to the edge of the bed. It was so hard to accept there was nothing now. There never had been a chance of a baby being born.

It was even harder to accept that the end of her pregnancy meant losing Mark. But she could hardly pretend that he would have considered a long-term relationship with her if it hadn't been for the baby.

When he'd made love to her, he'd whispered endearments so sweet they'd thrilled her to the bone, and had encouraged her to hope that he loved her. But he'd never repeated them in the cold light of day.

There was no avoiding the truth. Mark wouldn't

expect or want her to stay on without the baby. Yesterday's decision to leave had nearly killed her, but deep down she knew it was the right, the only thing to do. This morning, she had to find the quickest way to get back to England.

Mark was halfway down the highway when his phone rang.

'Mark, it's Sophie. I'm so glad I got through to you.'

Goosebumps broke out on his arms and back. 'Where are you? I tried to ring you at the hospital, but they said you'd checked out.'

'Yes. I'm fighting fit, apparently. I'm in a coffee shop in the main part of town. Where are you?'

'About an hour away. I've packed the rest of your things and I have them with me.'

'That's so kind of you.'

Kind? No, not kind—crazy!

'I've rung the airlines and booked my flights,' she said.

Mark swore. Hoped Sophie didn't hear it. The goose-bumps morphed into a cold sweat. 'When—uh—when are you planning to leave?'

'I've a flight to the coast that leaves around twelve.'

Twelve? He gripped the steering wheel so tightly, his knuckles almost snapped. 'Why? Why the rush?'

'I'll spend a couple of nights in Sydney,' she said, neatly avoiding his question. 'I can fly home on Friday.'

'But isn't that too soon? Don't you need a little more time to—to get over everything?'

'I'll be OK. It's best this way.'

Best? Sophie had to be joking. It was the worst news

possible. But there was no sense in having an argument with her when he was in the middle of the highway.

'I'll be cutting it a bit fine, but I'll make it,' he told her.

'I shouldn't keep you on the phone if you're driving, Mark. I'll head over to the airport and meet you there. See you in about an hour.'

'Wait!' he shouted. 'We need to talk, Sophie. It's important…'

But she'd already disconnected.

In the ladies' room in the airport, Sophie stood in front of the mirror. She was wearing the clothes Jill had packed for her, a purple T-shirt with a scooped neck and a short denim skirt. But in the harsh light of the overhead fluorescent tube she looked like a dying heroine in the final act of one of her mother's tragic operas.

Just thinking about her mother brought tears to her eyes. Last night she'd wanted to phone her, but she hadn't felt brave enough to tell her that everything had gone wrong, that she'd failed again.

She rubbed concealer into the shadows under her eyes, used a tinted moisturiser to blend everything together, added a little blush and some lip gloss, and then sifted her fingers through her hair in an attempt to plump up her curls.

She tried to smile at her reflection.

Come on, Sophie, you can do better than that.

Taking several deep breaths, she tried again. *Cringe!* She looked like a clown, with an artificially smiling mouth and tragic eyes.

She tried to picture Mark striding into the terminal—

her tall, strapping heartthrob in blue jeans. Her smile held until she got to the part where they began to say goodbye, and the reflection in the mirror cracked and crumpled. A glint of silver sparkled in her eyes.

No, no! She was not going to cry today. She had to steel herself. She was going to get through this. She would say farewell to Mark with a brave smile and without shedding a single tear.

She went to the airport kiosk. Her nerves were too on edge for more coffee, so she bought a magazine and a bottle of water, found a comfortable chair and sat down and pretended to read.

It didn't work, of course. The magazine was full of stories about celebrities with relationship problems. What did she care about their heartache when her own was off the scale? She turned to the crossword. The answers to the first few clues were easy, so she scribbled them in.

This was better; if she concentrated on the cross-word, she might be able to forget about...

Zap!

Sophie dropped her pen as long jeans-clad legs and brown elastic-sided boots entered her line of sight.

Her head jerked up and there was Mark, wearing a white long-sleeved shirt that showed off his tan, and looking a million times more gorgeous than any film star. Her heart began to race.

But then she saw his eyes, and the dark pain there made her so suddenly weak she was sure she would never get out of her chair.

'You made good time,' she said, trying to smile at him and failing miserably.

She couldn't think what to say next, knew that neither of them was in the mood for small talk.

Mark set her suitcase down, and she groped for her handbag on the seat beside her.

'I just need my passport,' she said, fishing in an inside pocket. 'And then I can check in.'

As she feared, her legs were wobbly when she tried to stand. Mark was beside her in an instant, his hand at her elbow, supporting her.

'Sophie, this is crazy. You're in no condition to be setting out on a long journey.'

She threw back her shoulders, pinned on a smile and tried hard to ignore the electrifying thrill of his hand on her arm. 'I'm fine, Mark. And I have two nights in Sydney before the long haul home.'

Gripping her other arm, he pulled her around so that she faced him, and his eyes blazed with an intensity that frightened her.

He spoke through tight lips. 'Tell me honestly that this is what you want.'

Startled, she cried, 'Of course it's what I want!' She willed herself to mean it, and couldn't let herself think otherwise, not for a fraction of a second.

'Honestly!' Mark hissed, gripping her harder. 'If you have even a shadow of a doubt about going home, say so now, Sophie.'

This was so unlike Mark. She waggled her passport in his face. 'There's no reason for me to stay now. You know that. You can get on with your life.'

'That's rubbish.' Still he gripped her. 'You haven't said it.'

Her throat was so full she couldn't breathe. Her vision blurred.

'Sophie.' Mark held her arms more tightly than ever. 'Can you really tell me that you can walk away with no regrets at all?'

She blinked to stop herself from weeping.

Mark stood very still, looking down at her with a face that seemed to be carved from stone. Except for his eyes. His eyes burned her.

'Don't for one moment imagine that I am free to get on with my life,' he said quietly. 'Not without you.'

'B-but there's no baby.'

'I know, and I'm really sorry about that, sweetheart.' Without warning, Mark loosened his grip, let his hands slide down her arms until he held her loosely at the wrists. 'Sophie, I'm very sorry there's just the two of us now. I mourn the loss of our baby more than you can possibly guess.'

The tears she'd been battling sprang into her eyes and trembled on the ends of her lashes.

'But don't you see what losing the baby means?' Mark gave her hands a gentle shake. 'This is only about *us* now. It's about how I feel about you, Sophie Felsham. You alone. And I'm telling you I can't let you get on that plane. I know I'll never see you again. And I—I can't bear to lose you.'

She stood very still, saw how very nervous Mark was, saw the unguarded truth in his eyes.

'Tell me, Sophie, short of throwing myself on the tarmac in front of the plane, what have I got to do?' He released her and held out his hands, offered her a disarming, trembling smile. 'There's nothing I won't do to keep you.'

She hardly dared to believe her ears. Each word Mark uttered was like a healing balm for her unravelled heart.

'I love you,' he said. 'What else can I say to persuade you to stay?'

'Oh Mark.' She gave him a weepy grin as she stumbled forward and reached for his hands. 'I think you've already said it.'

'I mean it, Sophie. I love you. I know you've had a man tell you this before, then turn around and hurt you. But I swear I mean it, darling. I'm not going to change my mind about loving you. You do understand that, don't you?

'Yes,' she said softly. 'I understand, Mark. It's almost too good to be true, but I do understand.'

'I love you so much, Sophie. I can't let you go. I don't believe I can live without you.'

Sophie lifted Mark's hand to her cheek, and it felt strong and good and wonderful. Steadfast.

'I know I'm asking a lot to expect you to live with me at Coolabah Waters,' he said. 'It's hardly the Ritz.'

'I don't want the Ritz, Mark. The Outback is an acquired taste, but it's growing on me fast. I'm not so sure that I belong in London any more. I was actually feeling very miserable at the thought of going back there.'

Heedless of the travellers milling about them, Mark gathered her in and kissed her with infinite tenderness.

Speaking softly so that only she could hear, he said, 'Ever since you arrived here, I've been falling more deeply in love with you. Every morning, every night, all day long. I would never have believed it's quite, quite possible to fall hopelessly, painfully in love in less than fortnight.'

'I believe.' Deeply moved, she touched her fingers to his lips. 'The same thing has happened to me.'

His face flooded with a smile as bright as the Australian sun.

'I promise I'll make you happy if you stay, Sophie.'

He cupped her face and they kissed, slowly, deeply.

Against his lips, Sophie whispered, 'I love you, too.' And then, 'Let's go home,' she said, eagerly linking her arm through Mark's.

'Best idea yet.'

They were halfway to the car when they remembered her suitcase, still sitting where Mark had left it in the middle of the terminal building.

Laughing, they hurried back to collect it. 'I almost forgot something else,' Mark said as he put the case in the back of the Range Rover. 'Your mother rang last night.'

'Really? What did she want?'

'She was worried about her baby daughter. Had a gut feeling that something was wrong.'

'Goodness.' Sophie marvelled at how warmed she was by her mum's unexpected concern. 'That's nice to know.'

'I told her what had happened, and she was terribly sorry and we had rather a long chat. I ended up inviting her out here for a visit.'

Sophie's jaw dropped. 'My mum wouldn't be able to come. She's always far too busy.'

Mark shook his head. 'She's coming all right. It's mid-season for the opera company, but she said her understudy will be delighted at the chance to sing this role.'

'Wow!' Sophie felt unbelievably chuffed to think her mother wanted to come all this way just to see her. But as she took this in a more puzzling thought struck. 'But—but how could you have invited her, when you didn't even know I was going to stay?'

'I guess…' Mark shrugged and smiled shyly. 'I wouldn't allow myself to consider the alternative.'

'Oh, Mark!'

'She'll be here in two days' time, and I thought it would be really nice if she could help co-ordinate our wedding.'

Sophie couldn't hold back a shriek of excitement. Tears flowed down her cheeks as she threw her arms about Mark and gave him an ecstatic hug. 'That is the most beautiful, beautiful suggestion I've ever heard.'

He rewarded her with a long, hard kiss.

Eventually, when they got into the vehicle and Sophie secured her seatbelt, she remembered another important piece of news. 'The doctor said we can try again for a baby in a month or two.'

Mark smiled. 'Of course we can. We can have a whole tribe of them.'

'I think I'd like to call our first baby Jack.'

'Jack Winchester?' He grinned as he fitted the key into the ignition. 'Sounds good, but what's wrong with Jane?'

'Nothing,' smiled Sophie. 'I'll settle for either.'

'We'll have both,' he said as he accelerated out of the car park.

And, as they turned and headed for home, Sophie saw no reason to doubt him.

MILLS & BOON®

Why shop at millsandboon.co.uk?

Each year, thousands of romance readers find their perfect read at millsandboon.co.uk. That's because we're passionate about bringing you the very best romantic fiction. Here are some of the advantages of shopping at millsandboon.co.uk:

* **Get new books first**—you'll be able to buy your favourite books before they hit the shops

* **Get exclusive discounts**—you'll also be able to buy our specially created monthly collections, with up to 50% off the RRP

* **Find your favourite authors**—latest news, interviews and new releases for all your favourite authors and series on our website, plus ideas for what to try next

* **Join in**—once you've bought your favourite books, don't forget to register with us to rate, review and join in the discussions

Visit **www.millsandboon.co.uk**
for all this and more today!